Prize Stories 1999

THE O. HENRY AWARDS

Past Jurors
1997: Louise Erdrich, Thom Jones, David Foster Wallace
1998: Andrea Barrett, Mary Gaitskill, Rick Moody

Past Magazine Award Winners
1997: *Epoch*
1998: *The New Yorker*

Prize Stories

1999

The O. Henry Awards

Edited and with an Introduction
by Larry Dark

ANCHOR BOOKS
A Division of Random House, Inc. New York

First Anchor Books Original Edition, October 1999

Copyright © 1999 by Random House, Inc.

All rights reserved under International and Pan-American Copyright
Conventions. Published in the United States by Anchor Books, a division of
Random House, Inc., New York, and simultaneously in Canada by Random
House of Canada Limited, Toronto.

Anchor Books and colophon are registered trademarks of Random House, Inc.

Owing to limitations of space, permissions appear on pages 441–443.

Library of Congress Cataloging-in-Publication Data

Prize stories, 1947–
New York, N.Y., Doubleday.
v. 22 cm.
Annual.
The O. Henry awards.
None published 1952–53.
Continues: O. Henry memorial award prize stories.
1. Short stories, American—Collected works.
PZ1.011   813'.01'08—dc19   21-9372

ISBN: 0-385-49358-4
www.randomhouse.com
Printed in the United States of America

10 9 8 7 6 5 4 3 2 1

Publisher's Note

WILLIAM SYDNEY PORTER, who wrote under the pen name O. Henry, was born in North Carolina in 1862. He started writing stories while in prison for embezzlement, a crime for which he was convicted in 1898 (it is uncertain if he actually committed the crime). His writing career was short and started late, but O. Henry proved himself a prolific and widely read short story writer in the twelve years he devoted to the craft, and his name has become synonymous with the American short story.

His years in Texas inspired many lively Westerns, but it was New York City that galvanized his creative powers, and his New York stories became his claim to fame. Loved for their ironic plot twists, which made for pleasing surprise endings, his highly entertaining tales appeared weekly in Joseph Pulitzer's *New York World*.

His best known story, "The Gift of the Magi," was written for the *World* in 1905 and has become an American treasure. Dashed off past deadline in a matter of hours, it is the story of a man who sells his watch to buy a set of hair combs as a Christmas present for his wife, who in the meantime has sold her luxurious locks to buy him a watch chain. "The Last Leaf" is another O. Henry favorite. It is the story of a woman who falls ill with pneumonia and pronounces that she will die when the last leaf of ivy she sees outside her Greenwich Village window falls away. She hangs on with the last stubborn leaf, which gives her the resolve to recover. She eventually learns that her inspirational leaf wasn't a real leaf at all, but rather a painting of a leaf. Her neighbor, who has always dreamed of painting a masterpiece, painted it on the wall and caught pneumonia in the process.

His work made him famous, but O. Henry was an extremely private man who, sadly, preferred to spend his time and money on drink, and ultimately it was the bottle that did him in. He died alone and penniless in 1910. O. Henry's legacy and his popularization of the short story was such that in 1918 Doubleday, in conjunction with the Society of Arts and Sciences, established the O. Henry Awards, an annual anthology of short stories, in his honor. At the end of the century the short story continues to flourish. Styles have radically changed and there can be no greater evidence of the evolution and high achievement today's short story writers enjoy than the contents of this 1999 edition of *Prize Stories: The O. Henry Awards* selected and compiled by the series editor, Larry Dark. Anchor Books and Doubleday are proud, with the seventy-ninth edition of the series, to continue the tradition of publishing this much beloved collection of outstanding short stories in O. Henry's name.

The twenty stories included in *Prize Stories 1999: The O. Henry Awards* were chosen by the series editor, Larry Dark, from among the three thousand or so short stories published during the course of the previous year in the magazines consulted for the series and listed on page 419. Blind copies of these twenty stories, that is copies with the names of the authors and magazines omitted, were then sent to the prize jury members. Each juror was instructed to vote for his or her top three choices, and the first-, second-, and third-prize winners were determined as a result of these votes. The jurors for the 1999 volume were Sherman Alexie, Stephen King, and Lorrie Moore. An introduction by one of the three jurors precedes each of the top-prize stories selected.

A short list of fifty other stories given serious consideration for *Prize Stories 1999: The O. Henry Awards,* along with brief summaries of each, can be found on page 409.

The Magazine Award is given to the magazine publishing the

best fiction during the course of the previous year, as determined by: the number of stories selected for *Prize Stories: The O. Henry Awards,* the placement of stories among the top-prize winners, and the number of short-listed stories. The Magazine Award winner for 1999 is *The New Yorker.* A citation for this award is provided on page 417.

Acknowledgments

Thanks to Alice Elliott Dark, Scott Conklin, and, at Anchor Books, Gerald Howard, Tina Pohlman, and Katy Burns-Howard.

Contents

Introduction

THE EXPERIENCE of reading a short story is intensely personal. Though the words on the page are the same for everyone who reads them, each person's experience of what the words add up to is different, sometimes vastly so. In this respect, "A Rose for Emily" is not "A Rose for Emily" is not "A Rose for Emily." Stories are a distillation of thought and experience that requires interpretation. The source of their effectiveness lies not only in what they give us but also in what they ask of us, and a good literary short story sometimes asks a lot.

The inherent subjectivity of the reading experience is one of the factors that make the task of explaining why I chose the stories I did so difficult. I would like to be able to lay out my criteria, to pinpoint the qualities and characteristics that make for an O. Henry Award–winning story. And it would be convenient to have the capacity to assess everything I read in a precise manner, to be equipped with a hard-edged instrument of objective degree that I could lay up against each story, one that would allow me to pronounce with certainty that: "This one measures up, this one nearly does, this one doesn't quite, and, sorry, this one not at all." But I can't provide reasons that would cover all of my choices this year and in years past and for the foreseeable future, because whenever I try to pinpoint what I believe to be the essential characteristics of the well-made story, I read something not encompassed by or anticipated by my notions. Though the short story is a well-defined form and a good subject for critical analysis, it is also wonderfully elastic and the potential for the creation of something new remains, no matter how many millions of stories are written. If there's one thing that I could say I look for in compiling this collection, it would be the story like no other story I have ever read.

I won't claim that every one of these twenty stories precisely fits that description, but they all reach toward it, some of them quietly, others in more obvious ways. I have, for instance never before encountered a story in which Richard Nixon serves as the muse for an actor facing his own mortality.[1] Nor have I ever read a wryly analytical study of depression that shows how prolonged navel-gazing can lead to a tragically isolating solipsism.[2] Or how about two hundred or so years in the history of the Pacific nation of Tonga through the eyes of a tortoise long favored by the island's monarchs?[3] And this situation is new to me as well: a broad pastiche of trailer park minimalism married to a gothic morality tale in which a male exotic dancer/waiter living with his sister, his cousin, and the girls' out-of-wedlock infants are visited by a maiden aunt returned from the dead.[4]

These are instances of artistic risk-taking in which the gambles pay off to reveal deeper truths about human nature. But a story doesn't need an outlandish concept to make it worthy of attention, and ambitious efforts in this direction often fail, reducing the characters rather than enlarging them. The examples above notwithstanding, most of the stories in this year's collection caught my attention with seemingly conventional approaches, yet each does something very well, whether it's capturing a milieu convincingly, speaking with a distinctive voice, or insightfully detailing the inner workings of a character or characters.

Among the interesting milieus visited in these stories are those of the rodeo circuit, where, against all good sense, compulsion drives a young man to risk life and limb riding bulls for the short-lived

---

[1] "Nixon Under the Bodhi Tree," Gerald Reilly.
[2] "The Depressed Person," David Foster Wallace.
[3] "A Tortoise for the Queen of Tonga," Julia Whitty.
[4] "Sea Oak," George Saunders.

difficulties[14]; a privileged but troubled American teen and a boy who has labored in a rug factory in Pakistan who find common ground despite their differences[15]; a businessman on his way to an appointment who stops in a village green to watch a girls' soccer game and recalls his youthful prowess at the sport[16]; and a woman impregnated by a rapist who decides to keep the baby, despite the strains it puts on her marriage.[17]

Though I have read many thousands of stories in three years of editing this series, all of these felt new to me. The ones I haven't yet mentioned are this year's top-prize winners, as selected and introduced by Sherman Alexie, Stephen King, and Lorrie Moore. I was impressed with the dedication, honesty, and generosity these writers brought to their role as jurors. I know from experience that it's difficult to read with an open mind and difficult to bestow special recognition on a few out of many. As Stephen King put it, "Reading the stories was a pleasure. Judging them was not."

What's most interesting this year is that few readers are likely to recognize the names of the first- and second-prize winners or to have read the magazines in which these stories were published. The truth this underscores is that the field of the short story is as wide open as the creative possibilities. While it's likely that an Alice Munro or a T. C. Boyle or a David Foster Wallace will write some of the best stories of the year, it is also possible that a Peter Baida or a Cary Holladay will. And while *The New Yorker* and *Harper's Magazine* can be expected to publish great fiction, there's also a good chance that *The Gettysburg Review* and the *Alaska Quarterly Review* will as well. Skill, talent, insight, inspiration, editorial acumen, and a propensity to take risks were all part of the mix in the stories published during the course of the year. May it ever be so.

LARRY DARK, 1999

[14] "Afterbirth," Sheila M. Schwartz.
[15] "Moon," Chaim Potok.
[16] "Watching Girls Play," W. D. Wetherell.
[17] "Son of the Wolfman," Michael Chabon.

adrenaline rush that makes him feel truly alive[5]; the sites of ancient Hindu ruins in India, toured by an Americanized Indian family and their romantically inclined native guide[6]; a whitewater rafting expedition on the Colorado River attempted under the most dangerous possible conditions, which becomes the backdrop for a pitched battle between the sexes[7]; the Pacific nation of Fiji, where a tribal woman educated abroad finds herself caught in the dangerous no-man's-land between Western-style politics and ancient traditions[8]; and turn-of-the-century Fresno, California, where an Italian laborer, frustrated in his dreams of establishing a winery, turns to his skill at digging as a last stab at redemption.[9]

Among the distinctive voices with which the stories in this year's collection speak are those of: a married woman who has suffered a series of miscarriages and who discovers what she believes to be the terrible reason she wasn't meant to have children[10]; a disaffected man and his equally disaffected girlfriend who, while driving back from a friend's wedding, stop for a strange couple who have just escaped from a burning building[11]; and a grown man who finds that he has eclipsed the accomplishments of an older brother who had once seemed to him the embodiment of perfection.[12]

The short story is perhaps at its best when it convincingly details the inner workings of its characters in a way that, though particular, sheds light on the human condition in general. Among the characters insightfully depicted in this collection are: a group of boys who out of morbid curiosity, cruelly prey upon a classmate whose accidentally severed feet were surgically reattached[13]; a wife and mother returning from a conference at which she betrayed her husband, who finds herself aboard a plane with serious mechanic

---

[5] "The Mud Below," Annie Proulx.
[6] "Interpreter of Maladies," Jhumpa Lahiri.
[7] "Cataract," Pam Houston.
[8] "Fork Used in Eating Reverend Baker," Kiana Davenport.
[9] "The Underground Gardens," T. Coraghessan Boyle.
[10] "Sign," Charlotte Forbes.
[11] "Burning," Robert Schirmer.
[12] "Mister Brother," Michael Cunningham.
[13] "Miracle Boy," Pinckney Benedict.

FIRST PRIZE

A Nurse's Story

By Peter Baida

Introduced by Sherman Alexie

Okay, so this is the nurse I remember most, the Navajo woman who came to my reservation in 1978 or 1979 and took care of us for three or four glorious months, as we all, men and women alike, gossiped about her beauty and her near-silence, re-arranging our schedules and inventing illnesses so that we could be seen by her, and waiting forever in the lobby because we refused to be seen by anybody else, even the doctors, a series of white men too old or young, too incompetent and ill-mannered, too poor at birth, or cursed with an altruistic streak that landed them in an Indian Health Service clinic in Wellpinit, Washington, a town of five hundred or one thousand depending on which welcome sign you read as you drove into our lives.

Yes, I remember that Navajo nurse, how she left, or was forced to leave, after a series of epileptic seizures. And that is all I know about that nurse's story.

So it was with great delight that I read Peter Baida's "A Nurse's Story," a decidedly quiet, yet cinematic story that shifts smoothly in time, takes us on a circular journey from past to present to future, taking us into the life of one Mary McDonald, a nurse who knows "The web that connects people in a small town is more tightly spun than the web that exists in a large city."

And her story is a mystery too, in which we first learn she is going to die, and only then discover how she lived, how she helped generations of others live and die.

There are no forced epiphanies here, no sermons on the roofs of churches or hospitals. There are union strikes, tragic deaths, and the small realization that "A good death. That's what everybody wants." And we want that because we can never be sure about our lives in small towns, on or off the reservation, in this nurse's story or in that nurse's story.

—SHERMAN ALEXIE

Peter Baida

A Nurse's Story

From *The Gettysburg Review*

T HE PAIN in Mary McDonald's bones is not the old pain that
she knows well, but a new pain. Sitting in her room in the
Booth-Tiessler Geriatric Center, on the third floor, in the bulky
chair by the window, Mary tries to measure this pain. She sits mo-
tionless, with a grave expression on her face, while the cheerless gray
sky on the other side of the window slowly fades toward evening.

Mary McDonald knows what this pain comes from. It comes
from a cancer that began in her colon and then spread to her liver
and now has moved into her bones. Mary McDonald has been a
nurse for forty years, she has retained the full use of her faculties,
and she understands perfectly where this pain comes from and what
it means.

"Union?" Eunice Barnacle says. "What do I want with a union?"

"Miss Barnacle," Mary McDonald says, looking at her from the
chair by the window, "do you think you're paid what you're
worth?"

Miss Barnacle is a lean, sharp-featured black woman in her middle twenties, with a straight nose, small teeth, wary eyes, and a
straightforward manner, who joined the staff at Booth-Tiessler
about a month ago. "This place can't afford to pay me what I'm
worth," she says.

"That's certainly what they want you to believe, Miss Barnacle. May I ask a nosy question?"

"I suppose."

"What do they pay you, Miss Barnacle?"

"That's my business."

"Eight-fifty per hour. Is that about right, Miss Barnacle?"

Miss Barnacle, in her white uniform, turns pale. She has paused with her hand on the doorknob, looking over the neatly made bed to the chair where Mary McDonald is sitting. Pearl gray light falls on a walker near the chair. Mary McDonald's hands are closed in her lap, over a green-and-gold quilt. Her face is solemn.

"Do you think this place *knows* what you're worth, Miss Barnacle?"

A good death. That's what everyone wants.

Mary McDonald still remembers, from her first year as a nurse, well over forty years ago, a little old woman named Ida Peterson, with a tumor in her neck near the carotid artery. The call bell at the nurses' station rang, and Mary McDonald walked down the hall, opened the door, and was struck squarely in the face by something warm, wet, and red.

Blood from a ruptured artery gushed out of Mrs. Peterson's tracheotomy opening, out of an ulcerated site on her neck, out of her nose, out of her mouth. Mary was stunned. She saw blood on the ceiling, on the floor, on the bed, on the walls.

Mrs. Peterson had wanted to die a peaceful, dignified death, in the presence of her husband. She had wanted to die a "natural" death. Now, as the life poured out of her, she lifted her hand to wipe her nose and mouth. With wide eyes, she looked at the blood on her hand.

Ida Peterson had wanted a natural death, in the presence of her husband, and she was getting one, in the presence of Mary McDonald, a nurse she had known for five minutes.

Mrs. Peterson's blue, terrified eyes looked into Mary McDonald's eyes for the full fifteen minutes it took her to bleed to death. Her hand gripped Mary's hand. Mary did nothing. Her orders were to allow Mrs. Peterson to die a natural death.

Mary had never before seen an arterial bleed. She still remembers the splash of blood on her face when she stepped into Mrs. Peterson's room. She still remembers how long it took Mrs. Peterson to die. You wouldn't think that a little woman could have so much blood in her.

"They tell me you were some good nurse," Eunice Barnacle says, taking Mary's blood pressure.

"I'm still a good nurse," Mary McDonald says.

"They tell me you helped start the nurses' union, over at the hospital."

"Who tells you?"

"Mrs. Pierce."

"Ah."

"Mrs. Pierce says those were the days."

"Maybe they were."

Eunice loosens the blood pressure cup from Mary's arm. "Mrs. McDonald?"

"Yes?"

"That union—" Eunice hesitates, looking at the floor.

"What about it?" Mary says.

"You think it helped you?"

Booth's Landing is an unpretentious town with a population of nearly nine thousand, located among gently rolling hills on the east side of the Hudson River, fifty miles north of New York City. In every generation, for as long as anyone can remember, the Booths and the Tiesslers have been the town's leading families. The Booth family descends from the town's founder, Josiah Booth, a merchant of the Revolutionary War period whom local historians describe as a miniature version of John Jacob Astor. The Tiessler family descends from Klaus Tiessler, an immigrant from Heidelberg who in 1851 founded a factory that makes silverware.

"A nice town," people who live in Booth's Landing say. "A nice place to bring up a family." That's how Mary McDonald has always felt, and that's what she has always said when people ask her about the place.

In every generation, for as long as anyone can remember, one member of the Booth family has run the town's bank, and one member of the Tiessler family has run the silverware factory. The town also supports one movie theater, two sporting goods stores, two opticians, three auto repair shops, one synagogue, and nine churches. Most of the people who die in Booth's Landing were born there. Many have died with Mary McDonald holding their hands.

Oh, not so many, Mary thinks, pursing her lips. Not that she has kept count. Why would anyone keep count?

You can do worse than to live and die in a place like Booth's Landing. The air is fresh. The streets are clean and safe. The leading families have paid steady attention to their civic and philanthropic responsibilities. If you're sick in Booth's Landing, you go to the Booth-Tiessler Community Hospital. If you want to see live entertainment, you buy tickets for the latest show at the Booth-Tiessler Center for the Performing Arts. If you can no longer take care of yourself, you arrange to have yourself deposited in the Booth-Tiessler Geriatric Center.

At the Booth-Tiessler Community College, nearly fifty years ago, Mary McDonald fulfilled the requirements for her nursing degree. Now, sitting by her window on the third floor in the Geriatric Center, looking over the cherry tree in the yard below toward the river, with the odor of overcooked turnips floating up from the kitchen on the first floor, she finds her mind drifting over her life, back and forth, here and there, like a bird that hops from place to place on a tree with many branches.

"I've never been a troublemaker."

That was what Mary McDonald said to Clarice Hunter when Clarice asked her to help form a nurses' union at the Booth-Tiessler Community Hospital in 1965.

"Hon," Clarice Hunter said, "do you know what the nurses get paid in New York City?"

"I don't live in New York City," Mary said.

"You know what the nurses get paid in Tarrytown?"

"I don't live in Tarrytown."

"It's only ten minutes drive."

"Okay. What do they get paid in Tarrytown?"

Clarice told her.

"Holy moly," Mary McDonald said.

"Will you help me?" Clarice said.

"Clarice, don't pester me."

"You call this pestering?"

Mary did not answer.

"What's the problem, Mary?"

"I'm not a big believer in unions."

"Being a doormat—is that what you believe in?"

Mary pursed her lips.

"It's your Catholic upbringing," Clarice said.

"What about it?"

"Mary, they *programmed* you. They programmed you to bow down to authority."

No doubt about that, Mary thought. Call me Bended Knee.

"Mary, your help would mean a lot to us."

"I've never been a troublemaker."

"I don't think I'll ever make much money."

That was what George McDonald told Mary, a long time ago.

Well, George, you were right about that.

Mary was twenty-one when she met him, in 1948. She had just taken her first job at the hospital, as a nurse in the emergency room.

George was twenty-seven. In the Pacific, he had fought in the Battle of the Coral Sea and in the Battle of Midway.

The first time Mary saw him, George was helping his father carry a sofa up the stairs into the apartment his sister had rented, on Jefferson Street. Mary was friends with the sister, Eleanor, a nurse at the hospital.

He was a big man, six foot three, with hair the color of fresh corn and a big, boyish smile. The war had left him with a scar six inches long, an angry pink dent, on his left shin.

Mary herself was a heavyset young woman, with a figure that lacked curves. Even in her twenties, she looked as if she had been carved from a block of wood. As she aged, she looked as if she'd been carved from a larger block.

I was stout, not fat.

On their first date, George took Mary to see a movie called *Johnny Belinda*. Then they went over to Krieger's, the luncheonette on Main Street. Mary had a hot fudge sundae.

George taught at Booth's Landing High School. He played the clarinet. He thought he would be satisfied teaching music and living in Booth's Landing for the rest of his life.

"I guess I'm not too ambitious," he said.

On the second date, George took Mary on a picnic, in Dabney Park. After lunch he took her rowing. At the far end of the lake, they paused in the shadows under tall trees. Kiss me, Mary thought. George crossed his hands over his knees.

"I don't think I'll ever make much money," he said. "I've never cared much about it."

"There's more to life than money," Mary said.

On the third date, George took Mary to see a movie called *The Snake Pit*. Would you like to go to Krieger's for a sundae, he asked when it was over.

"I don't want a sundae," Mary said. "Let's go walk by the river."

She took his hand as they walked down Tremont Street. The night was cool. His fingers were as thick as cigars.

Six months later they were married.

Mary still remembered the way his fingers felt, laced in hers.

Thirty-nine years together. Three kids, all of them grown now and moved away. No other women in his life, no other men in hers.

He died of kidney failure in 1988. A man who rarely lost his temper, a father who taught his sons how to scramble eggs and his daughter how to throw a baseball, a small-town music teacher who loved the clarinet.

Oh, George, I miss you. You can't imagine.

Maybe you can.

"How you feeling today, Mrs. M?" Dr. Seybold says. He is a large man with a friendly face, pink skin, and paprika-colored hair. His breath smells of peppermint.

"Well enough, Tom. How you feeling?"

"I'm fine, ma'am. Thank you."

"How's your family?"

"My mother broke her toe."

"Broke her toe? How'd she do that?"

"Bowling."

"Dropped a bowling ball?"

"No. Dropped a coffee mug. She tried to hop away, but she couldn't hop fast enough."

"None of us hop as fast as we used to."

"That's the truth, Mrs. M."

"You tell her I hope she feels better. Don't forget."

Forty years ago, in the years before Tom Seybold was born, his mother had two miscarriages. Mary still remembers the look in Laura Seybold's eyes after the second one. She had carried the child for six months, the happiest months of her life, and when she lost it, her life went out of her eyes, the spring went out of her step, and for a full year she wandered through town with a bleak, dazed, shellshocked look on her face. Mary still remembers taking care of Laura Seybold during the three days she spent in the hospital after the Saturday night when she swallowed every pill in the house.

Tom Seybold puts his hand gently on Mary's shoulder.

"You sure you're feeling fine, Mrs. M?"

A coffee mug. Broke her toe with a coffee mug.

"Tom, how long have you known me?"

"As long as I can remember."

"May I ask you an honest question?"

"Why sure, Mrs. M."

"Considering I've got a colon cancer that's chewing up my liver, just how well do you expect me to feel?"

Meat loaf.

If this is Monday, that gray-brown slab on Mary McDonald's plate must be meat loaf.

"What I want to know is where the money goes," Lucy Heywood says. "We *pay*. It's not as if we don't pay."

"What I want to know," Penny Mack says, "is what happens to us when the money's all gone."

"Moneymoneymoneymoney," Roy Quigley says. "If I had a dollar for every day I've spent worrying about money, I'd be a rich man."

"I'm tired of meat loaf," Barbara Collins says.

"Did you read in the paper about Frank Sinatra?" Lucy Heywood says.

"You're not tired of meat loaf," Mary McDonald says.

"I am," Barbara Collins says. "I certainly am."

"What happened to variety shows?" Penny Mack says. "Remember Garry Moore?"

"That man has no shame," Lucy Heywood says.

"Garry Moore?"

"Sinatra."

"Did you see those photos of Princess Di?"

"Whatever happened to Carol Burnett?"

"You're not tired of meat loaf," Mary McDonald says, leaning toward Barbara Collins. "You're tired of life."

"I'm *not*," Barbara Collins says, holding up a fork with a gravy-smeared piece of meat loaf on the end of it. "I'm *not* tired of life."

Mary McDonald's grandmother also died of colon cancer. *Also* is the word that comes into Mary's mind. Her grandmother died in 1957, or maybe 1958. If you lived long enough, Mary had noticed, you forgot when things happened. The only years she remembered were the years her kids were born.

Mary's parents took her grandmother down to New York City, to Columbia-Presbyterian, so a famous surgeon could operate. Mary could remember the look on the surgeon's face, after the operation, when he came into the room where Mary and her parents were waiting.

Mary sighs, sitting by the window in her room. Outside, in the yard below her window, a breeze stirs the leaves of the cherry tree. The sky is white today. Poor Grandma! The famous surgeon cut her open, looked inside, and sewed her up. Nothing he could do. Just as, nine months ago, a different surgeon had sewed up Mary.

My goose is cooked.

At Booth-Tiessler, in Grandma's final days, Clarice Hunter was the nurse on the day shift. Mary remembers her grandmother telling her how Clarice had bathed her, and combed her hair, and talked to her. Mary's grandmother was a plain-looking, plain-talking woman, with only an eighth-grade education, who expected nothing from life and generally got what she expected. But then, in the last days of her life, she got Clarice Hunter as her nurse.

"This woman is a jewel," Mary's grandmother said to Mary, while Clarice blushed. "This woman is a blessing."

"Just doing my job," Clarice said, checking Grandma's pulse.

At one o'clock in the morning on the night Mary's grandmother died, she insisted on seeing her family. The night nurse called Mary's parents, who came to the hospital with Mary.

"Where's Clarice?" Mary's grandmother said. "I want to see Clarice."

"It's the middle of the night," Mary said. "She'll be here in the morning."

"I need her *now,*" Mary's grandmother said, turning on Mary a look so fierce that Mary still remembered it.

Mary called Clarice, who came to the hospital at two in the morning. At three, Mary's grandmother fell asleep with her mouth wide open. At six, with a terrifying snort, she woke and died. Clarice helped the night nurse wash the body. Then she worked the day shift.

"Little stick," Eunice Barnacle says, leaning over. She pushes a tiny needle into a vein in Mary's hand. Blood flows back through the needle, into the tubing.

"Good shot," Mary said.

"Tell me about that strike. When was it?"

"1967."

"What was it made you want a union?"

"I didn't want one. Not at first."

"So what happened?"

At a sink in the nurses' lavatory, Clarice Hunter is crying. The year is 1965, ten years after the death of Mary McDonald's grandmother. Mary is thirty-eight; Clarice is ten years older. Mary walks over to the sink and, carefully, puts one hand on her friend's shoulder.

"You okay?" Mary asks.

"I guess." Clarice blows her nose. "Thanks."

Mary waits.

"Mary?"

"Yes."

"They're driving me crazy. They're running me off my feet."

"They're running all of us, dear."

"But it's making me crazy, Mary. I lost my temper with Mrs. Grbeck, I nearly got into a fight with Mr. Palermo's daughter, and I forgot all about Mr. Howard's pain medicine. That poor man waited *fifty* minutes for his pain medicine."

"We're all rushing, Clarice. We're all making mistakes."

"Mary, I have *twenty* patients."

"I know, dear."

"I can't take care of twenty patients."

"I know, dear."

"Mary?"

"Yes."

"You know how hard a nurse has to work."

"Of course."

"What'll I do, Mary? I can't take care of twenty patients. I can't. I just *can't.*"

"How about you, Mary?"

In the nurses' lounge, back in 1965, that was the question Ruth Sullivan asked, a few days after Mary McDonald had found Clarice Hunter crying at the sink in the nurses' lavatory.

In three weeks, the nurses would vote on whether to form a union. Mary had always expected to vote no.

"I think maybe I'll vote yes," Mary said.

"You'll vote yes?"

"I think so. Maybe."

"I thought you didn't believe in unions."

"I don't. But I think—oh, I don't know. I think I changed my mind. Maybe."

It hadn't occurred to Mary McDonald that anyone would care

how she voted. But if you talked to other nurses, you found out that Mary's opinion made a difference.

"I hear Mary McDonald's voting yes," a nurse would say.

"Really?"

"That's what I heard."

"I thought she didn't want a union."

"She changed her mind."

"Really?"

"That's what I heard."

The vote drew near. Arguments were made, pro and con. Tempers flared. In September 1965, the nurses voted in favor of a union.

In the nurses' lounge, Pam Ryder is leafing through a copy of *Family Circle* magazine.

"Well, it won't be long now," Eunice Barnacle says.

"What?" Pam Ryder says.

"Mrs. McDonald," Eunice Barnacle says.

"Poor woman," Pam Ryder says.

"She told me about that union, over at the hospital."

"We need one here," Pam Ryder says.

"You think so?"

"You don't?"

Eunice does not answer. Pam Ryder turns the page in her magazine. Eunice stirs her coffee.

"I know one thing," Eunice says.

Pam Ryder looks up, brushing a hair off her forehead.

"That union can't help her now," Eunice says.

"May I have this dance?"

Brad, her youngest, bends over Mary with his hand outstretched. Mary struggles to her feet. Brad takes her right hand with his left. His other hand settles on the small of her back. Barely moving, they dance.

In her chair, half dozing, Mary remembers that dance.

It was two months ago, on Mary's sixty-ninth birthday. All three of her children had come to Booth's Landing, with their families.

They know what's up.

George Jr. offered, again, to take her to Chicago.

"I want to die here," Mary said.

"But Mother—"

"No but."

A gangling, loose-jointed, long-armed boy, a star athlete, George Jr. has grown up to become an earnest, quiet-voiced man who dresses in rumpled suits. He's an attorney, but, of course, he can't win an argument with his mother. Who can? Though he's tall and moves gracefully, he's no longer slim. His face has grown puffy. His belly bulges over his belt.

"George," Mary said, on her birthday two months ago. "You need to lose weight."

"Yes, Mother," George said. The look in his eyes told her how sad he was to see her dying.

Oh, George, I'm sorry I nagged you. But it's true, you *should* lose weight.

Jane came from Boston, with her two little girls, cute as could be, but bored, and who could blame them? They didn't understand why Mommy had dragged them to see their grandmother.

"Jane, you look tired."

"Mother, I'm a *nurse*. You know what that means."

Three years ago, Jane had a drinking problem. Now she's licked it—maybe. But she bites her fingernails and smokes.

Jane, do you think I didn't notice?

Brad came all the way from Seattle, where he's worked for a decade. Everyone laughed again at the story about the phone call when he'd told his parents about the job.

"Microwhat?" Mary had said.

"Microsoft, Mother."

"You couldn't get a job with IBM?"

"Mother, I'm working for Bill Gates."

"Bill who?"

Mary turned a happy pink while Brad told the story.

"Look at Mom! Look at her face!"

Brad, my baby. That time when you ran full speed into the clothesline and busted your head open, and I held you while Dad drove us to the emergency room—I know you can't remember, but no one will ever love you the way I loved you on that ride to the hospital.

"Enough about me, Eunice. Tell me about yourself."

"I was born in Virginia, in Richmond," Eunice says. "My father was no good. My mother brought me up."

Outside, three black birds are flying toward the river.

"I don't like to talk about my family, Mrs. McDonald."

"That's all right. You don't have to."

Two days later, while Eunice gives Mary a back rub, the conversation resumes. The smell of rubbing alcohol makes Mary feel drowsy. Rain is drizzling from a bleak sky.

"My mother—she's in jail."

"Oh?"

"She had a boyfriend, Jethro, who beat her when he got drunk. So, about six years ago, Jethro got arrested, and she bailed him out. But then, when they got home, she killed him."

"Oh!"

"They gave her life in prison. I guess maybe they had to."

"Why did she bail him out?"

"That's the thing. She bought a shotgun. She bailed him out to kill him."

"Hmm."

"She's in Sing Sing. It's only thirty minutes drive. I visit every Sunday. You know what's funny?"

"What?"

"Sing Sing. It's in a town called Ossinning. I never knew that before."

Mary feels Eunice's fingers on her back.

"She's a good woman, my mother. But she did wrong. I know that."

Mary feels Eunice's fingers on her shoulder blades.

"That fellow Jethro, he pushed her too far."

George would give her a back rub, and then a front rub, and then—well, what's marriage for?

"My mother, she's only thirty-nine. She was sixteen when I was born."

□ □ □ □

A football, thrown with a perfect spiral, thrown forty yards through the gray November air, beneath a sky like the sky outside this minute, a football hurled forty yards and falling into the hands of the receiver, glancing over his shoulder at exactly the right moment, reaching up at exactly the right moment, making the catch, and sprinting into the end zone.

It was the winter of 1967. George Jr. threw the football, Warren Booth Jr. caught it, the Booth's Landing football team won the county championship, and life was as good as it gets.

Except for the strike.

The strike had begun in September, two years after the nurses organized their union.

What did the nurses want? That was the question that Richard Dill, a reporter on the Booth's Landing *Gazette,* asked Clarice Hunter, who was the head of the Strike Committee. Clarice told him.

Money.

Job security.

Some say in decisions relating to staffing levels.

No, no, no. That was what management said. So Mary McDonald, who never in her life, before or after the strike, ever voted for anyone but a Republican, found herself on a picket line.

Sister Rosa, the Executive Director, was a short, no-nonsense woman who made it her business to be seen, striding through the halls of Booth-Tiessler Community Hospital, waging war on dust, dirt, and disorder, encouraging nurses and nurses' aides, keeping doctors in line, looking for inefficiencies to eliminate, attacking problems, pushing for improvements.

"Mr. Dill," Sister Rosa said in the first interview that she gave after the strike began, "our nurses are wonderful, all our employees are wonderful, but we cannot let employees set their own salaries. We cannot let employees define the terms and conditions of employment. We cannot let employees set staffing levels."

Remembering, Mary McDonald sighs.

Oh, Sister Rosa, how I admired you! How I hated doing anything that might displease you. How I wanted you to *like* me. How I wanted to hear you say, "Good work, Mary. . . . Nice job, Mary."

"Mr. Dill, management must not run away from its responsibilities."

Five years before the strike, Mary McDonald worked with Sister Rosa on a project to improve the patient scheduling system in the radiation department. With Sister Rosa guiding the project, staff members collected and evaluated treatment time data. Then Sister Rosa designed a system that matched the time allotted for an appointment to the complexity of the treatment. A more flexible scheduling system was put in place. The result: a twenty percent decrease in patient waiting time, and a fifteen percent increase in physician and hospital revenue. Mary later used what she had learned from Sister Rosa to improve the patient scheduling system in the chemotherapy department.

"Mr. Dill, management must *manage.*"

One week before Thanksgiving. Outside, a nasty sky. Inside, the radiator clanks and rattles. Eunice has brought Mary McDonald a tiny white pill in a tiny white cup.

"You visiting your family for Thanksgiving, Mrs. McDonald?"

"No." Mary swallows her pill. "I'm too tired."

"Your family coming here?"

"They came for my birthday. That was enough. How about you, Eunice?"

"Guess I'll take my little girl to see my mom." Eunice has a daughter, three years old, in day care.

"That's nice." Mary looks at Eunice, who is looking at her watch while she checks Mary's pulse. Mary feels the pressure of Eunice's fingers—a nice feeling.

You're a good nurse, Eunice, but the two-year degree isn't enough. You should go back to school. Do it now, while you're young.

Mary hears those words in her head, but she does not say them aloud. Mary and Eunice often talk about Eunice's future, but Mary does not feel like talking today.

"I've got a new picture." Eunice opens her wallet, takes out a photo, and holds it out for Mary to see. The photo shows a bright-eyed little girl with twin pigtails sitting on a mechanical rocking horse, outside Tyler's Pharmacy.

"I heard from her daddy."

"Oh?"

"He lost his job, out in San Diego. Asked if I could send him some money."

Eunice is staring at the photo of her little girl.

"That man," Eunice says, shaking her head. "That man needs a brain transplant."

For six months, the nurses carried picket signs outside the hospital. Twenty nurses, on the picket line, every day and into the night. Mary still remembers the looks people gave them. Friendly looks, hostile looks, curious looks. She still remembers the sign she carried: TOGETHER WE WILL WIN.

The hospital hired a company that specialized in fighting strikes. The company flew in scab nurses. On the picket line, Mary sang: "UNION BUSTING, IT'S DISGUSTING."

In Booth's Landing, people took sides. Millie Tolliver said to Mary at a PTA meeting, "Mary, I'm surprised in you." Carl Usher, the plumber whose son took clarinet lessons from George, said, "Mrs. McDonald, I just don't see how you girls can walk out on your patients." In an interview on TV, Cheryl Hughes, a woman whom Mary had always liked, whose husband prepared Mary and George's tax returns, said, "If you ask me, it's an outrage. Let's just hope nobody dies. Those women ought to be ashamed."

The web that connects people in a small town is more tightly spun than the web that exists in a large city. In Booth's Landing, the man who will write Mary McDonald's obituary for the local newspaper is the son of the reporter who covered the nurses' strike of 1967.

Richard Dill, the father, lives on the same floor as Mary McDonald at the Booth-Tiessler Geriatric Center. Richard Dill sees that Mary has lost twenty pounds in the last six months, sees that her step is weaker each time she comes out of her room, sees that she comes out less and less often, and sees that her skin grows paler and paler, grayer and grayer, with every week.

Watching Mary fade away, Richard Dill remembers her as a sturdy woman carrying her picket sign, thirty years ago. He remembers her twenty years ago, nursing his wife after her surgery.

Roger Dill, the son, sometimes sees Mary in the hall with her walker when he visits his father, and he nods amiably in her direction, but he does not remember the nurses' strike of '67 because he was only three years old when it took place. Roger Dill does not remember that, when he was six, Mary's daughter Elizabeth was one of his camp counselors. He remembers the surgery his mother had when he was twelve, but he does not remember any of his mother's nurses.

"A nice boy," Mary thinks when she sees Roger Dill, though she merely nods as he walks with his father in the hall. Mary remembers Roger at the age of twelve, a skinny kid carrying a football helmet, visiting his mother in the hospital. Poor woman. What was her name? Jennifer. From a town called Mistletoe, in Mississippi. Mary taught her how to care for the colostomy bag that she needed after her surgery.

Two months into the strike, the hospital withdrew recognition of the union.

"Withdrew recognition?" Mary said to Clarice Hunter. "How can they do that?"

"They can't," Clarice Hunter said. "Not unless they've hired those scabs as permanent replacements."

"Sister Rosa wouldn't do that."

In fact, that was exactly what Sister Rosa had done.

"What'll we do?" Mary asked Clarice.

"We'll move into Phase Two."

Phase One: the nurses carried picket signs outside the hospital.

Phase Two: the nurses took their fight up to the top of Mountainview Drive.

Why Mountainview Drive? Because that was where Warren Booth, the Chairman of the Board, lived with his wife and children. Mary McDonald remembers Warren Booth, with a big frown on his broad, well-scrubbed face, when he came down the driveway from his mansion to confront the strikers. She remembers the tone of his voice, and the look in his eyes, and the way his jaw worked, and the way he turned on his heel and strode back up the driveway and into the house.

George Jr. said: "But, *Mom,* don't you see what you're doing? I'm the *quarterback,* and Warren Jr. is my best receiver."

In Booth's Landing, back in 1967, the public schools were good enough that the son of the richest man in town and the son of George and Mary McDonald could go to the same school and play on the same football team.

"Mom, Warren's my *teammate.*"

"Yes, George. I understand. But out in the world, where I work—well, let's just say that Warren's dad isn't my teammate."

Frank Gifford.

"If Frank Gifford ever comes to town," George used to say, "I'll have to lock Mary away from him."

Well, George, you may have been right about that.

Mary and the Giants. Everybody who knew Mary McDonald knew about her love affair with the Giants.

She was a knowledgeable fan. When the announcer said that the Giants had gone into their "prevent defense," Mary would shout: "No! Not the prevent! Anything but the prevent!" She'd seen the Giants lose too many games when the prevent defense failed to prevent anything.

Her other great love was beer, the darker the better. "I can't stand that piss-colored beer," she would tell people. Once she discovered Guinness, she never drank anything else.

It's true. I could use one right now.

She didn't like games. She didn't like to travel. She didn't have any hobbies. What she really liked was—nursing.

That's also true. I loved it from day one.

She knew things that only nurses know. If you smell an unpleasant odor coming from a patient's urine drainage bag, add ten milliliters of hydrogen peroxide to the bag when you empty it. If a nasogastric feeding tube becomes clogged, use diet cola to flush it. If you need to remove oil-based paint that is close to a patient's eyes or mouth, use mineral water, not turpentine.

In the neighborhood where George and Mary lived, phone calls to physicians were rare. People called Mary first, and Mary told them what to do.

"So they hired permanent replacements," Eunice Barnacle said. "Then what?"

"What you have to remember," Mary said, "is that Booth-Tiessler is part of a chain of hospitals. And it's a chain of *Catholic* hospitals. That's why nuns run the place."

"What difference does it make who runs it?"

"A big difference. Maybe all the difference."

Most of the striking nurses also were Catholic. They didn't merely picket outside the hospital. They prayed:

> Give us this day our daily bread,
> And forgive us our trespasses,
> As we forgive those who trespass against us.

And they chanted:

> United we bargain,
> Divided we beg!

And they sang:

> I dreamed I saw Joe Hill last night,
> Alive as you and me. . . .

On TV in those days, in and around Booth's Landing, people saw nurses on strike, with their picket signs lowered and their heads bowed in prayer. When people remembered the strike, years later, what they remembered was nurses praying on the sidewalk outside the hospital.

"If the hospital hadn't been run by an order of nuns," Mary

McDonald said to Eunice Barnacle, "I think we'd have lost. But we hit those nuns where it hurt. We appealed to their consciences."

The Sisters of Mercy—that's what the nuns were called. Somebody looked up their mission statement. It said that they were committed to act in solidarity with the poor, the weak, the outcast, the elderly, and the infirm.

On the chilliest day that winter, with her cheeks freezing and her breath visible in the air, Mary McDonald read the Sisters of Mercy mission statement out loud, while TV cameras rolled.

Then Beverly Wellstone began a fast. A nurse who had once been a nun, she was five feet tall, trim and intense, with bright blue eyes and cinnamon-colored hair. She fasted for thirty-three days, her eyes growing brighter and brighter as the flesh fell from her face. Other nurses fasted in support, usually for twenty-four or forty-eight hours. The TV cameras kept rolling.

"I am fasting in an effort to bring this strike to the attention of higher authorities," Beverly Wellstone said. The look in her eyes was the look you see in paintings, in the eyes of martyred saints.

Other strikers begged her to stop, but Beverly Wellstone declined with a nearly invisible movement of her parched lips.

"To represent the women on this picket line," Beverly Wellstone said, "is an honor and privilege I will never know again in my life."

A camera crew arrived from New York. One of the national networks had picked up the story. That night, millions of people learned about the striking nurses of Booth's Landing. From her cot in the basement of a local church, Beverly Wellstone whispered a few words about the role of faith in her life. Warren Booth Sr., entering the hospital for an emergency meeting of the Board, declined to comment. He looked haggard and distracted.

The next day, according to newspaper reports published later, a stranger arrived in Booth's Landing. Three days later, the strike was over.

"A stranger?" Eunice Barnacle said.

"An emissary of the Cardinal," Mary McDonald said.

"What did he do?"

"He carried a message to Sister Rosa."

"A message from the Cardinal?"

"Yes."

"Then what happened?"

"Talks resumed, but in a different spirit."

Eunice was leaning against the windowsill in Mary McDonald's room. The light that poured through the window from a clear winter sky made her skin shine. Mary McDonald, as she told the story, was sitting up comfortably in bed, her back supported by two pillows set on end.

"So you won?" Eunice Barnacle said.

"The scab nurses were dismissed," Mary said. "The striking nurses were rehired. The effort to decertify the union was abandoned."

"You got the salary increase you wanted?"

"No. We got about half the increase we wanted. But we also got something we wanted for our patients."

"What was that?"

"More staff on the medical and surgical floors. For the next three years, after we signed that contract, we had the staff to give the kind of care we wanted to give."

Thirty thousand dollars—that was what Sister Margaret calculated that Booth-Tiessler Community Hospital would save annually by buying less expensive surgical gloves. Sister Margaret's expertise in materials management dazzled everyone who worked with her at Booth-Tiessler. It was an expertise she had honed in years of hard work under the eye of her mentor and predecessor, Sister Rosa, whom she had succeeded as Executive Director in 1984.

Sister Margaret had turned on her dictaphone, with the intention of dictating a memorandum on the subject of surgical gloves, when Sister Celia softly entered the office with the latest pile of papers and reports for Sister Margaret's in-box. Something in Sister Celia's eyes—a flicker that suggested the desire to speak—led Sister Margaret to lift her own eyes with an inquiring look.

"Mary McDonald died this morning," Sister Celia said.

"Ah." The word came out of Sister Margaret's mouth as a sigh. When Mary McDonald was transferred from the Geriatric Center to the hospital, three days ago, Sister Margaret had suspected that the end was near. Now, memories of Mary McDonald mixed in Sister Margaret's mind with the thought that the time had come to take another look at soap prices.

What Sister Margaret said, looking at Sister Celia, was, simply: "A good nurse. . . . A *damned* good nurse." The word *damned* was pronounced with an emphasis that verged on audacity. Sister Margaret remembered the nurses' union, and the strike of '67, and the look on Sister Rosa's face in the days after the Cardinal had sent his emissary to Booth's Landing. "Of course," Sister Margaret said, "we had our differences."

Roger Dill, at his old-fashioned desk in the old-fashioned offices of the Booth's Landing *Gazette,* took a long sip of coffee, paused to savor the taste, paused to savor the warmth in his stomach, and typed: "Mary McDonald died at the Booth-Tiessler Nursing Home on December 16. She was sixty-nine."

Roger closed his eyes. When they opened, his fingers moved swiftly: "A graduate of Booth-Tiessler Community College, Mrs. McDonald worked for many years as a nurse at Booth-Tiessler Community Hospital. . . ."

Roger closed his eyes again. People of no great consequence died every week in Booth's Landing, and Roger Dill was required to write three to five paragraphs about them. It was not a task that he resented, but it was not one that excited or inspired him. How much could he say about a nurse he had never met?

"Mrs. McDonald is survived by three children. . . ."

Roger Dill suppressed a yawn and thought about the legs of his son's piano teacher. Even with coffee, he found that it was sometimes a challenge not to fall asleep with his fingers on the keyboard, the computer humming gently on his desk, and the conventional sentences taking shape in his head.

From his office on the top floor of the Booth's Landing Savings and Loan Association, a sturdy stone building at the intersection of

Tremont and Main Streets, Warren Booth Jr. could see the blue shimmer of the Hudson, sweeping south, and, beyond it, the fields and meadows of New Jersey. Though it had rained a few hours ago, the day had brightened. Warren Booth allowed his gaze to linger on the river, beneath the sparkling blue of the midafternoon sky.

The Booth's Landing *Gazette* lay open on Warren Booth's desk. Looking out over the river, the town's leading banker found himself falling into a strangely agitated mood. Nearly thirty years had passed, yet he still remembered the days when nurses picketed his family's house, while he tried to prepare for the biggest football game of his life.

In those days, nothing in the world had seemed more important to Warren Booth than the Booth's Landing football team. George McDonald had been the team's quarterback. Warren had been the team's primary receiver. The team itself had been outstanding—the best that anyone could remember. Yet Warren remembered the winter of 1967 as a painful and confusing time, because a group of nurses, including George McDonald's mother, had made life miserable for Warren's father. Why? *Why?*

With an exasperated sigh, Warren Booth shifted in his chair. He had inherited not merely his father's position in life but also his attitudes on matters pertaining to civic and business affairs. The nerve! The nerve of those women. What great enterprise had they ever managed? What did they know about worldly affairs?

Something that resembled a grimace appeared on the face of Warren Booth. The fact that he himself had never managed any great enterprise did not occur to him. Those women had made Warren's father out to be some Scrooge, and the press, the damned press—well, better not to think about the press.

Warren Booth took a deep breath. He would send a condolence card to George McDonald, in Chicago. Yes, he would do that. Hell, he would go to the funeral. Why not? Go to the funeral. Pay his respects. See old George. . . . Talk with old George? What would they say to one another? What could they possibly say to one another?

Sighing, Warren Booth leaned back in his chair, looked up at the ceiling, and closed his eyes. The look on his face was the look of a troubled man. He kept his eyes closed a long time.

Forget the funeral. Send a card.

Two blocks from the little red-brick apartment building where Eunice Barnacle lives, there is a park with swings and sliding boards and a jungle gym. Even in winter, on a sunny day, the park fills with children. With all the young voices squealing and shouting, and young feet running and jumping, it is as happy a place as you can find in Booth's Landing. This park is where Eunice Barnacle went, with her three-year-old daughter, on the day after Mary Mc-Donald died.

It was a Saturday, bright and cold, with a sky completely white. Eunice pushed her daughter on a swing, then sat on a green wooden bench, apart from the other mothers, while her daughter played in the sandbox. After a while, another woman sat down near Eunice. The women talked for a time, and then they sat without talking for nearly half an hour. Then Eunice said:

"You know what we need, Carrie?"

"What?"

"A union."

"Union? What do we need with a union?"

"You think you're paid what you're worth?"

"Eunice, what's got into you?"

"Nothing."

"That woman brainwashed you."

"Nobody brainwashed me."

"You could get us in trouble, Eunice."

"We're already in trouble."

"Not me. I'm not in trouble."

"That's what you think."

To a little girl in a bulky red jacket, in the sandbox, Eunice yelled: "Coretta, sweetie, five more minutes."

"Mommy, *no!*"

"Five minutes, Coretta."

The woman on the bench next to Eunice folded her arms across her chest. She was wearing an orange scarf over a silver-gray coat. Eunice was wearing a white scarf over a crimson coat.

"I've never been a troublemaker," the woman said. "One thing I've learned in life, Eunice. You go looking for trouble, you'll find it."

Eunice did not answer. The sun had gone behind a cloud. A chill came into the air.

A month ago, Eunice recalled, she had asked Mary McDonald if the union had really helped her. The old woman had thought a long time before she said, "To tell the truth, it had its good points and its bad points. Like most things." Eunice had asked her to explain the good points and the bad points. "Some other time," the old woman had said. "I'm tired now."

But the subject had never come up again, so now Eunice did not know what Mary McDonald would have said.

"Coretta! Sweetie!" Eunice called.

"But *Mommy!*"

"Time to go, honey."

The child opened her mouth as if to wail, paused, closed her mouth, stood, held out her arms, and toddled toward Eunice.

"Let's go home, sweetie. Mommy's tired."

At Santino's Funeral Home, Nick Santino and Harry Orbit were preparing the body of Mary McDonald for its final resting place.

"Here's one I'm sorry to see," Nick Santino said.

"Oh?"

"Mary McDonald."

"You knew her?"

"A nurse. Took care of my mother, back when she was dying."

Mary's body lay on a porcelain embalming table, under a sheet. Nick paused, looking at the face of the dead woman. The eyes were closed, the skin was wrinkled and pale, the lips were crooked. A white thread, half an inch long, lay on the face below the left eye. Nick lifted off the thread.

Nick and Harry washed Mary's body with warm water and a soapy solution. They cleaned Mary's fingernails. Through a needle that Nick placed in the jugular vein, they drained the blood from Mary's body.

Harry inserted cotton in both nostrils, to hold the nose straight. Nick sewed Mary's lips shut.

A machine pumped embalming fluid into Mary's body. After the fluid had entered Mary's hands, Nick crossed them over her chest. He applied adhesive glue to hold her fingers together.

Nick paused, looking at Mary's face. A refrigerator hummed in a corner of the room.

"This woman took care of my mother," Nick said, looking down at her. "She took care of my mother like she was taking care of her own mother."

Nick shooed away a fly that was buzzing near Mary's cheek. He touched Mary's hair with a gloved hand. He looked at Harry.

"This woman washed my mother's feet," Nick said, with sudden intensity. "This woman cleaned my mother's toes with a tooth-brush."

Mary McDonald, late in the last day of her life, fell into a sleep as deep as a child's sleep after an overactive day. Her eyes were closed, her head was tilted back, her lips were open, her breathing was steady, though not strong.

At one point a middle-aged woman in a nun's outfit came into the room, closing the door behind her. With a mild expression on her face and her hands crossed at her waist, the visitor stood looking down at the sleeping woman. Mary's eyes opened.

"Sister Rosa. How nice of you to visit."

"Don't mention it, dear. How are you?"

"Not long for this world, I'm afraid."

"Don't be afraid."

"No. I'm not."

"Have they given you something for pain, Mary?"

"Oh, yes. Thank God for morphine."

"I'll do that."

Mary thought for a moment, with a slightly puzzled expression on her face. Then she let the thought go.

"Sister Rosa?"

"Yes."

"When you died, *after* you died, was it—what you expected?"

"I'm not allowed to talk about that, dear."

"No. I guess not."

Mary closed her eyes again. She kept them closed for a long time. When she opened them again, the light in the room seemed different.

"Sister Rosa?"

"Yes, dear."

"Would you mind holding my hand?"

"Of course not, dear."

Sister Rosa put her hand on Mary's hand. The nun's hand was warm—warmer than Mary's, perhaps. Mary closed her eyes again, but opened them almost at once.

"There's something on my mind, Sister Rosa."

"What's that, dear?"

"The strike—you remember the strike?"

"Of course, dear."

"I hope you didn't take it the wrong way?"

"The wrong way, dear?"

"It wasn't about *you,* Sister Rosa. I hope you understand that."

"I do, dear."

"But the nurses—we couldn't let things go, the way they were going."

"I understand, dear."

"We couldn't roll over and die."

"Of course, dear. I understand."

"You do?"

"Mary, I'm *glad* you fought."

"You are?"

"Workers have to fight."

"You really think so?"

"The whole system depends on it."

"I'm not sure about that, Sister Rosa."

"Well, I am."

A sound came from the door, but no one was there. Sister Rosa looked at the door, then back at Mary.

"Would you like to see George?" Sister Rosa said.

"Is he here?"

"He's right outside."

"Could I see him?"

"Of course."

Mary closed her eyes. When she opened them, the light in the room was different. Sister Rosa had gone, but George had not come in. A woman in a white uniform was standing at the bedside, taking Mary's pulse. Mary felt the pressure of her fingers on her wrist.

"I'd like to see George," Mary said.

"George?"

From the foot of the bed, someone said: "That's her husband. My father."

"Jane?"

"I'm right here, Mom."

"How nice. I'm glad you've come, Jane."

"Me, too."

"Brad?"

Mary felt confused. The nurse let go of her wrist.

Mary looked on the other side of her bed. Brad was there, in a navy sweater, and George Jr., in a rumpled suit, with his hand reaching into a bag of pretzels.

"You had a good sleep," Brad said.

George said, "I'm right here, Mom. We're all here with you."

Mary looked at him. His belly bulged over his belt.

"You need to lose weight, George."

"Yes, Mom. I know."

"Promise."

George withdrew his hand from the bag without a pretzel.

"I promise, Mom."

I can't help myself, George. A mother's a mother till her dying breath.

But where was *her* George? Sister Rosa had said he was here.

Out loud Mary said, "I don't want a sundae. Let's go walk by the river."

The woman in the white uniform went out of the room. Mary's children talked softly to one another. Mary listened for a while with

her eyes closed. She could hear the voices, but the words escaped her. When she opened her eyes, her husband was standing by her bed. The smile on his face made Mary want to get up and throw her arms around his neck. He was young and tall, his hair was the color of fresh corn, his fingers were as thick as cigars, and he had his clarinet with him.

SECOND PRIZE

Merry-Go-Sorry

By Cary Holladay

Introduced by Stephen King

Good fiction shows us the inside of things—a community, a job, a relationship, the human heart. Great fiction can sometimes show all of these things working together; it lifts us briefly above the event horizon of our own day-to-day existences and gives us a dreamlike (and godlike) sense of understanding what life itself is about. Cary Holladay's "Merry-Go-Sorry" is one of those rare and always welcome stories.

Based on an actual event—how closely I don't know or want to know—it traces the aftermath of a triple murder. It is a story filled with marvelous details (Sid Treadway's "long scarred dumbfounded face," the yellow-haired Gulf Shores girl beside the green water and under the green sky, a nameless murderer vomiting at the side of the road as a rain shower pelts down) and illuminated by its passionate yet carefully controlled narration. Its real success, however, lies in Holladay's inspired (and sometimes eccentric) tracing of lives which come together in a blood knot and then wander away again on their own jagged courses. There is a pattern in the rebound, Holladay suggests, a blind evolutionary process that might be for the good as well as for the bad, and it is that mixed feeling which the title so beautifully evokes. Holladay shows us the inside of a senseless crime, where there is a pattern no tabloid headline can touch.

—STEPHEN KING

Cary Holladay

Merry-Go-Sorry

From *Alaska Quarterly Review*

And I will cast abominable filth upon thee, and make thee vile,
and will set thee as a gazingstock.
  —Nahum 3:6

IT BEGINS in an Arkansas courtroom: the trial of a young man
for the deaths of three boys. It begins in late May, a year after the
murders, on a day so hot that the air conditioning can't keep up
with the sweat on the seventeen-year-old defendant's face. He has
confessed, though his lawyer protests that the confession, taped in
hysterical segments by the police and existing too in written form,
signed in Sid's childlike scrawl, means nothing: Sid Treadway is
mentally retarded, he says, and the police coerced him.

Sid Treadway's long scarred dumbfounded face follows his lawyer's striding figure to the bench and back, and then Sid's mild
green eyes are distracted by a cicada thrumming on a courtroom
windowsill. He recalls the last such insect he saw, at his sister's
house, which died loudly, clatteringly, in a dish of lemons. He barely
hears his lawyer. In revulsion, his sister had thrown out the lemons,
which she had planned to use in a pie. She has not come to the
courtroom; only Sid's father is there for him, Big Sid, who when his
son was arrested had burst into sobs like a child. There will be
another trial for Sid's alleged conspirators, one of them widely re-

garded by an outraged public as the ringleader. Sid's trial is separate because he confessed, implicating the other two.

Sid Treadway helped to slay three young boys and left them hog-tied, bleeding and drowning in a ditch, says the prosecutor.

That is what the jury believes, swiftly convicting Sid Treadway, but that is just the prelude, the beginning.

It begins again in the trial of Benedict James, the devil-worshiping, girlfriend-biting, trailer-dwelling dropout who had tutored his disciples Sid Treadway and Robert Abt in evil (so the prosecutor says, six weeks later in the same courtroom), who had targeted his three victims (their eight-year-old faces—one slyly mugging, another somber, a third, the most lovable, expansively smiling—have decorated Tennessee and Arkansas newspapers for months now). If the trial of Sid Treadway was easy, the trial of Benedict James and Robert Abt is as simple as calling Satan by his name.

In Benedict's closet there's nothing but black T-shirts and black pants, a police officer testifies, and his diary has poems he wrote to the devil.

Benedict's pregnant girlfriend, Victorine Stark, sits every day in the back row. Sixteen, red-haired, beautiful, she has pointed to teethmark-scars on her white neck for the benefit of photographers. She is carrying the child of the man she loves; this is her fate, she says. Her mother, thirty-two but looking sixty, sits beside her embroidering the face of Jesus on a pillowcase. Nobody loves *her,* she tells reporters, and she'll be grandmother to the devil, but she has a sweet lovely daughter, she says; I want the best for my girl.

Benedict of the shaggy black hair, the fishbelly-white skin, the deeply scalloped underlip, the pedophile's eyes, gets sent to hell right there in the Arkansas courtroom, as daily the trial ends with a curse: the father of one of the victims (who will himself be on trial within the year, for stealing furniture from a neighbor's moving van), rushes Benedict in a ritual that the guards and the jury have come to enjoy: Burn in hell, murderer! You killed my little boy! he cries. The guards let him get within arm's length of Benedict before gently tugging him out the door. Benedict sits unmoved, only his large stomach moving fast with his breath, his T-shirt lifting up and down.

The other defendant, Robert Abt, is vocal, whereas Benedict says nothing and does not take the stand. Robert Abt denies it all, the luring of the three young victims, the cutting, the binding, the rapes. But he gets confused. To the prosecuting attorney, he explodes, Damn you, man, you're trying to mess me up. His lawyer tells the judge that he has advised his client against taking the stand, but Robert Abt, age sixteen, insisted. I'm innocent, Robert Abt cries from the witness stand.

Benedict James is eighteen but looks older; he could be twenty-four or five. When the judge sentences him to death and asks if he has anything to say, he replies, No, sir.

Within six months, he's on television, complaining to an eager, rabbit-eyed interviewer about the regular rapes and the blandness of prison food. Yes, he says, he did bite his girlfriend during sex, just a lick, and he demonstrates with his tongue, while the reporter shudders. I don't worship Satan. I'm a white witch, a Wiccan, he says. I never said nowise else. He will not talk about the three murdered boys, whose faces flash again on the TV screen as Benedict is led handcuffed back to his cell on Death Row. Facing the camera, the reporter assures viewers that Benedict will be under lock and key until his execution; within minutes, the TV station is flooded with calls from viewers who express the wish that Benedict be raped every day for as long as he lives.

The drainage ditch, called Ten Mile Bayou, where the three young boys' bodies were found, still trickles through West Memphis past the truck stops and car washes. Now and then, somebody still leaves a wreath of flowers there; other such offerings, of wire and withered white silk, lie askew in the sludge, stuck in the ditchbank. Victorine Stark, in the trailer she shares with her mother, cuddles her newborn, a boy, and names it Malachi. That means "my messenger," she announces, with middle name Destiny. She had a vision, she tells a reporter who follows up on her story: on the day before the baby's birth, she saw a crow with a long strand of something in its beak, a long piece of videotape. It gave me hope, she says, her red hair spread out on the pillowcase with the Jesus face on it, while in the background, the baby whimpers and Victorine's mother spoons macaroni and cheese onto paper plates, inviting the reporter to stay for supper.

What do you think was on the videotape? the reporter asks indulgently. The one that the crow was carrying?

Victorine laughs, a sad gurgle that has caught on lately among the girls at her school, who copy the laugh and the way she wears her plentiful hair—loose with a tiny braid encircling the crown of her head. That videotape would be something pretty. It don't have nothing to do, really, with the crow. It would show the future my baby will have. Rising from her narrow bed, Victorine announces, I have memorized something from the Bible, from the Book of Malachi: *"Bring ye all the tithes into the storehouse, that there may be meat in mine house, and prove me now herewith, saith the Lord of hosts, if I will not open you the windows of heaven, and pour you out a blessing, that there shall not be room enough to receive it."*

The reporter, a young man whose instincts keep him at bay from this girl, but who has loved her violently since he stepped into her trailer twenty minutes earlier, saw her on the narrow bed, and heard the Arkansas honey in her voice, says, That's beautiful. I've never heard it before because I don't read the Bible.

Victorine holds his gaze with her green eyes, undoes her flouncy white blouse, and nurses the baby. It's getting dark outside; her mother hovers nearby to light candles that smell of patchouli oil. Victorine says, I still love Benedict, no matter what. Here's my favorite picture of him. She nudges the baby from her breast to draw something from the pocket of her blouse: a newsprint photo of Benedict bare-chested, his arms flung out in the shape of the cross. That was took just a few days before he was arrested, Victorine says. Sid Treadway took it. They was drinking and clowning around. You can have it. I've looked at it till it's in my heart forever. I tell my baby about his dad.

The reporter turns the picture over and discovers on the other side a coupon for a casino in Tunica: SEAFOOD BUFFET HALF PRICE. Victorine sees it too and says, I can't wait till I'm old enough to go play those slot machines.

The reporter tells her, I hope things turn out just fine for you. And you too, ma'am, he says to her mother.

You got me thinkin', Victorine says.

The reporter drives back to Memphis, over the bridge, with the scent of patchouli candles in his hair. For years afterward, while he entertains eligible young women in restaurants, he grows moody over his wine, imagines rescuing Victorine, taking her to the casinos that she dreams of. He tells himself she'll be old and fat by nineteen, but it is because of her that he does not marry until he is forty and the memory of her has faded to an outline of Arkansas trailer and nursing infant.

Oh, it begins, it begins a thousand times, as many times and ways as a heart can beat or break. It began when the victims were conceived, three boys—one of whom, Matthew, had he lived, would have committed sins at least equal to those he suffered; this secret was written in his genes and known only to God and to his mother, who had seen something that terrified her in his eyes one day when he came riding his bike out of the woods, April wind streaming across his fresh blond buzz cut, declaring, I'm the czar; beat a drum and blow a trumpet for me. Two weeks later, Matthew was dead. His mother assumed he had learned the word "czar" in school; that look in his eyes had matched the word, somehow. Glossing her lips in the years after the murders, after the trial, she looks in her mirror and thanks God that there is nothing of her dead son's gaze in her own face.

Yes I loved him, she tells herself, but not like I love the others. Her other children are twins, docile and calm, with a gift for mimicry. They go with her to pull weeds from their dead brother's grave, but doing so they talk about homework, church, cartoons. Both twins can do lots of cartoon voices, to the point where their mother goes weak with laughter, yanking pokeweed mechanically from Matthew's granite monument. The expensive stone bears in the center a porcelain photograph of Matthew, the somber one that ran for months in the newspapers. Matthew's mother was assured by the monument company that the porcelain picture will outlast even the monument itself. In five hundred years, a thousand years, Matthew's face will still gaze across the yard of the Presbyterian church.

We're as high as a cat's back, the owner of the monument company had said proudly as Matthew's mother picked out the stone and made a down payment, but we've been in business forever.

Lady, monument companies come and go as fast as you can say tick, but we'll be here.

I didn't know the grave marker business had such a high turnover, Matthew's mother said, tearing from her checkbook a pastel check printed with a design of irises.

Yep, said the man, but not us. We been in business sixty years, and the last forty, the owner-manager's been me.

Because of the case, a newspaper photographer wins an award, having snapped a picture of the furious crowd outside the police station the day that Benedict James, Sid Treadway, and Robert Abt were arrested. The black-and-white image of those who gathered to see them brought into custody—the bared teeth, the lunging accusation, the scene electric with lynch-longing—finds a place in national news magazines and on the bulletin boards of thousands of newspapermen, amateur shutterbugs, and crime enthusiasts. In the picture, Sid and Robert hang their heads, their cuffed hands chafe at their backs. Benedict looks handsome in profile, his black hair tossed back from his high forehead, his nose shaped like Elvis Presley's, but he's in handcuffs too, and he's hearing the jeers of the crowd that wants him torn apart.

The West Memphis police chief, Merle Neville, receives the personal thanks of the Governor for cracking the case. Modestly he announces, I just listened to the buzz, meaning he has eyes and ears throughout the local subculture. I kept hearing Benedict James's name.

What of "Stonehenge," the abandoned cotton gin-house where Satanic rituals were long rumored to occur, Stonehenge, where word has it that Benedict used to sacrifice dogs, cats, rabbits, chickens? The farmer who owns it, burns the parts of it that will catch fire, and tears the rest of it down. It had sat so long on the edge of his cotton field, a high-roofed shed; not until after the arrests did it blossom with five-pointed stars and 666, and the farmer himself scratched its dirt floor for animal bones and found none, though he did discover charred circles, which the police deemed ritualistic. (Aw, somebody roasted marshmallows out there, the farmer told police, while his wife said, Henry, that cult stuff is true; you just don't want to believe it. There were *orgies* going on out there. Do you think it was anybody we know?)

Merle Neville reassures the public, Your German shepherds are safe now. That's what those devil-worshipers want, is German shepherds.

The farmer resists even that; he does not know anyone who owns a German shepherd, he tells his wife. Most everybody has hounds. The farmer owns a fat yellow Lab that lolls in the grass and snaps at flies as the farmer burns and dismantles his troublesome old cotton shed. To the dog he says, There were never any devil-worship meetings here. *You* know it and I know it.

Benedict James had played with a cat's skull, his classmates recall, jerking it up and down on a string in the second grade, when everybody else had yo-yos. He was seven, then; eleven years later he lured three little boys into the woods and with his two companions he sodomized and killed them, and then, according to Lyle Adair, a former friend of Benedict's who testified against him, Benedict bragged on it all. Victorine vouched that Benedict spent the night with her, but she could not account for the entire evening. She said it wasn't true that he wanted the baby named Lucifer.

He wanted me to give him a lullaby, but I wouldn't do it, Victorine had told the jury. He was with me right *after* them boys was killed. Don't get me wrong—he wouldn't do nothing so bad. But he wasn't with me at the time he said he was. So no lullaby.

She means alibi, her lawyer said.

There was another suspect, a man who had wandered into a Chicken Hooray restaurant the afternoon of the killings and covered the walls of the men's room in bloody handprints. The restaurant manager washed them off himself, disgusted, relieved when the man—wild, Indian-looking—went stumbling off without even ordering a meal. When the murders screamed into the news the next morning, the manager called the police and said, I saw the guy; he was here, all bloody. I knew something was wrong, but I didn't want to fool with him. I never saw him before nor since.

The restaurant sits on the highway close to the swampy field where the bodies were found. The investigators stopped by for fried chicken when the shifts changed and complained that the hot wings were too spicy and the chocolate malts too thin. That was when everybody thought some drifter had done it, a trucker or a hitchhiker stopping by to destroy kids who would have been out of school and into summer's liberty in just a few more weeks, kids who had played in the field and in the woods all their lives.

The restaurant manager weeps when Benedict, Sid, and Robert are convicted. To his wife and daughter, he says, They didn't do it. I saw the guy that did, but he's gone. I wish to God I'd left that blood on the walls. I wish I'd locked him in the men's room and called the cops. He did it, did it and got away with it.

The manager's wife says, Maybe he had just been in a fight. Those three creeps in jail, they're the ones did it.

Their daughter, Crystal, isn't listening. A wispy blonde fifteen-year-old with almost transparent skin, she is in love with Robert Abt, having fallen for him during the trial. She has even visited him in jail, secretly, making the trip by bus to the prison sixty miles away after telling her parents that she is at a friend's house, learning to sew.

Her father says, I will feel wrong for the rest of my life, like I'm wearing the wrong body.

His sobs sound wracking and unmanly to Crystal's distracted ears. She slips away to her room to write to Robert Abt, in a sacred ritual of pink stationery, calligraphic penmanship, and dabs of perfume on the envelope, always with a "LOVE" stamp, placed upside down. In school she had known Robert Abt vaguely; now she has pledged to herself that she will marry him, even if he stays in jail for the rest of their lives. Robert rarely answers her letters; she knows other girls love him too and that he could have his pick. Sid Treadway of the long pimply face and stigma of retardation and signed confession has no such following. Benedict James's admirers are the most varied, including the hardest-core of the tattooed high school girls, a number of quiet intellectual women who would never admit an attraction to him, and several stoned older women who alternately want to mother him and take him to bed.

The girls and the women, along with nearly everyone else in West Memphis, make donations to the reading grove that is established at the elementary school in honor of the murdered children: three sturdy benches donated by the local hardware store and a half-dozen oak saplings that will grow to shade the children of future years, who will linger there, the teachers hope, turning the pages of books, the oak leaves whispering above them.

Crystal, the daughter of the Chicken Hooray manager, gets A's in school without reading anything at all. She pays attention in class. I don't read, but I can write, she tells her friends, meaning her letters to Robert, letters so hot and loving that even the recipient, stupid and angry in his cell, catches his breath as he holds the pink-mist stationery in his hands, the charm of passion searing his blood. He recalls her then. She has visited him three times: a blurry girl who weeps more than she talks, with blonde hair so thin her ears poke through it, reminding him of a lop-eared rabbit, yes he remembers her now.

To her friends, Crystal says mysteriously, Robert *knows something* about what happened, but he didn't do it. When her friends scowl, she sticks out her chin and says, He'd of told me if it was different.

What of the crushed roll of peppermints found at the crime scene, and the scrap of a handkerchief printed with a picture of a Hot Springs bathhouse? Why was one victim, David, missing his shoes, and where is the third bicycle, only two having been recovered at the scene? Who cared about mints or handkerchiefs when the bodies showed treatment that only the devil could have invented, or carried out?

One detective asked the chief, Why don't we arrest that Lyle Adair. We got as much on him as on the others. His name comes up just as often. He was seen at a laundry washing clothes with mud on 'em, and hauling a smelly secret box in the back of his car. Why don't we arrest Lyle Adair.

But Lyle goes free, a rangy, skulking presence who skips out of West Memphis after the trial. The convicted ones are enough, and three is a magic number: Sid Treadway, Robert Abt, Benedict James; three killers for three victims.

Never mind that David would have grown up to be a brilliant folklorist, that even at eight he knew that the ballad "Barbara Allen" existed in at least ninety-two forms, of which he could sing several, in a high clear voice. Nobody knew where he got it, the curiosity about the old songs or the beautiful voice. His mother, a hair stylist, a tough gal who spends her Saturdays waxing her jeep, says David just loved old songbooks. She doesn't like those songs, she tells her friends; it used to bug her when David sang about some Barbara Allen asking for a grave long and narrow. He had a premonition, David's mother says moodily, snipping little v's into a client's bangs to give lift and volume, as the radio plays the Statler Brothers. If I'd gone ahead and given him that Game-Boy he wanted for his last birthday, he'd've put those creepy old ballads out of his head. His dad and I never sung 'em.

Not that she's with David's father anymore. Within six months of the murder convictions, she has divorced David's father. Matthew's parents were long divorced already. The parents of the other victim, Troy, had never married, though they had talked about it when they were not involved with others. They had last discussed it—and decided against it—at a Halloween costume party the year before the murders, a party for grown-ups and kids, he dressed as a crescent moon, she as the sea, with Troy in tow as an undercover cop. It was a great Halloween party, Troy told his mother, his fingers deep in the sticky icing of a cupcake, amidst the flaring jack-o-lanterns and the flowing orange punch, though he had to keep explaining his costume to all the other kids: his old jeans and dirty T-shirt gave no clues. He had a squirtgun in his pocket, though, and a plastic badge on his chest, and late in the party he cut armholes in a paper sack and announced it was a bullet-proof vest. His father, the moon, and his mother, the sea, got drunk enough on rum that they spent the night together, the crescent cardboard mask tossed on her bedroom floor, and her silver shawl, sequined in turquoise, catching the breeze from the window, that warm night. It is the crescent moon who rushes Benedict James in the courtroom some months later, daily during the trial, cursing him to hell and back until the final day when the judge sentences Benedict to death, until Benedict, when asked if he has anything to say, moves his scalloped underlip just enough to reply, No, sir.

❑ ❑ ❑ ❑

The animal part of the legend grows: it wasn't just dogs and chickens sacrificed in McKenzie's cotton shed, the buzz goes, but horses and pigs, sheep and cows and babies of girls who were themselves raised by goats and bore on their foreheads the mark of Baphomet, the head of a goat inside a pentagram, young girls so far gone in depravity that they killed their own infants; they set the babies on a rock and raised the knife and you can still see the blood, the buzz said, look for the dark stain on the biggest rock on the floor of the cotton shed that McKenzie tore down. Babies' blood will never wash away, even if it rains forever.

McKenzie says to his wife, That triple murder was a sex crime. Didn't have nothing to do with the devil. That was just hype that the police and the lawyers thought up.

Satan works through men, through us humans, his wife says.

This is what Troy, the son of the moon and the sea, had done on the day he died. At school that day, he had been impressed by the science lesson: the teacher, a young man impassioned in his love for wildlife, had described a field experiment during a college biology class, during which time he had gone from nest to nest in a swamp, shaking the eggs of birds who had laid them there, birds that had invaded the nests of the rightful owners, rare endangered creatures of milder temperament. Troy pictured his teacher seizing the big speckled invaders' eggs and shaking them hard enough to kill the embryos inside. The teacher was kind, so Troy could not grasp the kindness in his shaking the eggs. It seemed so cruel to kill the baby birds inside.

After school, Troy found his friends Matthew and David. All three had bikes. With little conversation, they planned to race and play in the woods as they always did.

When the man at the woods' edge beckoned them to follow him, Troy's mind was on those birds' eggs being shaken, even as he pedaled toward the forest with his friends. He felt sick at his stomach, thinking of his teacher shaking those eggs. Something tugged vaguely at his thoughts—*don't*—but his legs were churning and his bike sped into the darkness where the trees were and where the man waited.

❑ ❑ ❑ ❑

Humble dreams, Sid Treadway's: to be a trucker in one of the rigs that whiz along I-40 and I-55, staying up all night to cover, oh, six, seven hundred miles. Even after months in jail, he has not realized, not really, that this will not happen for him, that he will never drive such a truck, unless as a very old man straining to read highway signs, his eyes too bleared for driving after dark. It's the driving that has always attracted him, not so much the places, not Chicago or San Francisco or St. Louis, just the fast hard nonstop travel that is sexual for him, the idea of it.

When a damning piece of evidence—a knife—was retrieved from a pond behind Sid's house, Sid's lawyer argued that it was old, rusty, and unidentifiable as the murder weapon. The jury eyeballed it, still sharp as a spearpoint, its handle wrapped with leather thongs, and decided this was it: Those killers thought they'd fooled us, flipping it into the pond when they were through cutting.

After the trial, Sid's lawyer fumed to his friends, There's knives at the bottom of every damn pond in the world, and they said, We don't think so.

Sid had been to Memphis many times. Just before the three little boys were murdered, he had visited the Pink Palace Museum with his father (Sid had long since dropped out of school, abandoning his special education classes) to see a display of elaborate mechanical dinosaurs. At first Sid thought they were real. Roaring giants, they reared back, then lurched toward him, their claws flexing, their great tails thumping the polished museum floor. His father, Big Sid, dared reach across the velvet rope and slap the haunch of a stegosaurus. The creature rolled its eyes at him, and father and son cried out, only the father was laughing.

They got some kinda sensor in there, Big Sid said. It ain't alive. Look at them feet. You can see gears and stuff that they tried to hide with rocks and a clump of fake grass.

I want to go home, Sid said.

Who else, then, was in the cult? Besides Benedict, Robert, and Sid, (speculation ran), a harelipped housewife comes under suspicion. She lives on the edge of town; she might slip out of her house to buy a quart of milk, and instead make her way to Stonehenge. Maybe McKenzie was in on it, people say, and his wife. After all, Stonehenge was on his land. Victorine of course was in the cult although who could blame her; Benedict had brainwashed her and would have eaten their baby had he not been caught in time. A dozen trailer-park teens, grunge-dressed, their ears dulled by endless playing of heavy metal CDs, tell tales of chanting and spells and wild sex, tales about each other and strangers too.

Thirty miles away, in another county, a man and a woman run a shop that sells roach clips, black candles, and wands. A cherry bomb crashes through their plate-glass window and explodes. The couple collect the insurance money and open a tanning salon. Business had been terrible, anyway, ever since the occult rumors got started about the killings. They were never devil-worshipers at all, the couple says; they are Methodists. Their tanning parlor, Sun Worshipers, offers discount coupons in conjunction with the pizza parlor next door. It's a hit.

Where were *you* that afternoon, that witching-hour of suppertime and twilight, that full-moon evening of sticky mild air and fierce mosquitoes, when the boys disappeared, leaving two of their bicycles mangled deep in the woods? Can you account for where you were every minute and with whom, and what you did and why? Suppose it wasn't Benedict or Sid or Robert or the bloody Indian-looking man in Chicken Hooray?

Suppose there's a man who knows the woods well; he's driven the service road to the highway a million times. He killed the little boys in a place near the highway, where the whizz-a-mizz sounds of traffic covered up their shrieks. By the time he read about the boys' disappearance, maybe he was rocking on his heels in Las Vegas. Through the newspapers, he followed the trial from Oregon, say, where he was backhauling trash to a landfill. He's on a fishing trip in the Everglades when he reads about the convictions. Every morning he buys coffee and newspapers from an old man at a little bait store. How 'about them devil worshipers in Arkansas, the fisherman says, squirting milk into his Styrofoam coffee cup. The old man says, What about it. What is it you know. The old man has ears that could hear the splash of a body being rolled into a creek nine hundred miles to the northwest. He has God's eyes.

The fisherman grins into God's eyes and says, Fix me a egg sandwich, mister, and don't tell me you never wanted to bugger no little boy. He slaps Benedict's picture on the newspaper and says, This guy got fat during his trial, didden he? That's what happens when a vampire eats jail food. He was used to living off little boys' blood. He sucked blood from one of 'em's cock, old man.

He drives off in a car he stole in Georgia, a rusty alligator-green Crown Vic with a busted radio and bad shocks. When a hard morning storm catches him, he discovers the car leaks, rain splashing through the vinyl roof and onto his arm as he steers. No fishing that day. His stomach lurches, he has to pull over and roll out of the car into the brush to vomit. The egg sandwich, he thinks. He sees again the old man's eyes. His guts heave. He has heard of people dying from throwing up when they get snakebit. He thinks of that now as he convulses in the weeds, though he knows he wasn't bit. His money's almost gone. The rain stings the back of his neck and slashes his bare arms, exposed in the cut-off T-shirt. It feels like knives, but it's rain.

The moon's face is God's head turned backwards. That's what a teen, brought in for questioning, told the detectives as the investigation stalled, then picked up, then gathered steam. Backwards, yes sir, the girl said, identifying herself as a spirit sister of Victorine, picking at her chipped black nail polish. Yes, she said, I had sex with Benedict and Victorine both. We had went to a carnival in Jonesboro and then we came back to Victorine's trailer and we was drinking. Later on I found out Victorine was pregnant, the girl says, and I'm scared she'll have Siamese twins because of what we done. They're both so sexy, the girl said, Benedict and Victorine. I know I ought to care more about the three little boys that got killed, but the ones I love are Benedict and Victorine and the baby inside her, please let it be okay.

She told the detective, I knew we was going to all make love that night as we was heading to the fair. We crossed this field that smelled all sweet like hay, and in the distance I could see the ferris wheel lit up bright and I heard the music from the fair, and I just knew. It made me scared but so happy. I bet you didn't know anybody could be as happy as I was.

There was a word that Benedict loved, his mother says during the trial, speaking as if her son were already dead. It was an old word, something he found in a dictionary, a word that had not been used for centuries. The detectives write this word down: merry-go-sorry. It means a story with good news and bad, she says slowly, frowning, remembering. Joy and sorrow mixed together, yes, that's what my son used to say. He was always finding out old-timey stuff. Merry-go-sorry. Like if somebody had a lot of trouble in their life, but was still alive to tell about it. Ill fortune, Benedict used to say, and then something good happens to you. Good and bad smacking you in the face all the time. He's always been sad. He has not had much good in his life, but he's not an evil person. Just drugs and drink and getting that girl pregnant and no, he never killed no animals except maybe a bullfrog. He's on medication for sadness. I have tried. I have really tried. He seemed the happiest when we was living out in Washington state, a few years back, with his real dad. He went to school regular then and liked the snow and the mountains. Benedict James is the name he give hisself. When he was born, I named him Woodrow. His real daddy's last name is Gilson. He took his stepdad's name when he was twelve and searched through phone books looking for a first name. Benedict was the one he chose, so that's what he goes by and that's what them that loves him, calls him.

Luminol: what a beautiful word. It makes blood glow in the dark, the egg-shaking science teacher tells the class. Policemen use it to find where people were killed. They used it last year when your friends Troy, David, and Matthew were murdered. Luminol has to be used at night. The police are our friends. They went into the woods at night and sprayed the Luminol on the ground around the ditch where the boys were found, and it lit up like sunset. Phosphorescence: here let me write it on the board, but I've never been any good at spelling. Y'all are better spellers than I am. Everything leaves a trail. Do you pray for your friends who died? Let's all bow our heads right now.

Crystal, in love with Robert Abt and writing him every night now in the privacy of her own room, a room bedecked with angel sun-catchers, bowls of potpourri, and posters of handsome TV stars bare-chested in leather jackets, knows that sooner or later her mother will find out about the correspondence. Propped up on pillows on her pretty bed, she expects her mother to barge in, knock the clipboard and the pink-mist stationery off the bed, and seize her by the ear, declaring, Don't you *fool* with that killer, you hear me?

Yet weeks pass, and Crystal mails the letters each morning in secret at the mailbox near her high school. Growing bolder, she displays a picture of Robert Abt that she clipped from a yearbook. She sticks the picture in the frame of her mirror so she can look at his defiant face while she brushes her thin blonde hair. In dim light, his eyes follow her movements as she tosses her head, brushing her hair as if it's tresses, a word she doesn't know how she knows.

One night her mother enters the room with a basket of fresh clothes, spots the picture, and says, Who is this? Crystal puts down her pen and says, It's who I love.

Setting the laundry basket at the foot of Crystal's bed, her mother goes to the mirror, plucks the picture from the frame, and holds it up to the light. He's one of them three, she says, but with more caution than censure. Crystal waits for outrage, but her mother turns the picture this way and that, then chuckles. He could be in the church choir. Look at that stripe tie and that pressed shirt, she says.

I write to him every day, Crystal says, and sometimes I go visit him. I'm almost grown. Don't try to stop me.

How can anybody stop their kid from growing up? her mother says, laying the picture gently on Crystal's dresser. It's just 'cause he's in jail, and will be until he dies, that he seems like anything at all to you. You write to him all you want, but don't expect me to sew you any white gown for a jailbird wedding, if it gets that far. I bet he's got *sacks* of letters from girls.

Are you mad, Mama? Crystal asks, confused not by her mother's words—they're nearly what she expected—but by her tone, curiosity mixed with scorn and sadness.

Your daddy thinks that Indian-looking guy did it, the one came stumbling into Chicken Hooray, but I think the police got the right ones. Those three jerks in jail did it. The jury decided it and the judge just knew. If your Romeo got out tomorrow, he wouldn't seem so hot. Here's your bras and jeans I washed for you. Oh honey, Robert Abt can't take you to the prom. Find somebody who can.

I'm not going to any prom, Crystal says, glorying in the sacrifice of it all—turning down boys who would ask her. If she chose to, she could spend all afternoon with her hair in curlers, putting on her makeup, pulling on a tight dress with rhinestones on the straps, but she won't. She will take the bus to Cummins prison on that fine spring day and get home late, smelling the apple blossoms in the air and hearing the distant music over at a rented dance hall. Already there is talk among the juniors and seniors of holding the prom at the Holiday Inn, a place of such sophistication that Crystal's heart nearly bursts with longing to go there, but no, she tells herself, I will not.

Suit yourself, honey, her mother says. Proms is too expensive these days anyhow. Kids think they have to rent limos, for God's sake. Your daddy and I had one of them old-fashioned proms with crepe paper streamers strung up in the gym, and it was just as good that way.

Did y'all drink back then? Did you go all the way? Crystal sits up straight on her bed. She has never dared to ask her mother these things.

Of course we did. We still do, and I bet that shocks you more. Her mother laughs and leaves the room.

Crystal sits on her bed, the writing paper scattered across her lap, remembering something: the way her grandmother used to address her mother, Crystal's mother. She used to call her Daughter. Crystal's gaze falls on Robert's picture and it's her grandmother's voice she hears, saying, Daughter, I won't see you as a murderer's bride.

She picks up her pen again and writes to him. The memory of her dead grandmother has awakened something in her, a whole chain of memories. She writes them down for Robert: do you remember, she asks him, as if they are seventy-five instead of fifteen and sixteen. Do you remember the way our elementary school used to play chimes before the principal spoke over the intercom. We'd hear a xylophone and then Mr. Butsavage would speak. Isn't that a funny name. I never heard a funnier one.

Crystal writes many other memories in her letter, but that's the only one that Robert Abt reads. He remembers Mr. Butsavage too, and he hurls the letter to the floor of his cell with an oath. He still remembers a beating the guy gave him, the old wooden-paddle kind. But he can't remember why.

There was a boy in an Arkansas town who wore a long black coat even in summertime, who walked along the levee speaking in verse, waving his hands with their long fingernails at the sky, squinting at the sun. The prettiest thing he'd ever seen, he told his friends, was a little girl with long blonde hair down at Gulf Breeze, Florida. He'd been there long ago. Her hair was so yellow and the sea so green. The sky was green too, because it was about to rain, and Benedict liked rain.

He used to gesture across the river at Memphis and mention a famous movie star who lived there. He'd tell his friends, I know friends of *hers*. They say she's the person they used to go to back in high school when they wanted somebody beat up. She'd get somebody to do it, or she'd beat 'em up herself. Benedict would make his group of followers pause and stare across the river, through the haze that hung always above it, at a pale smudge of townhouses on the cliffs: see that white house on the bluffs? That's hers.

How do you know these people, these friends of hers, a doubter asked. I think you make stuff up.

Maybe I do, Benedict said, and maybe people tell me stuff. Secrets. I like to think about that movie star beating people up in high school. I'd like to take her on.

She's old, man, somebody said.

But she's pretty, said Benedict. One time I was with a lady who was fifty years old, and she was damn sexy. You got no idea, he said to his friends.

So he loved the memory of the little blonde girl by the green

Gulf. He loved the river, with its floods and the slow barges moving their cargoes of coal and timber from St. Paul to New Orleans. He loved the long flat Arkansas roads with cotton fields on either side, and mud puddles, and the painted wooden fake windows, nailed to the sides of small white churches, that serve as stained-glass "windows" for Arkansas congregations that don't have any money.

His own church was his room, where he wrote in his journal and burned his candles and loved and tormented his girlfriend, Victorine, on a bare mattress. The rest is all legend, what they say he did with animals and with those little boys.

Isn't it.

Another baby is growing inside Victorine's belly, this time a black man's child. She took a black man for a lover as easily as she might help herself to a slice of pie. Of all her lovers, and even at sixteen and a half she already has trouble keeping count of them, this man is the one she loves the most, the one who makes her forget about Benedict (whom she had loved despite—because of?—the neck-biting, the two-timing).

This man is a groundskeeper for an old cemetery in Memphis. She met him at a quick-mart where he was buying gas for his truck. He looked at her as she passed by him, a hungry look that held in it a dream, not just of sex but of something lasting. She waited in the store, resting the baby, Malachi Destiny, half on her hip, half on the frozen foods case. She had come to buy herself a Fudgsicle, but now in her mind there was only waiting. The man came in the store and paid for the gasoline and then came straight to her with his deep eyes, hungry and waiting, too.

He said, I noticed you came here on foot. Would you like a ride, you and the little baby.

Victorine opened the ice cream case, which steamed frozenly up into her face. She reached in and plucked out a cup of strawberry ice cream. The man stood beside her, all quietness, older she saw when she looked at him again, older than she'd thought at first, yet with energy and newness.

I'm tired, she told him. I'm tired of everything. I live in a trailer with my mother, and I have this little boy. We don't have a car.

What's your name, he asked her, and she told him.

I'm Zebulon, he said. He took the cup of ice cream from her hand and bought it for her, then held the door as she went outside into the beautiful day (it was February by then, and warm the way the Delta can be in late winter, with the trees already wreathed in palest green). The trials had been over for a few weeks, and the baby was fussy, wearing Victorine out in the trailer all day. Benedict, when she visited him in jail, did not care about anything, he said. Zebulon held the door of his truck open and Victorine climbed into the passenger side. The truck was neat and clean and smelled like the man. She thought about how Benedict would have made her buy the ice cream herself and buy some for him, too. When Zebulon got behind the steering wheel and started the truck, she turned to him and said, Make me laugh. I haven't laughed in a long time.

He held the baby while she ate her ice cream.

That very afternoon he took her to Elmwood, the cemetery where he worked. She had not known there were whole cities of the dead, with lanes marked like city streets and communities of sorts laid out: for the yellow fever victims, for the Memphis Jews and Memphis Chinese, for the Woodmen of the World (some old-fashioned self-help group, Zebulon said), and row after row of Confederate soldiers. Huge trees stretched out their massed limbs above the graves, so that the whole place was a garden, and the ground was hilly like the old Indian mounds that Victorine used to play on as a child. Eighty acres, but it feels like a thousand, said Zebulon, proud. He said: One evening I saw four men all dressed in white, at the tomb of that there Napoleon Hill (with a jerk of his chin he indicated a cotton factor's grave), and they were disappearing.

What do you mean? asked Victorine.

Fading away. And I saw a little child one time, sitting on that stone there, the one with an upside-down torch, meaning a life untimely ended, extinguished you might say.

I want to be buried here, Victorine said. Is there room?

Yes, but it's high, said Zebulon. He showed her a new grave and said, Just the marble itself cost a hundred thousand dollars.

The air grew darker and colder as they wandered, the baby asleep in Victorine's arms. She could hear the highway distantly on one side of the cemetery and a slow train moving behind the trees, but all around were just the silent graves.

Here's a man who went drinking on Front Street a hundred years ago and was never seen again, said Zebulon. Jasper Smith his name was. See the stone bale of cotton beside him. And here's two stone feet underneath a stone tree trunk—that's a lumberjack killed in Arkansas when a tree fell on him. His ma even had his feet measured so the stone feet could be made the right size.

But the stone that Victorine fell in love with was an angel, pointing to heaven with her fingers worn off by rain and time. She had a diadem in her hair, a diadem topped by a star. Victorine fell to her knees on the damp winter earth and wept. Zebulon knelt beside her and said, I have a wife and two daughters. I have always kept my marriage vows, but now I want to spend time with you.

That much felt familiar: Benedict had not been true to her either; she had not been his only girl. Victorine raised her eyes to the angel. Who is buried here, she said.

A slave dealer killed in a duel, he said. Here now, he said, don't wipe your eyes with that handfulla grass. Take my handkerchief.

The handkerchief was fresh and white, pressed as for church. He didn't touch her that day. That came later, and when it did, so lovely, even in her passion she remembered the angel, the clean handkerchief, the strawberry taste of ice cream on her tongue.

Where are they buried, the three little boys? None in the old cemetery in Memphis where Victorine's new lover mows the grass and listens to the silence and to the trains and the cars passing fast on the highway behind a screen of trees. One is buried in Alabama, where his mother's people are: that is Troy, whose mother customed herself as the sea. The cemetery is new, with the stones flat to the ground. Little David lies in Chicago, because his grandparents on his father's side pitched a fit lest he be laid to rest in the town where he was killed. Only Matthew was buried in Arkansas, Matthew who had he lived would have killed someone, too, and maybe many. His mother, who with her twins pulls weeds from his stone, wonders at how the weeds got a foothold so fast in the soil. She still hears the church bells ringing all over town as they did on the day of his funeral. Fine, she thinks, trying to end it. This is what was meant for him. I told him not to go into the woods. I told him.

You can drive the back roads of Arkansas for a hundred years, past Indian mounds, past swamps where turtles cling to logs and slip underwater when your car rumbles by. You can pass through towns so small they have no sidewalks, where the autumn leaves scuttle through unpaved streets; inside the old shotgun houses that used to be sharecroppers' cabins, people love and fight and worry about money and children. Getting on toward dusk, you pass a barred owl perched on a sign, a black-striped sign that indicates a small bridge over a creek. The owl's broad face swivels around to follow your car, its gaze so fierce you back up to look at it again: it doesn't scare. It will hunt into twilight, hunt the mice in the grass and the flocks of blackbirds that whirl like a spray of pepper above fields of cotton and beans.

All over the Mid-South, an ice storm strikes in the winter after the trials, a storm so brilliant and terrible that power is out for weeks in parts of Arkansas, western Tennessee, and northern Mississippi. What's beautiful happens by accident: at the Memphis Fairgrounds, used as a gathering site for toppled trees and piles of brush, tons of debris ignite spontaneously into a colossal, magnificent fire, visible even across the river in West Memphis, where people jump up from their supper tables to stare, glorying and fearing, for it puts them in mind of Judgment Day.

Merry-go-sorry: a word that Benedict wrote in his journal and taught to his mother, a word detectives pointed out as Satanic, though Benedict had merely looked up the phrase in the Oxford English Dictionary.

It begins with three boys alive, then dead, it begins when they were conceived, when the man or men who bound them and knifed them were boys themselves. It never ends, not with Crystal setting down her pen and dreaming of Robert Abt in jail, or with Victorine nursing her two babies, both biggity—that Arkansas word that just means big—a pale biggity son and a dark daughter ("Amaziah," she named the girl, untroubled by the fact that Amaziah in the Book of

Chronicles was a king who set up false gods and was ruined; she just loves the name)—Victorine with the two babies at her breasts, happy enough with her children, or with Farmer McKenzie gazing up into the high ceiling of his barn where a hayfork hangs suspended, its spiked jaws chilling him: one frayed spot in the rope and the rusty fork could fall. He wants to believe some phantom killed those kids, not three young men possessed by Satan, as so many of his neighbors say, or three young men not possessed.

From his farm it's not far to the woods where Ten Mile Bayou spills its dirty water through the forest and out into the fields. Sowing and reaping, he adds up what he knows and finds it wanting.

Save the Reaper

By Alice Munro

Introduced by Lorrie Moore

In Alice Munro's "Save the Reaper," as in Flannery O'Connor's "A Good Man Is Hard to Find," a grandmother on a road trip leads her grandchildren down a hidden and remote dirt road: both old women are in vague search of a house they recall from their girlhoods; both have memories of beautiful glass at its entryway. And though in each story the car ominously gets struck and dangerous men appear, Munro, who shares O'Connor's wicked eye but not her theological certitude, quickly parts company with O'Connor in favor of her own themes. Grace here is an accident of the human heart, a pardon from loneliness. Life's susceptible shape is determined by a half-mocking trick of the loins (in this case, the sexual touch of strangers; or, in the parlance of the grandson's game, "the signals offered by plausible-looking people in other cars or from somebody standing by a mailbox or even riding a tractor in a field"). As always in the fictional world of Munro, a character's fate pivots not on the penitential moment but on the erotic one. The penitential ones accumulate at the end of life, in a heap (of beautiful glass?) through which Munro's characters pick and sift, bittersweetly injuring themselves. The poisonous and bewildering contents of memory's store—a subject usually reserved for novels—is here, as in all her short fiction, Munro's signature subject.

Munro has rewritten the O'Connor story in honor of her own gods: Eros, Demeter, and Hermes—ideas of romance, of harvest, of mischievous and thieving fate. ("I learned Greek mythology and I didn't know where Greece was" complains the protagonist's daughter to her mother. "I didn't know *what* it was.") The stupefying power of love; the deep mourning of one's absent, married children; the inappropriate or foolish feeling of youthful inclinations in the old (and yet the mourning, too, of their fleetingness): all combine to make "Save the Reaper" a kind of pagan prayer. It is a masterful short story, from someone whose work in the genre continues to be complex, radical, and profound.

—LORRIE MOORE

Alice Munro

Save the Reaper

From *The New Yorker*

THE GAME THEY PLAYED was almost the same one that Eve had played with Sophie, on long dull car trips when Sophie was a little girl. Then it was spies—now it was aliens. Sophie's children, Philip and Daisy, were sitting in the backseat. Daisy was barely three and could not understand what was going on. Philip was seven, and in control. He was the one who picked the car they were to follow, in which there were newly arrived space travellers on their way to the secret headquarters, the invaders' lair. They got their directions from the signals offered by plausible-looking people in other cars or from somebody standing by a mailbox or even riding a tractor in a field. Many aliens had already arrived on earth and been translated—this was Philip's word—so that anybody might be one. Gas station attendants or women pushing baby carriages or even the babies riding in the carriages. They could be giving signals.

Usually Eve and Sophie had played this game on a busy highway where there was enough traffic that they wouldn't be detected. (Though once they had got carried away and ended up in a suburban drive.) On the country roads that Eve was taking today that wasn't so easy. She tried to solve the problem by saying that they might have to switch from following one vehicle to another because some were only decoys, not heading for the hideaway at all, but leading you astray.

"No, that isn't it," said Philip. "What they do, they suck the people out of one car into another car, just in case anybody is following. They can be like inside one body and then they go *schlup* through the air into another body in another car. They go into different people all the time and the people never know what was in them."

"Really?" Eve said. "So how do we know which car?"

"The code's on the license plate," said Philip. "It's changed by the electrical field they create in the car. So their trackers in space can follow them. It's just one simple little thing, but I can't tell you."

"Well no," said Eve. "I suppose very few people know it."

Philip said, "I am the only one right now in Ontario."

He sat as far forward as he could with his seat belt on, tapping his teeth sometimes in urgent concentration and making light whistling noises as he cautioned her.

"Unh-unh, watch out here," he said. "I think you're going to have to turn around. Yeah. Yeah. I think this may be it."

They had been following a white Mazda, and were now, apparently, to follow an old green pickup truck, a Ford. Eve said, "Are you sure?"

"Sure."

"You felt them sucked through the air?"

"They're translated simultaneously," Philip said. "I might have said 'sucked,' but that's just to help people understand it."

What Eve had originally planned was to have the headquarters turn out to be in the village store that sold ice cream, or in the playground. It could be revealed that all the aliens were congregated there in the form of children, seduced by the pleasures of ice cream or slides and swings, their powers temporarily in abeyance. No fear they could abduct you—or get into you—unless you chose the one wrong flavor of ice cream or swung the exact wrong number of times on the designated swing. (There would have to be some remaining danger, or else Philip would feel let down, humiliated.) But Philip had taken charge so thoroughly that now it was hard to manage the outcome. The pickup truck was turning from the paved

county road onto a gravelled side road. It was a decrepit truck w
no topper, its body eaten by rust—it would not be going far. Hor
to some farm, most likely. They might not meet another vehicle
switch to before the destination was reached.

"You're positive this is it?" said Eve. "It's only one man by him
self, you know. I thought they never travelled alone."

"The dog," said Philip.

For there was a dog riding in the open back of the truck, running
back and forth from one side to the other as if there were events to
be kept track of everywhere.

"The dog's one too," Philip said.

That morning, when Sophie was leaving to meet Ian at the Toronto
airport, Philip had kept Daisy occupied in the children's bedroom.
Daisy had settled down pretty well in the strange house—except for
wetting her bed every night of the holiday—but this was the first
time that her mother had gone off and left her behind. So Sophie
had asked Philip to distract her, and he did so with enthusiasm
(happy at the new turn events had taken?). He shot the toy cars
across the floor with angry engine noises to cover up the sound of
Sophie's starting the real rented car and driving away. Shortly after
that he shouted to Eve, "Has the B.M. gone?"

Eve was in the kitchen, clearing up the remains of breakfast and
disciplining herself. She walked into the living room. There was the
boxed tape of the movie that she and Sophie had been watching last
night.

The Bridges of Madison County.

"What does mean 'B.M.'?" said Daisy.

The children's room opened off the living room. This was a
cramped little house, fixed up on the cheap for summer rental. Eve's
idea had been to get a lakeside cottage for the holiday—Sophie's and
Philip's first visit with her in nearly five years and Daisy's first ever.
She had picked this stretch of the Lake Huron shore because her
parents used to bring her here with her brother when they were
children. Things had changed—the cottages were all as substantial
as suburban houses, and the rents were out of sight. This house half
a mile inland from the rocky, unfavored north end of the usable

beach had been the best she could manage. It stood in the middle of a cornfield. She had told the children what her father had once told her—that at night you could hear the corn growing.

Every day when Sophie took Daisy's hand-washed sheets off the line, she had to shake out the corn bugs.

"It means 'bowel movement,'" said Philip with a look of sly challenge at Eve.

Eve halted in the doorway. Last night she and Sophie had watched Meryl Streep sitting in the husband's truck, in the rain, pressing down on the door handle, choking with longing, as her lover drove away. Then they had turned and had seen each other's eyes full of tears and shook their heads and started laughing.

"Also it means 'Big Mama,'" Philip said in a more conciliatory tone. "Sometimes that's what Dad calls her."

"Well then," said Eve. "If that's your question, the answer to your question is yes."

She wondered if he thought of Ian as his real father. She hadn't asked Sophie what they'd told him. She wouldn't, of course. His real father had been an Irish boy who was travelling around North America trying to decide what to do now that he had decided not to be a priest. Eve had thought of him as a casual friend of Sophie's, and it seemed that Sophie had thought of him that way too, until she seduced him. ("He was so shy I never dreamed it would take," she said.) It wasn't until Eve saw Philip that Eve could really picture what the boy had looked like. Then she saw him faithfully repro-duced—the bright-eyed, pedantic, sensitive, scornful, fault-finding, blushing, shrinking, arguing young Irishman. Something like Sam-uel Beckett, she said, even to the wrinkles. Of course as the baby got older, the wrinkles tended to disappear.

Sophie was a full-time archaeology student then. Eve took care of Philip while she was off at her classes. Eve was an actress—she still was, when she could get work. Even in those days there were times when she wasn't working, or if she had daytime rehearsals she could take Philip along. For a couple of years they all lived together—Eve and Sophie and Philip—in Eve's apartment in Toronto. It was Eve who wheeled Philip in his baby carriage—and, later on, in his stroller—along all the streets between Queen and College and

Spadina and Ossington, and during these walks she would sometimes discover a perfect, though neglected, little house for sale in a
previously unknown to her two-block-long, tree-shaded, dead-end
street. She would send Sophie to look at it; they would go round
with the real-estate agent, talk about a mortgage, discuss what reno-
vations they would have to pay for, and which they could do themselves. Dithering and fantasizing until the house was sold to
somebody else, or until Eve had one of her periodic but intense fits
of financial prudence, or until somebody persuaded them that these
charming little side streets were not half so safe for women and
children as the bright, ugly, brash, and noisy street that they continued to live on.

Ian was a person Eve took even less note of than she had of the
Irish boy. He was a friend; he never came to the apartment except
with others. Then he went to a job in California—he was an urban
geographer—and Sophie ran up a phone bill which Eve had to
speak to her about, and there was a change altogether in the atmosphere of the apartment. (Should Eve not have mentioned the bill?)
Soon a visit was planned, and Sophie took Philip along, because Eve
was doing a summer play in a regional theater.

Not long afterwards came the news from California. Sophie and
Ian were going to get married.

"Wouldn't it be smarter to try living together for a while?" said
Eve on the phone from her boarding house, and Sophie said, "Oh,
no. He's weird. He doesn't believe in that."

"But I can't get off for a wedding," Eve said. "We run till the
middle of September."

"That's okay," said Sophie. "It won't be a *wedding* wedding."

And until this summer, Eve had not seen her again. There was
the lack of money at both ends, in the beginning. When Eve was
working she had a steady commitment, and when she wasn't working she couldn't afford anything extra. Soon Sophie had a job, too—
she was a receptionist in a doctor's office. Once Eve was just about
to book a flight, when Sophie phoned to say that Ian's father had
died and that he was flying to England for the funeral and bringing
his mother back with him.

"And we only have the one room," she said.

"Perish the thought," said Eve. "Two mothers-in-law in one house, let alone in one room."

"Maybe after she's gone?" said Sophie.

But that mother stayed till after Daisy was born, stayed till they moved into the new house, stayed eight months in all. By then Ian was starting to write his book, and it was difficult for him if there were visitors in the house. It was difficult enough anyway. The time passed during which Eve felt confident enough to invite herself. Sophie sent pictures of Daisy, the garden, all the rooms of the house.

Then she announced that they could come, she and Philip and Daisy could come back to Ontario this summer. They would spend three weeks with Eve while Ian worked alone in California. At the end of that time he would join them and they would fly from Toronto to England to spend a month with his mother.

"I'll get a cottage on the lake," said Eve. "Oh, it will be lovely."

"It will," said Sophie. "It's crazy that it's been so long."

And so it had been. Reasonably lovely, Eve had thought. Sophie hadn't seemed much bothered or surprised by Daisy's wetting the bed. Philip had been finicky and standoffish for a couple of days, responding coolly to Eve's report that she had known him as a baby, and whining about the mosquitoes that descended on them as they hurried through the shoreline woods to get to the beach. He wanted to be taken to Toronto to see the Science Centre. But then he settled down, swam in the lake without complaining that it was cold, and busied himself with solitary projects—such as boiling and scraping the meat off a dead turtle he'd lugged home, so he could keep its shell. The turtle's stomach contained an undigested crayfish, and its shell came off in strips, but none of this dismayed him.

Eve and Sophie, meanwhile, developed a pleasant, puttering routine of morning chores, afternoons on the beach, wine with supper, and late-evening movies. They were drawn into half-serious speculations about the house. What could be done about it? First strip off the living-room wallpaper, an imitation of imitation-wood panelling. Pull up the linoleum with its silly pattern of gold fleurs-de-lis turned brown by ground-in sand and dirty scrub water. Sophie was so carried away that she loosened a bit of it that had rotted in front of the sink and discovered pine floorboards that surely could be sanded. They talked about the cost of renting a sander (supposing, that is, that the house was theirs) and what colors they would choose for the paint on the doors and woodwork, shutters on the windows, open shelves in the kitchen instead of the dingy plywood cupboards. What about a gas fireplace?

And who was going to live here? Eve. The snowmobilers who used the house for a winter clubhouse were building a place of their own, and the landlord might be happy to rent it year-round. Or maybe sell it very cheaply, considering its condition. It could be a retreat, if Eve got the job she was hoping for, next winter. And if she didn't, why not sublet the apartment and live here? There'd be the difference in the rents, and the old-age pension she started getting in October, and the money that still came in from a commercial she had made for a diet supplement. She could manage.

"And then if we came in the summers we could help with the rent," said Sophie.

Philip heard them. He said, "Every summer?"

"Well you like the lake now," Sophie said. "You like it here now."

"And the mosquitoes, you know they're not as bad every year," Eve said. "Usually they're just bad in the early summer. June, before you'd even get here. In the spring there are all these boggy places full of water, and they breed there, and then the boggy places dry up, and they don't breed again. But this year there was so much rain earlier, those places didn't dry up, so the mosquitoes got a second chance, and there's a whole new generation."

She had found out how much he respected information and preferred it to her opinions and reminiscences.

Sophie was not keen on reminiscence either. Whenever the past that she and Eve had shared was mentioned—even those months after Philip's birth that Eve thought of as some of the happiest, the hardest, the most purposeful and harmonious, in her life—Sophie's face took on a look of gravity and concealment, of patiently withheld judgments. The earlier time, Sophie's own childhood, was a positive minefield, as Eve discovered, when they were talking about Philip's school. Sophie thought it a little too rigorous, and Ian thought it just fine.

"What a switch from Blackbird," Eve said, and Sophie said at once, almost viciously, "Oh, Blackbird. What a farce. When I think that you paid for that. You *paid*."

Blackbird was an ungraded alternative school that Sophie had gone to (the name came from "Morning Has Broken"). It had cost Eve more than she could afford, but she thought it was better for a child whose mother was an actress and whose father was not in evidence. When Sophie was nine or ten, it had broken up because of disagreements among the parents.

"I learned Greek myths and I didn't know where Greece was," said Sophie. "I didn't know *what* it was. We had to spend art period making antinuke signs."

Eve said, "Oh, no, surely."

"We did. And they literally badgered us—they badgered us—to talk about sex. It was verbal molestation. You *paid*."

"I didn't know it was as bad as all that."

"Oh well," said Sophie. "I survived."

"That's the main thing," Eve said shakily. "Survival."

Sophie's father was from Kerala, in the southern part of India. Eve had met him, and spent her whole time with him, on a train going from Vancouver to Toronto. He was a young doctor studying in Canada on a fellowship. He had a wife already, and a baby daughter, at home in India.

The train trip took three days. There was a half-hour stop in Calgary. Eve and the doctor ran around looking for a drugstore where they could buy condoms. They didn't find one. By the time they got to Winnipeg, where the train stopped for a full hour, it was too late. In fact—said Eve, when she told their story—by the time they got to the Calgary city limits, it was probably too late.

He was travelling in the day coach—the fellowship was not generous. But Eve had splurged and got herself a roomette. It was this extravagance—a last-minute decision—it was the convenience and privacy of the roomette that were responsible, Eve said, for the existence of Sophie and the greatest change in her, Eve's, life. That, and the fact that you couldn't get condoms anywhere around the Calgary station, not for love or money.

In Toronto she waved goodbye to her lover from Kerala, as you would wave to any train acquaintance, because she was met there by the man who was at that time the serious interest and main trouble in her life. The whole three days had been underscored by the swaying and rocking of the train—the lovers' motions were never just what they contrived themselves, and perhaps for that reason seemed guiltless, irresistible. Their feelings and conversations must have been affected, too. Eve remembered these as sweet and generous, never solemn or desperate. It would have been hard to be solemn when you were dealing with the dimensions and the projections of the roomette.

She told Sophie his Christian name—Thomas, after the saint. Until she met him, Eve had never heard about the ancient Christians in southern India. For a while when she was in her teens Sophie had taken an interest in Kerala. She brought home books from the library and took to going to parties in a sari. She talked about looking her father up, when she got older. The fact that she knew his first name and his special study—diseases of the blood—seemed to her possibly enough. Eve stressed to her the size of the population of India and the chance that he had not even stayed there. What she could not bring herself to explain was how incidental, how nearly unimaginable, the existence of Sophie would be, necessarily, in her father's life. Fortunately the idea faded, and Sophie gave up wearing the sari when all those dramatic, ethnic costumes became too commonplace. The only time she mentioned her father, later on, was when she was carrying Philip, and making jokes about keeping up the family tradition of flyby fathers.

No jokes like that now. Sophie had grown stately, womanly, graceful, and reserved. There had been a moment—they were getting through the woods to the beach, and Sophie had bent to scoop up Daisy, so that they might move more quickly out of range of the mosquitoes—when Eve had been amazed at the new, late manifestation of her daughter's beauty. A full-bodied, tranquil, classic beauty, achieved not by care and vanity but by self-forgetfulness and duty. She looked more Indian now, her creamed-coffee skin had darkened in the California sun, and she bore under her eyes the lilac crescents of a permanent mild fatigue.

But she was still a strong swimmer. Swimming was the only sport she had ever cared for, and she swam as well as ever, heading it seemed for the middle of the lake. The first day she had done it she said, "That was wonderful. I felt so free." She didn't say that it was because Eve was watching the children that she had felt that way, but Eve understood that it didn't need to be said. "I'm glad," she said—though in fact she had been frightened. Several times she had thought, Turn around now, and Sophie had swum right on, disregarding this urgent telepathic message. Her dark head became a spot, then a speck, then an illusion tossed among the steady waves. What Eve feared, and could not think about, was not a failure of strength but of the desire to return. As if this new Sophie, this grown woman so tethered to life, could be actually more indifferent to it than the girl Eve used to know, the young Sophie with her plentiful risks and loves and dramas.

"We have to get that movie back to the store," Eve said to Philip. "Maybe we should do it before we go to the beach."

Philip said, "I'm sick of the beach."

Eve didn't feel like arguing. With Sophie gone, with all plans altered, so that they were leaving, all of them leaving later in the day, she was sick of the beach, too. And sick of the house—all she could see now was the way this room would look tomorrow. The crayons, the toy cars, the large pieces of Daisy's simple jigsaw puzzle, all swept up and taken away. The storybooks gone that she knew by heart. No sheets drying outside the window. Eighteen more days to last, by herself, in this place.

"How about we go somewhere else today?" she said.

Philip said, "Where is there?"

"Let it be a surprise."

Eve had come home from the village the day before, laden with provisions. Fresh shrimp for Sophie—the village store was actually a classy supermarket these days, you could find almost anything— coffee, wine, rye bread without caraway seeds because Philip hated caraway, a ripe melon, the dark cherries they all loved, though Daisy had to be watched with the stones, a tub of mocha-fudge ice cream, and all the regular things to keep them going for another week.

Sophie was clearing up the children's lunch. "Oh," she cried. "Oh, what'll we do with all that stuff?"

Ian had phoned, she said. Ian had phoned and said he was flying into Toronto tomorrow. Work on his book had progressed more quickly than he had expected; he had changed his plans. Instead of waiting for the three weeks to be up, he was coming tomorrow to collect Sophie and the children and take them on a little trip. He wanted to go to Quebec City. He had never been there, and he thought the children should see the part of Canada where people spoke French.

"He got lonesome," Philip said.

Sophie laughed. She said, "Yes. He got lonesome for us."

Twelve days, Eve thought. Twelve days had passed of the three weeks. She had had to take the house for a month. She was letting her friend Dev use the apartment. He was another out-of-work actor, and was in such real or imagined financial peril that he answered the phone in various stage voices. She was fond of Dev, but she couldn't go back and share the apartment with him.

Sophie said that they would drive to Quebec in the rented car, then drive straight back to the Toronto airport, where the car was to be turned in. No mention of Eve's going along. There wasn't room in the rented car. But couldn't she have taken her own car? Philip riding with her, perhaps, for company. Or Sophie. Ian could take the children, if he was so lonesome for them, and give Sophie a rest. Eve and Sophie could ride together as they used to in the summer, travelling to some town they had never seen before, where Eve had got a job.

That was ridiculous. Eve's car was nine years old and in no condition to make a long trip. And it was Sophie Ian had got lonesome for—you could tell that by her warm averted face. Also, Eve hadn't been asked.

"Well that's wonderful," said Eve. "That he's got along so well with his book."

"It is," said Sophie. She always had an air of careful detachment when she spoke of Ian's book, and when Eve had asked what it was about she had said merely, "Urban geography." Perhaps this was the correct behavior for academic wives—Eve had never known any.

"Anyway you'll get some time by yourself," Sophie said. "After all this circus. You'll find out if you really would like to have a place in the country. A retreat."

Eve had to start talking about something else, anything else, so that she wouldn't bleat out a question about whether Sophie still thought of coming next summer.

"I had a friend who went on one of those real retreats," she said. "He's a Buddhist. No, maybe a Hindu. Not a real Indian." (At this mention of Indians Sophie smiled in a way that said this was another subject that need not be gone into.) "Anyway, you could not speak on this retreat for three months. There were other people around all the time, but you could not speak to them. And he said that one of the things that often happened and that they were warned about was that you fell in love with one of these people you'd never spoken to. You felt you were communicating in a special way with them when you couldn't talk. Of course it was a kind of spiritual love, and you couldn't do anything about it. They were strict about that kind of thing. Or so he said."

Sophie said, "So? When you were finally allowed to speak what happened?"

"It was a big letdown. Usually the person you thought you'd been communicating with hadn't been communicating with you at all. Maybe they thought they'd been communicating that way with somebody else, and they thought—"

Sophie laughed with relief. She said, "So it goes." Glad that there was to be no show of disappointment, no hurt feelings.

Maybe they had a tiff, thought Eve. This whole visit might have been tactical. Sophie might have taken the children off to show him something. Spent time with her mother, just to show him something. Planning future holidays without him, to prove to herself that she could do it. A diversion.

And the burning question was, Who did the phoning?

"Why don't you leave the children here?" she said. "Just while you drive to the airport? Then just drive back and pick them up and take off. You'd have a little time to yourself and a little time alone with Ian. It'll be hell with them in the airport."

Sophie said, "I'm tempted."

So in the end that was what she did.

Now Eve had to wonder if she herself had engineered that little change just so she could get to talk to Philip.

(Wasn't it a big surprise when your dad phoned from California?
He didn't phone. My mom phoned him.
Did she? Oh I didn't know. What did she say?
She said, "I can't stand it here, I'm sick of it, let's figure out some plan to get me away.")

Eve dropped her voice to a matter-of-fact level, to indicate an interruption of the game. She said, "Philip. Philip, listen. I think we've got to stop this. That truck just belongs to some farmer and it's going to turn in someplace and we can't go on following."

"Yes we can," Philip said.

"No we can't. They'd want to know what we were doing. They might be very mad."

"We'll call up our helicopters to come and shoot them."

"Don't be silly. You know this is just a game."

"They'll shoot them."

"I don't think they have any weapons," said Eve, trying another tack. "They haven't developed any weapons to destroy aliens."

Philip said, "You're wrong," and began a description of some kind of rockets, which she did not listen to.

When she was a child staying in the village with her brother and her parents, Eve had sometimes gone for drives in the country with her mother. They didn't have a car—it was wartime, they had come here on the train. The woman who ran the hotel was friends with Eve's mother, and they would be invited along when she drove to the country to buy corn or raspberries or tomatoes. Sometimes they would stop to have tea and look at the old dishes and bits of furniture for sale in some enterprising farm woman's front parlor. Eve's father preferred to stay behind and play checkers with some other men on the beach. There was a big cement square with a checker-board painted on it, a roof protecting it but no walls, and there, even in the rain, the men moved oversized checkers around in a deliber-ate way, with long poles. Eve's brother watched them or went swimming unsupervised—he was older. That was all gone now—the cement, even, was gone, or something had been built right on top of it. The hotel with its verandas extending over the sand was gone, and the railway station with its flower beds spelling out the name of the village. The railway tracks too. Instead there was a fake-old-fashioned mall with the satisfactory new supermarket and wineshop and boutiques for leisure wear and country crafts.

When she was quite small and wore a great hair bow on top of her head, Eve was fond of these country expeditions. She ate tiny jam tarts and cakes whose frosting was stiff on top and soft under-neath, topped with a bleeding maraschino cherry. She was not al-lowed to touch the dishes or the lace-and-satin pincushions or the sallow-looking old dolls, and the women's conversations passed over her head with a temporary and mildly depressing effect, like the inevitable clouds. But she enjoyed riding in the backseat imagining herself on horseback or in a royal coach. Later on she refused to go. She began to hate trailing along with her mother and being identi-fied as her mother's daughter. My daughter, Eve. How richly conde-scending, how mistakenly possessive, that voice sounded in her ears. (She was to use it, or some version of it, for years as a staple in some of her broadest, least accomplished acting.) She detested also her mother's habit of dressing up, wearing large hats and gloves in the country, and sheer dresses on which there were raised flowers, like warts. The oxford shoes, on the other hand—they were worn to favor her mother's corns—appeared embarrassingly stout and shabby.

"What did you hate most about your mother?" was a game that Eve would play with her friends in her first years free of home.

"Corsets," one girl would say, and another would say, "Wet aprons."

Hair nets. Fat arms. Bible quotations. "Danny Boy."

Eve always said. "Her corns."

She had forgotten all about this game until recently. The thought of it now was like touching a bad tooth.

Ahead of them the truck slowed and without signalling turned into a long tree-lined lane. Eve said, "I can't follow them any farther, Philip," and drove on. But as she passed the lane she noticed the gateposts. They were unusual, being shaped something like crude minarets and decorated with whitewashed pebbles and bit of colored glass. Neither one of them was straight, and they were half hidden by goldenrod and wild carrot, so that they had lost all reality as gateposts and looked instead like lost stage props from some gaudy operetta. The minute she saw them Eve remembered something else—a whitewashed outdoor wall in which there were pictures set. The pictures were stiff, fantastic, childish scenes. Churches with spires, castles with towers, square houses with square, lopsided, yellow windows. Triangular Christmas trees and tropical-colored birds half as big as the trees, a fat horse with dinky legs and burning red eyes, curly blue rivers, like lengths of ribbon, a moon and drunken stars and fat sunflowers nodding over the roofs of houses. All of this made of pieces of colored glass set into cement or plaster. She had seen it, and it wasn't in any public place. It was out in the country, and she had been with her mother. The shape of her mother loomed in front of the wall—she was talking to an old farmer. He might only have been her mother's age, of course, and looked old to Eve.

Her mother and the hotel woman did go to look at odd things on those trips; they didn't just look at antiques. They had gone to see a shrub cut to resemble a bear, and an orchard of dwarf apple trees.

Eve didn't remember the gateposts at all, but it seemed to her that they could not have belonged to any other place. She backed the car and swung around into the narrow track beneath the trees. The trees were heavy old Scotch pines, probably dangerous—you could see dangling half-dead branches, and branches that had already blown down or fallen down were lying in the grass and weeds on either side of the track. The car rocked back and forth in the ruts, and it seemed that Daisy approved of this motion. She began to make an accompanying noise. *Whoppy. Whoppy. Whoppy.*

This was something Daisy might remember—all she might remember—of this day. The arched trees, the sudden shadow, the interesting motion of the car. Maybe the white faces of the wild carrot that brushed at the windows. The sense of Philip beside her—his incomprehensible serious excitement, the tingling of his childish voice brought under unnatural control. A much vaguer sense of Eve—bare, freckly, sun-wrinkled arms, gray-blond frizzy curls held back by a black hairband. Maybe a smell. Not of cigarettes anymore, or of the touted creams and cosmetics on which Eve once spent so much of her money. Old skin? Garlic? Wine? Mouthwash? Eve might be dead when Daisy remembered this. Daisy and Philip might be estranged. Eve had not spoken to her own brother for three years. Not since he said to her on the phone, "You shouldn't have become an actress if you weren't equipped to make a better go of it."

There wasn't any sign of a house ahead, but through a gap in the trees the skeleton of a barn rose up, walls gone, beams intact, roof whole but flopping to one side like a funny hat. There seemed to be pieces of machinery, old cars or trucks, scattered around it, in the sea of flowering weeds. Eve had not much leisure to look—she was busy controlling the car on this rough track. The green truck had disappeared ahead of her—how far could it have gone? Then she saw that the lane curved. It curved; they left the shade of the pines and were out in the sunlight. The same sea foam of wild carrot, the same impression of rusting junk strewed about. A high wild hedge to one side, and there was the house, finally, behind it. A big house, two stories of yellowish-gray brick, an attic story of wood, its dormer windows stuffed with dirty foam rubber. One of the lower windows shone with aluminum foil covering it on the inside.

She had come to the wrong place. She had no memory of this house. There was no wall here around mown grass. Saplings grew up at random in the weeds.

The truck was parked ahead of her. And ahead of that she could see a patch of cleared ground where gravel had been spread and where she could have turned the car around. But she couldn't get past the truck to do that. She had to stop, too. She wondered if the man in the truck had stopped where he did on purpose, so that she would have to explain herself. He was now getting out of the truck in a leisurely way. Without looking at her, he released the dog, which had been running back and forth and barking with a great deal of angry spirit. Once on the ground, it continued to bark, but didn't leave the man's side. The man wore a cap that shaded his face, so that Eve could not see his expression. He stood by the truck looking at them, not yet deciding to come any closer.

Eve unbuckled her seat belt.

"Don't get out," said Philip. "Stay in the car. Turn around. Drive away."

"I can't," said Eve. "It's all right. That dog's just a yapper, he won't hurt me."

"Don't get out."

She should never have let that game get so far out of control. A child of Philip's age could get too carried away. "This isn't part of the game," she said. "He's just a man."

"I know," said Philip. "But *don't get out.*"

"Stop that," said Eve, and got out and shut the door.

"Hi," she said. "I'm sorry. I made a mistake. I thought this was somewhere else."

The man said something like "Hey."

"I was actually looking for another place," said Eve. "It was a place where I came once when I was a little girl. There was a wall with pictures on it all made with pieces of broken glass. I think a cement wall, whitewashed. When I saw those pillars by the road, I thought this must be it. You must have thought we were following you. It sounds so silly."

She heard the car door open. Philip got out, dragging Daisy behind him. Eve thought he had come to be close to her, and she put out her arm to welcome him. But he detached himself from Daisy and circled round Eve and spoke to the man. He had brought himself out of the alarm of a moment before and now he seemed steadier than Eve was.

"Is your dog friendly?" he said in a challenging way.

"She won't hurt you," the man said. "Long as I'm here, she's okay. She gets in a tear because she's not no more than a pup. She's still not no more than a pup."

He was a small man, no taller than Eve. He was wearing jeans and one of those open vests of colorful weave, made in Peru or Guatemala. Gold chains and medallions sparkled on his hairless, tanned, and muscular chest. When he spoke he threw his head back and Eve could see that his face was older than his body. Some front teeth were missing.

"We won't bother you anymore," she said. "Philip, I was just telling this man we drove down this road looking for a place I came when I was a little girl, and there were pictures made of colored glass set in a wall. But I made a mistake, this isn't the place."

"What's its name?" said Philip.

"Trixie," the man said, and on hearing her name the dog jumped up and bumped his arm. He swatted her down. "I don't know about no pictures. I don't live here. Harold, he's the one would know."

"It's all right," said Eve, and hoisted Daisy up on her hip. "If you could just move the truck ahead, then I could turn around."

"I don't know no pictures. See, if they was in the front part the house I never would've saw them because Harold, he's got the front part of the house shut off."

"No, they were outside," said Eve. "It doesn't matter. This was years and years ago."

"Yeah. Yeah. Yeah," the man was saying, warming to the conversation. "You come in and get Harold to tell you about it. You know Harold? He's who owns it here. Mary, she owns it, but Harold he put her in the Home, so now he does. It wasn't his fault, she had to go there." He reached into the truck and took out two cases of beer. "I just had to go to town, Harold sent me into town. You go on. You go in. Harold be glad to see you."

"Here Trixie," said Philip sternly.

The dog came yelping and bounding around them, Daisy squealed with fright and pleasure and somehow they were all on the route to the house, Eve carrying Daisy, and Philip and Trixie scrambling around her up some earthen bumps that had once been steps. The man came close behind them, smelling of the beer that he must have been drinking in the truck.

"Open it up, go ahead in," he said. "Make your way through. You don't mind it's got a little untidy here? Mary's in the Home, nobody to keep it tidied up like it used to be."

Massive disorder was what they had to make their way through—the kind that takes years to accumulate. The bottom layer of it made up of chairs and tables and couches and perhaps a stove or two, with old bedclothes and newspapers and window shades and dead potted plants and ends of lumber and empty bottles and broken lighting fixtures and curtain rods piled on top of that, up to the ceiling in some places, blocking nearly all the light from outside. To make up for that, a light was burning by the inside door.

The man shifted the beer and got that door open, and shouted for Harold. It was hard to tell what sort of room they were in now—there were kitchen cupboards with the doors off the hinges, some cans on the shelves, but there were also a couple of cots with bare mattresses and rumpled blankets. The windows were so successfully covered up with furniture or hanging quilts that you could not tell where they were, and the smell was that of a junk store, a plugged sink, or maybe a plugged toilet, cooking and grease and cigarettes and human sweat and dog mess and unremoved garbage.

Nobody answered the shouts. Eve turned around—there was room to turn around here, as there hadn't been in the porch—and said, "I don't think we should—" but Trixie got in her way and the man ducked round her to bang on another door.

"Here he is," he said—still at the top of his voice, though the door had opened. "Here's Harold in here." At the same time Trixie rushed forward, and another man's voice said, "Fuck. Get that dog out of here."

"Lady here wants to see some pictures," the little man said. Trixie whined in pain—somebody had kicked her. Eve had no choice but to go on into the room.

This was a dining room. There was the heavy old dining-room table and the substantial chairs. Three men were sitting down, playing cards. The fourth man had got up to kick the dog. The temperature in the room was about ninety degrees.

"Shut the door, there's a draft," said one of the men at the table. The little man hauled Trixie out from under the table and threw her into the outer room, then closed the door behind Eve and the children.

"Christ. Fuck," said the man who had got up. His chest and arms were so heavily tattooed that he seemed to have purple or bluish skin. He shook one foot as if it hurt. Perhaps he had also kicked a table leg when he kicked Trixie.

Sitting with his back to the door was a young man with sharp narrow shoulders and a delicate neck. At least Eve assumed he was young, because he wore his hair in dyed golden spikes and had gold rings in his ears. He didn't turn around. The man across from him was as old as Eve herself, and had a shaved head, a tidy gray beard, and bloodshot blue eyes. He looked at Eve without any friendliness but with some intelligence or comprehension, and in this he was unlike the tattooed man, who had looked at her as if she was some kind of hallucination that he had decided to ignore.

At the end of the table, in the host's or the father's chair, sat the man who had given the order to close the door, but who hadn't looked up or otherwise paid any attention to the interruption. He was a large-boned, fat, pale man with sweaty brown curls, and as far as Eve could tell he was entirely naked. The tattooed man and the blond man were wearing jeans, and the gray-bearded man was wearing jeans and a checked shirt buttoned up to the neck and a string tie. There were glasses and bottles on the table. The man in the host's chair—he must be Harold—and the gray-bearded man were drinking whiskey. The other two were drinking beer.

"I told her maybe there was pictures in the front but she couldn't go in there you got that shut up," the little man said.

Harold said, "You shut up."

Eve said, "I'm really sorry." There seemed to be nothing to do but go into her spiel, enlarging it to include staying at the village hotel as a little girl, drives with her mother, the pictures in the wall, her memory of them today, the gateposts, her obvious mistake, her apologies. She spoke directly to the graybeard, since he seemed the only one willing to listen or capable of understanding her. Her arm and shoulder ached from the weight of Daisy and from the tension which had got hold of her entire body. Yet she was thinking how she would describe this—she'd say it was like finding yourself in the middle of a Pinter play. Or like all her nightmares of a stolid, silent, hostile audience.

The graybeard spoke when she could not think of any further charming or apologetic thing to say. He said, "I don't know. You'll have to ask Harold. Hey. Hey Harold. Do you know anything about some pictures made out of broken glass?"

"Tell her when she was riding around looking at pictures I wasn't even born yet," said Harold, without looking up.

"You're out of luck, lady," said the graybeard.

The tattooed man whistled. "Hey you," he said to Philip. "Hey kid. Can you play the piano?"

There was a piano in the room behind Harold's chair. There was no stool or bench—Harold himself taking up most of the room between the piano and the table—and inappropriate things, such as plates and overcoats, were piled on top of it, as they were on every surface in the house.

"No," said Eve quickly. "No he can't."

"I'm asking him," the tattooed man said. "Can you play a tune?"

The graybeard said, "Let him alone."

"Just asking if he can play a tune, what's the matter with that?"

"Let him alone."

"You see I can't move until somebody moves the truck," Eve said. She thought, There is a smell of semen in this room.

Philip was mute, pressed against her side.

"If you could just move—" she said, turning and expecting to find the little man behind her. She stopped when she saw he wasn't there, he wasn't in the room at all, he had got out without her knowing when. What if he had locked the door?

She put her hand on the knob and it turned, the door opened with a little difficulty and a scramble on the other side of it. The little man had been crouched right there, listening.

Eve went out without speaking to him, out through the kitchen, Philip trotting along beside her like the most tractable little boy in the world. Along the narrow pathway on the porch, through the junk, and when they reached the open air she sucked it in, not having taken a real breath for a long time.

"You ought to go along down the road ask down at Harold's

cousin's place," the little man's voice came after her. "They got a nice place. They got a new house, she keeps it beautiful. They'll show you pictures or anything you want, they'll make you welcome. They'll sit you down and feed you, they don't let nobody go away empty."

He couldn't have been crouched against the door all the time, because he had moved the truck. Or somebody had. It had disappeared altogether, been driven away to some shed or parking spot out of sight.

Eve ignored him. She got Daisy buckled in. Philip was buckling himself in, without having to be reminded. Trixie appeared from somewhere and walked around the car in a disconsolate way, sniffing at the tires.

Eve got in and closed the door, put her sweating hand on the key. The car started, she pulled ahead onto the gravel—a space that was surrounded by thick bushes, berry bushes she supposed, and old lilacs, as well as weeds. In places these bushes had been flattened by piles of old tires and bottles and tin cans. It was hard to think that things had been thrown out of that house, considering all that was left in it, but apparently they had. And as Eve swung the car around she saw, revealed by this flattening, some fragment of a wall, to which bits of whitewash still clung.

She thought she could see pieces of glass embedded there, glinting.

She didn't slow down to look. She hoped Philip hadn't noticed— he might want to stop. She got the car pointed towards the lane and drove past the dirt steps to the house. The little man stood there with both arms waving and Trixie was wagging her tail, roused from her scared docility sufficiently to bark farewell and chase them partway down the lane. The chase was only a formality; she could have caught up with them if she wanted to. Eve had had to slow down at once when she hit the ruts.

She was driving so slowly that it was possible, it was easy, for a figure to rise up out of the tall weeds on the passenger side of the car and open the door—which Eve had not thought of locking—and jump in.

It was the blond man who had been sitting at the table, the one whose face she had never seen.

"Don't be scared. Don't be scared anybody. I just wondered if I could hitch a ride with you guys, okay?"

It wasn't a man or a boy; it was a girl. A girl now wearing a dirty sort of undershirt.

Eve said, "Okay." She had just managed to hold the car in the track.

"I couldn't ask you back in the house," the girl said. "I went in the bathroom and got out the window and run out here. They probably don't even know I'm gone yet. They're boiled." She took hold of a handful of the undershirt which was much too large for her and sniffed at it. "Stinks," she said. "I just grabbed this of Harold's, was in the bathroom. Stinks."

Eve left the ruts, the darkness of the lane, and turned onto the ordinary road. "Jesus I'm glad to get out of there," the girl said. "I didn't know nothing about what I was getting into. I didn't know even how I got there, it was night. It wasn't no place for me. You know what I mean?"

"They seemed pretty drunk all right," said Eve.

"Yeah. Well. I'm sorry if I scared you."

"That's okay."

"If I hadn't've jumped in I thought you wouldn't stop for me. Would you?"

"I don't know," said Eve. "I guess I would have if it got through to me you were a girl. I didn't really get a look at you before."

"Yeah. I don't look like much now. I look like shit now. I'm not saying I don't like to party. I like to party. But there's party and there's party, you know what I mean?"

She turned in the seat and looked at Eve so steadily that Eve had to take her eyes from the road for a moment and look back. And what she saw was that this girl was much more drunk than she sounded. Her dark-brown eyes were glazed but held wide open, rounded with effort, and they had the imploring yet distant expression that drunks' eyes get, a kind of last-ditch insistence on fooling you. Her skin was blotched in some places and ashy in others, her whole face crumpled with the effects of a mighty binge-ing. She was a natural brunette—the gold spikes were intentionally and provocatively dark at the roots—and pretty enough, if you dis-regarded her present dinginess, to make you wonder how she had ever got mixed up with Harold and Harold's crew. Her way of living and the style of the times must have taken fifteen or twenty natural pounds off her—but she wasn't tall and she really wasn't boyish. Her true inclination was to be a cuddly chunky girl, a dar-ling dumpling.

"Herb was crazy bringing you in there like that," she said. "He's got a screw loose, Herb."

Eve said, "I gathered that."

"I don't know what he does around there, I guess he works for Harold. I don't think Harold uses him too good, neither."

Eve had never believed herself to be attracted to women in a sexual way. And this girl in her soiled and crumpled state seemed unlikely to appeal to anybody. But perhaps the girl did not believe this possible—she must be so used to appealing to people. At any rate she slid her hand along Eve's bare thigh, just getting a little way beyond the hem of her shorts. It was a practiced move, drunk as she was. To spread the fingers, to grasp flesh on the first try, would have been too much. A practiced, automatically hopeful move, yet so lacking in any true, strong, squirmy, comradely lust that Eve felt that the hand might easily have fallen short and caressed the car upholstery.

"I'm okay," the girl said, and her voice, like the hand, struggled to put herself and Eve on a new level of intimacy. "You know what I mean? You understand me. Okay?"

"Of course," said Eve briskly, and the hand trailed away, its tired whore's courtesy done with. But it had not failed—not altogether. Blatant and halfhearted as it was, it had been enough to set some old wires twitching.

And the fact that it could be effective in any way at all filled Eve with misgiving, flung a shadow backwards from this moment over all the rowdy and impulsive as well as all the hopeful and serious, the more or less unrepented-of, couplings of her life. Not a real flare-up of shame, a sense of sin—just a dirty shadow. What a joke on her, if she started to hanker now after a purer past and a cleaner slate.

But it could be just that still, and always, she hankered after love.

She said, "Where is it you want to go?"

The girl jerked backwards, faced the road. She said, "Where you going? You live around here?" The blurred tone of seductiveness had changed, as no doubt it would change after sex, into a mean-sounding swagger.

"There's a bus goes through the village," Eve said. "It stops at the gas station. I've seen the sign."

"Yeah but just one thing," the girl said. "I got no money. See, I got away from there in such a hurry I never got to collect my money. So what use would it be me getting on a bus without no money?"

The thing to do was not to recognize a threat. Tell her that she could hitchhike, if she had no money. It wasn't likely that she had a gun in her jeans. She just wanted to sound as if she might have one.

But a knife?

The girl turned for the first time to look into the backseat.

"You kids okay back there?" she said.

No answer.

"They're cute," she said. "They shy with strangers?"

How stupid of Eve to think about sex, when the reality, the danger, were elsewhere.

Eve's purse was on the floor of the car in front of the girl's feet. She didn't know how much money was in it. Sixty, seventy dollars. Hardly more. If she offered money for a ticket the girl would name an expensive destination. Montreal. Or at least Toronto. If she said, "Just take what's there," the girl would see capitulation. She would sense Eve's fear and might try to push further. What was the best she could do? Steal the car? If she left Eve and the children beside the road, the police would be after her in a hurry. If she left them dead in some thicket, she might get farther. Or if she took them along while she needed them, a knife against Eve's side or a child's throat.

Such things happen. But not as regularly as on television or in the movies. Such things don't often happen.

Eve turned onto the county road, which was fairly busy. Why did that make her feel better? Safety there was an illusion. She could be driving along the highway in the midst of the day's traffic taking herself and the children to their deaths.

The girl said, "Where's this road go?"

"It goes out to the main highway."

"Let's drive out there."

"That's where I am driving," Eve said.

"Which way's the highway go?"

"It goes north to Owen Sound or up to Tobermory where you get the boat. Or south to—I don't know. But it joins another highway, you can get to Sarnia. Or London. Or Detroit or Toronto if you keep going."

Nothing more was said until they reached the highway. Eve turned onto it and said, "This is it."

"Which way you heading now?"

"I'm heading north," Eve said.

"That the way you live then?"

"I'm going to the village. I'm going to stop for gas."

"You got gas," the girl said. "You got over half a tank."

That was stupid. Eve should have said groceries.

Beside her the girl let out a long groan of decision, maybe of relinquishment.

"You know," she said, "you know. I might as well get out here if I'm going to hitch a ride. I could get a ride here as easy as anyplace."

Eve pulled over onto the gravel. Relief was turning into something like shame. It was probably true that the girl had run away without collecting any money, that she had nothing. What was it like to be drunk, wasted, with no money, at the side of the road?

"Which way you said we're going?"

"North," Eve told her again.

"Which way you said to Sarnia?"

"South. Just cross the road, the cars'll be headed south. Watch out for the traffic."

"Sure," the girl said. Her voice was already distant; she was calculating new chances. She was half out of the car as she said, "See you." And into the backseat, "See you guys. Be good."

"Wait," said Eve. She leaned over and felt in her purse for her wallet, got out a twenty-dollar bill. She got out of the car and came round to where the girl was waiting. "Here," she said. "This'll help you."

"Yeah. Thanks," the girl said, stuffing the bill in her pocket, her eyes on the road.

"Listen," said Eve. "If you're stranded I'll tell you where my house is. It's about two miles north of the village and the village is about half a mile north of here. North. This way. My family's there now, but they should be gone by evening, if that bothers you. It's got the name Ford on the mailbox. That's not my name, I don't know why it's there. It's all by itself in the middle of a field. It's got one ordinary window on one side of the front door and a funny-looking little window on the other. That's where they put in the bathroom."

"Yeah," the girl said.

"It's just that I thought, if you don't get a ride—"

"Okay," the girl said. "Sure."

When they had started driving again, Philip said, "Yuck. She smelled like vomit."

A little farther on he said, "She didn't even know you should look at the sun to tell directions. She was stupid. Wasn't she?"

"I guess so," Eve said.

"Yuck. I never ever saw anybody so stupid."

As they went through the village he asked if they could stop for ice-cream cones. Eve said no.

"There's so many people stopping for ice cream it's hard to find a place to park," she said. "We've got enough ice cream at home."

"You shouldn't say 'home,' " said Philip. "It's just where we're staying. You should say 'the house.' "

The big hay rolls in a field to the east of the highway were facing ends-on into the sun, so tightly packed they looked like shields or gongs or faces of Aztec metal. Past that was a field of pale soft gold tails or feathers.

"That's called barley, that gold stuff with the tails on it," she said to Philip.

He said, "I know."

"The tails are called beards sometimes." She began to recite, " 'But the reapers, reaping early, in among the bearded barley—' "

Daisy said, "What does mean 'pearly'?"

Philip said, "Bar-ley."

" 'Only reapers, reaping early,' " Eve said. She tried to remember. " 'Save the reapers, reaping early—' " "Save" was what sounded best. Save the reapers.

Sophie and Ian had bought corn at a roadside stand. It was for dinner. Plans had changed—they weren't leaving till morning. And they had bought a bottle of gin and some tonic and limes. Ian made the drinks while Eve and Sophie sat husking the corn. Eve said, "Two dozen. That's crazy."

"Wait and see," said Sophie. "Ian loves corn."

Ian bowed when he presented Eve with her drink, and after she had tasted it she said, "This is most heavenly."

Ian wasn't much as she had remembered or pictured him. He was not tall, Teutonic, humorless. He was a slim fair-haired man of medium height, quick moving, companionable. Sophie was less assured, more tentative in all she said and did, than she had seemed since she'd been here. But happier, too.

Eve told her story. She began with the checkerboard on the beach, the vanished hotel, the drives into the country. It included her mother's city-lady outfits, her sheer dresses and matching slips, but not the young Eve's feelings of repugnance. Then the things they went to see—the dwarf orchard, the shelf of old dolls, the marvellous pictures made of colored glass.

"They were a little like Chagall?" Eve said.

Ian said, "Yep. Even us urban geographers know about Chagall."

Eve said, "Sor-ry." Both laughed.

Now the gateposts, the sudden memory, the dark lane and ruined barn and rusted machinery, the house a shambles.

"The owner was in there playing cards with his friends," Eve said. "He didn't know anything about it. Didn't know or didn't care. And my God, it could have been nearly sixty years ago I was there—think of that."

Sophie said, "Oh, Mom. What a shame." She was glowing with relief to see Ian and Eve getting on so well together.

"Are you sure it was even the right place?" she said.

"Maybe not," said Eve. "Maybe not."

She would not mention the fragment of wall she had seen beyond the bushes. Why bother, when there were so many things she thought best not to mention? First, the game that she had got Philip playing, overexciting him. And nearly everything about Harold and his companions. Everything, every single thing about the girl who had jumped into the car.

There are people who carry decency and optimism around with them, who seem to cleanse every atmosphere they settle in, and you can't tell such people things, it is too disruptive. Ian struck Eve as being one of those people, in spite of his present graciousness, and Sophie as being someone who thanked her lucky stars that she had found him. It used to be older people who claimed this protection from you, but now it seemed more and more to be younger people, and someone like Eve had to try not to reveal how she was stranded in between. Her whole life liable to be seen as some sort of unseemly thrashing around, a radical mistake.

She could say that the house smelled vile, and that the owner and his friends looked altogether boozy and disreputable, but not that Harold was naked and never that she herself was afraid. And never what she was afraid of.

Philip was in charge of gathering up the corn husks and carrying them outside to throw them along the edge of the field. Occasionally Daisy picked up a few on her own, and took them off to be distributed around the house. Philip had added nothing to Eve's story and had not seemed to be concerned with the telling of it. But once it was told, and Ian (interested in bringing this local anecdote into line with his professional studies) was asking Eve what she knew about the breakup of older patterns of village and rural life, about the spread of what was called agribusiness, Philip did look up from his stooping and crawling work around the adults' feet. He looked at Eve. A flat look, a moment of conspiratorial blankness, a buried smile, that passed before there could be any need for recognition of it.

What did this mean? Only that he had begun the private work of storing and secreting, deciding on his own what should be preserved and how, and what these things were going to mean to him, in his unknown future.

If the girl came looking for her, they would all still be here. Then Eve's carefulness would go for nothing.

The girl wouldn't come. Much better offers would turn up before she'd stood ten minutes by the highway. More dangerous offers perhaps, but more interesting, likely to be more profitable.

The girl wouldn't come. Unless she found some homeless, heartless wastrel of her own age. (*I know where there's a place we can stay, if we can get rid of the old lady.*)

Not tonight but tomorrow night Eve would lie down in this hollowed-out house, its board walls like a paper shell around her, willing herself to grow light, relieved of consequence, with nothing in her head but the rustle of the deep tall corn which might have stopped growing now but still made its live noise after dark.

David Foster Wallace

The Depressed Person

THE DEPRESSED PERSON was in terrible and unceasing emotional pain, and the impossibility of sharing or articulating this pain was itself a component of the pain and a contributing factor in its essential horror.

Despairing, then, of describing the emotional pain or expressing its utterness to those around her, the depressed person instead described circumstances, both past and ongoing, which were somehow related to the pain, to its etiology and cause, hoping at least to be able to express to others something of the pain's context, its—as it were—shape and texture. The depressed person's parents, for example, who had divorced when she was a child, had used her as a pawn in the sick games they played. The depressed person had, as a child, required orthodonture, and each parent had claimed—not without some cause, given the Medicean legal ambiguities of the divorce settlement, the depressed person always inserted when she described the painful struggle between her parents over the expense of her orthodonture—that the other should be required to pay for it. And the venomous rage of each parent over the other's petty, selfish refusal to pay was vented on their daughter, who had to hear over and over again from each parent how the other was unloving and selfish. Both parents were well off, and each had privately expressed to the depressed person that s/he was, of course, if push came to shove, willing to pay for all the orthodonture the depressed person needed and then some, that it was, at its heart, a matter not of money or dentition but of "principle." And the depressed person always took care, when as an adult she attempted to describe to a trusted friend the circumstances of the struggle over the cost of her orthodonture and that struggle's legacy of emotional pain for her, to concede that it may very well truly have appeared to each parent to have been, in fact, just that (i.e., a matter of "principle"), though unfortunately not a "principle" that took into account their daughter's needs or her feelings at receiving the emotional message that scoring petty points off each other was more important to her parents than her own maxillofacial health and thus constituted, if considered from a certain perspective, a form of parental neglect or abandonment or even outright abuse, an abuse clearly connected— here the depressed person nearly always inserted that her therapist concurred with this assessment—to the bottomless, chronic adult despair she suffered every day and felt hopelessly trapped in. This was just one example. The depressed person averaged four interpolated apologies each time she recounted for supportive friends this type of painful and damaging past circumstance on the telephone, as well as a sort of preamble in which she attempted to describe how painful and frightening it was not to feel able to articulate the chronic depression's excruciating pain itself but to have to resort to recounting examples that probably sounded, she always took care to acknowledge, dreary or self-pitying or like one of those people who are narcissistically obsessed with their "painful childhoods" and "painful lives" and wallow in their burdens and insist on recounting them at tiresome length to friends who are trying to be supportive and nurturing, and bore them and repel them.

The friends whom the depressed person reached out to for support and tried to open up to and share at least the contextual shape of her unceasing psychic agony and feelings of isolation with numbered around half a dozen and underwent a certain amount of rotation. The depressed person's therapist—who had earned both a terminal graduate degree and a medical degree, and who was the self-professed exponent of a school of therapy which stressed the cultivation and regular use of a supportive peer-community in any endogenously depressed adult's journey toward healing—referred to these female friends as the depressed person's Support System. The approximately half-dozen rotating members of this Support System tended to be either former acquaintances from the depressed person's childhood or else girls she had roomed with at various stages of her school career, nurturing and comparatively undamaged women who now lived in all manner of different cities and whom the depressed person often had not seen in person for years and years, and whom she often called late in the evening, long-distance, for sharing and support and just a few well-chosen words to help her get some realistic perspective on the day's despair and get centered and gather together the strength to fight through the emotional agony of the next day, and to whom, when she telephoned, the depressed person always began by saying that she apologized if she was dragging them down or coming off as boring or self-pitying or repellent or taking them away from their active, vibrant, largely pain-free long-distance lives.

The depressed person also made it a point, when reaching out to members of her Support System, never to cite circumstances like her parents' endless battle over her orthodonture as the *cause* of her unceasing adult depression. The "Blame Game" was too easy, she said; it was pathetic and contemptible; and besides, she'd had quite enough of the "Blame Game" just listening to her fucking parents all those years, the endless blame and recrimination the two had exchanged over her, through her, using the depressed person's (i.e., the depressed person as a child's) own feelings and needs as ammunition, as if her valid feelings and needs were nothing more than a battlefield or theater of conflict, weapons which the parents felt they could deploy against each other. They had displayed far more interest and passion and emotional availability in their hatred of each other than either had shown toward the depressed person herself, as a child, the depressed person confessed to feeling, sometimes, still.

The depressed person's therapist, whose school of therapy rejected the transference relation as a therapeutic resource and thus deliberately eschewed confrontation and "should"-statements and all normative, judging, "authority"-based theory in favor of a more value-neutral bioexperiential model and the creative use of analogy and narrative (including, but not necessarily mandating, the use of hand puppets, polystyrene props and toys, role-playing, human sculpture, mirroring, drama therapy, and, in appropriate cases, whole meticulously scripted and storyboarded Childhood Reconstructions), had deployed the following medications in an attempt to help the depressed person find some relief from her acute affective discomfort and progress in her (i.e., the depressed person's) journey toward enjoying some semblance of a normal adult life: Paxil, Zoloft, Prozac, Tofranil, Welbutrin, Elavil, Metrazol in combination with unilateral ECT (during a two-week voluntary in-patient course of treatment at a regional Mood Disorders clinic), Parnate both with and without lithium salts, Nardil both with and without Xanax. None had delivered any significant relief from the pain and feelings of emotional isolation that rendered the depressed person's every waking hour an indescribable hell on earth, and many of the medications themselves had had side effects which the depressed person had found intolerable. The depressed person was currently taking only very tiny daily doses of Prozac, for her A.D.D. symptoms, and of Ativan, a mild nonaddictive tranquilizer, for the panic attacks which made the hours at her toxically dysfunctional and unsupportive workplace such a living hell. Her therapist gently but repeatedly shared with the depressed person her (i.e., the therapist's) belief that the very best medicine for her (i.e., the depressed person's) endogenous depression was the cultivation and regular use of a Support System the depressed person felt she could reach out to share with and lean on for unconditional caring and support. The exact composition of this Support System and its one or two most special, most trusted "core" members underwent a certain amount of change and rotation as time passed, which the therapist had encouraged the depressed person to see as perfectly normal and OK, since it was only by taking the risks and exposing the vulnerabilities required to deepen supportive relationships that an individual could discover which friendships could meet her needs and to what degree.

The depressed person felt that she trusted the therapist and made a concerted effort to be as completely open and honest with her as she possibly could. She admitted to the therapist that she was always extremely careful to share with whomever she called long-distance

apian drone of the dial tone and feeling even more isolated and inadequate and contemptible than she had before she'd called. These feelings of toxic shame at reaching out to others for community and support were issues which the therapist encouraged the depressed person to try to get in touch with and explore so that they could be processed in detail. The depressed person admitted to the therapist that whenever she (i.e., the depressed person) reached out long-distance to a member of her Support System she almost always visualized the friend's face, on the telephone, assuming a combined expression of boredom and pity and repulsion and abstract guilt, and almost always imagined she (i.e., the depressed person) could detect, in the friend's increasingly long silences and/or tedious repetitions of encouraging clichés, the boredom and frustration people always feel when someone is clinging to them and being a burden. She confessed that she could all too well imagine each friend now wincing when the telephone rang late at night, or during the conversation looking impatiently at the clock or directing silent gestures and facial expressions of helpless entrapment to all the other people in the room with her (i.e., the other people in the room with the "friend"), these inaudible gestures and expressions becoming more and more extreme and desperate as the depressed person just went on and on and on. The depressed person's therapist's most noticeable unconscious personal habit or tic consisted of placing the tips of all her fingers together in her lap as she listened attentively to the depressed person and manipulating the fingers idly so that her mated hands formed various enclosing shapes—e.g., cube, sphere, pyramid, right cylinder—and then appearing to study or contemplate them. The depressed person disliked this habit, though she would be the first to admit that this was chiefly because it drew her attention to the therapist's fingers and fingernails and caused her to compare them with her own.

The depressed person had shared with both the therapist and her Support System that she could recall, all too clearly, at her third boarding school, once watching her roommate talk to some unknown boy on their room's telephone as she (i.e., the roommate) made faces and gestures of repulsion and boredom with the call, this

at night her (i.e., the depressed person's) belief that it wou~~ld be~~
whiny and pathetic to blame her constant, indescribable adult ~~pain~~
on her parents' traumatic divorce or their cynical use of her w~~hile~~
they hypocritically pretended that each cared for her more than t~~he~~
other did. Her parents had, after all—as her therapist had helpe~~d~~
the depressed person to see—done the very best they could with the
emotional resources they'd had at the time. And she had, after all,
the depressed person always inserted, laughing weakly, eventually
gotten the orthodonture she'd needed. The former acquaintances
and roommates who composed her Support System often told the
depressed person that they wished she could be a little less hard on
herself, to which the depressed person often responded by bursting
involuntarily into tears and telling them that she knew all too well
that she was one of those dreaded types of people of everyone's grim
acquaintance who call at inconvenient times and just go on and on
about themselves and whom it often takes several increasingly awkward attempts to get off the telephone with. The depressed person
said that she was all too horribly aware of what a joyless burden she
was to her friends, and during the long-distance calls she always
made it a point to express the enormous gratitude she felt at having
a friend she could call and share with and get nurturing and support
from, however briefly, before the demands of that friend's full, joyful, active life took understandable precedence and required her (i.e.,
the friend) to get off the telephone.

The excruciating feelings of shame and inadequacy which the
depressed person experienced about calling supportive members of
her Support System long-distance late at night and burdening them
with her clumsy attempts to articulate at least the overall context of
her emotional agony were an issue on which the depressed person
and her therapist were currently doing a great deal of work in their
time together. The depressed person confessed that when whatever
empathetic friend she was sharing with finally confessed that she
(i.e., the friend) was dreadfully sorry but there was no helping it she
absolutely *had* to get off the telephone, and had finally detached the
depressed person's needy fingers from her pantcuff and gotten off
the telephone and back to her full, vibrant long-distance life, the
depressed person almost always sat there listening to the empty

self-assured, popular and attractive roommate finally directing at the depressed person an exaggerated pantomime of someone knocking on a door, continuing the pantomime with a desperate expression until the depressed person understood that she was to open the room's door and step outside and knock loudly on the open door so as to give the roommate an excuse to get off the telephone. As a schoolgirl, the depressed person had never spoken of the incident of the boy's telephone call and the mendacious pantomime with that particular roommate—a roommate with whom the depressed person hadn't clicked or connected at all, and whom she had resented in a bitter, cringing way that had made the depressed person despise herself, and had not made any attempt to stay in touch with after that endless sophomore second semester was finished—but she (i.e., the depressed person) had shared her agonizing memory of the incident with many of the friends in her Support System, and had also shared how bottomlessly horrible and pathetic she had felt it would have been to have been that nameless, unknown boy at the other end of that telephone, a boy trying in good faith to take an emotional risk and to reach out and try to connect with the confident roommate, unaware that he was an unwelcome burden, pathetically unaware of the silent pantomimed boredom and contempt at the telephone's other end, and how the depressed person dreaded more than almost anything ever being in the position of being someone you had to appeal silently to someone else in the room to help you contrive an excuse to get off the telephone with. The depressed person would therefore always implore any friend she was on the telephone with to tell her the very *second* she (i.e., the friend) was getting bored or frustrated or repelled or felt she had other more urgent or interesting things to do, to please for God's sake be utterly up-front and frank and not spend one second longer on the phone with the depressed person than she (i.e., the friend) was absolutely glad to spend. The depressed person knew perfectly well, of course, she assured the therapist, how pathetic such a need for reassurance might come off to someone, how it could all too possibly be heard not as an open invitation to get off the telephone but actually as a needy, self-pitying, contemptibly manipulative plea for the friend *not* to get off the telephone, *never* to get off the telephone. The therapist[1] was diligent, whenever the depressed person shared her concern about how some statement or action might "seem" or "appear," in supporting the depressed person in exploring how these beliefs about how she "seemed" or "came off" to others made her feel.

It felt demeaning; the depressed person felt demeaned. She said it felt demeaning to call childhood friends long-distance late at night when they clearly had other things to do and lives to lead and vibrant, healthy, nurturing, intimate, caring partner-relationships to be in; it felt demeaning and pathetic to constantly apologize for boring someone or to feel that you had to thank them effusively just for being your friend. The depressed person's parents had eventually split the cost of her orthodonture; a professional arbitrator had finally been hired by their lawyers to structure the compromise. Arbitration had also been required to negotiate shared payment schedules for the depressed person's boarding schools and Healthy Eating Lifestyles summer camps and oboe lessons and car and collision insurance, as well as for the cosmetic surgery needed to correct a malformation of the anterior spine and alar cartilage of the depressed person's nose which had given her what felt like an excruciatingly pronounced and snoutish pug nose and had, coupled with the external orthodontic retainer she had to wear twenty-two hours a day, made looking at herself in the mirrors of her rooms at her boarding schools feel like more than any person could possibly stand. And yet also, in the year that the depressed person's father had remarried, he—in either a gesture of rare uncompromised caring or a *coup de grâce* which the depressed person's mother had said was designed to make her own feelings of humiliation and superfluousness complete—had paid in toto for the riding lessons, jodhpurs,

---

[1] The multiform shapes the therapist's mated fingers assumed nearly always resembled, for the depressed person, various forms of geometrically diverse cages, an association which the depressed person had not shared with the therapist because its symbolic significance seemed too overt and simple-minded to waste their time together on. The therapist's fingernails were long and shapely and well maintained, whereas the depressed person's fingernails were compulsively bitten so short and ragged that the quick sometimes protruded and began spontaneously to bleed.

and outrageously expensive boots the depressed person had needed in order to gain admission to her second-to-last boarding school's Riding Club, a few of whose members were the only girls at this particular boarding school whom the depressed person felt, she had confessed to her father on the telephone in tears late one truly horrible night, even remotely accepted her and had even minimal empathy or compassion in them at all and around whom the depressed person hadn't felt so totally snout-nosed and brace-faced and inadequate and rejected that it had felt like a daily act of enormous personal courage even to leave her room to go eat dinner in the dining hall.

The professional arbitrator her parents' lawyers had finally agreed on for help in structuring compromises on the costs of meeting the depressed person's childhood needs had been a highly respected Conflict-Resolution Specialist named Walter D. ("Walt") DeLasandro Jr. As a child, the depressed person had never met or even laid eyes on Walter D. ("Walt") DeLasandro Jr., though she had been shown his business card—complete with its parenthesized invitation to informality—and his name had been invoked in her hearing on countless childhood occasions, along with the fact that he billed for his services at a staggering $130 an hour plus expenses. Despite overwhelming feelings of reluctance on the part of the depressed person—who knew very well how much like the "Blame Game" it might sound—her therapist had strongly supported her in taking the risk of sharing with members of her Support System an important emotional breakthrough she (i.e., the depressed person) had achieved during an Inner-Child-Focused Experiential Therapy Retreat Weekend which the therapist had supported her in taking the risk of enrolling in and giving herself open-mindedly over to the experience of. In the I.-C.-F.E.T. Retreat Weekend's Small-Group Drama-Therapy Room, other members of her Small Group had role-played the depressed person's parents and the parents' significant others and attorneys and myriad other emotionally toxic figures from the depressed person's childhood and, at the crucial phase of the drama-therapy exercise, had slowly encircled the depressed person, moving in and pressing steadily in together on her so that she could not escape or avoid or minimize, and had (i.e., the small group had) dramatically recited specially pre-scripted lines designed to evoke and awaken blocked trauma, which had almost immediately provoked the depressed person into a surge of agonizing emotional memories and long-buried trauma and had resulted in the emergence of the depressed person's Inner Child and a cathartic tantrum in which the depressed person had struck repeatedly at a stack of velour cushions with a bat made of polystyrene foam and had shrieked obscenities and had reexperienced long-pent-up and festering emotional wounds, one of which[2] being a deep vestigial rage over the fact that Walter D. ("Walt") DeLasandro Jr. had been able to bill her parents $130 an hour plus expenses for being put in the middle and playing the role of mediator and absorber of shit from both sides while she (i.e., the depressed person, as a child) had had to perform essentially the same coprophagous services on a more or less daily basis for *free,* for *nothing,* services which were not only grossly unfair and inappropriate for an emotionally sensitive child to be made to feel required to perform but about which her parents had then turned around and tried to make *her,* the depressed person *herself,* as a *child,* feel *guilty* about the staggering cost of Walter D. DeLasandro Jr. the Conflict-Resolution Specialist's services, as if the repeated hassle and expense of Walter D. DeLasandro Jr. were *her* fault and only undertaken on *her* spoiled little snout-nosed snaggletoothed behalf instead of simply because of her fucking parents' utterly fucking *sick* inability to communicate and share honestly and work through their own sick, dysfunctional issues with each other. This exercise and cathartic rage had enabled the depressed person to get in touch with some really core resentment-issues, the Small-Group Facilitator at the Inner-Child-Focused Experiential Therapy Retreat Weekend had said, and could have represented a real turning point in the depressed person's journey toward healing, had the rage and velour-cushion-pummeling not left the depressed person so emotionally shattered and drained and traumatized and embarrassed that she had felt she had no choice but to fly back home that night and miss the rest of the I.-C.-F.E.T.R. Weekend and the Small-Group Processing of all the exhumed feelings and issues.

[2] (i.e., one of which purulent wounds)

The eventual compromise which the depressed person and her therapist worked out together as they processed the unburied resentments and the consequent guilt and shame at what could all too easily appear to be just more of the self-pitying "Blame Game" that attended the depressed person's experience at the Retreat Weekend was that the depressed person would take the emotional risk of reaching out and sharing the experience's feelings and realizations with her Support System, but only with the two or three elite, "core" members whom the depressed person currently felt were there for her in the very most empathetic and unjudgingly supportive way. The most important provision of the compromise was that the depressed person would be permitted to reveal to them her reluctance about sharing these resentments and realizations and to inform them that she was aware of how pathetic and blaming they (i.e., the resentments and realizations) might sound, and to reveal that she was sharing this potentially pathetic "breakthrough" with them only at her therapist's firm and explicit suggestion. In validating this provision, the therapist had objected only to the depressed person's proposed use of the word "pathetic" in her sharing with the Support System. The therapist said that she felt she could support the depressed person's use of the word "vulnerable" far more wholeheartedly than she could support the use of "pathetic," since her gut (i.e., the therapist's gut) was telling her that the depressed person's proposed use of "pathetic" felt not only self-hating but also needy and even somewhat manipulative. The word "pathetic," the therapist candidly shared, often felt to her like a defense-mechanism the depressed person used to protect herself against a listener's possible negative judgments by making it clear that the depressed person was already judging herself far more severely than any listener could possibly have the heart to. The therapist was careful to point out that she was not judging or critiquing or rejecting the depressed person's use of "pathetic" but was merely trying to openly and honestly share the feelings which its use brought up for her in the context of their relationship. The therapist, who by this time had less than a year to live, took a brief time-out at this point to share once again with the depressed person her (i.e., the therapist's) conviction that self-hatred, toxic guilt, narcissism, self-pity, neediness, manipulation, and many of the other shame-based behaviors with which endogenously depressed adults typically presented were best understood as psychological defenses erected by a vestigial wounded Inner Child against the possibility of trauma and abandonment. The behaviors, in other words, were primitive emotional prophylaxes whose real function was to preclude intimacy; they were psychic armor designed to keep others at a distance so that they (i.e., others) could not get emotionally close enough to the depressed person to inflict any wounds that might echo and mirror the deep vestigial wounds of the depressed person's childhood, wounds which the depressed person was unconsciously determined to keep repressed at all costs. The therapist—who during the year's cold months, when the abundant fenestration of her home office kept the room chilly, wore a pelisse of hand-tanned Native American buckskin that formed a somewhat ghastlily moist-looking flesh-colored background for the enclosing shapes her joined hands formed in her lap as she spoke—assured the depressed person that she was not trying to lecture her or impose on her (i.e., on the depressed person) the therapist's own particular model of depressive etiology. Rather, it simply felt appropriate on an intuitive "gut" level at this particular point in time for the therapist to share some of her own feelings. Indeed, as the therapist said that she felt comfortable about positing at this point in the therapeutic relationship between them, the depressed person's acute chronic mood disorder could actually itself be seen as constituting an emotional defense-mechanism: i.e., as long as the depressed person had the depression's acute affective discomfort to preoccupy her and take up her emotional attention, she could avoid feeling or getting in touch with the deep vestigial childhood wounds which she (i.e., the depressed person) was apparently still determined to keep repressed.[3]

---

[3] The depressed person's therapist was always extremely careful to avoid appearing to judge or blame the depressed person for clinging to her defenses, or to suggest that the depressed person had in any way consciously *chosen* or *chosen to cling to* a chronic depression whose agony made her (i.e., the depressed person's) every waking hour feel like more than any person could possibly endure. This renunciation of judgment or imposed value was held by the therapeutic school in which the therapist's philosophy of healing had evolved over almost fifteen years of clinical experi-

Several months later, when the depressed person's therapist suddenly and unexpectedly died—as the result of what was determined by authorities to be an "accidentally" toxic combination of caffeine and homeopathic appetite suppressant but which, given the therapist's extensive medical background and knowledge of chemical interactions, only a person in very deep denial indeed could fail to see must have been, on some level, intentional—without leaving any sort of note or cassette or encouraging final words for any of the persons and/or clients in her life who had, despite all their debilitating fear and isolation and defense-mechanisms and vestigial wounds from past traumas, come to connect intimately with her and let her in emotionally even though it meant making themselves vulnerable to the possibility of loss- and abandonment-traumas, the depressed person found the trauma of this fresh loss and abandonment so shattering, its resultant agony and despair and hopelessness so unbearable, that she was, ironically, now forced to reach frantically and repeatedly out on a nightly basis to her Support System, sometimes calling three or even four long-distance friends in an evening, sometimes calling the same friends twice in one night, sometimes at a very late hour, sometimes even—the depressed person felt sickeningly sure—waking them up or interrupting them in the midst of healthy, joyful sexual intimacy with their partner. In other words, sheer survival, in the turbulent

---

ence to be integral to the combination of unconditional support and complete honesty about feelings which composed the nurturing professionalism required for a productive therapeutic journey toward authenticity and intrapersonal wholeness. Defenses against intimacy, the depressed person's therapist's experiential theory held, were nearly always arrested or vestigial survival-mechanisms; i.e., they had, at one time, been environmentally appropriate and necessary and had very probably served to shield a defenseless childhood psyche against potentially unbearable trauma, but in nearly all cases they (i.e., the defense-mechanisms) had become inappropriately imprinted and arrested and were now, in adulthood, no longer environmentally appropriate and in fact now, paradoxically, actually caused a great deal more trauma and pain than they prevented. Nevertheless, the therapist had made it clear from the outset that she was in no way going to pressure, hector, cajole, argue, persuade, flummox, trick, harangue, shame, or manipulate the depressed person into letting go of her arrested or vestigial defenses before she (i.e., the depressed person) felt ready and able to risk taking the leap of faith in her own internal resources and self-esteem and personal growth and healing to do so (i.e., to leave the nest of her defenses and freely and joyfully fly).

wake of her feelings of shock and grief and loss and abandonment and bitter betrayal following the therapist's sudden death, now compelled the depressed person to put aside her innate feelings of shame and inadequacy and embarrassment at being a pathetic burden and to lean with all her might on the empathy and emotional nurture of her Support System, despite the fact that this, ironically, had been one of the two areas in which the depressed person had most vigorously resisted the therapist's counsel.

Even on top of the shattering abandonment-issues it brought up, the therapist's unexpected death also could not have occurred at a worse time from the perspective of the depressed person's journey toward inner healing, coming as it (i.e., the suspicious death) did just as the depressed person was beginning to work through and process some of her core shame- and resentment-issues concerning the therapeutic process itself and the intimate therapist-patient relationship's impact on her (i.e., on the depressed person's) unbearable isolation and pain. As part of her grieving process, the depressed person shared with supportive members of her Support System the fact that she felt she had, she had realized, experienced significant trauma and anguish and isolation-feelings even in the therapeutic relationship itself, a realization which she said she and the therapist had been working intensively together to explore and process. For just one example, the depressed person shared long-distance, she had discovered and struggled in therapy to work through her feeling that it was ironic and demeaning, given her parents' dysfunctional preoccupation with money and all that that preoccupation had cost her as a child, that she was now, as an adult, in the position of having to pay a therapist $90 an hour to listen patiently to her and respond honestly and empathetically; i.e., it felt demeaning and pathetic to feel forced to *buy* patience and empathy, the depressed person had confessed to her therapist, and was an agonizing echo of the exact same childhood pain which she (i.e., the depressed person) was so very anxious to put behind her. The therapist—after attending closely and unjudgingly to what the depressed person later admitted to her Support System could all too easily have been interpreted as mere niggardly whining about the expense of therapy, and after a long and considered pause during which both the therapist and the depressed person had gazed at the ovoid cage which the therapist's mated hands in her lap at that moment composed[4]—had responded that, while on a purely intellectual or "head" level she might respectfully disagree with the substance or "propositional content" of what the depressed person was saying, she (i.e., the therapist) nevertheless wholeheartedly supported the depressed person in sharing whatever feelings the therapeutic relationship itself

---

[4] The therapist—who was substantially older than the depressed person but still younger than the depressed person's mother, and who, other than in the condition of her fingernails, resembled that mother in almost no physical or stylistic respects—sometimes annoyed the depressed person with her habit of making a digiform cage in her lap and changing the shapes of the cage and gazing down at the geometrically diverse cages during their work together. Over time, however, as the therapeutic relationship deepened in terms of intimacy and sharing and trust, the sight of the digiform cages irked the depressed person less and less, eventually becoming little more than a distraction. Far more problematic in terms of the depressed person's trust- and self-esteem-issues was the therapist's habit of from time to time glancing up very quickly at the large sunburst-design clock on the wall behind the suede easy chair in which the depressed person customarily sat during their time together, glancing (i.e., the therapist glancing) very quickly and almost furtively at the clock, such that what came to bother the depressed person more and more over time was not that the therapist was looking at the clock but that the therapist was apparently trying to *hide* or *disguise* the fact that she was looking at the clock. The depressed person—who was agonizingly sensitive, she admitted, to the possibility that anyone she was trying to reach out and share with was secretly bored or repelled or desperate to get away from her as quickly as possible, and was commensurately hypervigilant about any slight movements or gestures which might imply that a listener was conscious of the time or eager for time to pass, and never once failed to notice when the therapist glanced ever so quickly either up at the clock or down at the slender, elegant wristwatch whose timepiece rested hidden from the depressed person's view against the underside of the therapist's slim wrist—had finally, late in the first year of the therapeutic relationship, broken into sobs and shared that it made her feel totally demeaned and invalidated whenever the therapist appeared to try to hide the fact that she wished to know the exact time. Much of the depressed person's work with the therapist in the first year of her (i.e., the depressed person's) journey toward healing and intrapersonal wholeness had concerned her feelings of being uniquely and repulsively boring or convoluted or pathetically self-involved, and of not being able to trust that there was genuine interest and compassion and caring on the part of a person to whom she was reaching out for support; and in fact the therapeutic relationship's first significant breakthrough, the depressed person told members of her Support System in the agonizing period following the therapist's death, had come when the depressed person, late in the therapeutic relationship's second year, had gotten sufficiently in touch with her own inner worth and resources to be able

brought up in her (i.e., in the depressed person[5]) so that they could work together on processing them and exploring safe and appropriate environments and contexts for their expression.

The depressed person's recollections of the therapist's patient, attentive, and unjudging responses to even her (i.e., the depressed person's) most spiteful and childishly arrested complaints felt as if they brought on further, even more unbearable feelings of loss and

---

to share assertively with the therapist that she (i.e., the respectful but assertive depressed person) would prefer it if the therapist would simply look openly at the helioform clock or openly turn her wrist over to look at the underside's wristwatch instead of apparently believing—or at least engaging in behavior which made it appear, from the depressed person's admittedly hypersensitive perspective, as if the therapist believed—that the depressed person could be fooled by her dishonestly sneaking an observation of the time into some gesture that tried to look like a meaningless glance at the wall or an absent manipulation of the cagelike digiform shape in her lap.

Another important piece of therapeutic work the depressed person and her therapist had accomplished together—a piece of work which the therapist had said she personally felt constituted a seminal leap of growth and deepening of the trust and level of honest sharing between them—occurred in the therapeutic relationship's third year, when the depressed person had finally confessed that she also felt it was demeaning to be spoken to as the therapist sometimes spoke to her, i.e., that the depressed person felt patronized, condescended to, and/or treated like a child at those times during their work together when the therapist would start tiresomely lallating over and over and over again what her therapeutic philosophies and goals and wishes for the depressed person were; plus not to mention, while they were on the whole subject, that she (i.e., the depressed person) also sometimes felt demeaned and resentful whenever the therapist would look up from her lap's hands' cage at the depressed person and her (i.e., the therapist's) face would once again assume its customary expression of calm and boundless patience, an expression which the depressed person admitted she knew (i.e., the depressed person knew) was intended to communicate unjudging attention and interest and support but which nevertheless sometimes from the depressed person's perspective looked to her more like emotional detachment, like clinical distance, like mere professional interest the depressed person was purchasing instead of the intensely *personal* interest and empathy and compassion she often felt she had spent her whole life starved for. It made her angry, the depressed person confessed; she often felt angry and resentful at being nothing but the object of the therapist's professional compassion or of the putative "friends" in her pathetic "Support System" 's charity and abstract guilt.

[5] Though the depressed person had, she later acknowledged to her Support System, been anxiously watching the therapist's face for evidence of a negative reaction as she (i.e., the depressed person) opened up and vomited out all these potentially repulsive feelings about the therapeutic relationship, she nevertheless was by this

abandonment, as well as fresh waves of resentment and self-pity which the depressed person knew all too well were repellent in the extreme, she assured the friends who composed her Support System, trusted friends whom the depressed person was by this time calling almost constantly, sometimes now even during the day, from her workplace, dialing her closest friends' long-distance work numbers and asking them to take time away from their own challenging,

---

point in the session benefiting enough from a kind of momentum of emotional honesty to be able to open up even further and tearfully share with the therapist that it also felt demeaning and even somehow abusive to know that, for example, today (i.e., the day of the depressed person and her therapist's seminally honest and important piece of relationship-work together), at the moment the depressed person's time with the therapist was up and they had risen from their respective recliners and hugged stiffly goodbye until their next appointment together, that at that very moment all of the therapist's seemingly intensely personally focused attention and support and interest in the depressed person would be withdrawn and then effortlessly transferred onto the next pathetic contemptible whiny self-involved snaggle-toothed pig-nosed fat-thighed *shiteater* who was waiting out there right outside reading a used magazine and waiting to lurch in and cling pathetically to the hem of the therapist's pelisse for an hour, so desperate for a personally interested friend that they would pay almost as much per month for the pathetic temporary illusion of a friend as they paid in fucking *rent*. The depressed person knew all too perfectly well, she conceded—holding up a pica-gnawed hand to prevent the therapist from interrupting—that the therapist's professional detachment was in fact not at all incompatible with true caring, and that the therapist's careful maintenance of a professional, rather than a personal, level of caring and support and commitment meant that this support and caring could be counted on to always Be There for the depressed person and not fall prey to the normal vicissitudes of less professional and more personal interpersonal relationships' inevitable conflicts and misunderstandings or natural fluctuations in the therapist's own personal mood and emotional availability and capacity for empathy on any particular day; not to mention that her (i.e., the therapist's) professional detachment meant that at least within the confines of the therapist's chilly but attractive home office and of their appointed three hours together each week the depressed person could be totally honest and open about her own feelings without ever having to be afraid that the therapist would take those feelings personally and become angry or cold or judgmental or derisive or rejecting or would ever shame or deride or abandon the depressed person; in fact that, ironically, in many ways, as the depressed person said she was all too aware, the therapist was actually the depressed person's—or at any rate the isolated, agonized, needy, pathetic, selfish, spoiled, wounded-Inner-Child part of the depressed person's—absolutely *ideal* personal friend: i.e. here, after all, was a person (viz., the therapist) who would always Be There to listen and really care and empathize and be emotionally available and giving and to nurture and support the depressed person

stimulating careers to listen supportively and share and dialogue and help the depressed person find some way to process this grief and loss and find some way to survive. Her apologies for burdening these friends during daylight hours at their workplaces were elaborate, involved, vociferous, baroque, mercilessly self-critical, and very nearly constant, as were her expressions of gratitude to the Support System just for Being There for her, just for allowing her to begin

---

and yet would demand absolutely nothing back from the depressed person in terms of empathy or emotional support or in terms of the depressed person ever really caring about or even considering the therapist's own valid feelings and needs as a human being. The depressed person also knew perfectly well, she had acknowledged, that it was in fact the $90 an hour which made the therapeutic relationship's simulacrum of friendship so ideally one-sided: i.e. the only expectation or demand the therapist placed on the depressed person was for the contracted hourly $90; after that one demand was satisfied, everything in the relationship got to be for and about the depressed person. On a rational, intellectual, "head" level, the depressed person was completely aware of all these realities and compensations, she told the therapist, and so of course felt that she (i.e., the depressed person) had no rational reason or excuse for feeling the vain, needy, childish feelings she had just taken the unprecedented emotional risk of sharing that she felt; and yet the depressed person confessed to the therapist that she nevertheless still felt, on a more basic, emotionally intuitive or "gut" level, that it truly was demeaning and insulting and pathetic that her chronic emotional pain and isolation and inability to reach out forced her to spend $1,080 a month to purchase what was in many respects a kind of fantasy-friend who could fulfill her childishly narcissistic fantasies of getting her own emotional needs met by another without having to reciprocally meet or empathize with or even consider the other's own emotional needs, an other-directed empathy and consideration which the depressed person tearfully confessed she sometimes despaired of ever having it in her to give. The depressed person here inserted that she often worried, despite the numerous traumas she had suffered at the hands of attempted relationships with men, that it was in fact her own inability to get outside her own toxic neediness and to Be There for another and truly emotionally *give* which had made those attempts at intimate, mutually nurturing partner-relationships with men such an agonizingly demeaning across-the-board failure.

The depressed person had further inserted in her seminal sharing with the therapist, she later told the select elite "core" members of her Support System after the therapist's death, that her (i.e., the depressed person's) resentments about the $1,080/month cost of the therapeutic relationship were in truth less about the actual expense—which she freely admitted she could afford—than about the demeaning *idea* of paying for artificially one-sided friendship and narcissistic-fantasy-fulfillment, then had laughed hollowly (i.e., the depressed person had laughed hollowly during the original insertion in her sharing with the therapist) to indicate that she heard and acknowledged the unwitting echo of her cold, niggardly, emotionally unavail-

again to be able to trust and take the risk of reaching out, even just a little, because the depressed person shared that she felt as if she had been discovering all over again, and with a shattering new clarity now in the wake of the therapist's abrupt and wordless abandonment, she shared over her workstation's headset telephone, just how agonizingly few and far between were the people whom she could ever hope to really communicate and share with and forge healthy,

---

able parents in the stipulation that what was objectionable was not the actual expense but the idea or *"principle"* of the expense. What it really felt like, the depressed person later admitted to supportive friends that she had confessed to the compassionate therapist, was as if the $90 hourly therapeutic fee were almost a kind of ransom or "protection money," purchasing the depressed person an exemption from the scalding internal shame and mortification of telephoning distant former friends she hadn't even laid fucking *eyes* on in years and had no legitimate claim on the friendship of anymore and telephoning them uninvited at night and intruding on their functional and blissfully ignorantly joyful if perhaps somewhat shallow lives and leaning shamelessly on them and constantly reaching out and trying to articulate the essence of the depression's terrible and unceasing pain even when it was this very pain and despair and loneliness that rendered her, she knew, far too emotionally starved and needy and self-involved to be able ever to truly Be There in return for her long-distance friends to reach out to and share with and lean on in return, i.e. that hers (i.e., the depressed person's) was a contemptibly greedy and narcissistic omnineediness that only a complete idiot would not fully expect the members of her so-called "Support System" to detect all too easily in her, and to be totally repelled by, and to stay on the telephone with only out of the barest and most abstract human charity, all the while rolling their eyes and making faces and looking at the clock and wishing that the telephone call were over or that she (i.e., the pathetically needy depressed person on the phone) would call anyone else but her (i.e., the bored, repelled, eye-rolling putative "friend") or that she'd never historically been assigned to room with the depressed person or had never even gone to that particular boarding school or even that the depressed person had never been born and didn't even exist, such that the whole thing felt totally, unendurably pathetic and demeaning *"if the truth be told,"* if the therapist really wanted the *"totally honest and uncensored sharing"* she always kept *"alleging [she] want[ed],"* the depressed person later confessed to her Support System she had hissed derisively at the therapist, her face (i.e., the depressed person's face during the seminal but increasingly ugly and humiliating third-year therapy session) working in what she imagined must have been a grotesque admixture of rage and self-pity and complete humiliation. It had been the imaginative visualization of what her own enraged face must have looked like which had caused the depressed person to begin at this late juncture in the session to weep, pule, snuffle, and sob in real earnest, she shared later with trusted friends. For no, if the therapist really wanted the truth, the actual "gut"-level truth underneath all her childishly defensive anger and shame, the depressed person had shared from

open, trusting, mutually nurturing relationships to lean on. For example, her work environment—as the depressed person readily acknowledged she'd whined about at tiresome length many times before—was totally dysfunctional and toxic, and the totally unsupportive emotional atmosphere there made the idea of trying to bond in any mutually nurturing way with coworkers a grotesque joke. And the depressed person's attempts to reach out in her emotional

---

a hunched and near-fetal position beneath the sunburst clock, sobbing but making a conscious choice not to bother wiping her eyes or even her nose, the depressed person *really* felt that what was *really* unfair was that she felt able—even here in therapy with the trusted and compassionate therapist—that she felt able to share only painful circumstances and historical insights about her depression and its etiology and texture and numerous symptoms instead of feeling truly able to communicate and articulate and express the depression's terrible unceasing agony *itself,* an agony that was the overriding and unendurable reality of her every black minute on earth—i.e., not being able to share the way it truly *felt,* what the depression made her *feel like* inside on a daily basis, she had wailed hysterically, striking repeatedly at her recliner's suede armrests—or to reach out and communicate and express it to someone who could not only listen and understand and care but could or would actually *feel it* with her (i.e., feel what the depressed person felt). The depressed person confessed to the therapist that what she felt *truly* starved for and really *truly* fantasized about was having the ability to somehow really truly literally *"share"* it (i.e., the chronic depression's ceaseless torment). She said that the depression felt as if it was so central and inescapable to her identity and who she was as a person that not being able to share the depression's inner feeling or even really describe what it felt like felt to her for example like feeling a desperate, life-or-death need to describe the sun in the sky and yet being able or permitted only to point to shadows on the ground. She was so very tired of pointing at shadows, she had sobbed. She (i.e., the depressed person) had then immediately broken off and laughed hollowly at herself and apologized to the therapist for employing such a floridly melodramatic and self-pitying analogy. The depressed person shared all this later with her Support System, in great detail and sometimes more than once a night, as part of her grieving process following the therapist's death from homeopathic caffeinism, including her (i.e., the depressed person's) reminiscence that the therapist's display of compassionate and unjudging attention to everything the depressed person had finally opened up and vented and hissed and spewed and whined and puled about during the traumatically seminal breakthrough session had been so formidable and uncompromising that she (i.e., the therapist) had blinked far less often than any nonprofessional listener the depressed person had ever shared with face-to-face had ever blinked. The two currently most trusted and supportive "core" members of the depressed person's Support System had responded, almost verbatim, that it sounded as though the depressed person's therapist had been very special, and that the depressed person clearly missed her very much; and the one particularly valuable and empathetic and

isolation and try to cultivate and develop caring friends and relationships in the community through church groups or nutrition and
holistic stretching classes or community woodwind ensembles and
the like had proved so excruciating, she shared, that she had all but
begged the therapist to withdraw her gentle suggestion that the
depressed person try her best to do so. And then as for the idea of
girding herself once again and venturing out there into the emotionally Hobbesian meat market of the "dating scene" and trying once
again to find and establish any healthy, caring, functional connections with men, whether in a physically intimate partner-relation-
ship or even just as close and supportive friends—at this juncture in
her sharing the depressed person laughed hollowly into the headset
telephone she wore at the terminal inside her cubicle at her workplace and asked whether it was really even necessary, with a friend
who knew her as well as whatever member of her Support System
she was presently sharing with did, to go into why the depressed
person's intractable depression and highly charged self-esteem- and
trust-issues rendered that idea a pie-in-the-sky flight of Icarusian
fancy and denial. To take just one example, the depressed person
shared from her workstation, in the second semester of her junior
year at college there had been a traumatic incident in which the
depressed person had been sitting alone on the grass near a group of
popular, self-assured male students at an intercollegiate lacrosse
game and had distinctly overheard one of the men laughingly say, of
a female student the depressed person knew slightly, that the only
substantive difference between this woman and a restroom toilet
was that the toilet did not keep pathetically following you around
after you'd used it. Sharing with supportive friends, the depressed
person was now suddenly and unexpectedly flooded with emotional
memories of the early session during which she had first told the
therapist of this incident: they had been doing basic feelings-work

---

elite, physically ill "core" friend whom the depressed person leaned on more heavily
than on any other support during the grieving process suggested that the single most
loving and appropriate way to honor both the therapist's memory and the depressed
person's own grief over her loss might be for the depressed person to try to become
as special and caring and unflaggingly nurturing a friend to herself as the late
therapist had been.

together during this awkward opening stage of the therapeutic process, and the therapist had challenged the depressed person to identify whether the overheard slur had made her (i.e., the depressed person) feel primarily more angry, lonely, frightened, or sad.[6, 6(A)]

By this stage in the grieving process following the therapist's possible death by her own (i.e., by the therapist's own) hand, the

[6] The depressed person, trying desperately to open up and allow her Support System to help her honor and process her feelings about the therapist's death, took the risk of sharing her realization that she herself had rarely if ever used the word "sad" in the therapeutic process's dialogues. She had usually used the words "despair" and "agony," and the therapist had, for the most part, acquiesced to this admittedly melodramatic choice of words, though the depressed person had long suspected that the therapist probably felt that her (i.e., the depressed person's) choice of "agony," "despair," "torment," and the like was at once melodramatic—hence needy and manipulative—on the one hand, and minimizing—hence shame-based and toxic—on the other. The depressed person also shared with long-distance friends during the shattering grieving process the painful realization that she had never once actually come right out and asked the therapist what she (i.e., the therapist) was thinking or feeling at any given moment during their time together, nor had asked, even once, what she (i.e., the therapist) actually thought of her (i.e., of the depressed person) as a human being, i.e. whether the therapist personally liked her, didn't like her, thought she was a basically decent v. repellent person, etc. These were merely two examples.

[6(A)] As a natural part of the grieving process, sensuous details and emotional memories flooded the depressed person's agonized psyche at random moments and in ways impossible to predict, pressing in on her and clamoring for expression and processing. The therapist's buckskin pelisse, for example, though the therapist had seemed almost fetishistically attached to the Native American garment and had worn it, seemingly, on a near-daily basis, was always immaculately clean and always presented an immaculately raw- and moist-looking flesh-tone backdrop to the varioform cagelike shapes the therapist's unconscious hands composed—and the depressed person shared with members of her Support System, after the therapist's death, that it had never been clear to her how or by what process the pelisse's buckskin was able to stay so clean. The depressed person confessed to sometimes imagining narcissistically that the therapist wore the immaculate flesh-colored garment only for their particular appointments together. The therapist's chilly home office also contained, on the wall opposite the bronze clock and behind the therapist's recliner, a stunning molybdenum desk-and-personal-computer-hutch ensemble, one shelf of which was lined, on either side of the deluxe Braun coffeemaker, with small framed photographs of the late therapist's husband and sisters and son; and the depressed person often broke into fresh sobs of loss and despair and self-excoriation on her cubicle's headset telephone as she confessed to her Support System that she had never once even asked the therapist's loved ones' names.

depressed person's feelings of loss and abandonment had become so intense and overwhelming and had so completely overridden her vestigial defense-mechanisms that, for example, when whatever long-distance friend the depressed person had reached out to finally confessed that she (i.e., the "friend") was dreadfully sorry but there was no helping it she absolutely *had* to get off the telephone and back to the demands of her own full, vibrant, undepressed life, a primal instinct for what felt like nothing more than basic emotional survival now drove the depressed person to swallow every last pulverized remnant of pride and to beg shamelessly for two or even just one more minute of the friend's time and attention; and, if the "empathetic friend," after expressing her hope that the depressed person would find a way to be more gentle and compassionate with herself, held firm and gracefully terminated the conversation, the depressed person now spent hardly any time at all listening dully to the dial tone or gnawing the cuticle of her index finger or grinding the heel of her hand savagely into her forehead or feeling anything much at all beyond sheer primal desperation as she hurriedly dialed the next ten-digit number on her Support System Telephone List, a list which by this point in the grieving process had been photocopied several times and placed in the depressed person's address book, workstation terminal's PHONE.VIP file, billfold, zippered interior security compartment of her purse, mini-locker at the Holistic Stretching and Nutrition Center, and in a special homemade pocket inside the back cover of the leatherbound Feelings Journal which the depressed person—at her late therapist's suggestion—carried with her at all times.

The depressed person shared, with each available member of her Support System in turn, some portion of the flood of emotionally sensuous memories of the session during which she had first opened up and told the late therapist of the incident in which the laughing men had compared the female college student to a toilet, and shared that she had never been able to forget the incident, and that, even though she had not had much of a personal relationship or connection to the female student whom the men had compared to a toilet or even known her very well at all, the depressed person had, at the intercollegiate lacrosse game, been filled with horror and empathic despair at the pathos of the idea of that female student being the object of such derision and laughing intergender contempt without her (i.e., the female student, to whom the depressed person again admitted she had had very little connection) ever even knowing it. It seemed to the depressed person very likely that her (i.e., the depressed person's) whole later emotional development and ability to trust and reach out and connect had been deeply scarred by this incident; she chose to make herself open and vulnerable by sharing—albeit only with the one single most trusted and elite and special "core" member of her current Support System—that she had admitted to the therapist that she was, even today, as a putative adult, often preoccupied with the idea that laughing groups of people were often derisive and demeaning of her (i.e., of the depressed person) without her knowledge. The late therapist, the depressed person shared with her very closest long-distance confidante, had pointed to the memory of the traumatic incident in college and the depressed person's reactive presumption of derision and ridicule as a classic example of the way an adult's arrested vestigial emotional defense-mechanisms could become toxic and dysfunctional and could keep the adult emotionally isolated and deprived of community and nurturing, even from herself, and could (i.e., the toxic vestigial defenses could) deny the depressed adult access to her own precious inner resources and tools for both reaching out for support and for being gentle and compassionate and affirming with herself, and that thus, paradoxically, arrested defense-mechanisms helped contribute to the very pain and sadness they had originally been erected to forestall.

It was while sharing this candid, vulnerable four-year-old reminiscence with the one particular "core" Support System–member whom the grieving depressed person felt she now most deeply trusted and leaned on and could really communicate over the headset telephone with that she (i.e., the depressed person) suddenly experienced what she would later describe as an emotional realization nearly as traumatic and valuable as the realization she had experienced nine months prior at the Inner-Child-Focused Experiential Therapy Retreat Weekend before she had felt simply too cathartically drained and enervated to be able to continue and had

had to fly home. I.e., the depressed person told her very most trusted and supportive long-distance friend that, paradoxically, she (i.e., the depressed person) appeared to have somehow found, in the extremity of her feelings of loss and abandonment in the wake of the therapist's overdose of natural stimulants, the resources and inner respect for her own emotional survival required for her finally to feel able to risk trying to follow the second of the late therapist's two most challenging and difficult suggestions and to begin openly asking certain demonstrably honest and supportive others to tell her straight out whether they ever secretly felt contempt, derision, judgment, or repulsion for her. And the depressed person shared that she now, finally, after four years of whiny and truculent resistance, proposed at last really to begin actually asking trusted others this seminally honest and possibly shattering question, and that because she was all too aware of her own essential weakness and defensive capacities for denial and avoidance, she (i.e., the depressed person) was choosing to commence this unprecedentedly vulnerable interrogative process now, i.e., with the elite, incomparably honest and compassionate "core" Support System–member with whom she was sharing via her workstation's headset right this moment.[7] The depressed person here paused momentarily to insert the additional fact that she had firmly resolved to herself to ask this potentially deeply traumatizing question without the usual pathetic and irritating defense-mechanisms of preamble or apology or interpolated self-criticism. She wished to hear, with no holds barred, the depressed person averred, the one very most valuable and intimate friend in her current Support System's brutally honest opinion of her as a

---

[7] The singularly valuable and supportive long-distance friend to whom the depressed person had decided she was least mortified about posing a question this fraught with openness and vulnerability and emotional risk was an alumna of one of the depressed person's very first childhood boarding schools, a surpassingly generous and nurturing divorced mother of two in Bloomfield Hills, Michigan, who had recently undergone her second course of chemotherapy for a virulent neuroblastoma which had greatly reduced the number of responsibilities and activities in her full, functional, vibrantly other-directed adult life, and who thus was now not only almost always at home but also enjoyed nearly unlimited conflict-free availability and time to share on the telephone, for which the depressed person was always careful to enter a daily prayer of gratitude in her Feelings Journal.

person, the potentially negative and judging and hurtful parts as well as the positive and affirming and supportive and nurturing parts. The depressed person stressed that she was serious about this: whether it sounded melodramatic or not, the brutally honest assessment of her by an objective but deeply caring other felt to her, at this point in time, like an almost literal matter of life and death.

For she was frightened, the depressed person confessed to the trusted and convalescing friend, profoundly, unprecedentedly frightened by what she was beginning to feel she was seeing and learning and getting in touch with about herself in the grieving process following the sudden death of a therapist who for nearly four years had been the depressed person's closest and most trusted confidante and source of support and affirmation and—with no offense in any way intended to any members of her Support System—her very best friend in the world. Because what she had discovered, the depressed person confided long-distance, when she took her important daily Quiet Time[8] now, during the grieving process, and got quiet and centered and looked deep within, was that she could neither feel nor identify any real feelings within herself for the therapist, i.e. for the therapist as a person, a person who had died, a person who only somebody in truly stupefying denial could fail to see had probably taken her own life, and thus a person who, the depressed person posited, had possibly herself suffered levels of emotional agony and isolation and despair which were comparable to or perhaps—though it was only on a "head" or purely abstract intellectual level that she seemed to be able even to entertain this possibility, the depressed person confessed over the headset telephone—even exceeded the depressed person's own. The depressed person shared that the most frightening implication of this (i.e., of the fact that, even when she centered and looked deep within herself, she felt she could locate no real feelings for the therapist as an autonomously valid human being) appeared to be that all her ago-

---

[8] (i.e., carefully arranging her morning schedule to permit the twenty minutes the therapist had long suggested for quiet centering and getting in touch with feelings and owning them and journaling about them, looking inside herself with a compassionate, unjudging, almost clinical detachment)

nized pain and despair since the therapist's suicide had in fact been all and only for *herself*, i.e. for *her* loss, *her* abandonment, *her* grief, *her* trauma and pain and primal affective survival. And, the depressed person shared that she was taking the additional risk of revealing, even more frightening, that this shatteringly terrifying set of realizations, instead now of awakening in her any feelings of compassion, empathy, and other-directed grief for the therapist as a person, had—and here the depressed person waited patiently for an episode of retching in the especially available trusted friend to pass so that she could take the risk of sharing this with her—that these shatteringly frightening realizations had seemed, terrifyingly, merely to have brought up and created still more and further feelings in the depressed person about *herself*. At this point in the sharing, the depressed person took a time-out to solemnly swear to her long-distance, gravely ill, frequently retching but still caring and intimate friend that there was no toxic or pathetically manipulative self-excoriation here in what she (i.e., the depressed person) was reaching out and opening up and confessing, only profound and unprecedented fear: the depressed person was frightened for herself, for as it were "[her]*self*"—i.e. for her own so-called "character" or "spirit" or as it were "soul" i.e. for her own capacity for basic human empathy and compassion and caring—she told the supportive friend with the neuroblastoma. She was asking sincerely, the depressed person said, honestly, desperately: what kind of person could seem to feel nothing—*"nothing,"* she emphasized—for anyone but herself? Maybe not *ever?* The depressed person wept into the headset telephone and said that right here and now she was shamelessly begging her currently very best friend and confidante in the world to share her (i.e., the friend with the virulent malignancy in her adrenal medulla's) brutally candid assessment, to pull no punches, to say nothing reassuring or exculpatory or supportive which she did not honestly believe to be true. She trusted her, she assured her. For she had decided, she said, that her very life itself, however fraught with agony and despair and indescribable loneliness, depended, at this point in her journey toward true healing, on inviting—even if necessary laying aside all possible pride and defense and *begging for,* she interpolated—the judgment of certain trusted and very carefully

selected members of her supportive community. So, the depressed
person said, her voice breaking, she was begging her now single
most trusted friend to share her very most private judgment of the
depressed person's "character"'s or "spirit"'s capacity for human
caring. She needed her feedback, the depressed person wept, even if
that feedback was partly negative or hurtful or traumatic or had the
potential to push her right over the emotional edge once and for
all—even, she pleaded, if that feedback lay on nothing more than
the coldly intellectual or "head" level of objective verbal description;
she would settle even for that, she promised, hunched and trembling
in a near-fetal position atop her workstation cubicle's ergonomic
chair—and therefore now urged her terminally ill friend to go on,
to not hold back, to let her have it: what words and terms might be
applied to describe and assess such a solipsistic, self-consumed, endless emotional vacuum and sponge as she now appeared to herself to
be? How was she to decide and describe—even to herself, looking
inward and facing herself—what all she'd so painfully learned said
about her?

Pam Houston

Cataract

From *CutBank*

I GUESS I SHOULD have known the trip was doomed from the start.

When Josh forgot the Coleman stove *and* the five-gallon water thermos but only remembered to tell me about the stove on the truck-stop phone, and Henry's plane, four hours late into Salt Lake City from Chicago, he and Thea fighting over the Wagoneer's front seat, baiting each other like teenagers before we even got on the I-15 headed south.

I put in a Leonard Cohen tape, which Thea exchanged for something grungy and indecipherable, which Henry exchanged for Jimmy Buffett's *Living and Dying in ¾ Time.*

Thea said, "Henry's not happy unless the music he listens to exploits at least three cultures simultaneously."

It had been three years since Josh had come into my life wanting to know how to run rivers, two years since I taught him to row, six months since he decided he knew more about the river than I did, two weeks since he stopped speaking, since he started forgetting indispensable pieces of gear.

By the time we got to Hite's Crossing, ready to leave the truck at the take-out, we couldn't find the pilot who was supposed to fly us back upriver.

The little Beachcraft 270 sat on the runway, wings flexing against the wire tiedowns and I knew that meant we were paying for ground time while we all walked around separate coves and inlets trying to find the pilot, hands over our eyes, over our sunglasses, trying to fend off the glare and the hot wind and the waves of dizzying afternoon heat.

By the time we did find him the wind was up further, and he said it was too rough to fly, and would we mind keeping him posted while he ran down to the trailers where he had a little girlfriend, and it wouldn't—he winked at Henry—take him but a minute to go down there and see about her.

Thea and I sat on the short runway in the shade of the plane's left wing and looked out across the surface of Lake Powell, almost turquoise in the late-in-the-day sun, and the white and rust colored mesa tops that receded into forever beyond it.

"Not a bird, not a tree, not even a blade of grass," Thea said. "What precise level of hell is this?"

I looked at the scaly bathtub ring that circled the canyon walls thirty feet above the lake's present surface, at the log and silt jam that floated in the dead space where what used to be the Colorado River once came roaring through.

"Somebody's bright idea," I said. "Land of many uses."

The wind howled across the surface of the lake making a hundred thousand rows of diamonds moving toward us fast.

"And there's really a river up there?" Thea said, pointing with her chin to the north, to the other side of the log jam, a hundred miles beyond that to the put-in where Russell and Josh and the boats had been ready for hours, to the place the plane would take us if the wind would ever stop.

"Thirty miles up-canyon," I said, "is the wildest whitest water in America. The wind can howl up that canyon all day sometimes, and once you get through the rapids, once you hit lake level, you can row as hard as you want to—you won't be going anywhere but upstream in a blow even half this strong."

"Lucy," she said, "you're always going upstream."

"I know," I said, "but not as bad as that."

I looked along the shore to where the pilot had disappeared and tried not to think about the river level, 61,000 cubic feet of water per second and rising. Everybody who ran Cataract Canyon knew the sixty thousands were the most difficult level to negotiate, not counting, of course, the hundred-year flood.

I'd been running rivers a lot of years by then but I didn't overwhelm anybody with my level of confidence, hadn't ever acquired what I would call an athlete's natural grace.

It all went back to my father, I guess, as most things did, how he'd wanted me to be Chris Evert—not to be *like* her, understand, but *be* her. And *being her* always meant *to the exclusion of me.*

I got decent on the tennis court when I was seven and twelve and fourteen but could never move my feet fast enough across the hard clay surface to win a first place prize.

I'm strong for a girl, and stubborn enough not to give up without a dogfight. I took to the river because I believed it talked to me.

I believed that I could read the river, that I could understand its language, that I could let it tell me, sometimes even mid-rapid, exactly where it wanted me to be.

Thea said, "So how *are* things between Josh and you anyway."

"Stagnant," I said, "is the word that comes to mind."

"You invited Josh to go to sleep," Henry said, startling us from behind. "He accepted."

"Easy thing to do, sleep," I said, "when you keep your eyes closed all the time."

"You're getting smarter," Henry said, "slowly."

"That's quite the blessing," Thea said, "coming from you." She turned back to me. "I, by the way, have ended things with Charlie."

"Charlie," I said. "Did I know about Charlie?"

"He was in love with me," Thea said. "I was in love with the Universe."

"You can't be fussy," Henry said, "if you're gonna fuck 'em all."

"When are you gonna bring one of these guys down the river," I asked her.

"With us?" she said, "With you? Never in a hundred billion years."

❏ ❏ ❏ ❏

Henry and Thea had come into my life in the same year and both because of photography. Thea was my student at a semester-long seminar I taught in Denver, and Henry had bought one of my prints out of a gallery in Chicago and liked it so well he'd hunted me down. They had taken an instantaneous dislike to each other at a party I'd had the summer before to celebrate the summer solstice. I was running four or five rivers a year in those days and Thea hardly ever missed a launch date. Cataract was Henry's first trip.

I had been down Cataract Canyon three times before, but always in the drought years, thumping along through the Big Drops in the slow motion of six or eleven or fifteen thousand cubic feet per second while the Park Service waited for the one big snow that was going to come down from the high country as melt water and fill the reservoir to the top again.

Now the river had come back with a vengeance, filling the lake and threatening daily to burn up the dam's sluggish turbines. The spillways were carrying too much water, and the sandstone was being eaten away on either side of the dam. Thirty miles upriver, five people were dead at the bottom of Satan's Gut already, the season barely three weeks old.

"Tell me about the people who died," Thea said, and I blinked at her, my eyes dry as sockets in the wind. She read my mind like that a couple times daily. It still unsettled me.

"Well," I said, "two of 'em were that father and son that came down the Green in their powerboat, got to the confluence and turned the wrong way."

Thea nodded and I knew she'd have studied the maps before she came.

She didn't have a lot of experience but she wanted it bad, was the best student of the river I'd ever trained. When we were in the boat all I'd have to do was think of something I needed—a throw line or a spare oar blade, even a drink of water—and I'd open my mouth to ask her for it and there she'd be already putting it into my hand.

"And another one," I said, "was that crazy who tried to swim the whole series at high-water each year."

"Twenty-six rapids?" Thea said.

"In the drought years the water is warmer," I said, "and there's ages of time between falls. They say he wore three life jackets, one right on top of the other. I know it sounds impossible, but there were witnesses, five years in a row."

"Not this year," Henry said.

"No," I said, "he was dead before he even got to the Big Drops."

"And the other two?" Henry said.

"The other two were experienced boaters," I said, "out to have a little fun."

"Just like us," Thea said.

"Yep," I said. "Just like us."

The wind died right at seven like an alarm clock, and the pilot flew along the tops of the canyon walls, our flight path winding like a snake no more than two thousand feet above the surface of the water.

To the east we could see the heaved-up blocks of the Devil's Kitchen, the white humped back of Elephant Hill, the red and yellow spires of the Needles District, lit up like big bouquets of roses by the setting sun.

To the west was Ernie's Country, the Fins, and the Maze, multicolored canyon walls repeating and repeating themselves like God gone mad with the Play-doh.

After thirty miles the long finger of lake turned into a moving river again, the canyon walls squeezed even tighter, and in two more bends we could see the falls that were known as the Big Drops.

The rapids in Cataract Canyon are not named but numbered, 1 through 26, a decision that said to me *for serious practitioners only*. The rapids come after three whole days of hot and silent floating without so much as an eddy, a riffle, a pool.

Numbers 20, 21, and 22 are bigger and badder by far than the others, deserve to be named a second time and are: Big Drop 1, Big Drop 2, Big Drop 3. Big Drop 2 is famous for being the third highest runable falls in America. Big Drop 3 is famous for the wave in the dead center of it: an unavoidable twenty-foot curler by the name of Satan's Gut.

Even from that far above them, I could feel the rapids roar, and my stomach did flip-flops while the pilot dipped first one wing, and then the other so that Henry and Thea and I could see.

I could see the rock in Big Drop 2, dangerously close to the only safe run and bigger than a locomotive, saw the havoc it created in the river on every side.

Below it, in 3, the Gut surged and receded, built to its full height and toppled in on itself. Bits of broken metal and brightly painted river gear winked up at us from the rock gardens on either side.

People said I was good at running rivers and I'd come to believe that they liked me because of it. I never gave much thought to what would happen if I stopped. I just kept taking each river on, like I took on every other thing my life served up to me: not an *if,* but a *how.*

The nineteen rapids above the Big Drops sailed under us like an old-time movie in reverse, and before we knew it we were over Spanish Bottom.

The pilot circled the confluence, the place where the waters of the Green and the Colorado come together. The waters don't mix right away, but flow along side by side for almost a mile before mingling, the greenish Colorado, the browner Green finally becoming indistinguishable in the bend that leads to rapid #1.

The pilot dipped his wing one more time before turning for the airstrip, and pointed toward the severed brown and green edges of the formation called Upheaval Dome.

"They used to think the dome was made of salt," he said, "squeezed out of the ground hundreds of thousands of years ago, built up and up like a pillar before time collapsed it, before weather turned it into the crater you see. But now they think it's the site, not of a rise but of an impact, the place where a meteorite one third of a mile in diameter crashed into the side of the earth."

I talked the pilot into driving us to the City Market so we could replace the cook stove, talked him further into taking us the eighteen miles to the put-in, out of town and back down-river, near the mostly defunct Potash Mine.

By the time we got there it was almost nine o'clock, near dark with a full moon on the rise right above the canyon, the mosquitoes so thick I was worried for the grocery bags of food.

Josh and Russell had the boats in the water and were trying to keep the bugs off by drinking beer and smoking fat cigars. Russell was a sports photographer from San Diego who had been a conference buddy of mine until the day he met Josh and our friendship instantly receded.

"Took you long enough," was the first thing Josh said, and then when he saw me put the new stove into my boat he said, "Oh yeah, I forgot the water thermos too."

We studied each other in the moonlight for a minute.

"It's not like it's any big deal," he said. "We can manage without it."

And technically speaking he was right. But it was July 15, the quick-baked middle of the hottest month on the river, and we had four full days to get ourselves good and dehydrated under the Utah summer sun in the bottom of a canyon that didn't know the meaning of the word shade.

The drinking water would heat up to ninety degrees in no time, would taste like the hot insides of a melting plastic jug. A thermos would keep ice through the first day, maybe into the second. We could steal a half a block a day from the food cooler after that.

The mosquitoes weren't going to let anyone sleep, that was clear, and I was too mad at Josh to lie next to him, so I set out walking for the City Market, which I knew was open twenty-four hours a day.

"Where the hell do you think you're going?" Josh called after me, and I didn't turn around, even though I had set out without a water bottle, and I could already feel my throat start to close, even in the first half mile, even in the dark of the night.

The summer triangle hung bright in the sky above me, and the tamarisk, still in their spring blossoms, scraped the canyon walls in a wind that had all of a sudden rekindled itself. A couple of tiny stones skittered down the wall and onto the road in front of me and I strained my eyes upward in the twilight looking for whatever it was, wild sheep or coyote, that might have knocked them off.

My throat got drier still and I was almost ready to give up and turn back when I saw headlights behind me, moving slow and from a long ways off.

I thought briefly about the part of the world I was in, a place so far away from the city that the danger curve had bottomed out and started to rise again, a place where raping a woman and cutting her up into little pieces could be seen either as violence or religion, depending upon your point of view.

Then I thought about how mad I was at Josh, how dry my throat was, how dry it would be in five days without a water cooler, and I smiled into the oncoming lights and stuck out my thumb.

He worked the late shift, just off duty from the Potash plant. He was born again, recently, had sworn off liquor and cocaine. He was a big fan of Red Skelton, was picking up part-time work as an extra in a movie they were making in Lavender Canyon. He played a cowboy, he said, and the funny thing was he'd never gotten near a horse in his life.

The more he talked the slower he drove. But every time he got to saying how lonely he was, how in need of female company, I just sat up straight like one of the boys and said I knew that if he stayed sober one day soon something good would come his way.

When he stopped the car in front of the market I was out the door and running before his hand was off the gear shift and I didn't stop until I felt the whoosh behind me of the automatic doors.

I bought the thermos, filled it with ice cubes and started the long walk back to Potash. The town was deserted, except for the trucks that lined the roadway, their decorator lights glowing, their radios murmuring softly in the dark.

"Where do you think that little girl's going with a great big water jug at this time of night?" a husky voice crackled loud across the citizens' band.

I hunched my shoulders over and didn't lift my eyes. Eighteen miles was a long way, but I had water now, and by first light I'd have more than half the distance behind me and there would be friendlier cars on the road by that time, mountain bikers and climbers, and everything would look different than it did in this eerie 2 a.m.

I walked through the portal, the big sandstone gate that says soon the Colorado River will start to plunge again. Above me lay The Land Behind the Rocks: a wilderness of knobs and chutes and pinnacles, a playground for mountain lions and coyotes, for lizards, tarantulas and snakes.

I considered climbing the broken rock wall a couple thousand feet up and into it. Taking my thermos and getting lost back there for as long as I could make the water last. Staying up there till the level of the river ran itself back down into the fifty thousands. Till Josh and Russell and Henry had floated on down deep into the heart of the canyon. Then Thea and I would make our run, barely speaking, never shouting, the boat moving through the rapids as easily as if it had wings.

Russell was pretty impressed that I came up with the water cooler before he'd even gotten out of his sleeping bag, and Henry was impressed generally. Being from the city, even the put-in felt like a million miles from anywhere to him. Thea just smiled as if doing a thirty-six mile turnaround in the middle of the night without a vehicle was the most logical thing in the world.

Henry said, "I think that girl's in awe of you."

And Josh said, "I'm afraid it's even worse than that."

We launched early, before the sun crawled over the canyon wall, Russell and Henry in Josh's sixteen-foot Riken, Thea and I in my Achilles, a foot shorter than Josh's boat, and the tubes less than half as big around.

"Damned if it isn't hot already," Henry said.

We hooked the boats together with a caribiner and let them float down the river, all the way to Dead Horse Point with only a few words between us, the sun climbing higher in the sky, the canyon walls slick with desert varnish, the heat pressing down on us, not a breath of breeze, too hot it seemed even to lift the water jug to our lips.

Then it got hotter still and we lay stretched out across the tubes like sea lions, hands and feet dangling in the water. We could have all slept like that till nightfall, till three days later when we'd hit the rapids, till the late summer rains came at last to cool us down.

"Well, what I think," Henry said, breaking at least an hour's silence, "is that things will never get right in the world until women are willing to give up some of their rights and privileges."

That's how it was with Henry, always had been, when the silence got too much.

"Say that again . . ." Thea said, and then they were off and into it: custody rights and fetal tissue, maternity leaves and female sportscasters in locker rooms, job quotas and income tax breaks.

I picked up the oars for a minute and gave the boats a nudge away from the bank, back toward the center of the river.

"Okay," Henry said, "if we're all so equal, then tell me this. Why is everybody so goddamned accepting of hetero girls falling in love with each other." He looked from Josh to Russell and then back to Thea. "Why's there no similar deal between heterosexual men?"

I watched both Russell and Josh startle, watched them arc their bodies slightly away from Henry as if in a dance.

"Maybe in your fantasies, Henry," Thea said, not quite under her breath.

"Lugs," I said, louder than I meant to, trying to remember, and all four heads turned my way. "Lesbians until graduation," I said. "In college we called them Lugs."

"It's not that it's unacceptable," Russell said, his voice rising. "Men just aren't attracted in that way to other men."

"I hope that isn't true," Thea said, "for all your sakes."

"But it is." Henry said. "Women are trained to appreciate each other's bodies. Men aren't. Josh, for instance, would never tell Russell that he had a nice ass."

"Even if he did," I said, and winked at Russell.

My mind was running three days ahead to the rapids, and how our lives might depend on resolving our sociological differences if we all found ourselves in the water, needing to work together just to survive.

"It's just not something I'm interested in," Russell said, "and don't tell me I'm in denial."

"When a woman meets someone," Thea said, "she decides whether or not she is attracted to them prior to noticing if it's a man or a woman."

"*Prior to?*" said Henry.

"Separate from, if you like," said Thea, "but I really do mean prior to."

"Let me put it this way," Russell said. "I've never gotten a hard-on for a man. That's the bottom line, isn't it?"

"How lucky for you," Thea said, "to have such an infallible bottom line."

Thea unhooked the caribiner that held the two rafts together and gave their boat a push. We floated to the other side of the river and began my favorite girl's boat conversation, naming in order all the men we'd made love to in our lives.

My total always came out somewhere between twenty-three and twenty-seven, depending on how sharp my memory was that day, and also what we'd all agreed would count. Thea had had only half as many, but she was five years younger and, because of her stepfather, a whole world angrier at men than me.

We camped that night on a fin of Navajo Sandstone and listened to the thunder rumble, watched far-off lightning flash a warning in the darkening sky. I made Josh and Russell cool their beer in the river which made Josh even madder, though he was the one who told me aluminum eats up cooler ice fastest of all.

After dinner we ran out of talk so Thea started us singing songs we could all agree on: *Pancho and Lefty* and old Janis Joplin, *Moon River, You Don't Know Me,* and *Light as a Breeze.*

"So Thea," Henry said before we'd been floating five minutes the next morning, "who's the better river runner, Lucy or Josh?"

"Please let's talk about something else," I said.

"Josh has a lot of strength," Thea said. "Lucy has a lot of patience."

"Patience?" Russell said. "Like for what?"

In the days when I called Josh and me the perfect couple, I said it was because his carelessness tempered my exactitude; I had too many fears, he had none.

Josh was strong enough to get himself out of tight corners where the river tossed him, and brave enough to go for the odds-against run. He had no fear of the river, which only I saw as a problem. Everything he knew about reading water would fit on the blade of an oar. I still led us into all the major rapids, but I knew those days were numbered, maybe even gone.

"Lucy waits on the river," Thea said, "waits for it to help her. Like her goal—once in the rapid—is not to have to use the oars."

"That's lovely, Thea," I said.

"I've seen her use her oars a few times," Josh said.

"Okay," I said, "can we please talk about something else?"

"I don't know why she wouldn't use them," Russell said, kicking Josh's oar with his foot. "They don't weight a third of what these do. Have you felt Lucy's oars, Henry? They're like toothpicks, like feathers, compared to these."

"But generally speaking, Thea," Henry said, "you have to admit that the average man is better equipped to run rivers than the average woman."

"Not," Thea said, "unless it's one of those special trips where the only thing you're allowed to use is your dick."

"Is everybody drinking enough water?" I said. "Has everybody peed at least once today?"

"Yes, your majesty," Josh said, "oh great protectress of the block ice."

I sent Thea and Russell hiking up and over a big sandstone fin that the river took six miles to circle, folding back on itself and winding up, as the crow flies less than a hundred yards from where I dropped them off. Then I made Henry row my boat the six miles.

The only good thing about how hot it was, was that it might stop the river rising, that with heat so severe and no rain, evaporation and usage would start to surpass runoff; not too long after that, the river would fall.

In the afternoon, thunder rumbled again in some far-off corner of the sky, and by the time we entered Meander Canyon a few clouds were sailing in the wind that must have been whipping somewhere high above the canyon, and a rainbow stretched above us, reaching from rim to rim.

On the third day we came to the confluence and Russell dove into the place where the rivers ran alongside each other and tried to mix the two strips of colored water together with his hands. We stopped at the huge salmon-colored danger sign to take pictures, and I wondered how the men in the powerboat could have missed it, wondered how any boatman could be mistaken about whether he was moving upstream or down.

We camped that night in Spanish Bottom, two miles up-river from the start of the rapids, knew we'd hear them roaring all night long. Thea and Russell and I climbed up the canyon rim to the Doll's House, its candy-striped spires like a toll booth, taking tickets for Cataract's wild ride. We goofed around at the base of the towers, took pictures of each other and laughed a lot, and I thought how different the trip might have been without Henry, who caused trouble everywhere he went, and Josh, who could get so far inside himself that the sound of his laughter would make everybody feel hollow and afraid.

To the north Junction Butte rose like the Hall of Justice on the horizon, and behind it the big flat mesa top called Island in the Sky. Russell went off to explore on his own and left Thea and me sitting on a big slab of orange rock.

"If the Doll's House were my Doll's House," I said, "I wouldn't have wanted to play ball with the boys."

"Lucy," Thea said, "have you ever made love to a woman?"

"I've been in love with a woman," I said. "More than one."

"That's not what I asked you," she said. "It's not the same thing."

"No it isn't," I said. "No I haven't."

"And *no* to the next question," Thea said. "And *no,* and *no,* and *no* again."

During dinner we watched a thunderstorm roll down the canyon, turning the clouds behind the mesa tops black and lifting the sand into Tasmanian devils all around us. The sun broke low out of the clouds just before setting and lit the buttes bright orange against the black.

Then we heard a rumble above our heads, a noise I first associated with an earthquake in a city, highway overpasses tumbling into each other, apartment buildings buckling and collapsing in on themselves.

We jumped out of the low folding chairs and ran to the top of a dune and looked back toward the Doll's House.

"There," Thea said, pointing. We followed her finger to a large wash that plummeted into Spanish Bottom just north of the Doll's House. A thick ribbon of what looked like molten chocolate had just crested the rim and was thundering down the vertical face of the wash. It took something like ten seconds for the front of it to reach the bottom, where it exploded into a giant fan, covering half the floor of Spanish Bottom.

As it got closer we could see the cargo it carried: tree trunks, car parts, something that looked like the desiccated carcass of a sheep.

"You think the tents are all right?" I said to Josh.

"Yeah," he said. "The ground is a little higher here, and anyway, this thing won't last."

As if in response to his voice the fan closed itself down by a third in that instant, and the thunder coming down the face of the wash changed into a much duller roar.

A rumble began out of sight down canyon, and then another beyond it, even farther down.

"I guess we don't have to worry about the river falling to below sixty thousand now," Josh said.

The next day, we all hit the rapids smiling.

Thea and I strapped everything down twice, threw our shoulders into it and hauled on the straps, fastened each other's life jackets and pulled the buckles tight. The water was thick after last night's thunderstorms, roiling, still the color of hot milk chocolate.

I led us out among the tree limbs and tires that the flood had brought down, wondered if the debris would give us any trouble, but forgot my worry instantly as I felt the tug of the V-slick in rapid #1.

We rambled through the first several rapids in short order, me pulling hard on the oars, Thea watching for holes and bailing. We got knocked around pretty good in 9, and we filled the boat in the upper reaches of 15, and in 19 I had to spin around backwards to make the final cut.

I was feeling a little out-muscled by the river, feeling like maybe it was trying to tell me something I ought to hear, but as we pulled over to scout Big Drop 1 we were still smiling and, thanks to the sun, almost dry.

In the sixty thousands Big Drop 1 is huge, but not technical, and Thea and I eased through it with so much finesse it was a little scary, the water pounding all around us, my hands strong on the oars. Thea was ready to bail at any second, but we were so well lined up, so precise in our timing, and the river so good to us we hardly took on enough water to make it worthwhile.

We pulled to the side and watched Josh bring his big boat through the rapid. Then we walked downriver to look at Big Drops 2 and 3. There was no way to stop between them. If you flipped in 2 you swam Satan's Gut, sacrificed yourself to it like a kamikaze.

I looked hard at the boat carnage that littered the sides of the canyon: broken oars, cracked water bottles, even rafts damaged so badly they were unsalvageable, their tubes split open on the toothy rocks, their frames twisted beyond repair.

I knew the river was telling me not to run it. *Not in that little boat,* it said, *not with only the two of you, not during the highest water in a decade,* not when it was roaring past me, pounding in my ears, telling me *no.*

I watched Josh's jaw twitch just slightly as he stared at the rapid and I knew we wouldn't have to portage. He was gonna go for it. And if he didn't die taking his big boat through, he'd like nothing better than a second chance at it in mine.

"I don't want to run it," I said, for the very first time in my boating career. "It's too big for me."

Henry and Russell lowered their eyes, as if I'd just taken off my shirt.

"It's a piece of cake," Josh said. "No problem. Why don't you follow me this time, if you're nervous. Then you don't have to worry about where to be."

I looked at the big rock I'd seen from the airplane, the size of a seven-story apartment building, and at the torrent of water going over its top.

"I don't know," Henry said, "it doesn't look all that bad to me."

"You take my boat through then, Henry," I said, and he smacked me on the butt with his life jacket and turned to Josh, who shrugged.

"It's not a piece of cake," Thea said. "It's a son of a bitch, but I believe you can do it."

"Okay," I said, tugging the straps on her lifejacket down and tight, "then let's just the hell go."

We agreed that we were going to try to enter the rapid just right of a medium-sized rock that was showing mid-stream, then we'd turn our noses to the right and keep pulling left and away from the seven-story rock, which we'd leave to our right as we entered the heart of the rapid. Once through the biggest waves we'd have to row like hell to get far enough back to the right again to be in position for Big Drop 3.

I was worried about a funny little wave at the top of 2 on the right-hand side, a little curler that wouldn't be big enough to flood my boat but might turn it sideways, and I needed to hit every wave that came after it head on.

Josh said that wave was no problem, and it wasn't for his boat and his big tubes, but I decided I was going to try to miss it by staying slightly to the right of wherever he went in.

We pulled away from the bank, my heart beating so fast I could feel it there between my palms and the oar handles. I watched Josh tie his hat to his boat frame, take a last-minute drink of water.

"Watch the goddamn rapid," I muttered, and finally he looked up.

"Does he seem too far right to you?" Thea said, fear edging into her voice.

"There's no way to tell with him right in front of us," I said. "We'll just have to take him at his word."

It was right about then that I saw the funny little wave I had wanted to miss more than thirty yards to the left of us and then I saw Josh's boat disappear, vertically, as if it had fallen over a cliff, and I realized in that moment we *were* too far right, *way* too far right, and we were about to go straight down over the seven-story rock. We would fall through the air off the face of that rock, land at the bottom of a seven-story waterfall, where there would be nothing but rocks and tree limbs and sixty-some thousand feet per second of pounding white water which would shake us and crush us and hold us under until we drowned.

I don't know what I said to Thea in that moment, as I made one last desperate effort, one hard long pull to the left. I don't know if it was *Oh shit* or *Did you see that* or just my usual *Hang on* or if there was, in that moment between us, only a silent stony awe.

And as we went over the edge of the seven-story boulder down, down, into the snarling white hole, not only wide and deep and boat-stopping but corkscrew-shaped besides, time slowed down to another version of itself, started moving like rough-cut slow motion, one frame at a time in measured stops and starts. And of all the stops and starts I remember, all the frozen frames I will see in my head for as long as I live, as the boat fell through space, as it hit the corkscrew wave, as its nose began to rise again, the one I remember most clearly is this:

My hands are still on the oars and the water that has been so brown for days is suddenly as white as lightning. It is white, and it is alive and it is moving toward me from both sides, coming at me like two jagged white walls with only me in between them, and Thea is airborne, is sailing backwards, is flying over my head, like a prayer.

Then everything went dark, and there was nothing around me but water and I was breathing it in, helpless to fight it as it wrapped itself around me and tossed me so hard I thought I would break before I drowned. Every third moment my foot or arm would catch a piece of Thea below me, or was it above me, somewhere beside me doing her own watery dance.

Then we popped up, both of us almost together, out of the back wave and moving by some miracle downstream. The boat popped up next to us, upside down and partly deflated, but I grabbed onto it, and so did Thea and that's when the truth about where we were got a hold of me and I screamed, though it was more of a yowl than a scream, an animal sound, the sound maybe of the river itself inside me. And though there were words involved, words that later we decided were "Heeeeeeellllllllpppppppp uuuuuuusssss!" it was some part of me I didn't recognize that made that noise in the rapid, a part just scared enough and mad enough to turn into the face of the river and start fighting like hell for its life.

Thea's eyes got big. "It's okay," she said. "Come here."

I smiled, a little embarrassed and human again, as if to say I was only kidding about the scream . . . and Thea laughed with me for a moment, though we both knew it had been the other voice that was the truest thing.

The waves were getting smaller, only pulling us under every now and again and I knew we were in the calmer water between 2 and 3. I got a glimpse of Josh's boat, somehow still topside, Russell and Henry bailing like crazy, Josh's face wild with fear and red.

"Help us," I screamed again, like a human being this time, and Josh's eyes widened like his face was slapped and I knew that his boat was full of water, way too heavy to move and that he was as out of control as we were, and that Thea and I were going to have to face Satan's Gut in our life jackets after all.

"Leave the boat and swim to the right," Josh screamed, and it took me a minute to realize he was right, to picture the way the rapids lined up when we scouted, to realize that the raft was headed straight into another rock fall, one that would snap our bodies like matchsticks before we had time to say casualties number six and seven, and that our only chance of surviving was to get hard and fast to the right.

I took off swimming, hoping to God Thea was behind me, but I only got about ten strokes in when I saw Josh's boat disappear sideways into the heart of the Gut, which meant that I was too far to the left of him, and Thea farther left still, maybe already in the rock garden, maybe dead on impact, maybe drowning in her own blood.

This is the one that gets me, I thought, as I rode the V-slick right into the heart of Satan's Gut and all twenty feet of back wave crashed over my head. The white water grabbed me for a minute and shook me hard, like an angry airport mother, and then just as roughly it spat me out, it let me go.

Wave after wave crashed over my head, but I knew I was past the Gut so I just kept breathing every time I got near the surface, choking down water as often as air. My knee banged into a rock during one of the poundings and I braced for the next rock, the bigger one that would smash my back or my spine, but it never came.

Finally the waves started getting smaller, so small that I could ride on top of them, and that's when in between them, I got a glimpse of Josh's boat, still topside, and Thea inside it, safe.

"Throw the rope!" Josh said to Russell, and he did throw it, but behind me, and too far to the left. He pulled it in fast to throw it again but by that time I was well past him, not very far from exhaustion, and headed for the entrance to rapid 23.

That's when the water jug popped up beside me, and I grabbed for it, got it, and stuffed it between my legs. Rapid 23 isn't big, unless it's high-water and you are sitting not in a boat but on a five-gallon thermos. I gripped the thermos between my thighs like it was the wildest horse I'd ever been on and rode the series of rollers down the middle, my head above water, my feet ready to fend off the rocks.

Then the rapid was over, and Josh was rowing toward me, and Russell had the throw rope again in his hands. This time he threw it well and I caught it, wrapped my hands around it tight. Henry hauled me to the boat and then into it, and I found myself for a moment back under the water that filled it, clawing my way up Russell's leg, trying just to get my head high enough to breathe.

"Grab that oar," Josh shouted to Henry, and he did, and I saw that it was one of mine, floating near to us, and for the first time I wondered how the wreck of my boat would look.

Josh got us to shore and the three men went back to look for the boat while Thea and I coughed and sputtered and hugged and cried together there on the sand.

The boys came back lining my boat down the side of the river, one tube punctured and deflating badly, the spare oar gone to the bottom of the river, but other than that, not too much the worse for wear. I looked for a minute toward the remaining rapids, zipped up my life jacket and jumped in the boat.

"Come on," I said to Thea. "Let's get through the rest of these mothers before we run out of air."

❑ ❑ ❑ ❑

All we had left before us was a long pull out of the canyon. We'd lose the current gradually over the next twenty miles, and eventually—ten miles from the take-out—we'd hit the backwash of Lake Powell and lose it altogether.

We agreed to float until our progress slowed to less than three miles an hour, then we'd row in half-hour shifts, all night if it was required, to miss the winds that would start early in the morning and could keep us from getting across that last long arm of the lake.

For the first time we all sat together on Josh's boat and I made sandwiches. Thea and I couldn't stop burping up river water, and every now and then one or the other of us would erupt into a fit of the chills.

Henry and I sang *A Pirate Looks and Forty,* and Thea and I sang *Angel From Montgomery* and then Thea sang *Duncan* all by herself. My boat, half deflated, limped along in tow.

"Well," Henry said, raising his sandwich, "now that we're all safe and sound and feeding our faces, I'd like to tell you that *I,* for one, have had the perfect day."

"Here, here," Russell said. "Here's to Josh, river guide extraordinaire." He raised the bilge pump to his forehead in salute. "I would go anywhere with this man."

I could feel Thea's eyes on me but I kept my head down.

"It was good fun," Josh said, waving away the bilge pump, "nothing more or less than that."

"You girls should have seen it," Henry said. "You should have heard the way Josh shouted those commands."

I handed Thea her sandwich and the back of her hand rested, for a moment, on mine.

"I'm telling you guys," Henry said, "the day couldn't have been any better."

"Good fun," Josh said again, like it was an expression he was learning.

"Henry," Thea said, "weren't you ever just a little concerned that one of us might not make it?"

"I know what you're saying," Henry said, "I do. But Josh had it under control right from the beginning. And what a rush it was."

He grabbed my elbow. "I wish I had a photo of your face when I pulled you in."

"I would go anywhere with that man," Russell said again, dozing now, his words little more than a murmur.

"What I always wish," Josh said, "is that we could go back up there and do it again."

I studied his profile in the rose-colored light of a sun long gone behind the canyon wall.

"I saw your face while I was in the water," I said, "I know you were scared."

"What do you mean?" he said.

"Your face," I said. "It was red. You were worried about me, I know."

A light snore came from Russell's lips. Henry jiggled his shoulder.

"What color do you think my face should have been?" Josh said. "I was trying to move 200 gallons of water."

Night fell on the canyon softly just as we decided we'd crossed the three-mile-an-hour line, but the sky in the east was already bright with the moon, the canyon walls so well defined that rowing all night would be no problem.

Russell took the first shift, then Henry, then Thea, then me. Josh slept in a hammock he'd rigged up between his frame and the oarlocks on my boat.

"You know, Lucy," Henry said, "I know you were only kidding when you said I should have taken the boat through the Big Drops, but looking back now . . . I really think I could have done it."

Thea snorted, didn't speak.

"Josh's turn," I said, when my watch beeped.

"Let him sleep," Henry said. "I'll cover him. He's done enough for one day."

I turned the oars over to Henry, watched the moon rise into fullness on the rim of the canyon, saw in its reflection everything wrong with how I'd come to the river, everything wrong with why I stayed.

"They'll never get it," Thea said. "You can't expect them to."

But I was thinking, in fact, about my father, who wasn't now and never would be on that river, how even if I made a hundred runs through the Big Drops, I'd never be Chris Evert, not in a hundred billion years.

Thea and I moved to the back of the raft and sang every song we could think of with Continental Divide in the lyrics until it was our turn to row again.

"What I wanted just one of them to say," Thea said, "is that they were glad we made it."

"What I wanted one of them to say," I said, "is tell me what it felt like under there."

Eventually, Russell and Henry faded, and Thea and I took fifteen-minute shifts till we crossed under the bridge that meant the reservoir, the parking lot, civilization, and a world once again bigger than just us five.

The moon was high in the sky by then, and lighting the canyon walls like daylight. We'd rowed ourselves right into the log jam and I couldn't see the edges of it, so I said we should try to sleep until first light, which I knew couldn't be far.

I could see the lights in the trailer court and tried to imagine which one belonged to the pilot's girlfriend. The marina would be a ghost town, they said, before the end of the century, completely silted in and useless, a graveyard for cows and cottonwoods and car parts, every dead thing the river brought down.

We were cold by then, sick from the river water, and shaken from the ten-minute swim, the long night of rowing, and all that remained unspoken between us, though I didn't know whether it was terror, or love.

"Lucy," Thea said, "if you were to kill yourself ever, what would it be over?"

"A man," I said, though I didn't have a face for him. "It would only be over a man. And you?"

"I don't think so," she said. "Maybe something, not that."

"What then?" I said. But she didn't answer.

"If you are ever about to kill yourself over a man," she said, "get yourself to my house. Knock on my door."

"You do the same," I said. "For any reason."

"We'll talk about what it was like being under the water," she said, "what it was like when we popped out free."

"Maybe we should talk about that now," I said.

"I don't think so," she said. "Not quite yet."

On the long drive home from Cataract, Thea and I slept in the back of the Wagoneer curled around each other like puppies while the boys told and retold the story, trying to keep Josh and each other awake.

I dreamed of the place where the scream lived inside me. I dreamed I was a meteor returned again to crash into the top of Upheaval Dome. I dreamed of riding the V-slick again and again into the dark heart of a rapid. I dreamed of a life alone inside the Land Behind the Rocks.

"Christ almighty," I heard Henry say, "did you see the way Josh passed that semi?"

The sun beat down through the windows and the sweat poured out of me and I couldn't tell Thea's breathing from my own. In my dream everything around us was soft and bright, like water.

George Saunders

Sea Oak

From *The New Yorker*

AT TEN Mr. Frendt comes on the P.A. and shouts, "Welcome to Joysticks!" Then he announces Shirts Off. We take off our flight jackets and fold them up. We take off our shirts and fold them up. Our scarves we leave on. Thomas Kirster's our beautiful boy. He's got long muscles and bright-blue eyes. The minute his shirt comes off two fat ladies hustle up the aisle and stick some money in his pants and ask will he be their Pilot. He says sure. He brings their salads. He brings their soup. My phone rings and the caller tells me to come see her in the Spitfire mockup. Does she want me to be her Pilot? I'm hoping. Inside the Spitfire is Margie, who says she's been diagnosed with Chronic Shyness Syndrome, then hands me an Instamatic and offers me ten bucks for a closeup of Thomas's tush.

Do I do it? Yes I do.

It could be worse. It is worse for Lloyd Betts. Lately he's put on weight and his hair's gone thin. He doesn't get a call all shift and waits zero tables and winds up sitting on the P-51 wing, playing solitaire in a hunched-over position that gives him big gut rolls.

I Pilot six tables and make thirty dollars in tips plus five an hour in salary.

After closing we sit on the floor for Debriefing. "There are times," Mr. Frendt says, "when one must move gracefully to the next station in life, like for example certain women in Africa or Brazil, I forget which, who either color their faces or don some kind of distinctive headdress upon achieving menopause. Are you with me? One of our ranks must now leave us. No one is an island in terms of being thought cute forever, and so today we must say goodbye to our friend Lloyd. Lloyd, stand up so we can say goodbye to you. I'm sorry. We are all so very sorry."

"Oh God," says Lloyd. "Let this not be true."

But it's true. Lloyd's finished. We give him a round of applause, and Mr. Frendt gives him a Farewell Pen and the contents of his locker in a trash bag and out he goes. Poor Lloyd. He's got a wife and two kids and a sad little duplex on Self-Storage Parkway.

"It's been a pleasure!" he shouts desperately from the doorway, trying not to burn any bridges.

What a stressful workplace. The minute your Cute Rating drops you're a goner. Guests rank us as Knockout, Honeypie, Adequate, or Stinker. Not that I'm complaining. At least I'm working. At least I'm not a Stinker like Lloyd.

I'm a solid Honeypie/Adequate, heading home with forty bucks cash.

At Sea Oak there's no sea and no oak, just a hundred subsidized apartments and a rear view of FedEx. Min and Jade are feeding their babies while watching "How My Child Died Violently." Min's my sister. Jade's our cousin. "How My Child Died Violently" is hosted by Matt Merton, a six-foot-five blond who's always giving the parents shoulder rubs and telling them they've been sainted by pain. Today's show features a ten-year-old who killed a five-year-old for refusing to join his gang. The ten-year-old strangled the five-year-old with a jump rope, filled his mouth with baseball cards, then locked himself in the bathroom and wouldn't come out until his parents agreed to take him to FunTimeZone. The audience is shrieking threats at the parents of the killer while the parents of the victim urge restraint and forgiveness to such an extent that finally the audience starts shrieking threats at them, too. Then it's a commercial. Min and Jade put down the babies and light cigarettes and pace the room while quizzing each other for their G.E.D.s. It doesn't look good. Jade says "regicide" is a virus. Min locates Biafra one planet from Saturn. I offer to help and they start yelling at me for condescending.

"You're lucky, man!" my sister says. "You did high school. You got your frigging diploma. We don't. That's why we have to do this G.E.D. shit. If we had our diplomas we could just watch TV and not be all distracted."

"Really," says Jade. "Now shut it, chick! We got to study. Show's almost on."

They debate how many sides a triangle has. They agree that Churchill was in opera. Matt Merton comes back and explains that last week's show on suicide, in which the parents watched a reenactment of their son's suicide, was a healing process for the parents, then shows a video of the parents admitting it was a healing process.

My sister's baby is Troy. Jade's baby is Mac. They crawl off into the kitchen and Troy gets his finger caught in the heat vent. Min rushes over and starts pulling.

"Jesus freaking Christ!" screams Jade. "Watch it! Stop yanking on him and get the freaking Vaseline. You're going to give him a really long arm, man!"

Troy starts crying. Mac starts crying. I go over and free Troy no problem. Meanwhile Jade and Min get in a slap fight and nearly knock over the TV.

"Yo, chick!" Min shouts at the top of her lungs. "I'm sure you're slapping me? And then you knock over the freaking TV? Don't you care?"

"I care!" Jade shouts back. "You're the slut who nearly pulled off her own kid's finger for no freaking reason, man!"

Just then Aunt Bernie comes in from DrugTown in her DrugTown cap and hobbles over and picks up Troy and everything calms way down.

"No need to fuss, little man," she says. "Everything's fine. Everything's just hunky-dory."

"Hunky-dory," says Min, and gives Jade one last pinch.

Aunt Bernie's a peacemaker. She doesn't like trouble. Once this guy backed over her foot at FoodKing and she walked home with ten broken bones. She never got married, because Grandpa needed her to keep house after Grandma died. Then he died and left all his money to a woman none of us had ever heard of, and Aunt Bernie started in at DrugTown. But she's not bitter. Sometimes she's so non-bitter it gets on my nerves. When I say Sea Oak's a pit she says she's just glad to have a roof over her head. When I say I'm tired of being broke she says Grandpa once gave her pencils for Christmas and she was so thrilled she sat around sketching horses all day on the backs of used envelopes. Once I asked was she sorry she never had kids and she said no, not at all, and besides, weren't we her kids?

And I said yes we were.

But of course we're not.

For dinner it's beanie-wienies. For dessert it's ice cream with freezer burn.

"What a nice day we've had," Aunt Bernie says once we've got the babies in bed.

"Man, what an optometrist," says Jade.

Next day is Thursday, which means a visit from Ed Anders, from the Board of Health. He's in charge of insuring that our penises never show. Also that we don't kiss anyone. None of us ever kisses anyone or shows his penis except Sonny Vance, who does both, because he's saving up to buy a FaxIt franchise. As for our Penile Simulators, yes, we can show them, we can let them stick out the top of our pants, we can even periodically dampen our tight pants with spray bottles so our Simulators really contour, but our real penises, no, those have to stay inside our hot uncomfortable oversized Simulators.

"Sorry fellas, hi fellas," Anders says as he comes wearily in. "Please know that I don't like this any better than you do. I went to school to learn how to inspect meat, but this certainly wasn't what I had in mind. Ha ha!"

He orders a Lindbergh Enchilada and eats it cautiously, as if it's alive and he's afraid of waking it. Sonny Vance is serving soup to a table of hair stylists on a bender when, for a twenty, he shoots them a quick look at his unit.

Just then Anders glances up from his Lindbergh.

"Oh for crying out loud," he says, and writes up a Shutdown and we all get sent home early. Which is bad. Every cent counts. Lately I've been sneaking toilet paper home in my briefcase. I can fit three rolls in. By the time I get home they're usually flat and don't work so great on the roller but still it saves a few bucks.

I clock out and cut through the strip of forest behind FedEx. Very pretty. A raccoon scurries over a fallen oak and starts nibbling at a rusty bike. As I come out of the woods I hear a shot. At least I think it's a shot. It could be a backfire. But no, it's a shot, because then there's another one, and some kids sprint across the courtyard yelling that Big Scary Dawgz rule.

I run home. Min and Jade and Aunt Bernie and the babies are huddled behind the couch. Apparently they had the babies outside when the shooting started. Troy's walker got hit. Luckily, he wasn't in it. It's supposed to look like a duck but now the beak's missing.

"Man, fuck this shit!" Min shouts.

"Freak this crap, you mean," says Jade. "You want the babies growing up with shit-mouths like us? Crap-mouths, I mean?"

"I just want them growing up, period," says Min.

"Boo-hoo, Miss Dramatic," says Jade.

"Fuck off, Miss Ho," shouts Min.

"I mean it, jagoff, I'm not kidding," shouts Jade and punches Min in the arm.

"Girls, for crying out loud!" says Aunt Bernie. "We should be thankful. At least we got a home. And at least none of them bullets actually hit nobody."

"No offense, Bernie?" says Min. "But you call this a freaking home?"

Sea Oak's not safe. There's an adhoc crackhouse in the laundry room and last week Min found some brass knuckles in the kiddie pool. If I had my way I'd move everybody up to Canada. It's nice there. Very polite. We went for a weekend last fall and got a flat tire and these two farmers with bright-red faces insisted on fixing it, then springing for dinner, then starting a college fund for the babies. They sent us the stock certificates a week later, along with a photo of all of us eating cobbler at a diner. But moving to Canada takes bucks. Dad's dead and left us nada and Ma now lives with Freddie, who doesn't like us, plus he's not exactly rich himself. He does phone polls. This month he's asking divorced women how often they backslide and sleep with their exes. He gets ten bucks for every completed poll.

So not lucrative, and Canada's a moot point.

I find the beak of Troy's duck and fix it with Elmer's.

"Actually, you know what?" says Aunt Bernie. "I think that looks even more like a real duck now. Because sometimes their beaks are cracked? I seen one like that downtown."

"Oh my God," says Min. "The kid's duck gets shot in the face and she says we're lucky."

"Well, we are lucky," says Bernie.

"Somebody's beak is cracked," says Jade.

"You know what I do if something bad happens?" Bernie says. "I don't think about it. Don't take it so serious. It ain't the end of the world. That's what I do. That's what I always done. That's how I got where I am."

My feeling is, Bernie, I love you, but where are you? You work at DrugTown for minimum. You're sixty and own nothing. You were basically a slave to your father and never had a date in your life.

"I mean, complain if you want," she says. "But I think we're doing pretty darn good for ourselves."

"Oh, we're doing great," says Min, and pulls Troy out from behind the couch and brushes some duck shards off his sleeper.

Joysticks reopens on Friday. It's a madhouse. They've got the fog on. A bridge club offers me fifteen bucks to oil-wrestle Mel Turner. So I oil-wrestle Mel Turner. They offer me twenty bucks to feed them chicken wings from my hand. So I feed them chicken wings from my hand. The afternoon flies by. Then the evening. At nine the bridge club leaves and I get a sorority. They sing intelligent nasty songs and grope my Simulator and say they'll never be able to look their boyfriends' meagre genitalia in the eye again. Then Mr. Frendt comes over and says phone. It's Min. She sounds crazy. Four times in a row she shrieks get home. When I tell her calm down, she hangs up. I call back and no one answers. No biggie. Min's prone to panic. Probably one of the babies is puky. Luckily I'm on FlexTime.

"I'll be back," I say to Mr. Frendt.

"I look forward to it," he says.

I jog across the marsh and through FedEx. Up on the hill there's a light from the last remaining farm. Sometimes we take the boys to the adjacent car wash to look at the cow. Tonight, however, the cow is elsewhere.

At home Min and Jade are hopping up and down in front of Aunt Bernie, who's sitting very very still at one end of the couch.

"Keep the babies out!" shrieks Min. "I don't want them seeing something dead!"

"Shut up, man!" shrieks Jade. "Don't call her something dead!" She squats down and pinches Aunt Bernie's cheek.

"Aunt Bernie?" she shrieks. "Fuck!"

"We already tried that like twice, chick!" shrieks Min. "Why are you doing that shit again? Touch her neck and see if you can feel that beating thing!"

"Shit, shit, shit!" shrieks Jade.

I call 911 and the paramedics come out and work hard for twenty minutes, then give up and say they're sorry and it looks like she's been dead most of the afternoon. The apartment's a mess. Her money drawer's empty and her family photos are in the bathtub.

"Not a mark on her," says one cop.

"I suspect she died of fright," says another. "Fright of the intruder?"

"My guess is yes," says a paramedic.

"Oh God," says Jade. "God, God, God."

I sit down beside Aunt Bernie. I think: I am so sorry. I'm sorry I wasn't here when it happened and sorry you never had any fun in your life and sorry I wasn't rich enough to move you somewhere safe. I remember when she was young and wore pink stretch pants and made us paper chains out of DrugTown receipts while singing "Froggie Went A-Courting." All her life she worked hard. She never hurt anybody. And now this.

Scared to death in a crappy apartment.

Min puts the babies in the kitchen but they keep crawling out. Aunt Bernie's in a shroud on this sort of dolly and on the couch are a bunch of forms to sign.

We call Ma and Freddie. We get their machine.

"Ma, pick up!" says Min. "Something bad happened! Ma, please freaking pick up!"

But nobody picks up.

So we leave a message.

Lobton's Funeral Parlor is just a regular house on a regular street. Inside there's a rack of brochures with titles like "Why Does My Loved One Appear Somewhat Larger?" Lobton looks healthy. Maybe too healthy. He's wearing a yellow golf shirt and his biceps keep involuntarily flexing. Every now and then he touches his delts as if to confirm they're still big as softballs.

"Such a sad thing," he says.

"How much?" asks Jade. "I mean, like for basic. Not super-fancy."

"But not crappy either," says Min. "Our aunt was the best."

"What price range were you considering?" says Lobton, cracking his knuckles. We tell him and his eyebrows go up and he leads us to something that looks like a moving box.

"Prior to usage we'll moisture-proof this with a spray lacquer," he says. "Makes it look quite woodlike."

"That's all we can get?" says Jade. "Cardboard?"

"I'm actually offering you a slight break already," he says, and does a kind of pushup against the wall. "On account of the tragic circumstances. This is Sierra Sunset. Not exactly cardboard. More of a fibreboard."

"I don't know," says Min. "Seems pretty gyppy."

"Can we think about it?" says Ma.

"Absolutely," says Lobton. "Last time I checked this was still America."

I step over and take a closer look. There are staples where Aunt Bernie's spine would be. Down at the foot there's some writing about folding Tab A into Slot B.

"No freaking way," says Jade. "Work your whole life and end up in a Mayflower box? I doubt it."

We've got zip in savings. We sit at a desk and Lobton does what he calls a Credit Calc. If we pay it out monthly for seven years we can afford the AmberMist, which includes a double-thick balsa box and two coats of lacquer and a one-hour wake.

"But seven years, jeez," says Jade.

"We got to get her the good one," says Min. "She never had anything nice in her life."

So AmberMist it is.

We bury her at St. Leo's, on the hill up near BastCo. Her part of the graveyard's pretty plain. No angels, no little rock houses, no flowers, just a bunch of flat stones like parking bumpers and here and there a Styrofoam cup. Father Brian says a prayer and then one of us is supposed to talk. But what's there to say? She never had a life. Never married, no kids, work, work, work. Did she ever go on a cruise? All her life it was buses. Buses, buses, buses. Once she went with Ma on a bus to Quigley, Kansas, to gamble and shop at an outlet mall. Someone broke into her room and stole her clothes and took a dump in her suitcase while they were at the Roy Clark show. That was it. That was the extent of her tourism. After that it was DrugTown, night and day. After fifteen years as Cashier she got demoted to Greeter. People would ask where the Cold Remedies were and she'd point to some big letters on the wall that said Cold Remedies.

Freddie, Ma's boyfriend, steps up and says he didn't know her very long but she was an awful nice lady and left behind a lot of love, etc., etc., blah blah blah. While it's true she didn't do much in her life, still she was very dear to those of us who knew her and never made a stink about anything but was always content with whatever happened to her, etc., etc., blah blah blah.

Then it's over and we're supposed to go away.

"We gotta come out here like every week," says Jade.

"I know I will," says Min.

"What, like I won't?" says Jade. "She was so freaking nice."

"I'm sure you swear at a grave," says Min.

"Since when is freak a swear, chick?" says Jade.

"Girls," says Ma.

"I hope I did O.K. in what I said about her," says Freddie in his full-of-crap way, smelling bad of English Navy. "Actually I sort of surprised myself."

"Bye-bye, Aunt Bernie," says Min.

"Bye-bye, Bern," says Jade.

"Oh my dear sister," says Ma.

I scrunch my eyes tight and try to picture her happy, laughing, poking me in the ribs. But all I can see is her terrified on the couch. It's awful. Out there, somewhere, is whoever did it. Someone came in our house, scared her to death, watched her die, went through our stuff, stole her money. Someone who's still living, someone who right now might be having a piece of pie or running an errand or scratching his ass, someone who, if he wanted to, could drive west for three days or whatever and sit in the sun by the ocean.

We stand a few minutes with heads down and hands folded.

Afterward Freddie takes us to Trabanti's for lunch. Last year Trabanti died and three Vietnamese families went in together and bought the place, and it still serves pasta and pizza and the big oil of Trabanti is still on the wall but now from the kitchen comes this very pretty Vietnamese music and the food is somehow better.

Freddie proposes a toast. Min says remember how Bernie always called lunch dinner and dinner supper? Jade says remember how when her jaw clicked she'd say she needed oil?

"She was a excellent lady," says Freddie.

"I already miss her so bad," says Ma.

"I'd like to kill that fuck that killed her," says Min.

"How about let's don't say fuck at lunch," says Ma.

"It's just a word, Ma, right?" says Min. "Like pluck is just a word? You don't mind if I say pluck? Pluck, pluck, pluck?"

"Well, shit's just a word, too," says Freddie. "But we don't say it at lunch."

"Same with puke," says Ma.

"Shit puke, shit puke," says Min.

The waiter clears his throat. Ma glares at Min.

"I love you girls' manners," Ma says.

"Especially at a funeral," says Freddie.

"This ain't a funeral," says Min.

"The question in my mind is what you kids are gonna do now," says Freddie. "Because I consider this whole thing a wakeup call, meaning it's time for you to pull yourselfs up by the bootstraps like I done and get out of that dangerous craphole you're living at."

"Mister Phone Poll speaks," says Min.

"Anyways it ain't that dangerous," says Jade.

"A woman gets killed and it ain't that dangerous?" says Freddie.

"All's we need is a dead bolt and a eyehole," says Min.

"What's a bootstrap?" says Jade.

"It's like a strap on a boot, you doof," says Min.

"Plus where we gonna go?" says Min. "Can we move in with you guys?"

"I personally would love that, and you know that," says Freddie. "But who would not love that is our landlord."

"I think what Freddie's saying is it's time for you girls to get jobs," says Ma.

"Yeah right, Ma," says Min. "After what happened last time?"

When I first moved in, Jade and Min were working the Info booth at HardwareNiche. Then one day we picked the babies up at day care and found Troy sitting naked on top of the washer and Mac in the yard being nipped by a Pekingese and the day-care lady sloshed and playing KillerBirds on Nintendo.

So that was that. No more HardwareNiche.

"Maybe one could work, one could babysit?" says Ma.

"I don't see why I should have to work so she can stay home with her baby," says Min.

"And I don't see why I should have to work so she can stay home with her baby," says Jade.

"It's like a freaking veece versa," says Min.

"Let me tell you something," says Freddie. "Something about this country. Anybody can do anything. But first they gotta try. And you guys ain't. Two don't work and one strips naked? I don't consider that trying. You kids make squat. And therefore you live in a dangerous craphole. And what happens in a dangerous craphole? Bad tragic shit. It's the freaking American way—you start out in a dangerous craphole and work hard so you can someday move up to a somewhat less dangerous craphole. And finally maybe you get a mansion. But at this rate you ain't even gonna make it to the somewhat less dangerous craphole."

"Like you live in a mansion," says Jade.

"I do not claim to live in no mansion," says Freddie. "But then again I do not live in no slum. The other thing I also do not do is strip naked."

"Thank God for small favors," says Min.

"Anyways he's never actually naked," says Jade.

Which is true. I always have on at least a T-back.

"No wonder we never take these kids out to a nice lunch," says Freddie.

"I do not even consider this a nice lunch," says Min.

For dinner Jade microwaves some Stars-n-Flags. They're addictive. They put sugar in the sauce and sugar in the meat nuggets. I think also caffeine. Someone told me the brown streaks in the Flags are caffeine. We have like five bowls each.

After dinner the babies get fussy and Min puts a mush of ice cream and Hershey's syrup in their bottles and we watch "The Worst That Could Happen," a half hour of computer simulations of tragedies that have never actually occurred but theoretically could. A kid gets hit by a train and flies into a zoo, where he's eaten by wolves. A man cuts his hand off chopping wood and while wandering around screaming for help is picked up by a tornado and dropped on a preschool during recess and lands on a pregnant teacher.

"I miss Bernie so bad," says Min.

"Me too," says Jade sadly.

The babies start howling for more ice cream.

"That is so cute," says Jade. "They're like, *Give it the fuck up!*"

"We'll give it the fuck up, sweeties, don't worry," says Min. "We didn't forget about you."

Then the phone rings. It's Father Brian. He sounds weird. He says he's sorry to bother us so late. But something strange has happened. Something bad. Something sort of, you know, unspeakable. Am I sitting? I'm not, but I say I am.

Apparently someone has defaced Bernie's grave.

My first thought is there's no stone. It's just grass. How do you deface grass? What did they do, pee on the grass on the grave? But Father's nearly in tears.

So I call Ma and Freddie and tell them to meet us, and we get the babies up and load them into the K-car.

"Deface," says Jade on the way over. "What does that mean, deface?"

"It means like fucked it up," says Min.

"But how?" says Jade. "I mean, like what did they do?"

"We don't know, dumbass," says Min. "That's why we're going there."

"And why?" says Jade. "Why would someone do that?"

"Check out Miss Shreelock Holmes," says Min. "Someone done that because someone is a asshole."

"Someone is a big-time asshole," says Jade.

Father Brian meets us at the gate with a flashlight and a golf cart.

"When I saw this," he says, "I literally sat down in astonishment. Nothing like this has ever happened here. I am so sorry. You seem like nice people."

We're too heavy and the wheels spin as we climb the hills, so I get out and jog alongside.

"O.K., folks, brace yourselves," Father says, and shuts off the engine.

Where the grave used to be is just a hole. Inside the hole is the AmberMist, with the top missing. Inside the AmberMist is nothing. No Aunt Bernie.

"What the hell," says Jade. "Where's Bernie?"

"Somebody stole Bernie?" says Min.

"At least you folks have retained your feet," says Father Brian. "I'm telling you I literally sat right down. I sat right down on that pile of dirt. I dropped as if shot. See that mark? That's where I sat."

On the pile of grave dirt is a butt-shaped mark.

The cops show up and one climbs down in the hole with a tape measure and a camera. After three or four flashes he climbs out and hands Ma a pair of blue pumps.

"Her little shoes," says Ma. "Oh my God."

"Are those them?" says Jade.

"Those are them," says Min.

"I am freaking out," says Jade.

"I am totally freaking out," says Min.

"I'm gonna sit," says Ma, and drops into the golf cart.

"What I don't get is who'd want her?" says Min.

"She was just this lady," says Jade.

"Typically it's teens?" the cop says. "Typically we find the loved one nearby? Once we found the loved one nearby with, you know, a cigarette between its lips, wearing a sombrero? These kids today got a lot more nerve than we ever did. I never would've dreamed of digging up a dead corpse when I was a teen. You might tip over a stone, sure, you might spray-paint something on a crypt, you might, you know, give a wino a hotfoot."

"But this, jeez," says Freddie. "This is a entirely different ballgame."

"Boy howdy," says the cop, and we all look down at the shoes in Ma's hands.

Next day I go back to work. I don't feel like it, but we need the money. The grass is wet and it's hard getting across the ravine in my dress shoes. The soles are slick. Plus they're too tight. Several times I fall forward on my briefcase. Inside the briefcase are my T-backs and a thing of mousse.

Right off the bat I get a call from a tableful of MediBen women seated under a banner that says "BEST OF LUCK, BEATRICE, NO HARD FEELINGS." I take off my shirt and serve their salads. I take off my flight pants and serve their soup. One drops a dollar on the floor and tells me feel free to pick it up.

I pick it up.

"Not like that, not like that," she says. "Face the other way, so when you bend we can see your crack."

I've done this about a million times, but somehow I can't do it now.

I look at her. She looks at me.

"What?" she says. "I'm not allowed to say that? I thought that was the whole point."

"That is the whole point, Phyllis," says another lady. "You stand your ground."

"Look," Phyllis says. "Either bend how I say or give back the dollar. I think that's fair."

"You go, girl," says her friend.

I give back the dollar. I return to the Locker Area and sit awhile. For the first time ever, I'm voted Stinker. There are thirteen women at the MediBen table and they all vote me Stinker. Do the MediBen women know my situation? Would they vote me Stinker if they did? But what am I supposed to do, go out and say, please, ladies, my aunt just died, plus her body's missing?

Mr. Frendt pulls me aside.

"Perhaps you need to go home," he says. "I'm sorry for your loss. But I'd like to encourage you not to behave like one of those Comanche ladies who bite off their index fingers when a loved one dies. Grief is good, grief is fine, but too much grief, as we all know, is excessive. If your aunt's death has filled your mouth with too many bitten-off fingers, for crying out loud, take a week off, only don't take it out on our guests, they didn't kill your dang aunt."

But I can't afford to take a week off. I can't even afford to take a few days off.

"We really need the money," I say.

"Is that my problem?" he says. "Am I supposed to let you dance without vigor just because you need the money? Why don't I put an ad in the paper for all sad people who need money? All the town's sad could come here and strip. Goodbye. Come back when you feel halfway normal."

From the pay phone I call home to see if they need anything from the FoodSoQuik.

"Just come home," Min says stiffly. "Just come straight home."

"What is it?" I say.

"Come home," she says.

Maybe someone's found the body. I imagine Bernie naked, Bernie chopped in two, Bernie posed on a bus bench. I hope and pray that something only mildly bad's been done to her, something we can live with.

At home the door's wide open. Min and Jade are sitting very still on the couch, babies in their laps, staring at the rocking chair, and in the rocking chair is Bernie. Bernie's body.

Same perm, same glasses, same blue dress we buried her in.

What's it doing here? Who could be so cruel? And what are we supposed to do with it?

Then she turns her head and looks at me.

"Sit the fuck down," she says.

In life she never swore.

I sit. Min squeezes and releases my hand, squeezes and releases, squeezes and releases.

"You, mister," Bernie says to me, "are going to start showing your cock. You'll show it and show it. You go up to a lady, if she wants to see it, if she'll pay to see it, I'll make a thumbprint on the forehead. You see the thumbprint, you ask. I'll try to get you five a day, at twenty bucks a pop. So a hundred bucks a day. Seven hundred a week. And that's cash, so no taxes. No withholding. See? That's the beauty of it."

She's got dirt in her hair and dirt in her teeth and her hair is a mess and her tongue when it darts out to lick her lips is black.

"You, Jade," she says. "Tomorrow you start work. Andersen Labels, Fifth and Rivera. Dress up when you go. Wear something nice. Show a little leg. And don't chomp your gum. Ask for Len. At the end of the month, we take the money you made and the cock money and get a new place. Somewhere safe. That's part one of Phase One. You, Min. You babysit. Plus you quit smoking. Plus you learn how to cook. No more food out of cans. We gotta eat right to look our best. Because I am getting me so many lovers. Maybe you kids don't know this but I died a freaking virgin. No babies, no lovers. Nothing went in, nothing came out. Ha ha! Dry as a bone, completely wasted, this pretty little thing God gave me between my legs. Well, I am going to have lovers now, you fucks! Like in the movies, big shoulders and all, and a summer house, and nice trips, and in the morning in my room a big vase of flowers, and I'm going to get my nipples hard standing in the breeze from the ocean, eating shrimp from a cup, you sons of bitches, while my lover watches me from the veranda, his big shoulders shining, all hard for me, that's one damn thing I will guarantee you kids! Ha ha! You think I'm joking? I ain't freaking joking. I never got nothing! My life was shit! I was never even up in a freaking plane. But that was that life and this is this life. My new life. Cover me up now! With a blanket. I need my beauty rest. Tell anyone I'm here, you all die. Plus they die. Whoever you tell, they die. I kill them with my mind. I can do that. I am very freaking strong now. I got powers! So no visitors. I don't exactly look my best. You got it? You all got it?"

We nod. I go for a blanket. Her hands and feet are shaking and she's grinding her teeth and one falls out.

"Put it over me, you fuck, all the way over!" she screams, and I put it over her.

We sneak off and whisper in the kitchen.

"It looks like her," says Min.

"It is her," I say.

"It is and it ain't," says Jade.

"We better do what she says," Min says.

"No shit," Jade says.

All night she sits in the rocker under the blanket, shaking and swearing.

All night we sit in Min's bed, fully dressed, holding hands.

"See how strong I am!" she shouts around midnight, and there's a cracking sound, and when I go out the door's been torn off the microwave but she's still sitting in the chair.

In the morning she's still there, shaking and swearing.

"Take the blanket off!" she screams. "It's time to get this show on the road."

I take the blanket off. The smell is not good. One ear is now in her lap. She keeps absent-mindedly sticking it back on her head.

"You, Jade!" she shouts. "Get dressed. Go get that job. When you meet Len, bend forward a little. Let him see down your top. Give him some hope. He's a sicko, but we need him. You, Min! Make breakfast. Something homemade. Like biscuits."

"Why don't you make it with your powers?" says Min.

"Don't be a smartass!" screams Bernie. "You see what I did to that microwave?"

"I don't know how to make freaking biscuits," Min wails.

"You know how to read, right?" Bernie shouts. "You ever heard of a recipe? You ever been in the grave? It sucks so bad! You regret all the things you never did. You little bitches are gonna have a very bad time in the grave unless you get on the stick, believe me! Turn down the thermostat! Make it cold. I like cold. Something's off with my body. I don't feel right."

I turn down the thermostat. She looks at me.

"Go show your cock!" she shouts. "That is the first part of Phase One. After we get the new place, then that's the end of the first part of Phase Two. You'll still show your cock, but only three days a week. Because you'll start community college. Pre-law. Pre-law is best. You'll be a whiz. You ain't dumb. And Jade'll work weekends to make up for the decrease in cock money. See? See how that works? Now get out of here. What are you gonna do?"

"Show my cock?" I say.

"Show your cock, that's right," she says, and brushes back her hair with her hand, and a huge wad comes out, leaving her almost bald on one side.

"Oh God," says Min. "You know what? No way me and the babies are staying here alone."

"You ain't alone," says Bernie. "I'm here."

"Please don't go," Min says to me.

"Oh, stop it," Bernie says, and the door flies open and I feel a sort of invisible fist punching me in the back.

Outside it's sunny. A regular day. A guy's changing his oil. The clouds are regular clouds and the sun's the regular sun and the only non-regular thing is that my clothes smell like Bernie, a combo of wet cellar and rotten bacon.

Work goes well. I manage to keep smiling and hide my shaking hands, and my mid-shift rating is Honeypie. After lunch this older woman comes up and says I look so much like a real Pilot she can hardly stand it.

On her forehead is a thumbprint. Like Ash Wednesday, only sort of glowing.

I don't know what to do. Do I just come out and ask if she wants to see my cock? What if she says no? What if I get caught? What if I show her and she doesn't think it's worth twenty bucks?

Then she asks if I'll surprise her friend with a birthday table dance. She points out her friend. A pretty girl, no thumbprint. Looks somehow familiar.

We start over and at about twenty feet I realize it's Angela.

Angela Silveri.

We dated senior year. Then Dad died and Ma had to take a job at Patty Melt Depot. From all the grease Ma got a bad rash and could barely wear a blouse. Plus Min was running wild. So Angela would come over and there'd be Min getting high under a tarp on the carport and Ma sitting in her bra on a kitchen stool with a fan pointed at her gut. Angela had dreams. She had plans. In her notebook she'd pasted a picture of an office from the J. C. Penney catalogue and under it wrote, "My (someday?) office." Once we saw this black Porsche and she said very nice but make hers red. The last straw was Ed Edwards, a big drunk, one of Dad's cousins. Things got so bad Ma rented him the utility room. One night Angela and I were making out on the couch late when Ed came in soused and started peeing in the dishwasher.

What could I say? He's only barely related to me? He hardly ever does that?

Angela's eyes were like these little pies.

I walked her home, got no kiss, came back, cleaned up the dishwasher as best I could. A few days later I got my class ring in the mail and a copy of "The Prophet."

"You will always be my first love," she'd written inside. "But now my path converges to a higher ground. Be well always. Walk in joy. Please don't think me cruel, it's just that I want so much in terms of accomplishment, plus I couldn't believe that guy peed right on your dishes."

No way am I table-dancing for Angela Silveri. No way am I asking Angela Silveri's friend if she wants to see my cock. No way am I hanging around here so Angela can see me in my flight jacket and T-backs and wonder to herself how I went so wrong, etc., etc.

I hide in the kitchen until my shift is done, then walk home very,

very slowly because I'm afraid of what Bernie's going to do to me when I get there.

Min meets me at the door. She's got flour all over her blouse and it looks like she's been crying.

"I can't take any more of this," she says. "She's like falling apart. I mean shit's falling off her. Plus she made me bake a freaking pie."

On the table is a very lumpy pie. One of Bernie's arms is now disconnected and lying across her lap.

"What are you thinking of!" she shouts. "You didn't show your cock even once? You think it's easy making those thumbprints? You try it, smartass! Do you or do you not know the plan? You gotta get us out of here! And to get us out, you gotta use what you got. And you ain't got much. A nice face. And a decent unit. Not huge, but shaped nice."

"Bernie, God," says Min.

"What, Miss Priss?" shouts Bernie, and slams the severed arm down hard on her lap and her other ear falls off.

"I'm sorry, but this is too fucking sickening," says Min. "I'm going out."

"What's sickening?" says Bernie. "Are you saying I'm sickening? Well, I think you're sickening. So many wonderful things in life and where is your mind? You think with your lazy ass. Whatever life hands you, you take. You're not going anywhere. You're staying home and studying."

"I'm what?" says Min. "Studying what? I ain't studying. Chick comes into my house and starts ordering me to study? I freaking doubt it."

"You don't know nothing!" Bernie says. "What fun is life when you don't know nothing? You can't find your own town on the map. You can't name a single President. When we go to Rome you won't know nothing about the history. You're going to study the World Book. Do we still have those World Books?"

"Yeah right," says Min. "We're going to Rome."

"We'll go to Rome when he's a lawyer," says Bernie.

"Dream on, chick," says Min. "And we'll go to Mars when I'm a stockbreaker."

"Don't you dare make fun of me!" Bernie shouts, and our only vase goes flying across the room and nearly nails Min in the head.

"She's been like this all day," says Min.

"Like what?" shouts Bernie. "We had a perfectly nice day."

"She made me help her try on my bras," says Min.

"I never had a nice sexy bra," says Bernie.

"And now mine are all ruined," says Min. "They got this sort of goo on them."

"You ungrateful shit!" shouts Bernie. "Do you know what I'm doing for you? I'm saving your boy. And you got the nerve to say I made goo on your bras! Troy's gonna get caught in a crossfire in the courtyard. In September. September 18th. He's gonna get thrown right off his little trike. With one leg twisted under him and blood pouring out of his ear. It's a freaking prophecy. You know that word? It means prediction. You know that word? You think I'm bullshitting? Well, I ain't bullshitting. I got the power. Watch this: All day Jade sat licking labels at a desk by a window. Her boss bought everybody subs for lunch. She's bringing some home in a green bag."

"That ain't true about Troy, is it?" says Min. "Is it? I don't believe it."

"Turn on the TV!" Bernie shouts. "Give me the changer."

I turn on the TV. I give her the changer. She puts on "Nathan's Body Shop." Nathan says washboard abs drive the women wild. Then there's a closeup of his washboard abs.

"Oh yes," says Bernie. "Them are for me. I'd like to give those a lick. A lick and a pinch. I'd like to sort of straddle those things."

Just then Jade comes through the door with a big green bag.

"Oh God," says Min.

"Told you so!" says Bernie, and pokes Min in the ribs. "Ha ha! I really got the power!"

"I don't get it," Min says, all desperate. "What happens? Please. What happens to him? You better freaking tell me."

"I already told you," Bernie says. "He'll fly about fifteen feet and live about three minutes."

"Bernie, God," Min says, and starts to cry. "You used to be so nice."

"I'm still so nice," says Bernie, and bites into a sub and takes off the tip of her finger and starts chewing it up.

Just after dawn she shouts out my name.

"Take the blanket off," she says. "I ain't feeling so good."

I take the blanket off. She's basically just this pile of parts: both arms in her lap, head on the arms, heel of one foot touching the heel of the other, all of it sort of wrapped up in her dress.

"Get me a washcloth," she says. "Do I got a fever? I feel like I got a fever. Oh, I knew it was too good to be true. But O.K. New plan. New plan. I'm changing the first part of Phase One. If you see two thumbprints, that means the lady'll screw you for cash. We're in a fix here. We gotta speed this up. There ain't gonna be nothing left of me. Who's gonna be my lover now?"

The doorbell rings.

"Son of a bitch," Bernie snarls.

It's Father Brian with a box of doughnuts. I step out quick and close the door behind me. He says he's just checking in. Perhaps we'd like to talk? Perhaps we're feeling some residual anger about Bernie's situation? Which would of course be completely understandable. Once when he was a young priest someone broke in and drew a mustache on the Virgin Mary with a permanent marker, and for weeks he was tortured by visions of bending back the finger of the vandal until he or she broke into tears of apology.

"I knew that wasn't appropriate," he says. "I knew that by indulging in that fantasy I was honoring violence. And yet it gave me pleasure. I also thought of catching them in the act and boinking them in the head with a rock. I also thought of jumping up and down on their backs until something in their spinal column cracked. Actually I had about a million ideas. But you know what I did instead? I scrubbed and scrubbed our Holy Mother, and soon she was as good as new. Her statue, I mean. She herself of course is always good as new."

From inside comes the sound of breaking glass. Breaking glass and then something heavy falling, and Jade yelling and Min yelling and the babies crying.

"Oops, I guess?" he says. "I've come at a bad time? Look, all I'm trying to do is urge you, if at all possible, to forgive the perpetrators, as I forgave the perpetrators that drew on the Virgin Mary. The thing lost, after all, is only your aunt's body, and what is essential, I assure you, is elsewhere, being well taken care of."

I nod. I smile. I say thanks for stopping by. I take the doughnuts and go back inside.

The TV's broke and the refrigerator's tipped over and Bernie's parts are strewn across the living room like she's been shot out of a cannon.

"She tried to get up," says Jade.

"I don't know where the hell she thought she was going," says Min.

"Come here," the head says to me, and I squat down. "That's it for me. I'm fucked. As per usual. Always the bridesmaid, never the bride. Although come to think of it I was never even the freaking bridesmaid. Look, show your cock. It's the shortest line between two points. The world ain't giving away nice lives. You got a trust fund? You a genius? Show your cock. It's what you got. And remember: Troy in September. On his trike. One leg twisted. Don't forget. And also. Don't remember me like this. Remember me like how I was that night we all went to Red Lobster and I had that new perm. Ah Christ. At least buy me a stone."

I rub her shoulder, which is next to her foot.

"We loved you," I say.

"Why do some people get everything and I got nothing?" she says. "Why? Why was that?"

"I don't know," I say.

"Show your cock," she says, and dies again.

We stand there looking down at the pile of parts. Mac crawls toward it and Min moves him back with her foot.

"This is too freaking much," says Jade, and starts crying.

"What do we do now?" says Min.

"Call the cops," Jade says.

"And say what?" says Min.

We think about this awhile.

I get a Hefty bag. I get my winter gloves.

"I ain't watching," says Jade.

"I ain't watching either," says Min, and they take the babies into the bedroom.

I close my eyes and wrap Bernie up in the Hefty bag and twistie-tie the bag shut and lug it out to the trunk of the K-car. I throw in a shovel. I drive up to St. Leo's. I lower the bag into the hole using a bungee cord, then fill the hole back in.

Down in the city are the nice houses and the so-so houses and the lovers making out in dark yards and the babies crying for their moms and I wonder if, other than Jesus, this has ever happened before. Maybe it happens all the time. Maybe there's angry dead all over, hiding in rooms, covered with blankets, bossing around their scared embarrassed relatives. Because how would we know?

I for sure don't plan on broadcasting this.

I smooth over the dirt and say a little prayer: If it was wrong for her to come back, forgive her, she never got beans in this life, plus she was trying to help us.

At the car I think of an additional prayer: But please don't let her come back again.

When I get home the babies are asleep and Jade and Min are watching a phone-sex infomercial, three girls in leather jumpsuits eating bananas in slo-mo while across the screen runs a constant disclaimer: "Not Necessarily the Girls Who Man the Phones! Not Necessarily the Girls Who Man the Phones!"

"Them chicks seem to really be enjoying those bananas," says Min in a thin little voice.

"I like them jumpsuits, though," says Jade.

"Yeah, them jumpsuits look decent," says Min.

Then they look up at me. I've never seen them so sad and beat and sick.

"It's done," I say.

Then we hug and cry and promise never to forget Bernie the way she really was, and before bed I use some Resolve on the rug and they do a little reading in their World Books.

Next day I go in early. I don't see a single thumbprint. But it doesn't matter. I get with Sonny Vance and he tells me how to do it. First you ask the woman would she like a private tour. Then you show her the fake P-40, the Gallery of Historical Aces, the shower stall where we get oiled up, etc., etc., and then in the hall near the rest room you ask if there's anything else she'd like to see. It's sleazy. It's gross. But when I do it I think of September. September and Troy in the crossfire, his little leg bent under him, etc., etc.

Most say no but quite a few say yes.

I've got a place picked out at a complex called Swan's Glen. They've never had a shooting or a knifing and the public school is great and every Saturday they have a nature walk for kids behind the clubhouse.

For every hundred bucks I make, I set aside five for Bernie's stone.

What do you write on something like that? LIFE PASSED HER BY? DIED DISAPPOINTED? CAME BACK TO LIFE BUT FELL APART? All true, but too sad, and no way I'm writing any of those.

BERNIE KOWALSKI, it's going to say. BELOVED AUNT.

Sometimes she comes to me in dreams. She never looks good. Sometimes she's wearing a dirty smock. Once she had on handcuffs. Once she was naked and dirty and this mean cat was clawing its way up her front. But every time it's the same thing.

"Some people get everything and I got nothing," she says. "Why? Why did that happen?"

Every time I say I don't know.

And I don't.

Jhumpa Lahiri

Interpreter of Maladies

From *Agni*

AT THE TEA STALL Mr. and Mrs. Das bickered about who should take Tina to the toilet. Eventually Mrs. Das relented when Mr. Das pointed out that he had given the girl her bath the night before. In the rearview mirror Mr. Kapasi watched as Mrs. Das emerged slowly from his bulky white Ambassador, dragging her shaved, largely bare legs across the back seat. She did not hold the little girl's hand as they walked to the rest room.

They were on their way to see the Sun Temple at Konarak. It was a dry, bright Saturday, the mid-July heat tempered by a steady ocean breeze, ideal weather for sightseeing. Ordinarily Mr. Kapasi would not have stopped so soon along the way, but less than five minutes after he'd picked up the family that morning in front of Hotel Sandy Villa, the little girl had complained. The first thing Mr. Kapasi had noticed when he saw Mr. and Mrs. Das, standing with their children under the portico of the hotel, was that they were very young, perhaps not even thirty. In addition to Tina they had two boys, Ronny and Bobby, who appeared very close in age and had teeth covered in a network of flashing silver wires. The family looked Indian but dressed as foreigners did, the children in stiff, brightly colored clothing and caps with translucent visors. Mr. Kapasi was accustomed to foreign tourists; he was assigned to them regularly because he could speak English. Yesterday he had driven an elderly couple from Scotland, both with spotted faces and fluffy white hair so thin it exposed their sunburnt scalps. In comparison, the tanned, youthful faces of Mr. and Mrs. Das were all the more striking. When he'd introduced himself, Mr. Kapasi had pressed his palms together in greeting, but Mr. Das squeezed hands like an American so that Mr. Kapasi felt it in his elbow. Mrs. Das, for her part, had flexed one side of her mouth, smiling dutifully at Mr. Kapasi, without displaying any interest in him.

As they waited at the tea stall, Ronny, who looked like the older of the two boys, clambered suddenly out of the back seat, intrigued by a goat tied to a stake in the ground.

"Don't touch it," Mr. Das said. He glanced up from his paperback tour book, which said "INDIA" in yellow letters and looked as if it had been published abroad. His voice, somehow tentative and a little shrill, sounded as though it had not yet settled into maturity.

"I want to give it a piece of gum," the boy called back as he trotted ahead.

Mr. Das stepped out of the car and stretched his legs by squatting briefly to the ground. A clean-shaven man, he looked exactly like a magnified version of Ronny. He had a sapphire blue visor, and was dressed in shorts, sneakers, and a T-shirt. The camera slung around his neck, with an impressive telephoto lens and numerous buttons and markings, was the only complicated thing he wore. He frowned, watching as Ronny rushed toward the goat, but appeared to have no intention of intervening. "Bobby, make sure that your brother doesn't do anything stupid."

"I don't feel like it," Bobby said, not moving. He was sitting in the front seat beside Mr. Kapasi, studying a picture of the elephant god taped to the glove compartment.

"No need to worry," Mr. Kapasi said. "They are quite tame." Mr. Kapasi was forty-six years old, with receding hair that had gone completely silver, but his butterscotch complexion and his unlined brow, which he treated in spare moments to dabs of lotus-oil balm, made it easy to imagine what he must have looked like at an earlier age. He wore gray trousers and a matching jacket-style shirt, tapered at the waist, with short sleeves and a large pointed collar, made of a thin but durable synthetic material. He had specified both the cut and the fabric to his tailor—it was his preferred uniform for giving tours because it did not get crushed during his long hours behind the wheel. Through the windshield he watched as Ronny circled around the goat, touched it quickly on its side, then trotted back to the car.

"You left India as a child?" Mr. Kapasi asked when Mr. Das had settled once again into the passenger seat.

"Oh, Mina and I were both born in America," Mr. Das announced with an air of sudden confidence. "Born and raised. Our parents live here now, in Assansol. They retired. We visit them every couple years." He turned to watch as the little girl ran toward the car, the wide purple bows of her sundress flopping on her narrow brown shoulders. She was holding to her chest a doll with yellow hair that looked as if it had been chopped, as a punitive measure, with a pair of dull scissors. "This is Tina's first trip to India, isn't it, Tina?"

"I don't have to go to the bathroom anymore," Tina announced.

"Where's Mina?" Mr. Das asked.

Mr. Kapasi found it strange that Mr. Das should refer to his wife by first name when speaking to the little girl. Tina pointed to where Mrs. Das was purchasing something from one of the shirtless men who worked at the tea stall. Mr. Kapasi heard one of the shirtless men sing a phrase from a popular Hindi love song as Mrs. Das walked back to the car, but she did not appear to understand the words of the song, for she did not express irritation, or embarrassment, or react in any other way to the man's declarations.

He observed her. She wore a red-and-white-checkered skirt that stopped above her knees, slip-on shoes with a square wooden heel, and a close-fitting blouse styled like a man's undershirt. The blouse was decorated at chest-level with a calico appliqué in the shape of a strawberry. She was a short woman, with small hands like paws, her frosty pink fingernails painted to match her lips, and was slightly plump in her figure. Her hair, shorn only a little longer than her husband's, was parted far to one side. She was wearing large dark brown sunglasses with a pinkish tint to them, and carried a big straw bag, almost as big as her torso, shaped like a bowl, with a water bottle poking out of it. She walked slowly, carrying some puffed rice tossed with peanuts and chili peppers in a large packet made from newspapers. Mr. Kapasi turned to Mr. Das.

"Where in America do you live?"

"New Brunswick, New Jersey."

"Next to New York?"

"Exactly. I teach middle school there."

"What subject?"

"Science. In fact, every year I take my students on a trip to the Museum of Natural History in New York City. In a way we have a lot in common, you could say, you and I. How long have you been a tour guide, Mr. Kapasi?"

"Five years."

Mrs. Das reached the car. "How long's the trip?" she asked, shutting the door.

"About two and a half hours," Mr. Kapasi replied.

At this Mrs. Das gave an impatient sigh, as if she had been traveling her whole life without pause. She fanned herself with a folded Bombay film magazine written in English.

"I thought that the Sun Temple is only eighteen miles north of Puri," Mr. Das said, tapping on the tour book.

"The roads to Konarak are poor. Actually it is a distance of fifty-two miles," Mr. Kapasi explained.

Mr. Das nodded, readjusting the camera strap where it had begun to chafe the back of his neck.

Before starting the ignition, Mr. Kapasi reached back to make sure the crank-like locks on the inside of each of the back doors were secured. As soon as the car began to move the little girl began to play with the lock on her side, clicking it with some effort forward and backward, but Mrs. Das said nothing to stop her. She sat a bit slouched at one end of the back seat, not offering her puffed rice to anyone. Ronny and Tina sat on either side of her, both snapping bright green gum.

"Look," Bobby said as the car began to gather speed. He pointed with his finger to the tall trees that lined the road. "Look."

"Monkeys!" Ronny shrieked. "Wow!"

They were seated in groups along the branches, with shining black faces, silver bodies, horizontal eyebrows, and crested heads.

Their long gray tails dangled like a series of ropes among the leaves. A few scratched themselves with black leathery hands, or swung their feet, staring as the car passed.

"We call them the hanuman," Mr. Kapasi said. "They are quite common in the area."

As soon as he spoke, one of the monkeys leaped into the middle of the road, causing Mr. Kapasi to brake suddenly. Another bounced onto the hood of the car, then sprang away. Mr. Kapasi beeped his horn. The children began to get excited, sucking in their breath and covering their faces partly with their hands. They had never seen monkeys outside of a zoo, Mr. Das explained. He asked Mr. Kapasi to stop the car so that he could take a picture.

While Mr. Das adjusted his telephoto lens, Mrs. Das reached into her straw bag and pulled out a bottle of colorless nail polish, which she proceeded to stroke on the tip of her index finger.

The little girl stuck out a hand. "Mine too. Mommy, do mine too."

"Leave me alone," Mrs. Das said, blowing on her nail and turning her body slightly. "You're making me mess up."

The little girl occupied herself by buttoning and unbuttoning a pinafore on the doll's plastic body.

"All set," Mr. Das said, replacing the lens cap.

The car rattled considerably as it raced along the dusty road, causing them all to pop up from their seats every now and then, but Mrs. Das continued to polish her nails. Mr. Kapasi eased up on the accelerator, hoping to produce a smoother ride. When he reached for the gearshift the boy in front accommodated him by swinging his hairless knees out of the way. Mr. Kapasi noted that this boy was slightly paler than the other children. "Daddy, why is the driver sitting on the wrong side in this car, too?" the boy asked.

"They all do that here, dummy," Ronny said.

"Don't call your brother a dummy," Mr. Das said. He turned to Mr. Kapasi. "In America, you know . . . it confuses them."

"Oh yes, I am well aware," Mr. Kapasi said. As delicately as he could, he shifted gears again, accelerating as they approached a hill in the road. "I see it on *Dallas,* the steering wheels are on the left-hand side."

"What's *Dallas*?" Tina asked, banging her now naked doll on the seat behind Mr. Kapasi.

"It went off the air," Mr. Das explained. "It's a television show."

They were all like siblings, Mr. Kapasi thought as they passed a row of date trees. Mr. and Mrs. Das behaved like an older brother and sister, not parents. It seemed that they were in charge of the children only for the day; it was hard to believe they were regularly responsible for anything other than themselves. Mr. Das tapped on his lens cap, and his tour book, dragging his thumbnail occasionally across the pages so that they made a scraping sound. Mrs. Das continued to polish her nails. She had still not removed her sunglasses. Every now and then Tina renewed her plea that she wanted her nails done, too, and so at one point Mrs. Das flicked a drop of polish on the little girl's finger before depositing the bottle back inside her straw bag.

"Isn't this an air-conditioned car?" she asked, still blowing on her hand. The window on Tina's side was broken and could not be rolled down.

"Quit complaining," Mr. Das said. "It isn't so hot."

"I told you to get a car with air conditioning," Mrs. Das continued. "Why do you do this, Raj, just to save a few stupid rupees. What are you saving us, fifty cents?"

Their accents sounded just like the ones Mr. Kapasi heard on American television programs, though not like the ones on *Dallas*.

"Doesn't it get tiresome, Mr. Kapasi, showing people the same thing every day?" Mr. Das asked, rolling down his own window all the way. "Hey, do you mind stopping the car. I just want to get a shot of this guy."

Mr. Kapasi pulled over to the side of the road as Mr. Das took a picture of a barefoot man, his head wrapped in a dirty turban, seated on top of a cart of grain sacks pulled by a pair of bullocks. Both the man and the bullocks were emaciated. In the back seat Mrs. Das gazed out another window, at the sky, where nearly transparent clouds passed quickly in front of one another.

"I look forward to it, actually," Mr. Kapasi said as they continued on their way. "The Sun Temple is one of my favorite places. In that way it is a reward for me. I give tours on Fridays and Saturdays only. I have another job during the week."

"Oh? Where?" Mr. Das asked.

"I work in a doctor's office."

"You're a doctor?"

"I am not a doctor. I work with one. As an interpreter."

"What does a doctor need an interpreter for?"

"He has a number of Gujarati patients. My father was Gujarati, but many people do not speak Gujarati in this area, including the doctor. And so the doctor asked me to work in his office, interpreting what the patients say."

"Interesting. I've never heard of anything like that," Mr. Das said.

Mr. Kapasi shrugged. "It is a job like any other."

"But so romantic," Mrs. Das said dreamily, breaking her extended silence. She lifted her pinkish brown sunglasses and arranged them on top of her head like a tiara. For the first time, her eyes met Mr. Kapasi's in the rearview mirror: pale, a bit small, their gaze fixed but drowsy.

Mr. Das craned to look at her. "What's so romantic about it?"

"I don't know. Something." She shrugged, knitting her brows together for an instant. "Would you like a piece of gum, Mr. Kapasi?" she asked brightly. She reached into her straw bag and handed him a small square wrapped in green-and-white-stripped paper. As soon as Mr. Kapasi put the gum in his mouth a thick sweet liquid burst onto his tongue.

"Tell us more about your job, Mr. Kapasi," Mrs. Das said.

"What would you like to know, madame?"

"I don't know," she shrugged, munching on some puffed rice and licking the mustard oil from the corners of her mouth. "Tell us a typical situation." She settled back in her seat, her head tilted in a patch of sun, and closed her eyes. "I want to picture what happens."

"Very well. The other day a man came in with a pain in his throat."

"Did he smoke cigarettes?"

"No. It was very curious. He complained that he felt as if there were long pieces of straw stuck in his throat. When I told the doctor he was able to prescribe the proper medication."

"That's so neat."

"Yes," Mr. Kapasi agreed after some hesitation.

"So these patients are totally dependent on you," Mrs. Das said. She spoke slowly, as if she were thinking aloud. "In a way, more dependent on you than the doctor."

"How do you mean? How could it be?"

"Well, for example, you could tell the doctor that the pain felt like a burning, not straw. The patient would never know what you had told the doctor, and the doctor wouldn't know that you had told the wrong thing. It's a big responsibility."

"Yes, a big responsibility you have there, Mr. Kapasi," Mr. Das agreed.

Mr. Kapasi had never thought of his job in such complimentary terms. To him it was a thankless occupation. He found nothing noble in interpreting people's maladies, assiduously translating the symptoms of so many swollen bones, countless cramps of bellies and bowels, spots on people's palms that changed color, shape, or size. The doctor, nearly half his age, had an affinity for bell-bottom trousers and made humorless jokes about the Congress party. Together they worked in a stale little infirmary where Mr. Kapasi's smartly tailored clothes clung to him in the heat, in spite of the blackened blades of a ceiling fan churning over their heads.

The job was a sign of his failings. In his youth he'd been a devoted scholar of foreign languages, the owner of an impressive collection of dictionaries. He had dreamed of being an interpreter for diplomats and dignitaries, resolving conflicts between people and nations, settling disputes of which he alone could understand both sides. He was a self-educated man. In a series of notebooks, in the evenings before his parents settled his marriage, he had listed the common etymologies of words, and at one point in his life he was confident that he could converse, if given the opportunity, in English, French, Russian, Portuguese, and Italian, not to mention Hindi, Bengali, Orissi, and Gujarati. Now only a handful of European phrases remained in his memory, scattered words for things like saucers and chairs. English was the only non-Indian language he spoke fluently anymore. Mr. Kapasi knew it was not a remarkable talent. Sometimes he feared that his children knew better English than he did, just from watching television. Still, it came in handy for the tours.

He had taken the job as an interpreter after his first son, at the age of seven, contracted typhoid—that was how he had first made the acquaintance of the doctor. At the time Mr. Kapasi had been teaching English in a grammar school, and he bartered his skills as an interpreter to pay the increasingly exorbitant medical bills. In the end the boy had died one evening in his mother's arms, his limbs burning with fever, but then there was the funeral to pay for, and the other children who were born soon enough, and the newer, bigger house, and the good schools and tutors, and the fine shoes and the television, and the countless other ways he tried to console his wife and to keep her from crying in her sleep, and so when the doctor offered to pay him twice as much as he earned at the grammar school, he accepted. Mr. Kapasi knew that his wife had little regard for his career as an interpreter. He knew it reminded her of the son she'd lost, and that she resented the other lives he helped, in his own small way, to save. If ever she referred to his position, she used the phrase "doctor's assistant," as if the process of interpretation were equal to taking someone's temperature, or changing a bedpan. She never asked him about the patients who came to the doctor's office, or said that his job was a big responsibility.

For this reason it flattered Mr. Kapasi that Mrs. Das was so intrigued by his job. Unlike his wife, she had reminded him of its intellectual challenges. She had also used the word "romantic." She did not behave in a romantic way toward her husband, and yet she had used the word to describe him. He wondered if Mr. and Mrs. Das were a bad match, just as he and his wife were. Perhaps they, too, had little in common apart from three children and a decade of their lives. The signs he recognized from his own marriage were there—the bickering, the indifference, the protracted silences. Her sudden interest in him, an interest she did not express in either her husband or her children, was mildly intoxicating. When Mr. Kapasi thought once again about how she had said "romantic," the feeling of intoxication grew.

He began to check his reflection in the rearview mirror as he drove, feeling grateful that he had chosen the gray suit that morning and not the brown one, which tended to sag a little in the knees. From time to time he glanced through the mirror at Mrs. Das. In addition to glancing at her face he glanced at the strawberry between her breasts, and the golden brown hollow in her throat. He decided to tell Mrs. Das about another patient, and another: the young woman who had complained of a sensation of raindrops in her spine, the gentleman whose birthmark had begun to sprout hairs. Mrs. Das listened attentively, stroking her hair with a small plastic brush that resembled an oval bed of nails, asking more questions, for yet another example. The children were quiet, intent on spotting more monkeys in the trees, and Mr. Das was absorbed by his tour book, so it seemed like a private conversation between Mr. Kapasi and Mrs. Das. In this manner the next half hour passed, and when they stopped for lunch at a roadside restaurant that sold fritters and omelette sandwiches, usually something Mr. Kapasi looked forward to on his tours so that he could sit in peace and enjoy some hot tea, he was disappointed. As the Das family settled together under a magenta umbrella fringed with white and orange tassels, and placed their orders with one of the waiters who marched about in tricornered caps, Mr. Kapasi reluctantly headed toward a neighboring table.

"Mr. Kapasi, wait. There's room here," Mrs. Das called out. She gathered Tina onto her lap, insisting that he accompany them. And so, together, they had bottled mango juice and sandwiches and plates of onions and potatoes deep-fried in graham-flour batter. After finishing two omelette sandwiches Mr. Das took more pictures of the group as they ate.

"How much longer?" he asked Mr. Kapasi as he paused to load a new roll of film in the camera.

"About half an hour more."

By now the children had gotten up from the table to look at more monkeys perched in a nearby tree, so there was a considerable space between Mrs. Das and Mr. Kapasi. Mr. Das placed the camera to his face and squeezed one eye shut, his tongue exposed at one corner of his mouth. "This looks funny. Mina, you need to lean in closer to Mr. Kapasi."

She did. He could smell a scent on her skin, like a mixture of whiskey and rosewater. He worried suddenly that she could smell his perspiration, which he knew had collected beneath the synthetic material of his shirt. He polished off his mango juice in one gulp and smoothed his silver hair with his hands. A bit of the juice dripped onto his chin. He wondered if Mrs. Das had noticed.

She had not. "What's your address, Mr. Kapasi?" she inquired, fishing for something inside her straw bag.

"You would like my address?"

"So we can send you copies," she said. "Of the pictures." She handed him a scrap of paper which she had hastily ripped from a page of her film magazine. The blank portion was limited, for the narrow strip was crowded by lines of text and a tiny picture of a hero and heroine embracing under a eucalyptus tree.

The paper curled as Mr. Kapasi wrote his address in clear, careful letters. She would write to him, asking about his days interpreting at the doctor's office, and he would respond eloquently, choosing only the most entertaining anecdotes, ones that would make her laugh out loud as she read them in her house in New Jersey. In time she would reveal the disappointment of her marriage, and he his. In this way their friendship would grow, and flourish. He would possess a picture of the two of them, eating fried onions under a magenta umbrella, which he would keep, he decided, safely tucked between the pages of his Russian grammar. As his mind raced, Mr. Kapasi experienced a mild and pleasant shock. It was similar to a feeling he used to experience long ago when, after months of translating with the aid of a dictionary, he would finally read a passage from a French novel, or an Italian sonnet, and understand the words, one after another, unencumbered by his own efforts. In those moments Mr. Kapasi used to believe that all was right with the world, that all struggles were rewarded, that all of life's mistakes made sense in the end. The promise that he would hear from Mrs. Das now filled him with the same belief.

When he finished writing his address Mr. Kapasi handed her the paper, but as soon as he did so he worried that he had either misspelled his name, or accidentally reversed the numbers of his postal code. He dreaded the possibility of a lost letter, the photograph never reaching him, hovering somewhere in Orissa, close but ultimately unattainable. He thought of asking for the slip of paper again, just to make sure he had written his address accurately, but Mrs. Das had already dropped it into the jumble of her bag.

They reached Konarak at two-thirty. The temple, made of sandstone, was a massive pyramid-like structure in the shape of a chariot. It was dedicated to the great master of life, the sun, which struck three sides of the edifice as it made its journey each day across the sky. Twenty-four giant wheels were carved on the north and south sides of the plinth. The whole thing was drawn by a team of seven horses, speeding as if through the heavens. As they approached, Mr. Kapasi explained that the temple had been built between 1243 and 1255 A.D., with the efforts of twelve hundred artisans, by the great ruler of the Ganga dynasty, King Narasimhadeva the first, to commemorate his victory against the Muslim army.

"It says the temple occupies about a hundred and seventy acres of land," Mr. Das said, reading from his book.

"It's like a desert," Ronny said, his eyes wandering across the sand that stretched on all sides beyond the temple.

"The Chandrabhaga River once flowed one mile north of here. It is dry now," Mr. Kapasi said, turning off the engine.

They got out and walked toward the temple, posing first for pictures by the pair of lions that flanked the steps. Mr. Kapasi led them next to one of the wheels of the chariot, higher than any human being, nine feet in diameter.

" 'The wheels are supposed to symbolize the wheel of life,' " Mr. Das read. " 'They depict the cycle of creation, preservation, and achievement of realization.' Cool." He turned the page of his book. " 'Each wheel is divided into eight thick and thin spokes, dividing the day into eight equal parts. The rims are carved with designs of birds and animals, whereas the medallions in the spokes are carved with women in luxurious poses, largely erotic in nature.' "

What he referred to were the countless friezes of entwined naked bodies, making love in various positions, women clinging to the necks of men, their knees wrapped eternally around their lovers' thighs. In addition to these were assorted scenes from daily life, of hunting and trading, of deer being killed with bows and arrows and marching warriors holding swords in their hands.

It was no longer possible to enter the temple, for it had filled with rubble years ago, but they admired the exterior, as did all the tourists Mr. Kapasi brought there, slowly strolling along each of its sides. Mr. Das trailed behind, taking pictures. The children ran ahead, pointing to figures of naked people, intrigued in particular by the Nagamithunas, the half-human, half-serpentine couples who were said, Mr. Kapasi told them, to live in the deepest waters of the sea. Mr. Kapasi was pleased that they liked the temple, pleased especially that it appealed to Mrs. Das. She stopped every three or four paces, staring silently at the carved lovers, and the processions of elephants, and the topless female musicians beating on two-sided drums.

Though Mr. Kapasi had been to the temple countless times, it occurred to him, as he, too, gazed at the topless women, that he had never seen his own wife fully naked. Even when they had made love she kept the panels of her blouse hooked together, the string of her petticoat knotted around her waist. He had never admired the backs of his wife's legs the way he now admired those of Mrs. Das, walking as if for his benefit alone. He had, of course, seen plenty of bare limbs before, belonging to the American and European ladies who took his tours. But Mrs. Das was different. Unlike the other women, who had an interest only in the temple, and kept their noses buried in a guidebook, or their eyes behind the lens of a camera, Mrs. Das had taken an interest in him.

Mr. Kapasi was anxious to be alone with her, to continue their private conversation, yet he felt nervous to walk at her side. She was lost behind her sunglasses, ignoring her husband's requests that she pose for another picture, walking past her children as if they were strangers. Worried that he might disturb her, Mr. Kapasi walked ahead, to admire, as he always did, the three life-sized bronze avatars of Surya, the sun god, each emerging from its own niche on the temple facade to greet the sun at dawn, noon, and evening. They wore elaborate headdresses, their languid, elongated eyes closed, their bare chests draped with carved chains and amulets. Hibiscus petals, offerings from previous visitors, were strewn at their gray-green feet. The last statue, on the northern wall of the temple, was

Mr. Kapasi's favorite. This Surya had a tired expression, weary after a hard day of work, sitting astride a horse with folded legs. Even his horse's eyes were drowsy. Around his body were smaller sculptures of women in pairs, their hips thrust to one side.

"Who's that?" Mrs. Das asked. He was startled to see that she was standing beside him.

"He is the Astachala-Surya," Mr. Kapasi said. "The setting sun."

"So in a couple of hours the sun will set right here?" She slipped a foot out of one of her square-heeled shoes, rubbed her toes on the back of her other leg.

"That is correct."

She raised her sunglasses for a moment, then put them back on again. "Neat."

Mr. Kapasi was not certain exactly what the word suggested, but he had a feeling it was a favorable response. He hoped that Mrs. Das had understood Surya's beauty, his power. Perhaps they would discuss it further in their letters. He would explain things to her, things about India, and she would explain things to him about America. In its own way this correspondence would fulfill his dream, of serving as an interpreter between nations. He looked at her straw bag, delighted that his address lay nestled among its contents. When he pictured her so many thousands of miles away he plummeted, so much so that he had an overwhelming urge to wrap his arms around her, to freeze with her, even for an instant, in an embrace witnessed by his favorite Surya. But Mrs. Das had already started walking.

"When do you return to America?" he asked, trying to sound placid.

"In ten days."

He calculated: A week to settle in, a week to develop the pictures, a few days to compose her letter, two weeks to get to India by air. According to his schedule, allowing room for delays, he would hear from Mrs. Das in approximately six weeks' time.

The family was silent as Mr. Kapasi drove them back, a little past four-thirty, to Hotel Sandy Villa. The children had bought miniature granite versions of the chariot's wheels at a souvenir stand, and they turned them round in their hands. Mr. Das continued to read his book. Mrs. Das untangled Tina's hair with her brush and divided it into two little ponytails.

Mr. Kapasi was beginning to dread the thought of dropping them off. He was not prepared to begin his six-week wait to hear from Mrs. Das. As he stole glances at her in the rearview mirror, wrapping elastic bands around Tina's hair, he wondered how he might make the tour last a little longer. Ordinarily he sped back to Puri using a shortcut, eager to return home, scrub his feet and hands with sandalwood soap, and enjoy the evening newspaper and a cup of tea that his wife would serve him in silence. The thought of that silence, something to which he'd long been resigned, now oppressed him. It was then that he suggested visiting the hills at Udayagiri and Khandagiri, where a number of monastic dwellings were hewn out of the ground, facing one another across a defile. It was some miles away, but well worth seeing, Mr. Kapasi told them.

"Oh yeah, there's something mentioned about it in this book," Mr. Das said. "Built by a Jain king or something."

"Shall we go then?" Mr. Kapasi asked. He paused at a turn in the road. "It's to the left."

Mr. Das turned to look at Mrs. Das. Both of them shrugged.

"Left, left," the children chanted.

Mr. Kapasi turned the wheel, almost delirious with relief. He did not know what he would do or say to Mrs. Das once they arrived at the hills. Perhaps he would tell her what a pleasing smile she had. Perhaps he would compliment her strawberry shirt, which he found irresistibly becoming. Perhaps, when Mr. Das was busy taking a picture, he would take her hand.

He did not have to worry. When they got to the hills, divided by a steep path thick with trees, Mrs. Das refused to get out of the car. All along the path, dozens of monkeys were seated on stones, as well as on the branches of the trees. Their hind legs were stretched out in front and raised to shoulder level, their arms resting on their knees.

"My legs are tired," she said, sinking low in her seat. "I'll stay here."

"Why did you have to wear those stupid shoes?" Mr. Das said. "You won't be in the pictures."

"Pretend I'm there."

"But we could use one of these pictures for our Christmas card this year. We didn't get one of all five of us at the Sun Temple. Mr. Kapasi could take it."

"I'm not coming. Anyway, those monkeys give me the creeps."

"But they're harmless," Mr. Das said. He turned to Mr. Kapasi. "Aren't they?"

"They are more hungry than dangerous," Mr. Kapasi said. "Do not provoke them with food, and they will not bother you."

Mr. Das headed up the defile with the children, the boys at his side, the little girl on his shoulders. Mr. Kapasi watched as they crossed paths with a Japanese man and woman, the only other tourists there, who paused for a final photograph, then stepped into a nearby car and drove away. As the car disappeared out of view some of the monkeys called out, emitting soft whooping sounds, and then walked on their flat black hands and feet up the path. At one point a group of them formed a little ring around Mr. Das and the children. Tina screamed in delight. Ronny ran in circles around his father. Bobby bent down and picked up a fat stick on the ground. When he extended it, one of the monkeys approached him and snatched it, then briefly beat the ground.

"I'll join them," Mr. Kapasi said, unlocking the door on his side. "There is much to explain about the caves."

"No. Stay a minute," Mrs. Das said. She got out of the back seat and slipped in beside Mr. Kapasi. "Raj has his dumb book anyway." Together, through the windshield, Mrs. Das and Mr. Kapasi watched as Bobby and the monkey passed the stick back and forth between them.

"A brave little boy," Mr. Kapasi commented.

"It's not so surprising," Mrs. Das said.

"No?"

"He's not his."

"I beg your pardon?"

"Raj's. He's not Raj's son."

Mr. Kapasi felt a prickle on his skin. He reached into his shirt pocket for the small tin of lotus-oil balm he carried with him at all times, and applied it to three spots on his forehead. He knew that

Mrs. Das was watching him, but he did not turn to face her. Instead he watched as the figures of Mr. Das and the children grew smaller, climbing up the steep path, pausing every now and then for a picture, surrounded by a growing number of monkeys.

"Are you surprised?" The way she put it made him choose his words with care.

"It's not the type of thing one assumes," Mr. Kapasi replied slowly. He put the tin of lotus-oil balm back in his pocket.

"No, of course not. And no one knows, of course. No one at all. I've kept it a secret for eight whole years." She looked at Mr. Kapasi, tilting her chin as if to gain a fresh perspective. "But now I've told you."

Mr. Kapasi nodded. His throat felt suddenly parched, and his forehand was warm and slightly numb from the balm. He considered asking Mrs. Das for a sip of her water, then decided against it.

"We met when we were very young," she said. She reached into her straw bag in search of something, then pulled out the packet of puffed rice. "Want some?"

"No, thank you."

She put a fistful in her mouth, sank into the seat a little and looked away from Mr. Kapasi out the window on her side of the car. "We married when we were still in college. We were in high school when he proposed. We went to the same college, of course. Back then we couldn't stand the thought of being separated, not for a day, not for a minute. Our parents were best friends who lived in the same town. My entire life I saw him every weekend, either at our house or theirs. We were sent upstairs to play together while our parents joked about our marriage. Imagine! They never caught us at anything, though in a way I think it was all more or less a setup. The things we did those Friday and Saturday nights, while our parents sat downstairs drinking tea . . . I could tell you stories, Mr. Kapasi."

As a result of spending all her time in college with Raj, she continued, she did not make many close friends. There was no one to confide in about him at the end of a difficult day, or to share a passing thought or a worry. Her parents now lived on the other side of the world, but she had never been very close to them, anyway.

After marrying so young she was overwhelmed by it all, having a child so quickly, and nursing, and warming up bottles of milk and testing their temperature against her wrist while Raj was at work, dressed in sweaters and corduroy pants, teaching his students about rocks and dinosaurs. Raj never looked cross or harried, or plump as she had become after the first baby.

Always tired, she declined invitations from her one or two college girl friends, to have lunch or shop in Manhattan. Eventually the friends stopped calling her, so that she was left at home all day with the baby, surrounded by toys that made her trip when she walked or wince when she sat, always cross and tired. Only occasionally did they go out after Ronny was born, and even more rarely did they entertain. Raj didn't mind; he looked forward to coming home from teaching and watching television and bouncing Ronny on his knee. She had been outraged when Raj told her that a Punjabi friend, someone whom she had once met but did not remember, would be staying with them for a week for some job interviews in the New Brunswick area.

Bobby was conceived in the afternoon, on a sofa littered with rubber teething toys, after the friend learned that a London pharmaceutical company had hired him, while Ronny cried to be freed from his playpen. She made no protest when the friend touched the small of her back as she was about to make a pot of coffee, then pulled her against his crisp navy suit. He made love to her swiftly, in silence, with an expertise she had never known, without the meaningful expressions and smiles Raj always insisted on afterward. The next day Raj drove the friend to JFK. He was married now, to a Punjabi girl, and they lived in London still, and every year they exchanged Christmas cards with Raj and Mina, each couple tucking photos of their families into the envelopes. He did not know that he was Bobby's father. He never would.

"I beg your pardon, Mrs. Das, but why have you told me this information?" Mr. Kapasi asked when she had finally finished speaking, and had turned to face him once again.

"For God's sake, stop calling me Mrs. Das. I'm twenty-eight. You probably have children my age."

"Not quite." It disturbed Mr. Kapasi to learn that she thought of him as a parent. The feeling he had had toward her, that had made him check his reflection in the rearview mirror as they drove, evaporated a little.

"I told you because of your talents." She put the packet of puffed rice back into her bag without folding over the top.

"I don't understand," Mr. Kapasi said.

"Don't you see? For eight years I haven't been able to express this to anybody, not to friends, certainly not to Raj. He doesn't even suspect it. He thinks I'm still in love with him. Well, don't you have anything to say?"

"About what?"

"About what I've just told you. About my secret, and about how terrible it makes me feel. I feel terrible looking at my children, and at Raj, always terrible. I have terrible urges, Mr. Kapasi, to throw things away. One day I had the urge to throw everything I own out the window, the television, the children, everything. Don't you think it's unhealthy?"

He was silent.

"Mr. Kapasi, don't you have anything to say? I thought that was your job."

"My job is to give tours, Mrs. Das."

"Not that. Your other job. As an interpreter."

"But we do not face a language barrier. What need is there for an interpreter?"

"That's not what I mean. I would never have told you otherwise. Don't you realize what it means for me to tell you?"

"What does it mean?"

"It means that I'm tired of feeling so terrible all the time. Eight years, Mr. Kapasi, I've been in pain eight years. I was hoping you could help me feel better, say the right thing. Suggest some kind of remedy."

He looked at her, in her red plaid skirt and strawberry T-shirt, a woman not yet thirty, who loved neither her husband nor her children, who had already fallen out of love with life. Her confession depressed him, depressed him all the more when he thought of Mr. Das at the top of the path, Tina clinging to his shoulders, taking pictures of ancient monastic cells cut into the hills to show his students in America, unsuspecting and unaware that one of his sons was not his own. Mr. Kapasi felt insulted that Mrs. Das should ask him to interpret her common, trivial little secret. She did not resemble the patients in the doctor's office, those who came glassy-eyed and desperate, unable to sleep or breathe or urinate with ease, unable, above all, to give words to their pains. Still, Mr. Kapasi believed it was his duty to assist Mrs. Das. Perhaps he ought to tell her to confess the truth to Mr. Das. He would explain that honesty was the best policy. Honesty, surely, would help her feel better, as she'd put it. Perhaps he would offer to preside over the discussion, as a mediator. He decided to begin with the most obvious question, to get to the heart of the matter, and so he asked, "Is it really pain you feel, Mrs. Das, or is it guilt?"

She turned to him and glared, mustard oil thick on her frosty pink lips. She opened her mouth to say something, but as she glared at Mr. Kapasi some certain knowledge seemed to pass before her eyes, and she stopped. It crushed him; he knew at that moment that he was not even important enough to be properly insulted. She opened the car door and began walking up the path, wobbling a little on her square wooden heels, reaching into her straw bag to eat handfuls of puffed rice. It fell through her fingers, leaving a zigzagging trail, causing a monkey to leap down from a tree and devour the little white grains. In search of more, the monkey began to follow Mrs. Das. Others joined him, so that she was soon being followed by about half a dozen of them, their velvety tails dragging behind.

Mr. Kapasi stepped out of the car. He wanted to holler, to alert her in some way, but he worried that if she knew they were behind her, she would grow nervous. Perhaps she would lose her balance. Perhaps they would pull at her bag or her hair. He began to jog up the path, taking a fallen branch in his hand to scare away the monkeys. Mrs. Das continued walking, oblivious, trailing grains of puffed rice. Near the top of the incline, before a group of cells fronted by a row of squat stone pillars, Mr. Das was kneeling on the ground, focusing the lens of his camera. The children stood under the arcade, now hiding, now emerging from view.

"Wait for me," Mrs. Das called out. "I'm coming."

Tina jumped up and down. "Here comes Mommy!"

"Great," Mr. Das said without looking up. "Just in time. We'll get Mr. Kapasi to take a picture of the five of us."

Mr. Kapasi quickened his pace, waving his branch so that the monkeys scampered away, distracted, in another direction.

"Where's Bobby?" Mrs. Das asked when she stopped.

Mr. Das looked up from the camera. "I don't know. Ronny, where's Bobby?"

Ronny shrugged. "I thought he was right here."

"Where is he?" Mrs. Das repeated sharply. "What's wrong with all of you?"

They began calling his name, wandering up and down the path a bit. Because they were calling, they did not initially hear the boy's screams. When they found him, a little farther down the path under a tree, he was surrounded by a group of monkeys, over a dozen of them, pulling at his T-shirt with their long black fingers. The puffed rice Mrs. Das had spilled was scattered at his feet, raked over by the monkeys' hands. The boy was silent, his body frozen, swift tears running down his startled face. His bare legs were dusty and red with welts from where one of the monkeys struck him repeatedly with the stick he had given to it earlier.

"Daddy, the monkey's hurting Bobby," Tina said.

Mr. Das wiped his palms on the front of his shorts. In his nervousness he accidentally pressed the shutter on his camera; the whirring noise of the advancing film excited the monkeys, and the one with the stick began to beat Bobby more intently. "What are we supposed to do? What if they start attacking?"

"Mr. Kapasi," Mrs. Das shrieked, noticing him standing to one side. "Do something, for God's sake, do something!"

Mr. Kapasi took his branch and shooed them away, hissing at the ones that remained, stomping his feet to scare them. The animals retreated slowly, with a measured gait, obedient but unintimidated. Mr. Kapasi gathered Bobby in his arms and brought him back to where his parents and siblings were standing. As he carried him he was tempted to whisper a secret into the boy's ear. But Bobby was stunned, and shivering with fright, his legs bleeding slightly where the stick had broken the skin. When Mr. Kapasi delivered him to his parents, Mr. Das brushed some dirt off the boy's T-shirt and put the visor on him the right way. Mrs. Das reached into her straw bag to find a bandage which she taped over the cut on his knee. Ronny offered his brother a fresh piece of gum. "He's fine. Just a little scared, right, Bobby?" Mr. Das said, patting the top of his head.

"God, let's get out of here," Mrs. Das said. She folded her arms across the strawberry on her chest. "This place gives me the creeps."

"Yeah. Back to the hotel, definitely," Mr. Das agreed.

"Poor Bobby," Mrs. Das said. "Come here a second. Let Mommy fix your hair." Again she reached into her straw bag, this time for her hairbrush, and began to run it around the edges of the translucent visor. When she whipped out the hairbrush, the slip of paper with Mr. Kapasi's address on it fluttered away in the wind. No one but Mr. Kapasi noticed. He watched as it rose, carried higher and higher by the breeze, into the trees where the monkeys now sat, solemnly observing the scene below. Mr. Kapasi observed it too, knowing that this was the picture of the Das family he would preserve forever in his mind.

Gerald Reilly

Nixon Under the Bodhi Tree

From *The Gettysburg Review*

EVERY NIGHT it takes Dallas Boyd at least two hours to become Richard Nixon, and after the performance it takes just as long to get cleaned up and find a taxi to drive him home. He has started spending nearly the whole afternoon before a show getting ready, and the people at the theatre are used to it, they've already let him bring in some furniture, a reclining chair, an old oriental carpet, even a hot plate so he can brew his herb teas, whatever he needs within reason to make things a little more comfortable. He loves his dressing room. *I could live in a dressing room,* he has confided to the makeup artist named Gwen. He tells himself this is more than just a juicy part: it's become Dallas Boyd's defining moment, his crowning achievement. His entire life has shrunken around the role, he doesn't have energy left over for anything else.

The play is called *Nixon at Colonus,* and he's never liked the title—this play is more Mamet than Sophocles, it hardly offers Tricky Dick anything like the apotheosis that he deserves—but he loves the play all the same. The script is pretty hard on the president by way of being sympathetic. Tough love. Whatever softness Dallas has been able to insert is purely around the edges. No ducking the truth here, no claims that the only problem was being too soft-hearted, as though Nixon was ever softhearted.

Dallas Boyd loves the author too, a sweetheart of a playwright

named Lester Feltzer who still shows up occasionally at performances. Feltzer is straight, but the most softhearted, gushiest heterosexual friend that Dallas has ever known. At the end of the summer,
Les moved out to Los Angeles to write for the movies, but things
haven't gone well for him on the coast—the studio declined to exercise its option—and so Les is already planning a return to New
York. Whenever he visits the theatre, he brings tasty health food
offerings with him that he dispenses to Dallas like a Jewish grandmother, and then they sit down and talk.

On the very last visit, he told Les that he felt he was starting to
finally get deeper into the part. He's been doing the play for more
than fourteen months already, but at last it feels like all the unyielding discipline and concentration is paying off. With Feltzer he never
talks about his fears. Or that he has no idea how long he's going to
be able to continue. Even as he's drawn himself in and focussed all
his energies, inner and outer, on the role, he can feel the life forces
fading. The ironies of this are rich: almost Nixonian. Forty-three
years old, after twenty years of freak shows and supporting roles, he
lands the perfect part, complete with terrific notices and interest
from film casting people; all this, and he doesn't have the slightest
idea how much longer he can stick it out. He knows for certain he
will not be able to move on to some other role, so he has no choice
but to keep settling deeper and deeper into the personality. In his
recent performances he feels like he has finally mastered the physical
Dick Nixon. He never had to struggle to achieve the unmistakable
clipped speech cadences that always seemed to be uttering just the
wrong sentiment, and early on Gwen managed the pasty-face
makeup that forever appeared in desperate need of a shave. Now he
effortlessly takes on the awkward play of the shoulders as the president thrusts yet another absurdly inappropriate victory sign heaven-
ward with both hands. Gwen needs well over an hour to do the hair
and face, but he knows the resemblance wouldn't add up to much if
he doesn't inhabit that makeup with the bristling awkwardness of
the man himself.

When he is in character, all the lighting technicians and stage-
hands call him Mr. President. This started out as a joke, but right
away the star understood this helped him get deeper into the part.

At one point when he was struggling to improve his Nixon shuffle, he actually requested Vinnie, the chief stageman, to address him the same way. At first Vinnie looked vaguely insulted, as though he was outraged by the notion, as though going along with such absurdity was not only *not* required by the union handbook but absolutely against all good sense.

"It helps get me in character," the actor explained. "If you feel I *am* the president, I'll feel that way too."

Over time Vinnie has turned out to be his best friend at the theatre. Every week or two he brings in Italian food that his wife has cooked up, and whether his appetite is strong or not, Dallas tries to eat it as best he can, even on those nights when the smell of meatballs and veal nearly turns his stomach, and he always follows the dining with extravagant compliments to the chef and insistent requests for more.

But even Vinnie has been acting strangely tonight. Earlier he noticed something was wrong with Gwen, when she put on his face, but for once he didn't press her for details. Instead, it falls to Vinnie to bring him the news. It is almost six-thirty, and Gwen has long since finished her work and left him alone, sitting in character, when Vinnie knocks on the door.

"Want some tea?" Dallas offers as he always offers. He knows right away something is wrong. Vinnie shakes his head about the tea and stands there with an awkwardness that Dallas picks up immediately.

"How are you today, Vin?"

"Okay. How you feeling, Mr. President?"

"Terrific. Is something wrong, Vinnie?"

"You haven't heard the news?"

"No. What news?"

"That's what Gwen said. She didn't think you knew yet."

The stagehand removes the *New York Post* carefully from behind his back. For once Vinnie looks utterly abashed, like he's doing something that has to be done but gives him no pleasure. The huge front page announces that Richard Nixon is dead. A *New York Times* follows. The news overwhelms Dallas, surely more than it should. Nixon's health has been shaky, he was in the hospital early in the week, but before this exact moment Dallas has never been willing to allow the possibility of Richard Nixon's death, much less to explore its potential symbolic significance to his own inner life. And this is especially odd because he has so often contemplated his own death.

His eyes search for details to hang on to. One columnist is named Apple. The time of death is listed as nine o'clock in the evening. Which means he was onstage even as the president died. It occurs to him fleetingly that it might be good for box office receipts, at least from a short-term perspective, and then Dallas blushes deeply at the utter shallowness of that reaction. He thinks that everyone must have been shielding him, avoiding any mention of it with him, as though he were too fragile for the shock. Who knows, maybe they were right. He lives in such a focussed world that he hadn't even gotten the news on his own. He blushes again, realizing that he has been ignoring Vinnie, who has been standing in the dressing room watching him the whole time.

"I just thought you should know."

"Of course you were right. Thank you, Vinnie." Their eyes meet. "I guess I'm living in a cocoon. Even news like this comes to me a day late."

Alone, Dallas looks in the bright makeup mirror and asks himself what he is going to do. He considers medication, but settles on a mere pair of aspirin that he extracts from the forest of medicine bottles. Prescription bottles are laid out on surfaces everywhere, and Dallas carries a satchel packed with medications wherever he goes. He has become an expert at painkillers, and Dr. Reynolds has given him considerable latitude. There's Vicodin and Hydracordone. When things get more painful, there's Atavin and an open prescription for morphine, which he doesn't imagine needing till much later on, but which is a reassuring presence even in prescription form. He feels like he's been enormously lucky. He's gone for monthly blood tests and he keeps track of his T cells, but he's resigned to the course of the disease. They tried AZT for almost six months, and he's happy to be free of that drug's ugly side effects. He keeps reducing the circle of his days, reducing distractions of any sort. His performances are all that he can manage to get through. And the round of performances never ends. On Mondays, when he finally has a day off, he doesn't budge from his apartment. He lies in bed all day, dressed in a bathrobe with slippers no matter what the temperature outside. Lately, he always feels a chill. Silk long underwear, the thick wool Irish leg warmers, double layer of socks—nothing helps much.

He begins doing the now-familiar *tonglen* meditation. In recent days he has taken to studying all sort of crazy things: New Age books on channeling and astrology, theosophic tracts, even ancient Buddhist texts. Some might call it desperation, a lame attempt to stave off the idea of his mortality, but it's anything but escapism. In this meditation he mentally exchanges his own best feelings with another's suffering, all to the rhythm of his respiration—breathing in Nixon's anger and hatred and breathing out all the most peaceful, wonderful feelings.

It feels different with the news that the president has left the human realm. Dallas's mind roams back over the presidential career, and for once he doesn't fight his wandering mind. He tries only to keep the bare touch of the rhythm of his breathing and the exchange, the dark light in, the white light out, and slowly he feels himself steadying. It is simply indescribable doing this meditation with Dick Nixon. He finds himself thinking about Cambodia and all the bombs that were dropped and the black karma coming so thick that it clouds out the sun until Dallas feels he can barely keep breathing and then, just before he panics, he is letting go, all bliss and blue skies exhaling out to Nixon. It works counter to everything in the life of a struggling, up-and-coming actor, what's supposed to make up your most basic nature, your survival instinct. *You've changed,* friends told him. He knew he had grown altogether more somber. He felt like he was wearing a jacket and tie all the time now. He was dying, and yet he was worrying about poor Dick Nixon.

He often wondered what the president would think about his performance, even while knowing beyond the slightest doubt that Nixon would never have subjected himself to such a play. For years he's hated Nixon in that strange, superficial way that you can feel emotions about somebody existing so far from your daily life. He knows the written record only too well. At home he has two shelves overflowing with Nixon books, and he keeps a few beloved duplicates on hand in the dressing room, but rarely needs them. The sight of himself made up as Nixon is inspiration enough. There's so much juicy stuff. All the swear words that embarrassed Nixon so terribly afterwards, all the antisemitic jabs, the compulsive hate talk. How he ranted about all the Jews and liberals out to get him just because he wasn't as charming or Ivy-League connected as Jack Kennedy. It's gotten worse since he left the White House. Nixon has remained totally unrepentant. He claims only that he was too soft-hearted, even as one after another of his underlings and friends went to jail for him. In the media every few years, there arises that periodic drone—Nixon is back, Nixon is back—every chorus of it more carefully orchestrated than the last one.

But maybe the real Richard Nixon, the spirit Nixon, will finally get the chance to perceive his performance in this latest, disincarnate form. Watching a play must be entirely different for a consciousness that has left its body. Maybe Richard Nixon will be able to see past the prejudices and stubborn self-images that would have marred his appreciation in the first place. Maybe Nixon will feel Dallas's performance for what it is: a life-and-death role, a veritable inhabitation of the dead man's just departed career and life story.

He has already journeyed through a lifetime of his own karma in the last few years. Jorgen went back to Stockholm as soon as he tested positive, and back then Dallas knew it was only a matter of time before he tested positive. A few months later he got the call to play Nell in *Uncle Tom's Cabin,* and two years after that he was chosen to become Richard Nixon, but only after a pair of unsuccessful tryouts separated by almost a month. From transvestite glitter to the White House, but by then Dallas was all alone with his diagnosis. Such isolation was just perfect for Nixon. It was the way Dallas first slipped into the part. Nixon was a genius at loneliness, and now Dallas Boyd was utterly alone and undistracted with him too.

Dallas doesn't know how long he's been sitting by himself when there's a knock on the door and he answers, "Come in," and the dressing room door opens to reveal Les Feltzer.

"As soon as I heard the news, I thought of you."

For the first time Dallas feels like he might start crying. For the first time he feels like part of himself has died tonight. He motions to the empty chair.

"Sit with me for a few minutes."

Dallas knows Lester understands, maybe Lester alone in the entire world. They'd had long talks about the role. "I understand why you're acting even though you're sick," he said after the first week of previews. "We do what we do right up until the end," Lester said. "I'm exactly the same. I'll write until I can't hold a pen up. Then I'll probably talk into a microphone and have it transcribed. We're all terminal cases, and the lucky ones, like you and me, we know what we want—no, what we *have* to do right up till the bitter end." That was months ago, and the stakes have only gotten more intense in the interim.

"Want some tea, Lester?"

"Do you have something stronger?"

Suddenly Dallas is laughing at the obvious *just rightness* of the idea of sharing a stiff drink. Of course it has to be booze. He looks quickly around the dressing room. It is not often that he drinks anything much stronger than green tea, but he sees that he's better stocked than even he realized. He goes out and returns with a tiny cardboard pail of ice courtesy of Vinnie's refrigerator.

"I can just about manage martinis."

"Just the thing."

"I think I'll join you too. One for the president, that bastard. A stiff one for the road."

He pours quantities of gin and vermouth into cups used for his tea rituals and mixes them carefully, even using the bamboo tea whisk, he'll worry about cleaning that off later. Yes, just the thing. Both of them clink their cups as gingerly as if they are drinking highballs at Sardis or Twenty-one.

"I'm glad you're here tonight, Les. I hope you stay for the show."

"Wouldn't miss it for the world."

"You know I've been thinking a lot about Cambodia. I keep thinking about what he did, what we all did, how it's all been forgotten."

Les nods. He is listening with great care. He has spent the afternoon apartment hunting, planning his move back to New York in the next few months, and certainly he hadn't expected to have this impromptu wake in honor of Richard Nixon. He watches Dallas sniff the martini, and then they both take deep drafts of their respective potions. Les has been startled by the signs of physical deterioration that he sees up close, behind his friend's makeup. The actor looks haggard, appears to have aged even since the last time he visited, barely a month ago. All of it contributes to the character, no question. Because it's not just the physical appearance.

"I've taken your play and turned it into a religion," Dallas whispers, exaggerating only slightly. "I live and breathe and shit Richard Nixon. I dream his dreams."

Lester leans forward, but doesn't answer. He senses that the actor, this particular terminal case, is a vehicle for something special tonight.

"Most people, if I told them I was playing Nixon right up until the day I died, you know what they'd say. Say I was crazy. Absolutely certifiable crazy. Sometimes I think that too."

Lester says nothing, staying focussed, centered.

"But you know why I'm doing this?"

Lester admits he doesn't have a clue exactly what he's getting at.

"I'm teaching Nixon to forgive himself." He empties his cup. "I've already forgiven myself. It's all for Tricky Dick from here on out. Every night the soul of Richard Nixon is going to be hearing me, hearing all these prayers you wrote for him. And feeling the play too."

Lester cannot speak now. He feels like he's seen a ghost, it's not just this figure that looks like Richard Nixon—it's everything he knows about Dallas, about the fact that the actor is going to die.

"The real Nixon's with me tonight," says Dallas. "I've been reaching out to him night after night," he reaches up toward the ceiling of the dressing room, "and now he's reaching back from wherever he's journeying."

"You *feel* him?"

He nods. "I felt him last night. I didn't know it then, on stage, but now I know what it was. All that suffering. No wonder I didn't want to see a newspaper. But now I'm going to be able to reach him so much easier. There's nothing separating us anymore. We're all suffering, but poor fucks like Dick Nixon and me, we're just *swimming* in all the suffering." Then before Les can finish his martini or say no, Dallas has slipped a religious book in front of his friend and placed a xerox copy of the same text on his own lap. The actor has a huge stack of meditations and prayers for the dying, but his favorite one is right on top.

"What's this?" the playwright asks, not dreaming for a moment of offering the slightest resistance.

"The Heart Sutra. One of the most sacred Buddhist texts. Now I'm going to read this slowly, and don't worry if the words don't exactly seem clear or even make much sense. The important thing is the feeling you have. And imagine that Nixon's in the room with us. Just meditate on the words as I say them."

Lester is visibly moved, if nothing else by the intensity with which Dallas is directing this improvised moment. And as always Dallas—while he knows that his Tibetan teacher wouldn't agree with whatever extras he's adding, how he's turning a simple prayer recitation into something closer to a séance—Dallas feels completely right about what he is doing for the dead president and for himself. Already, even as he begins to read, Dallas is certain that Nixon is with them: his soul is present in the room. Lester is completely spooked by now—goose-bump-flesh spooked—he cannot see any of this of course, but his body is registering that they're not alone in the dressing room. The five skandhas are enumerated, each of the components of the psyche, and they are liberated in the text, found to be no different than the selflessness of pure experience, all things marked by emptiness—not born, not destroyed. In the few seconds it takes for Dallas to finish the text, scarcely a page long, Lester sees again that the actor is going to die very soon: first Nixon, then Dallas Boyd. They sit in silence for a little while after the prayer's finished. They can hear backstage sounds, but they are listening to something else.

Then Vinnie is knocking on the door. "Ten minutes to curtain."

Lester reaches out and squeezes his hands, "I love you, man."

"I love you too," Dallas answers back.

The actor spends the last few minutes by himself. Already he feels exhausted. He looks at himself in the mirror and doesn't know how he will have the energy to perform for two hours. Outside, the theatre seats will be filling up. The electronic bell tone will be signalling that the curtain is about to go up, though he can hear this only in his imagination.

He stands up. He is sure that it is not merely his own power carrying him forward any longer. He pauses before opening the door and pauses again in the darkness outside the dressing room. Ahead, the bright rim of stage lights awaiting him. A few more steps and he can feel the audience in the darkness, all of them focussed on his movements as he enters their view and sits down at the replica presidential desk. The dark space around him has evaporated: he feels as though they're sitting in a space as large as an airplane hangar, but a hangar so very vast that you can't even see the walls supporting it. Thousands of Cambodians are sitting in long aisles, the four dead youngsters from Kent State are there; the actor's parents and his grandparents and poor Jorgen Lindgren too. Even Pat Nixon has joined the rest of them: saints, arhats, martyrs, bodhisattvas. But by far, mostly simple people, as flawed as Dallas, as flawed as Richard Nixon, all of them merely seeking a glimpse of the truth. What do the souls say to each other in the endless space after their bodies are shed? Soon enough he will know. He looks up through the branches and sees the Milky Way twinkling clearly above. Then he looks down at the dark space that is his audience and begins speaking with a resonance that surprises even himself, loud enough that even the backmost rows can hear clearly.

"I *am* the president."

Michael Cunningham

Mister Brother

From *DoubleTake*

MISTER BROTHER is shaving for a date. Mister Brother likes getting ready, and he likes having had sex. Everything in between is just business.

"Hey, Twohey," he says. "Better take it easy on the sheets tonight, Mom's out of bleach."

Twohey (that's you, if you're willing to wear the skin for a while) says, "Shut up, you moron."

"Ow," Mister Brother says, expertly stroking his jaw with Schick steel. "Don't call me a moron, you know how upset it gets me."

Mister Brother, seventeen years old, looks dressed even when he's naked. His flesh has a serenely unsurprised quality, not common in the male nude since the last of the classical Greek sculptors cut his last torso. Mom and Dad, modest people, terrorized people, are always begging Mister Brother to put something on.

"Shut up," you tell him. "Just shut up."

You, Twohey, I'm sorry to say, are plump and pink as a birthday cake. You are never naked.

"Twohey, m'dear," Mister Brother says, "haven't you got any pressing business, ahem, elsewhere?"

You say, "You bet I do."

And yet you stay where you are, perched on the edge of the bathtub, watching Mister Brother, naked as a gladiator, prepare himself for Saturday night. You can't seem to imagine being anywhere else.

Mister Brother says, "Honestly, if you don't let up on me, I'm going to start crying. I'm going to just fall apart, and won't that make you happy?"

Mister Brother is a wicked mimic. When you tease him, he tends to answer in your mother's voice, but he performs only her hysterical aspect. He omits her undercurrent of bitter, muscular competence.

You laugh. For a moment your mother, not you, is the fool of the house. Mister Brother smiles into the mirror. You watch as he plucks a stray eyebrow hair from the bridge of his nose. Later, as the future starts springing its surprises and you find yourself acquainted with a drag queen or two, you will note that they do not extend to their toilets quite the level of ecstatic care practiced by Mister Brother before the medicine cabinet mirror.

"Hey, honey, come on now, don't cry, I didn't mean it," you say, in an attempt at your father's stately and mortified manner. Imitation is not, unfortunately, the area in which your main talents lie, and you sound more like Daffy Duck than you do like a rueful middle-aged tax attorney. You try to hold the moment by laughing. You do not mean your laughter to sound high-pitched or whinnying.

Mister Brother plucks another hair, rapt as a neurosurgeon. He says, "Twohey, man." He says nothing more. You understand. Work on that laugh, OK?

"Where are you going?" you ask, hoping to be loved for your selfless interest in the lives of others.

"O-U-T," he says. "Into the night. Don't wait up."

"You going out with Sandy?"

"I am, in fact."

"Sandy's a skank."

Mister Brother preens, undeterred. "And what've you got lined up for tonight, buddy?" he says. "A little *Bonanza,* a little self-abuse?"

"Shut *up,*" you say. He is, as usual, dead right, and you're starting to panic. How is it possible that the phrase "lonely, plump, and petulant" could apply to you? There is another you, lean and knowing, desired, and he's right here, under your skin. All you need is a little help getting him out into the world.

"So, Twohey," Mister Brother says. "How would you feel about shedding your light someplace else for a while? A man needs his privacy, dig?"

"Sayonara," you say, but you can't quite make yourself leave the bathroom. Here, right here, in this small chamber of tile and mirror, with three swan decals floating serenely over the bathtub, is all you hope to know about love and ardor, the whole machinery of the future. Everything else is just your house.

"Twohey, brave little chap, I'm serious, kapeesh? Run along, now. On to further adventures."

You nod, and remain. Mister Brother has created a wad of shifting muscles between his shoulder blades. The ropes of his triceps are big enough to throw shadows onto his skin.

You decide to deliver a line devised some time ago, and held in reserve. You say, "Why do you bother with Sandy? Why don't you just date yourself? You know you'll put out, and you can save the price of a movie."

Mister Brother looks at your reflected face in the mirror. He says, "Out, faggot." Now he is imitating no one but himself.

You would prefer to be unaffected by such a cheap shot. It would help if it wasn't true. Given that it is true, you would prefer to have something more in the way of a haughty, crushing response. You would prefer not to be standing here, fat in the fluorescent light, with hippopotamus tears suddenly streaming down your face.

"Christ," Mister Brother says. "Will you just fucking get out of here? Please?"

You will. In another moment, you will. But even now, impaled as you are, you can't quite remove yourself from the presence of your brother's stern and certain beauty.

What can the world possibly do but ruin him? Mister Brother, at seventeen, can have anything he wants, and sees nothing extraordinary about the fact. So what can the world do but marry him (to Carla, not Sandy), find him a job, arrange constellations over his head just the way he likes them, and then slowly start shutting down the power? It's one of the oldest stories. There's the beautiful wife who refuses, obdurately, mysteriously, to be as happy as she'd like to be. There's the baby, then another, then (oops, hey, she must be putting pinholes in my condoms) a third. There's the corporate job (money's no joke anymore, not with three kids at home) where charm counts for less and less, and where Ossie Ringwald, who played cornet in the high school band, joins the firm three years after Mister Brother does and takes less than two years to become his boss.

All that is waiting, and you and Mister Brother probably know it, somehow, here on this spring night in Pasadena, where the scents of honeysuckle and chaparral are extinguished by Mister Brother's Aramis and Right Guard, and where the souped-up cars of Mister Brother's friends and rivals leave rubber behind on the street. Why else would you love and despise each other so ardently, you who have nothing but blood in common? Looking at that present from this present, it seems possible that you both sense somewhere, beneath the level of language, that some thirty years later he, full of Scotch, picked bloody by his flock of sorrows, will suffer a spasm of tears and then fall asleep on your sofa with his head in your lap.

That night is now. Here you are, forty-five years old, showing Mister Brother around the new hilltop house you've bought. As Mister Brother walks the premises, Scotch in hand, appreciating this detail or that, you feel suddenly embarrassed by the house. It's too grand. No, it's grand in the wrong way. It's cheesy, Gatsbyesque. The sofa is so . . . faggot baroque. How had you failed to notice? What made you choose white suede? It had seemed like a brave, reckless disregard of the threat of stains. At this moment, though, it seems possible—it does not seem impossible—that men don't stay around because they can't imagine sitting with you, night after night, on a sofa like this. Maybe that's why you're still alone.

Tonight you sit on the sofa with Mister Brother, who lays his head in your lap. You tell him lots of people go through bad spells in their marriage. You tell him things at work will turn around after the election. Although you still call him by that name this man is not, strictly speaking, Mister Brother at all. This is a forty-eight-year-old, nattily dressed, semi-bald guy with a chain around his neck. This is a tax attorney. Here he is and here you are, speaking softly and consolingly as the more powerful constellations begin to show themselves outside your sliding glass doors.

And here you are at fourteen, in this suburban bathroom. You stand another moment with Mister Brother, livid, ashamed, sniveling, and then you finally force yourself to perform the singular act that should, all along, have been so simple. You leave him alone.

"So long, asshole," you say weepily as you exit. "And fuck you, too."

If he thought more of you, he'd lash out. He wouldn't continue plucking his eyebrows in the mirror.

You go and lie on your bed, running your fingers over the stylish houndstooth blanket you insisted on; worried, as always, about the stains it covers. You hear Mister Brother downstairs flirting with Mom, shadowboxing with Dad. You hear his Mustang fire up in the driveway. You lie on your bed in the room that will become a guest room, a junk room, a home office, and then the bedroom of a stranger's child. You plan to lose weight and get handsome. You plan to earn in the high five figures before you turn forty. You plan to be somebody other people need to know. These plans will largely, astonishingly, come true.

As Mister Brother roars away, radio blasting, you plan a future in which he respects and admires you. You plan to see him humbled, weeping, penitent. You plan to look pityingly down at him from your own pinnacle of strength and love. These plans will not come true. When the time arrives, reparations will be negotiated between a handsome, lonely man and a much older-looking guy in Dockers and a Bill Blass jacket; an exhausted family man who's had a few too many Scotches. Mister Brother won't come at all. Mister Brother is too fast. Mister Brother is too cool. Mister Brother is off to further adventures, and in his place he's sent a husband and father for you to hold, as the city sparkles beyond the blue brightness of your pool and cars pass by on the street below, leaving snatches of music behind.

Chaim Potok

Moon

From *Image*

MOON VINTEN, recently turned thirteen, was short for his age and too bony, too thin. He had a small pale face, dark angry eyes, and straight jet-black hair. A tiny silver ring hung from the lobe of his right ear, and a ponytail sprouted below the thick band at the nape of his neck and ran between his angular shoulder blades. The ponytail, emerging like a waterfall from the flat-combed dark hair, was dyed the clear blue color of a morning sky.

Moon marched into the family den one autumn evening and announced to his parents that he wanted to build a recording studio for himself and his band.

His parents, short, slender people in their late forties, had been talking together quietly on the sofa. Moon's father, annoyed by his son's brusque interruption of the conversation, thought: First, those drums; then the earring and the ponytail. And now, a *recording studio?* In a restrained tone, he asked, "What, exactly, does that involve?"

"A big table, microphones, stands, extension cords, rugs or carpets for soundproofing, a mixing board," said Moon.

"And how, exactly, will you pay for all that?"

"With the money I got for my birthday."

Patience is the desired mode here, Moon's father told himself.

"I'll remind you again. That money has been put away for your college tuition."

"The band will make lots of money, Dad."

"Then buy the equipment with that money."

"We'll need money to buy the equipment so we can make really high-quality recordings," said Moon, trying to keep calm. "We'll demo the recordings and send them out, and start making money from the gigs we'll get. It takes money to make money, Dad."

Moon's father turned to Moon's mother. "Where is he learning these things, Julia?"

"He's your son, too, Kenneth," said Moon's mother. "Why don't you ask him?" She had her mind at that moment on another matter: the face of a boy in Pakistan.

"He's only thirteen years old, for God's sake," Moon's father said.

Moon hated it when they talked about him as if he weren't there. His parent who were physicians, often spoke to one another clinically about their patients, and at times about Moon as if he were a patient. It was one more irritant in the list of things that made him angry.

"We shouldn't attach an 'only' to a thirteen year-old," said his mother, still seeing the face of the Pakistani boy, whose photograph had come to her office in the morning mail. "A thirteen-year-old is not a child."

Moon's father, a precise man with a dry, intimidating manner, looked at Moon and asked, "Where, exactly, do you plan to put all that equipment?"

"In the garage," Moon replied.

His parents stared at him. Calm is called for, his father thought, and remained silent. Inside Moon's mother, an unassuming woman of gentle demeanor, the picture of the gaunt, brown-faced Pakistani boy—dry thin lips, small straight nose, enormous frightened eyes— abruptly winked out.

She said quietly to Moon, "Dear, we keep our cars in the garage."

Moon said, "Then I'll put it in the basement."

"We've been through all that," said Moon's father. The clamor erupting from the basement and streaming through the air ducts

and filling the house with the booming drumming twanging pande-
monium they call music. "Let's talk about it another time."

"When, Dad?"

"Soon."

"But when?"

His father said, "Morgan, I have very important calls to make."
Morgan was Moon's given name, first on the list of things that made
him angry. A jovial older cousin had called him Moon some years
ago, for a reason Moon could no longer remember. His parents and
teachers still called him Morgan.

"I need the phone to call the guys in the band," said Moon.

"Whoever is on the phone, if an overseas call comes in on call-
waiting, please tell me immediately," said Moon's mother.

"I need the phone," said Moon again.

"Don't you have any homework?" his father asked.

"Dad, I really really really need to talk to the guys in my band,"
said Moon.

Moon's parents sat very quietly on the couch, looking at their son.
Even excited or angered, his face still retained its pallid look. But his
dark eyes glittered, and his thin lips drew back tight over his small
white teeth as if keeping a seal on a poisonous boil of words.

The telephone rang.

Moon's father picked up the receiver and said crisply, "Dr.
Vinten." He listened and handed the receiver to Moon's mother.
"Pakistan," he said.

Moon, his hands clenched, turned and left the den.

He took the carpeted stairs two at a time to the second floor, and
as he threw open the door to his room, the anger erupted. His heart
raced, his hands shook. He felt the rage like a scalding second skin.
He slammed the door shut. The large color poster of the Beatles,
loosely tacked to the inside of the door, fluttered briefly; the Beatles
seemed to be dancing and undulating in their exotic costumes.

He flopped down on his bed.

Always with the fury came fear. Occasional tantrums had accompanied him through childhood and in recent years had become too-
frequent fits of rage that rose suddenly from deep inside him and
sometimes took possession of his body. He lay on his back, tight and

quivering. "When you feel it coming, stop what you're doing," Mrs. Graham, the school counselor, had advised. "Take deep breaths and count slowly." He counted: One . . . two . . . three. . . . Mrs. Graham was in her forties, a round-faced, good-hearted woman. "If you feel you're losing control, walk out of the classroom. I've told your teachers it's all right for you to do that." Four . . . five . . . six. . . . After his fight with Tim Wesley two weeks ago, when they pummelled one another and tumbled down the wide staircase into the school's main entrance hall . . . seven . . . eight . . . nine. . . . Later, Moon couldn't remember why the fight had begun. His parents and Mrs. Graham had discussed the possibility of Moon getting help. A therapist, a total stranger. Everything I'd say would be written down, probably recorded. Ten . . . eleven . . . twelve. . . . Maybe go up to the third floor and play the drums awhile. But I need the telephone.

Was that someone at the door?

He got off the bed, pulled the door open, and saw his mother standing in the hallway.

She said gently, "I keep reminding you, if you close your door, we can't communicate with you. Closed doors often turn into stone walls."

His mother's frequent moralizing was definitely on the list of things that made Moon angry. "Can I use the phone now?" he asked.

She sighed. "I came up to tell you that we'll be having a guest."

"Who?" asked Moon.

"A boy from Pakistan."

Children with rare diseases came to his parents from all over the world for diagnosis and treatment. But always to the hospital, never to the house.

He asked, "Why is he staying with us if he's sick?"

His mother said, "He's not sick, dear. An organization your father and I belong to is bringing him into the country. You'll hear about it in school."

"He's coming to my school?"

"Yes. Be nice to him, dear."

But Moon was imagining the boy wandering around the house

and coming upon the small room on the third floor. He took a deep breath and said, "Can I use the phone now, Mom?"

Moon's mother remembered when her second son had gone off to college the year before. She had said to her husband, "It's difficult to let go, but it's much worse to hold on." Moon, listening nearby, had suddenly and unaccountably run up to his room and slammed the door, cracking the paint near the ceiling of the hallway wall, much to the annoyance of his father. His mother now stood gazing with disquiet at her youngest son. He was so different from the older ones. Andrew in engineering and football; Colin in pre-med and crew. And Morgan—so edgy and sullen, so fixed upon himself.

"Yes, dear, you may use the phone," she said. She was still standing in the hallway looking at Moon when he closed the door.

He sat at his cluttered desk and dialed the telephone. Pete's father answered. "Peter is doing his homework," he said.

"This won't take long, Mr. Weybridge, I promise," said Moon.

"You just make sure of that," said Pete's father.

While waiting for Pete to come to the phone, Moon sat looking at the large posters of John Bonham and Stewart Copeland playing the drums on the wall across from his bed. And at the posters on the wall near his bed: George and Paul with their guitars; Ringo at his drums; John singing. He imagined himself sauntering over to them and taking the sticks from Ringo and starting with a light *tik tik tik tik* on the hi-hat, and then—

"Hey, hey," came Pete's voice over the phone. "How you doin', Moon?"

"We can jam after school tomorrow, Pete."

"That's cool."

"Hey, Pete, there's a kid from Pakistan who's going to be staying in my house."

"Is he stayin' with you? Hey, that's real cool!"

"You know about him?"

"Everybody knows."

"How come I never heard anything about him?"

"Hey, you're asleep half the time. And the other half, you're so angry you don't know what's happenin'."

"I need to call Ronnie and John about tomorrow."

"Stay cool, Moon," said Pete.

Moon called Ronnie Klein and then John Wood. Just as he was telling John the time of their jam session, he heard the beep of the call-waiting, and told John to hang up. Another item on the list of things that angered him: the call-waiting, the way it broke into his conversations with his only friends, the members of his band. The low beep: once, twice; most of the calls were for his parents. No, they wouldn't give him his own telephone; they didn't want him talking on it for hours on end; his brothers hadn't had their own telephones and neither would he.

"This is Imram Moraes," a voice said in a strange accent. "I am phoning from Pakistan for Dr. Julia Vinten."

"One minute, please," said Moon and opened his door to call downstairs. "Mom, it's for you."

"Thank you, dear," Moon heard his mother's voice coming to him from the den.

When he returned to his desk, he put the receiver to his ear and heard, "Yes, Dr. Vinten, the boy will arrive early tomorrow. He will no doubt be tired, but he is—"

Moon hung up the telephone.

He had not thought to ask his mother where the boy would sleep. In Andy's room? In Colin's room? He feared the dusky silences in the house that enlarged the absence of his brothers and magnified invisible presences, like the noises made by the squirrels scampering inside the walls. Moon imagined he heard his brothers' voices: they were teaching him to hold a bat, catch a hardball, throw a football, dribble a basketball; they were teasing him, calling him the skinny runt of the family; they were helping him with his homework; they were bickering with Mom and Dad over cars and girls and late nights out. The thought of the boy from Pakistan staying in the room of one of his brothers. . . .

Feeling an outrage at the very center of himself, Moon began counting. One . . . two . . . three . . . four. . . . He inserted a Pearl Jam CD into his player . . . five . . . six . . . seven . . . and put on his earphones and opened one of the textbooks on the desk. He tapped his index and middle fingers on the desk, *doom-d-d-ka-doom-doom-d-ka-doom-d-d-ka-doom-doom-d-ka,* playing as if he were at a drum and snare. The words in the book flickered and pulsated in the torrent of drums and music.

Moon sat slumped in the seat, dimly aware of the TV cameras and crews in the back of the crowded auditorium, the empty chairs on the stage, and the whispering among the students and teachers. School assemblies—almost always full of monotonous, preachy, fake talk—were high on the list of things that annoyed Moon and made him angry.

He was especially angry that morning. Mrs. Woolston had raked him for not handing in the weekly English essay. A fat, ugly woman, with thick glasses and a voice like ice water. She wanted the essay tomorrow, and absolutely no excuses. He'd sensed the smirks of his classmates and saw out of the corner of his eye Pete's sympathetic look. He hadn't been able to think of anything to write about and, listening to Mrs. Woolston's public scolding, had felt heat rise to his face and considered walking out of the room. Instead, he'd remained at his desk, counting to himself, fingers tapping silently on his knees—until the assistant principal's reedy voice came over the public address system, announcing the assembly.

The crowd in the auditorium had fallen silent. Moon, still slumped in his sea watched as some people emerged from the dark right wing of the stage and walked toward the chairs. The first was Dr. Whatley, the school principal; then came two men Moon didn't know, both dressed in dark suits; then a tall, brown-skinned man with glasses and wearing a baggy light-brown suit, followed by a brown-skinned boy about Moon's age but an inch or two shorter than Moon. He looked gaunt. His eyes were dark and enormous. He wore dark trousers and a sky-blue woolen sweater and a white shirt and tie. His neck stuck out from the collar of the shirt like the neck of a plucked bird.

Behind the boy walked Moon's mother and father.

Moon watched as they all sat down in the chairs on the stage. The boy, looking tense and fearful, seemed not to know what to do with his hands. He sat on the edge of his chair, leaning forward and staring apprehensively at the crowded auditorium.

Dr. Whatley approached the podium and began to speak. Moon closed his eyes and wondered how he could convince his parents to let him build a recording studio. Maybe ask them for an addition to the garage. How much would that cost? Dr. Whatley droned on, the public address system amplifying his words.

Moon felt itchy, impatient. There was a scattering of applause and some more talk.

A moment later, an odd-sounding voice filled the air, small and breathless and high, and Moon opened his eyes and saw the boy standing behind the podium, only his face and neck visible. Alongside the boy stood the brown-skinned man.

Moon vaguely recalled having heard that the boy's name was Ashraf.

The boy said something in a foreign language, and the man, who had been introduced as Mr. Khan, translated.

The boy spoke again. He was talking about someone named Mr. Malik and the dozen boys who worked in his carpet factory. He said the boys had been bought by Mr. Malik from their parents.

Bought? thought Moon. *Bought?*

The boy said that he himself had been bought at the age of five for twelve dollars. Sitting on a bench fifteen hours a day as a carpet weaver with the others in a long, airless room and two weak light bulbs burning from a ceiling fixture and the temperature often over 100 degrees and the mud walls hot when he put his hands to them and the single window closed against carpet-eating insects. But that was better than working in a quarry, hauling and loading stones onto carts for the building of roads, or in the sporting-goods factory owned by one of the many nephews of Mr. Malik, making soccer balls by hand eighty hours a week in silence and near-darkness. At the carpet looms, he'd worked from six in the morning to eight at night and sometimes around the clock, tying short lengths of thin thread to a lattice of heavy white threads. His fingers often bled, and the blood mixed with the colors of the threads.

"Look," he said, thrusting his hands palms upward across the podium, his thin wrists jutting like chicken bones from the sleeves of his sweater, and Moon, listening to the quavery words of the boy and the deep voice of Mr. Khan, tried to make out the fingers from across the length of the auditorium and could not, and gazed at his own long, bony fingers and tapped them restlessly on his knees.

The audience was silent.

The boy went on talking in his high, breathless voice. Three weeks ago, in the village where he worked, two men in suits accompanied by two uniformed policemen, had entered Mr. Malik's carpet factory and taken him away, along with four younger boys and three older ones. What a shouting Mr. Malik had raised! How dare they take away his workers, his boys? All legally acquired from their parents, he had the papers to prove it, documents signed and recorded with the proper authorities! The boy paused and then said, "Was it right that children were made to labor at carpet factories, at brick and textile factories, at tanneries and steelworks?" He said, "People in America shouldn't buy the carpets made in his country. If the carpet makers couldn't sell their carpets, they wouldn't have any reason to use children as cheap labor."

He stopped, peering uncertainly at Mr. Khan, who nodded and smiled. The boy thanked the audience for listening to him and walked back to his chair and sat down. He put his hands on his knees and gazed at the floor. All the adults on the stage were looking at him.

There was an uneasy stirring in the audience and nervous, scattered applause.

Moon sat very still, looking at the boy.

Mr. Whatley stepped to the podium and introduced one of the two strangers, who turned out to be the governor of the state. The second stranger was the head of the organization that had brought the boy to the United States. Moon didn't listen to them. Nor did he pay much attention to the brief talks given by his parents; both said something about the need to raise the consciousness of Americans. Americans. He was watching the boy, who still sat on the edge of his chair, leaning forward and appearing a little lost—and wasn't it strange how right there on the stage, in front of everyone, as first the governor and then the head of the organization and then Moon's parents spoke, wasn't it strange how Ashraf had begun to tap with his fingers on his knees, lightly and silently tapping in small movements to some inner music he seemed to be hearing. Moon watched the rhythm and pattern of Ashraf's tapping, an odd sort of tempo, unlike anything Moon had ever seen before, and found himself tapping along with him. A one one one and a two and a one and a two and. . . .

In the school lunchroom later that day, Moon was at a table with Pete and the two other members of his band when Ashraf entered with Mr. Khan. He saw them go along the food line and then carry their trays to a table and sit with some other students. Moon watched Ashraf eating and heard him respond to questions put to him by the students and translated by Mr. Khan. Where had he been born? What sort of food did he like? Had he ever heard of McDonald's or Walt Disney or Tom Hanks? Did he like rock music?

As the last question was translated, Ashraf's eyes grew wide and bright, and he nodded. What was his favorite band? He said radiantly, smiling for the first time, "The Beatles," pronouncing it, "Bee-ah-tles."

"He says," Mr. Khan translated, "that someone near the carpet factory played recordings of the Beatles very often and very loud." Students crowded around the table, blocking Moon's view. Someone asked who was Ashraf's favorite Beatle, and Moon heard the eager, high-voiced answer: "Ringo."

Minutes later the crowd around Ashraf thinned and Moon saw him drumming lightly on the table surface with a knife and fork. Next to him sat Mr. Khan, finishing his meal. About a half-dozen students stood near the table, watching Ashraf's drumming.

"Hey, man," Moon heard Pete say. "You talk to your mom and dad about the recording studio?"

"Yeah," said Moon, looking at Ashraf.

"What'd they say?"

"They're thinking about it."

"Man, that'd be so cool," said Pete. "Our own studio and everything."

Moon wished Pete would be quiet so he could see and hear more clearly Ashraf's oddly-rhythmed drumming.

❑　❑　❑　❑

"What's up, man?" said Pete into the telephone later that afternoon. "I got one foot out the door."

"We can't jam today, Pete," said Moon.

"What's happenin'?"

"The kid from Pakistan and his interpreter, they're in my house, sleeping. We can't make any noise."

"He must be tired, man."

"I don't like him sleeping in Andy's bed. And the man, he's in Colin's bed."

"Hey, you know what my daddy once said to me? He said, 'You have your own house, you can decide who sleeps there.' "

"We'll jam tomorrow."

"Tomorrow I got my guitar lesson. The day after."

"Okay, Pete."

"Stay cool, man."

Moon called the other two members of the band. Then he sat at the desk in his room, listening to the silence in the house. Two hours at the drums—gone. He thought of Ashraf's head on Andy's pillow. Did they carry diseases? Mom would know about that. His parents were at the hospital, and that evening they were to have dinner with Ashraf and Mr. Khan, along with the governor and the mayor. Moon would eat alone at home, as he did on occasion. He would put a CD into the stereo player in the den, fill the air with swelling, pounding music that drove away the ominous silences and muffled the occasional chittering and scurrying of the squirrels inside the walls of the house.

A noise took him from his thoughts: barely audible voices in the next room. Ashraf and Mr. Khan. Moon rose and left his room. He walked past his parents' bedroom to the door at the end of the hallway and climbed the wooden staircase to the third floor.

The sloping roof of the large stone and brick house left space for three third-story rooms beneath the angled beams: one, a cedar closet; another, a storage area for his parents' files; the third, the room where Moon played his drums and jammed with his band. It was a small room, with barely enough space for the chairs and the music stands and the table with the CD player and the small cassette recorder they used to tape some of their sessions. The crowded room was the only place in the house his parents would permit Moon and his band to play.

He removed the covers from his drums, sat down, popped The Police into the CD player, put on the earphones, and took up his sticks. He knew by heart Stewart Copeland's stroke and beat, and played with deft precision. The blue-dyed ponytail moved from side to side and bobbed on his shoulders and back.

He played for some while, felt himself gliding off into the surge and crash of the drums and lifted into the cascades of thumping rhythms—and then sensed an alien presence behind him, and stopped and turned.

Ashraf and Mr. Khan were in the room.

Moon stared at them. He turned off the CD player and removed his earphones.

"We apologize if we are disturbing you," said Mr. Khan very politely.

"It's okay," said Moon, trying to keep the anger out of his voice. This was what he had feared most. An invasion of his most secret place. Slow, deep breaths. . . . One . . . two. . . .

Mr. Khan said, "Ashraf has asked me to tell you that your walls make sounds. He heard noises that woke him."

"Those are squirrels," said Moon. "Sometimes they get inside our walls. Usually we only hear them at night." Three . . . four . . . five. . . .

Mr. Khan spoke to Ashraf, who nodded and responded.

"He says to tell you the walls of the factory where he worked were filled with insects and sometimes he would hear them at night."

Moon said, "We once had a nest of honey bees in one of our walls. My parents had to bring in a man who raised bees to take away the nest with the bees still in it." Why am I telling him this? Six . . . seven. . . .

Ashraf listened attentively to the translation, nodding, then spoke softly.

"He says he does not know your name," said Mr. Khan.

"My name is Moon."

Mr. Khan looked puzzled.

"M-o-o-n," said Moon, spelling his name.

"Ah, yes?" said Mr. Khan. "Moon." He spoke to Ashraf, who responded.

"He asks why are you named Moon."

"It's my name, that's all," said Moon.

Mr. Khan spoke to Ashraf, who gazed intently at Moon. Dark, glittering pupils inside enormous, curious, eager eyes.

"Ashraf says he was drawn here by the sound of your drums and asks if he may speak frankly and put certain—um, how to say it?— personal questions to you."

"Personal? What do you mean, personal?"

"He says he will not be hurt if you do not answer."

"What questions?"

"First, he wishes to ask why you wear a ring in your ear."

"Why I wear the earring? I just do, that's all."

"Ashraf says he does not understand your answer."

"It makes me feel different. You know, not like everyone else."

"He asks why you dye your long hair blue."

"I saw it in a magazine."

"He says if you saw it in a magazine and are doing what others do, how does it make you different?"

Moon felt heat rising to his face. "No one else in my school does it."

"He asks if he may touch your hair."

"What?"

"May he touch your hair?"

Moon took a deep breath. All those questions, and now this. Touch my hair. Why not? He turned his head to the side. The ponytail swayed back and forth, dangling blue and loose from its root of raven hair. Ashraf leaned forward, ran his fingers gently through the ponytail, touching and caressing the sky-blue strands, a look of wonder on his thin face. Then he withdrew his hand. Moon saw him examining his fingers and heard him speak softly to Mr. Khan.

"He says he likes the way your hair looks and feels," Mr. Khan said to Moon.

Moon looked at Ashraf, who smiled back at him shyly and spoke again to Mr Khan.

"Now he asks why you play the drums."

Moon said, after a brief hesitation, "I just like to."

"He says to tell you that he plays drums because it is sometimes a good feeling to hit something."

"Yeah I feel that way, too . . . sometimes."

Moon had never before talked about these matters with anyone.

"He says to thank you for your answers."

"Can I ask a question?"

"Of course."

"Why did he work in that factory? Why didn't he just run away?"

Mr. Khan translated and Ashraf lowered his eyes as he responded.

"He says there was nowhere to run. He was hundreds of miles from his home and would have starved to death or been caught and brought back to his master and very severely beaten and perhaps chained to his workbench or sold off to work in the quarries."

"Why did his parents sell him?"

Ashraf listened to the translation and seemed to fill with shame.

"They needed the money to feed themselves and their other children."

"Does he have to go back?"

"Oh, yes. He feels obligated to return. Our organization will send him to school, and he will continue in the struggle to help other boys like him."

"Please say that I wish him good luck."

Mr. Khan translated and Ashraf replied.

"He thanks you and asks if he may request of you a small favor."

"Sure."

"He asks if he may play your drums."

Moon, surprised, was silent. His drums! No one touched his drums, ever. He looked at Ashraf, who, after a moment, spoke again.

218 / CHAIM POTOK

"He says he will not damage them," said Mr. Khan.

"Well, okay," Moon said.

Ashraf's eyes lit up as he extended his fingers toward Moon. Moon handed him his sticks and slid off the chair. Ashraf took the sticks and sat in Moon's chair and tapped on Moon's drums. He tapped on the drums and the hi-hat, a bit awkwardly and with no apparent rhythm, and after a while he put down the sticks and picked up the bongos from the floor near the hi-hat. Holding the bongos between his knees, he began to tap out with his calloused fingers and palms the odd rhythm he had played in the auditorium and lunchroom, a one one one and a two and a one and a two and. . . .

Moon reached over and switched on the tape recorder.

Ashraf drummed on. Moon, standing next to him, felt the power and pull of the strange rhythm. Ashraf played for some while, *dum dat, dum dat, dum dat,* and sweat formed on his brow and beads of sweat flecked off his face as he played and his fingers became a blur, *dum dat, dum dat, dum dat*—and abruptly he stopped. His eyes were like glowing coals. Sweat streamed down his brown face. He placed the bongos on the floor.

Moon switched off the recorder.

There was a silence before Ashraf spoke.

"He thanks you for the opportunity to play your drums," said Mr. Khan.

"Well, sure, it's okay, you're welcome," said Moon.

"He says you and he will probably never see each other again, but he will remember you."

Moon looked at Ashraf, who briefly spoke again.

"He says we must leave and prepare for this evening's dinner," said Mr. Khan.

Ashraf extended his hand. Moon took it and was startled by its boniness, its coarse, woodlike callous covering. Smiling shyly, Ashraf shook Moon's hand and then turned and left the small room, followed by Mr. Khan.

Moon rewound a portion of the tape, checked to see that it had recorded properly, and took it down to his room.

❑ ❑ ❑ ❑

Pete asked, "Hey, you see him on TV?"

"See who?" replied Moon. They were walking up the crowded stairs to their English class.

"That kid, what's his name, Ashraf."

"Was he on TV?"

"Man, what planet you livin' on? He was on the news last night, and on the *Today* show this mornin'."

"I was writing that essay for Mrs. Woolston."

"Is he still at your house?"

"He left before I woke up," said Moon.

That evening he sat with his parents in the den, watching a national news report that showed Ashraf speaking at a high school in Baltimore. He looked small and frightened behind the podium, but he thrust out his hands defiantly to show his fingers. Mr. Khan stood beside him, translating.

The next evening Ashraf was seen on television appearing before a committee of Congress. He wore a dark suit and a tie, and his neck protruded from the collar of his white shirt. He sat at a long table with Mr. Khan. Moon saw Ashraf's fingers tapping silently from time to time on the edge of the table.

One of the Congressmen asked a question. Ashraf thrust his hands toward the members of the committee, showing his fingers.

"Spunky kid," said Moon's father. "He's going back to a bad situation."

"Nothing will happen to him, Kenneth. Too many eyes are watching," said Moon's mother.

When Moon came down to breakfast the following morning, he found his father at the kitchen table, tense and upset. His mother, almost always too cheerful for Moon in the early hours of the day, looked troubled.

"What's happening?" Moon asked.

"See for yourself," said his father and, handing Moon the morning newspaper, pointed to the final paragraph of an essay titled "Blunt Reply to Crusading Boy," on the Op-Ed page.

In conclusion, we hold that there is room for improvement in any society. But we feel that the present situation is acceptable the way it is. The National Assembly must not rush through reforms without first evaluating their impact on productivity and sales. Our position is that the government must avoid so-called humanitarian measures that harm our competitive advantages.

The essay was signed by Imram Malik.

Moon asked, "What does it mean, Dad?"

"You're thirteen years old, what do you think it means?"

"I don't know," said Moon, afraid he understood it too well.

"They would not dare harm him," said his mother.

Moon felt a coldness in his heart and the impotence that was the prologue to rage.

In the weeks that followed he played the recording often, at times taking it upstairs to the third floor and listening to it and remembering the darkly glittering blaze in Ashraf's eyes when he'd played the bongos. And that's where Moon was the winter night the portable telephone rang on the table where he'd set it near the tape recorder. It was someone from Washington, D.C., calling his mother. His parents weren't home, he said, and wrote down an unfamiliar name and number. He turned off the telephone and immediately it rang again, and a man's voice asked for his father. Moon was writing down the man's name and number when he heard the beep of the call-waiting and felt himself growing angry—what was he, his parents' secretary or something? He'd come upstairs to play the drums, not to take their phone calls, one after the other like that.

"Hey, Moon." It was Pete.

"Hey, Pete. What's up?"

"You heard the news, man?"

"What news?"

"It was just on TV. That Ashraf kid. He's dead."

"What?"

"He's dead, man. Run down on his bike by a truck. Hit and run."

Moon's hands began to shake.

"They're sayin' it was an accident, but no one believes it for a minute," said Pete.

A fury was boiling in Moon's stomach and flaring red in his eyes. He remained quiet.

"Hey, man," said Pete. "You there?"

"Yeah," said Moon.

"Your parents home?"

"No."

"You want me to come over?"

"No."

"You sure you're okay?"

"Yeah."

"I gotta go. It's late. We'll talk tomorrow."

Moon turned off the telephone and the tape recorder and sat for a while in the silent room. He removed the tape from the recorder, brought it down to his room, and placed it in his desk drawer. Then he sat down at his desk and began to tap a rhythm on its surface with his hands. He played rudiments and patterns and flams. Right right left left right right left left . . . right left right right . . . left right left left . . . flamadiddle paradiddle. . . .

Was that someone at his door? He got up and opened the door and saw his parents in the hallway. They were in dinner clothes.

Moon and his parents looked at each other a moment.

"I see you know what happened," said his father.

"Pete called me," said Moon.

"It's horrible," his mother said. Her eyes were red, her face pale. She was seeing Ashraf vividly inside her head.

"Did they really kill him?" asked Moon.

"Our people in Washington are investigating it," said his father.

"We were up on the third floor together," said Moon. "I made a tape recording of him playing my bongos."

"You did?" said his father, looking surprised.

"I liked him," said Moon.

Moon saw his parents glance at each another.

"Oh, you poor dear," said his mother.

"We had no idea at all those people would do something like that," said his father.

Moon's heart pounded and his skin burned. He stepped back into his room, closing the door. The poster of the Beatles flapped briefly.

The telephone rang twice, and stopped. A moment later someone tapped on his door again.

It was his mother. "Dear, I keep reminding you, if you keep your door closed we can't communicate with you. Your English teacher is on the phone."

Moon left the door open and went over to the desk and lifted the receiver. "Hello," he said.

Mrs. Woolston said, "Morgan, the essay you handed in about your meeting with Ashraf is very good. You wrote that you made a tape recording of him playing the bongos. Is that right?"

"Yeah," said Moon.

"Please bring it with you tomorrow."

"Bring the recording to school?"

"Will you do that?"

"Sure," Moon heard himself say.

"And will you bring your drums?"

"My drums?"

"There will be a memorial service for Ashraf."

"Well, yeah, sure, I'll bring my drums," Moon said.

He sat for a while at the desk, then went downstairs and asked if he could borrow his father's tape recorder. Back in his room, he duplicated the tape of Ashraf playing the bongos.

The next morning he and his father loaded the drums into the car. Moon sat in the back while his parents rode in front, his father behind the wheel. It was a cold windy day, the sky ice-blue. They said nothing to each other during the trip to the school.

Pete met them in the parking lot and helped Moon carry his drums into the auditorium and set them up on the stage near the podium.

Later that morning, the entire school filed silently into the auditorium. From the dark right wing of the stage emerged Dr. Whatley, followed by the mayor, Moon's parents, and Moon. They sat down in chairs on the stage. Dr. Whatley stepped up to the podium and said that they had assembled to honor the memory of the brave boy named Ashraf who had spoken in their school some weeks ago and been killed in an accident the other day in Pakistan. He talked about how some people left behind records of their lives—books and music, works of art, deeds. He said that Ashraf had decided to live a life of deeds on behalf of young people his age. He announced that a special school fund would be set up in his memory.

Moon sat in his chair on the stage, listening.

The mayor spoke; then Moon's parents. Then, at a nod from Dr. Whatley, Moon went over to his drums and sat down.

A moment passed and then over the public address system came the sound of the bongos being played by Ashraf.

Moon waited a minute or two and then began to play an accompaniment to the bongos inside the spaces of Ashraf's beat, a one e and a two e and a three e. His hi-hat played the ands, the snare snapped two and four, and he added ghost notes to the snare to make it dance, and then added the bell and slipped into the Seattle sound, *doom-do'ak-doom-d'doom-ak,* and the bongos went *dum dat, dum dat, dum dat* in that strange rhythm, and then Moon took the drums higher in volume and then was taking them higher still, his sticks beating a frenzied cadence, a rhythm of scalding outrage, and he was thumping, driving, throbbing, tearing through his instruments, pouring onto the world a solid flood of sound, and he felt the outrage in his arms and shoulders and heart and the sublime sensation of secret power deep in the very darkest part of his soul.

The bongos fell silent. With a crashing flurry, Moon climaxed the drumming, washed in sweat, strands of his blue-dyed hair clinging to his face and neck. He sat with his head bowed, breathing hard and feeling an exhilaration that he knew would be too quickly gone.

A void followed, a gap in time, and utter silence from the audience. Moon, slowly raising his head, saw his parents staring at him, their faces like suddenly illumined globes. Over the public address system came the hollow hissing sound that signaled the end of the recording of Ashraf playing the bongos.

Robert Schirmer

Burning

From *Fiction*

NICKI AND I were driving back from the doomed wedding of two old friends, drinking cheap wine out of plastic champagne glasses less out of celebration than our mutual need to forget, when we came across the rumbling house on my side of the road.

At first we couldn't fathom the situation. The house convulsed, a window popped blackened glass, rags of smoke swirled like dust devils forming. An explosion followed, splitting one porch pillar, crumbling the second fully off its foundation. Twin flames punched through the roof, heaving shingles and nails, and somersaulted to the far end of the house, where they snapped at the stripped trees, red and feral whips.

The truth was, I might have driven right past. I'd drunk some whiskey before the wedding, more than was reasonable, and listened while my buddy Pete sobbed in the bathroom for Marcia, his ex-wife, whom he still dreamed at night of holding. "But she's gone for good," he said, wiping his tearing eyes and the scratches on his neck, which I guessed he'd earned from a careless morning's shave. "I could be lying on the side of a road with both my legs broken, Christ, my hips too, Drake, don't you see, I could cut every goddamn vein in both goddamn wrists, it wouldn't matter to her."

He seized the front of my shirt, and in an instant he was sitting on the edge of the tub, quietly holding his face. I had known Pete since we were boys pilfering cigarettes and skin magazines from a backroom tobacco shop, and still there seemed no comfort I could offer him that would matter now. So I abandoned Pete with his grief and stepped onto the porch solely for the smell of the crisp November air haunted by juniper. There was not a juniper in sight. I breathed to clear my head of several black doubts and while doing so spotted Linda smoking a joint and staring into one of the desolate fields that unfolded toward the house from all sides. Unfolded toward, unfolded away from? The white lace dress she wore looked yellowed and slept upon. I could tell she was stoned; her eyes were artificially moist and without focus. "He doesn't love me," she announced dreamily, smoothing down her skirt's most dramatic creases. "That bitch Marcia is holding his heart for more than a ransom."

I said of course Pete loved her, meaning Linda, he loved Linda, but she must have misinterpreted my generosity, or in my desire to please her I'd generated the wrong hormones, because soon she was leaning into me, one unwarm hand pressed to my thigh. In that way we smoked the joint down, growing agitated as we inhaled and exhaled. "God, what am I *doing?*" Linda asked. "Nicki doesn't know how to handle a sweetheart like you, do you hear?"

From such early promise, weddings proceed, this one in the center of Pete and Linda's scanty farmhouse living room, made unserious by dust balls, dog hairs, and crepe paper Nicki had looped around the fireplace in some misguided attempt to be festive. We stood stoically beside our friends, Nicki and me, the silent witnesses, our ring hands like granite and our knees, fizz. Two years together and I'd never fully cheated on Nicki once, yet at one time or another hadn't I also betrayed her in nearly every way a lover could? All the while the holy roller preacher Pete had met and commissioned in a bar spoke with zeal of love and enchantment, resurrection, Lazarus, bread and wine. We focused on him with more than a little terror. Before he declared Pete and Linda husband and wife, he paused to cough into the hand he blessed them with. Everyone looked toward me, as if I alone possessed the will to navigate a path out of our rubble of lies.

And what did I do? What any man would who has pot on his

breath and the smell of another woman on his hands and some displaced ache inside him that some people might call a conscience. I turned away and looked down at my shoes, scuffed.

Maybe I started to drive past the burning house because I didn't recognize, in the first moments, what it was I was looking at.

Or maybe I knew exactly what, and that was why I drove on.

"Stop!" Nicki cried, and my foot floated to the spongy brakes. The car jolted to a halt. A door to the house opened, a barefoot man and woman spilled out, their clothes and hair smoking. Nicki stumbled from the car in her heels and crushed taffeta, dropping her imitation champagne glass into the snow. I understood there was nothing left for me but to follow. The man lurched across the frosted yard, peering at us in shame and apology. With bare hands he patted smoke off the woman's shoulders, delivering into the air his disjointed, white-breathed words: "don't . . . baby . . . loose."

One of his shirt sleeves was on fire. The flame coiled around his arm and crawled into his hair. I watched the flame jitter, gathering force, a riot of color and heat, before I tossed the jacket of my tux over him. I rolled him around in the dead winter grass and the snow pockets until I'd put him out and also the manic unearthly glow in his eyes. He didn't seem much interested in being helped to his feet. "Please," he muttered, "see to Sybil."

The woman—Sybil—was hunched low to the ground, peering dazed at the house and at Nicki and me, her stylish rescuers. Despite her face, which looked finger-painted with soot, I could see she was younger than this man by a full ten years, and that she was good-looking but in a swiftly decaying way linked not at all to age. It had to do with smoke, whiskey, bad sex, and false hopes, this kind of dissolution, with mute phones and jukebox bars stocked with sixties love ballads and too much time spent drifting among strangers as misdirected and loveless as oneself. The blanket she clutched around her was in an Indian weave. Maroon coyotes howled at dusky suns, bloody moons. Someday I planned to visit a place with coyotes and bloody moons, but Nicki feared the desert. The scorpions, she said, and rattlers and flesh-eating birds, as if that were all the desert had to offer.

Clutched in Sybil's hand were a blouse, a pair of sandals, and a framed photograph of a sad-mouthed woman. "It was all I could reach," she said. "I put out my hands and there they were."

The man sat up, his shirt hanging open in scorched flags, exposing white shoulders, lean chest, the prison of his ribcage. On the verge of leading us, he settled back onto the ground as if having thought better of it.

And we might have stayed like that until the first knee-deep snow, the four of us, watching the house devoured. A couple of teens leaned out the window of their passing car, pressing the horn, their ruddy boyish faces spun out of Ovaltine and midwestern bible school, reminding us of time and space and a different kind of life. "We're on our way to the hospital!" I yelled to them, as if I knew exactly where we were headed.

Once we were seated in the car and on our way, I realized someone might be badly burned. The possibility came to me first as a smell—a rich, opiate smell, sweet and repellent, stinging my nostrils. Nicki rolled down her window, her eyes wide and woozy, a smear blemishing the front of her dress. But was it a dirt smear, smudged blood? None of us were bleeding; I couldn't imagine that.

"We're all okay, right?" Nicki asked, a question we left unanswered. I suppose for some small solace, she lay her hand on my thigh in the exact place and manner Linda had settled her own fingers in those final fitful moments before the wedding. "What?" I asked Nicki, and she said, "All right, then" and dipped her hand back into her lap.

Sometimes it was as if I didn't know her, I thought hotly. Or we knew each other, but a falseness had crept in.

"My name's Cooper," the man in the back said.

He sat very near Sybil with his head rested in a broken way on her shoulder, which, if you asked me, did nothing to close an unseen dark space between them. Sybil shivered into her desert blanket, so with regret I tossed Cooper the rented jacket I'd used to save his life, invested now with value and significance. He hugged it to his chest and sighed deeply into the collar.

"The place just blew," Sybil said. "A place can't just blow like that."

"Houses have temperaments." The words sounded wrong, twisted coming from Cooper's mouth. "You can't always keep them from ruin, but sometimes you can be more prepared."

"We were in the back room," Sybil said. "The cot."

We drove through a silence so fragile it felt cupped in someone's hands. Traces of snow slanted across the windshield to dizzy us. *The ways in which people can be brought together,* I thought. The pot tasted rank on my breath. "You name the hospital," I said.

"Who said anything about a hospital?"

After a healthy silence, Nicki said, "Excuse me?"

"Don't listen to him." Sybil smelled deeply of ashes, corn husks, and Cherry Chapstick. "He thinks all hospitals are the death factory since he lost Arlene—"

"Eileen. And you didn't know her, so you shouldn't talk like you did, sweetheart. I'll tell you what I want," Cooper continued, to me. "Down the road a few miles there's a church. Same church where I was baptized, married Eileen, buried Eileen. Some things just keep coming back to you. She was young when she went. That's what makes death mystifying. I promised Sybil I'd show her the altar and the stained glass."

"Now?" I was trying to remember something, the fire only minutes before or something farther back, until what came to me was how I'd watched a cow bleed into the snow when I was a boy. The cow was old, the farmer had said, and in her dull and bovine old age, she had followed a windswept burlap sack into a barbed wire fence, thinking the sack a hobbled calf she'd borne years before and lost. Once snared, the deceived animal fought and chewed, managing only to tear herself open in her efforts to escape. That was the farmer's explanation, at any rate. He was old himself and smelled of scotch and carrion. A false and a real thing looked the same to the lonely dreamer, he muttered through his stained, uneven teeth. He stroked the cow into a blissful silence, and shot her once while the ice breathed around us. "Let that be a lesson to you," the farmer said and trudged off in a different direction from the one from which he'd come.

"A fine church," Cooper continued now. "We just sat all morning, singing gospel. We listened to scripture and ate raisin cake and buried our dead, young and old."

With his rough hands he stroked the veins of Sybil's wrists. He moistened his thumb with his tongue and wiped away the soot beneath her eyes. She gazed at him in mild revulsion but didn't pull away. I looked over at Nicki because for a moment I doubted that she was still inside the car. I drove us into a glen of oaks that embraced over the road—shameless dead trees, waving their speared branches, some imitation of living things.

"We're not agreeing to this?" Nicki asked.

"Of course not." At the same time I wasn't convinced fully this was the truth. I snapped on the radio. The Doors, "Riders on the Storm," everything had turned at once unclear and overly meaningful, who could keep up with it? Who could translate?

"My God," Sybil said. "Cooper, look at your hands."

I watched with my own eyes as white blisters formed across his hands and spread like quick-moving acid up the backs of his hands to his wrists and forearms. I held my breath until my lungs felt like crushed weights. The blisters had not been there one moment, and in the next moment, a flourishing. Such moments could sway a man toward believing the stories of the ancient saints, whose palms opened up and bled in glory to God, or the Dark Age nuns who levitated over their beds at the dream of Christ's hands laid upon their exhausted foreheads.

"Amazing," I said, and I resented driving just then, because it forced my attention away from Cooper and onto the road. A deserted intersection lay ahead, indicating Saint Joseph's Hospital, left turn.

"The church is to the right," Cooper offered. "Don't you see the hospital is just a trap?"

"A trap," I repeated. "Nicki?" I whispered.

"A left." She clung to her door as if expecting it to fly open. "Of course, a left."

I had to focus my hands and my mind to make that necessary left turn, which expelled us suddenly out of the trees and into a frozen field of icy silos and trampled corn stalks. A dozen blackbirds rose to the sky and beat their wings over the car, filling me at once with hope and a nameless resignation. I laughed openly, I unnoosed my tie, feeling wildly joyful, desperately bold, for no more reason than neither Cooper nor Sybil had noticed the direction in which I'd turned. How long could I go without casting a shadow?

"What's funny?" Nicki asked, and I shrugged, my head light as birthday cake. "I wish I had the slightest clue what's so funny about any of this."

"Now you're turning blue," Sybil said.

The second discoloration reached from Cooper's temple down his cheek to form a V at the base of his neck. The left side of his face subtly shifted shades and even texture before our eyes, his flesh alive with its own defiant will, or so it seemed to me in the altered atmosphere of the car. Do I confess my horror and envy of this man? In his presence my own face, my hands, everything about me, down to the way I inhaled, seemed standard and unchanging. "Skin trauma," Nicki said, and Cooper nodded, sure.

"Did you leave the gas on, is that how this happened?" Sybil asked. "A gas leak? A pilot light?"

"Those are the easy explanations." Cooper peeled strips of damaged skin from his hands and dropped them like petals to the floor. *The bones of this man will soon be visible in pale light,* I thought in a distant voice not my own.

"I have a right to know, Cooper." She leaned forward, distracted. Cooper's name shuddered through my hair and whispered down my shirt. What I wanted most in that moment was to brush my hand back there, to feel Cooper's name adrift in my hair, not only his name but his name spoken by Sybil, whose breath only moments ago had been drawn in the midst of flame. "Damn you!" she said. "Look what you've done to me!"

"Don't think I enjoy always being the sensible one, Drake." Nicki's breathing had taken on an enervated sound. "There's no joy in it."

"Sometimes the mysteries of life cannot be explained by pilot lights and gas leaks," Cooper muttered, wrapped still in my empty arms. "Funny," he added. "I don't remember taking this road to church."

❏ ❏ ❏ ❏

The blizzard moved in without warning. The snow slanted in front of the headlights, a quiet, movie-set ash, and soon a blinding dustbowl white swept across the roads, rattling the car's frame, pushing up through the floor cracks beneath our feet. The wind, the frosting windows . . . Cooper sat up suddenly and stared at his unrecognizable hands. "Where are you taking us?" he asked.

The hospital materialized through the wet and falling snow. A pair of ambulance vans were parked haphazardly in the front, one van's back door flapping open. No one was visible inside either vehicle. "This isn't where we asked to go," Cooper said. "We trusted you and this isn't where we asked to go."

Cooper's admonishments raked against my ears as I veered us into a side lot. Cooper stumbled over Sybil, forgetting, I suppose, that he had a workable door on his own side. Without sound he stepped from the car before I'd come to a full stop. He kneeled into a snowbank and shoveled snow over the fire he could suddenly feel in his arms, face, blistered hands.

We all climbed out after Cooper but, once exposed, stood somber in the accumulating drift. Sybil stared at me, not Cooper, and her eyes seemed inflated with cold wind. She had stepped into her sandals—feeble against the snow—but still clutched her blouse and the photograph.

As for me, I badly needed something from this couple, but what that might be had grown faint and unreachable once the hospital came into view.

I pinned both Cooper's arms to his side and pulled him to his feet. He trembled against me, muscle against bone, generating heat, a man possessed, I thought, my head crackling with its own energy. "Stop!" I said, although secretly I marveled at the force radiating through my arms, reminding them of passion and a life beyond the transparent.

"I can't go inside," Sybil gripped my arm. "I'll wait out here for you."

"No," Nicki said, "of course, you have to be examined too." Nicki cupped an arm around Sybil's waist from behind, and that's how we all briefly stood, the four of us entangled, breathing ice into our lungs.

Cooper was wheeled into a strangely desolate ER for treatment, Sybil was ushered into a different room to sign forms, there was a brief rushing blur of doctors, nurses, gurneys, terse instructions back and forth, and when the activity ceased, Nicki and I stood abandoned in the hall, a spectacle, it seemed, in our disheveled formal wear. A janitor with a buzz cut doused his mop into a bucket and stared at us with misplaced joy. I turned away from him. The lighting overhead was too bright; with everything lighted so fully, how were any of us to see with any clarity?

I sat down on a small cushioned seat. Past the janitor were a chapel and a bathroom. A couple walked into the hall, a hunched woman clutching her side. A moment passed, and the couple turned and walked away. I stared down at the shirt I was wearing. It wasn't even mine. Pete had loaned it to me. He had stressed the importance of my wearing just the right shirt for his wedding. Apparently the right shirt was his own, still laced with smells that would remind Pete of himself.

I met Nicki in a hospital. I had broken my knee in a car accident. She was a nurse's aide. "You're killing me!" I'd screamed at Nicki, who fluffed pillows across the room while the head nurse stuck a hot needle into my leg.

See what a hospital can do to a person's thoughts? All that false light.

I had a sense of Nicki speaking, and when I glanced up, she was facing a boyish doctor dressed in scrubs and a jauntily polished stethoscope. He was Italian or possibly Greek—I was in no position to distinguish. A darkly exotic doctor, at any rate. "You're the wife?" he asked Nicki.

"Passerby," I said.

The doctor cast me a glance that implied he knew my sort well. "That may be true," he said to Nicki. "Still, if you'd care to know about his condition—?"

Nicki looked at me, shrugged, and followed the doctor down the hall. Twice abandoned, I thought. I had no idea why I was being excluded from Cooper's diagnosis. The doors to the ER swung open and two nurses in poorly scrubbed whites wheeled Cooper out on a stretcher. He was still awake, but his eyes had lost the gleam of inner fire. Now he was an older, medicated man, ordinary and unsurprising as bread.

"Where are you taking him?" I asked the younger nurse, determined to be a part, at least, of this.

"Burn unit." Her hair glittered with clashing barrettes.

"My wife died in this hospital," Cooper said. "She had a troubled heart and your doctors couldn't bring her around."

"None of us," the older, gloomier nurse advised, "should expect miracles."

They wheeled Cooper down the hall. I followed because it seemed someone should, and I didn't want to break away from him yet. Already I missed what had existed among the four of us in the car, whatever that had been.

"I'll tell you about miracles," Cooper said. "That Sybil and I ever found our way to each other, that's some degree of miracle." The sound of her name coming from his own mouth startled him. "Where is she?" And when no one answered, he tightened his hand on my shirt sleeve.

"The admitting desk," I said.

"Thief." For a moment I expected him to sit up and squeeze my throat with his disfigured hands. "You haven't fooled me."

His furious words faded and he lay back on the gurney. The nurses plied apart his fingers, and in an instant they'd whisked him around the corner and were gone. Thief? I stared at my forearm, the pale marks from his grip diminishing from sight. I slouched back to the ER hallway. Sybil sat on the cushioned seat, still bowed into the sunset of her blanket. The soot had been scrubbed from her face, giving it a raw, unhealed look. "Cooper's been transferred to the burn unit," I said.

She nodded and unspooled the blanket's loose threads. "We're not married," she said. "I don't even live with him, as long as you're pressing this."

Down the hall the doctor was still speaking to Nicki, his thick lips shaping soundless words. A bastard's language, I thought. And didn't I have a right to be bitter? He was barely old enough to be swabbing baby's butts, this man—what did he have to say that I couldn't hear? But it was Nicki—her complete absorption in the doctor's words, her sudden ease—that held my attention.

"I don't know why I'm here," Sybil said, not bothering to lower her voice. "I don't know how I ended up with him."

"You're in love."

"No, that's not it." She stumbled into the chapel, taking the blouse with her but leaving behind the picture of the sad-mouthed woman. In love—what had I meant by that?

I stepped into the tiny chapel after her, holding out the forgotten photograph. And at that moment the blanket slipped away from Sybil's shoulders, revealing, as if by accident, her startlingly pale back, with a spine clearly lined and delicately rendered as a wind-pipe. A rash of violet pimples scattered like drifting pollen across her shoulders, which were slightly more stout and rounded than I'd imagined. The blanket shuddered beneath my gaze, yielded, slumped to the drafty floor, long enough so I caught sight of her standing in her underpants, the drama of her spine ending there, then she'd slipped on the blouse and rearranged the blanket around herself, in a movement so gradual, so deliberate, I was torn between thinking I'd witnessed something very remarkable and that I'd in-dulged in a church peep show.

She turned to face me. I had no idea what to do with myself. My arms felt grafted onto my body through some unholy surgery. Sad, I felt sad. The church was cold so I rubbed my hands together. At least there was that. A velvet curtain hung in front, offering us a woman bathing the Son of God's feet with the loose blue river of her hair. The curtain was more sensual than reverent, Christ him-self more a shy lover than the savior of fallen men. To think Nicki had never washed my feet or my hands or any part of my body with her hair.

As for Sybil, she showed no surprise or embarrassment at my presence. "Because I'm not staying here," she said.

"What about Cooper?"

"Cooper?" She glared at me. "You have to get me away from here, please."

I shook my head dumbly. I was trying hard not to think of her powerful spine.

"I don't care, do you hear, I don't care." Her voice fought against itself, asserting and pleading. "I want to get out before someone expects me to go to him."

I couldn't catch my breath . . . a knife might as well have been stuck into my lungs, leaking air from the inside. I imagined I smelled ethanol.

"He's not my husband." She spoke swiftly, her words flying at me like stung sparrows. "The truth is, I'm married. Do you see? But not to Cooper. You want the whole story? The whole story is I've got a husband. Kids. Two of them, and they're expecting me soon."

An old woman wearing a smudged overcoat with a fake-fur collar stepped into the chapel and settled herself into the front pew, clutching a string of mismatched beads. The beads were not rosaries. "Don't you see how this will look?" Sybil whispered.

I shook my head again, solely for the feel of motion.

"You have to give me a lift. Back to my place. Now."

What I felt inside: a tangle of wires and cables, as if I had been invented on random parts and energized by sudden jolts of electricity. Any move or decision I made now would verge on the monstrous. "It's not like I'm leaving him alone here," she continued desperately. "He has doctors. Nurses. He's being cared for." The old woman signed a cross in the air, shook her beaded fist, slipped the beads around her neck. "If you won't give me a ride back, I'll walk. So there. I'll walk. Is that what I should do?"

"You can't walk."

"Well, then."

She moved toward the door, scornful of the photograph I held out to her. "Leave it," she said. "Better yet, give her back to Cooper. He's the one who lost her."

I could feel there was something not right in this, more not-right than it appeared; this unrightness moved through me like false blood, turning me bold. A quick exit began to make sense, if a forbidden wrong sense—but then, how had any of us ended up here or anywhere?

As soon as we stepped back into the hall, we ran into Nicki, finished at last with her secretive Italian doctor. I sensed instantly she wouldn't understand, yet I explained the story as best I could in my mangled shorthand. "I'll take Sybil home," I stammered. "It shouldn't take that long."

"Careful!" She took the photograph from me. Once it was in her hands, I thought she meant to smash it. "She's *leaving?*" she whispered.

"Yes, well, it's what she says she wants."

"Where does she live?" Nicki asked, and I shrugged. Seconds crawled around us. "You want me to go with you?"

I shrugged. "I suppose someone should stay with Cooper."

Nicki nodded and shook her head in one movement. "My God," she whispered. "What is this, Drake? What is she thinking?"

She touched my cheek and pulled her hand away, staring at her fingers displaced in air. The bones in my face trembled, missing her in some way. "What about Cooper?" Nicki stroked her own collarbone. "He's hurt. He needs skin grafts. My God, the doctors . . . Cooper's expecting her."

I took hold of Nicki's hand. I felt so near to crying suddenly, the kind of crying that rises not from one thing but all things. "I can't explain. There are complications. I don't know what she's thinking, you see." If my words had felt connected to my mind or my heart, I was sure I would sound less covert. "I'll drive her to the main road near her place; I'll drop her off. I shouldn't be more than a half hour."

Briefly our breath rose and fell, jagged and frail, scented with smoke. Or I smelled smoke, tasted smoke, whether it was on our breath or not. Sybil disappeared down the hall, dragging the blanket behind her, a regal robe, igniting some primal force back into my legs. I kissed Nicki's pale forehead. "I'll be back soon," I said.

I turned away and walked down the hall. I felt rather than saw Nicki lean against the wall, the portrait of Cooper's dead wife in her hand. She stared after me as the door closed.

As the sound of my boots crunching in the snow was lifted and carried off by the storm, a memory.

"I lied," Sybil said.

We had been driving for several minutes, past the first exit and the second, my hands locked on the wheel. "I lied," she repeated, and I nodded. Now we were getting somewhere, to the lost and corroded heart of some matter. "I'm not married. I just said that so you'd take me away from there. I have no kids, nothing. I have nothing."

"You're not married." I was trying it out, the concept.

"I've only known Cooper for three months. Three months! You could never tell it from the way he talks. You don't know what it was like with him. All his talk of love . . . but that's all it was! Talk, talk, talk! Do you know what we were doing just before the fire?"

The blizzard had slackened some, but in my mind it was still swirling, white and hot stars. I remembered how snow fallen on Nicki's hair took a long, sweet time in melting.

"Nothing," she said. "We were lying together, nude, just *lying* there, Cooper and me. A study in restraint. Maybe it's a nineties thing. But I say fuck the nineties, just fuck them."

The billboards we passed promised hearty meals, comfortable lodging, youth and song. It was not so long ago that I'd known them all. "So where am I taking you?" I asked.

"I don't know." Her voice sounded thin as kite string. "Where?"

I shook my head. I didn't want to know what I was doing. My body knew, in all its need. Sitting beside Sybil, I could feel myself growing hard and was lost to it, this misplaced yearning, this desire. Lust, was that all this was? She was beautiful and desperate, I couldn't shake the thought, and rootless too, being loved so openly by the wrong man. "Pull over and drop me off, if you want," Sybil said. "I'll find somewhere to go."

I didn't pull over. We were beyond pulling over.

Sybil slid closer and rested her hand on my thigh. I could smell her, you see—the flames, the heat—and this overpowered my lingering thoughts of the hospital, Cooper, the snow in Nicki's hair.

"I don't have much money, if you want the truth. Everything I owned I lost back there, in the fire."

I nodded. I supposed Sybil and I would get a motel room somewhere, cheap, and we would spend the weekend together, in bed with the blinds drawn, adrift in the remainder of passion the fire had ignited between us.

But where was there to go, once the thrill and the shock of the fire and our own shameful exits had worn away?

Sybil patted my shoulder and rested her head. "Don't leave me," she whispered, her voice hopeful as a child's.

The ways people can be brought together, I thought, *and the ways they can be divided.* I'd driven us so far back in the direction we'd come that I could see, across a rubbled field, Pete and Linda's house, gray and peeling in the distance. If for this one weekend, I could banish them from memory, I would. Pete's tears, Linda's hands, the preacher's joyless blessing to their union of quiet desperation.

My own silence as Pete and Linda, without love for the other in their hearts, promised themselves unto death.

I pressed Sybil's hand to my mouth and kissed each finger. "Don't worry," I lied. "No one's leaving anyone."

W. D. Wetherell

Watching Girls Play

From *The Georgia Review*

QUICKER, quick as he'd been in college, he could have speeded up the car just enough to head the ball off the top of the windshield and rocket it toward goal. As things are, he eases into it too slowly, the ball coming down obliquely against the roof, bouncing there three times like an angry fist trying to get his attention, then rolling back down over the flattened antenna. The car is instantly surrounded by girls or parts of girls—brown legs, red knees, pink elbows—reaching for the ball, laughing, draping themselves over the hood, blotting out the sun, then just as suddenly parting again, the dimpled ball nudged and herded back to where it belonged by ponytails, shag cuts, and curls.

Dolger smiles, knowing this is expected of him, but the girls are already gone back to their field. A funny incident . . . well, not so funny, he could have easily run over one if he hadn't been driving so carefully . . . and he surprises himself by taking the further step of stopping the car and getting out. It's autumn, this is country, and he hadn't been so deep in country in a very long time, so this is working on him, too—the feeling he should at least make a token communion with the brightness, the color and smells. That there is a soccer game about to begin on the common before a neat village church has nothing to do with it, not in his opinion. It's a kind of bonus, an extra added attraction to what is a badly needed break from the car.

He locks the doors from habit, then walks slowly toward where the first spectators are arranging their blankets and lawn chairs around the base of a tall, sloppy-looking elm. It's late enough in October that the leaves have mostly fallen, and what color hits him hardest comes from the perfect green of the field. A little later, looking at it more professionally, he will note the flinty patches scrubbed bare by cleats, the actual mud there by the south goal, a pronounced dip in the same direction. But that first glance comes to him right through the lungs, as if he's breathing in pure green adrenaline, so it's all he can do not to break into the relaxed, negligent kind of lope that once had been so much a part of him and to head for his usual position there in midfield.

Easy fella, he tells himself—he's still at the smiling stage, the taking it all in. Up above the field the sky is a deep and perfect blue, decorated by a flower or two of broken cloud. No scrub marks there, no dips or depressions. He can remember being exhausted toward the end of hard games, and how he would deliberately blast the ball high toward the sky just to soak in some of that exhilaration, the coach not daring to yell at him because he was the star. The kind of thing you couldn't teach a younger player, but there you are—there were lots of tricks you couldn't teach. He swings wide around the tree toward the far edge of the field, not stopping until his newly polished loafers come against the powder of the end stripe and take on some whiteness. Knowing it's foolish, unable to stop himself, he glances around at the spectators to see if anyone is watching. Being this close to a field is something of an exile's return, and he can't help expecting someone to acknowledge his presence there, to point, whisper, or stare.

Soccer is big at home, of course. Youth leagues, clinics, everyone playing. Often, driving to the home office or simply on his way to the bank, he would pass a game in progress, but it always seemed off in the distance, behind a haze, nothing that concerned him. If Andrea were in the car she would turn and look the other way, unable to bear any reminder of children. There was a time earlier in their marriage when he would have enjoyed coaching, but there was no way around her hurt, and in time he came to avoid the games, too, taking long detours just so he wouldn't brush up against the happy blur of color spinning around the maypole of that black and white ball, the dance he had once been so good at himself.

But this is different—he feels he can trust himself here for a few spare moments before driving on toward Boston. Down by the south goal is the home team dressed in long-sleeved red shirts and black nylon shorts. These are the girls who had surrounded the car in pursuit of their ball—sixth-graders probably, girls of eleven, womanly in their legs but not much above that, except for a couple of overweight ones who can barely touch their toes during drills. They laugh a lot, jump and laugh, and the tallest, a redhead, leads them in a warm-up that involves slapping the inside and outside of their knees like Swiss folk dancers. The goalie, dressed in an elaborately patterned jersey that suggests camouflage, has a crown on her head, a papery silver one, and everyone on the team takes turns wearing it, like it's part of their ritual.

Warm-ups over, they take shots at goal, fed balls by their coach who stands to their left with a farmer's patient stoop. He wears green work clothes and suspenders, a balding man in his fifties, calls out to them to listen up and concentrate, acting as the gentle damper on their high spirits. Dolger approves of him immediately. Yes, that's the way. Let them pour their exuberance out early, then pull them back slowly to the work at hand.

The visitors, the blue-and-yellow team, are slow in getting off their bus, and Dolger's first impression is that the wrong team has shown up. They're much bigger than the home team, twelve-year-olds at least, and there is one girl, dressed in a purple jogging suit, who looks to be high school age. They run down toward the north goal and immediately begin their drills—serious, unsmiling, mechanically filling the goal with balls that, unlike the home team's, are drilled in and hammered rather than tapped, shunted, and nudged.

This doesn't seem to worry anyone but him. The little knot of spectators by the elm has thinned out along the sideline, but they seem more intent on gossiping among themselves than paying attention to the field. Young women in wool shirts putting babies on the ground to toddle toward other babies. Older brothers and sisters kicking beach balls toward the road, getting yelled at. The fathers, what few there are, leaning against the pickup trucks which make a shiny chrome barrier behind the far end of the field. A much larger group of parents accompanies the visitors. They're older on average, better dressed, and much more caught up in the action. They slap their hands together, yell out encouragement with what seems to Dolger's ears, given the beauty of the day, a distinct note of discordance, even harshness. One thing is obvious: they have not come to see their team lose.

At midfield is a rickety set of risers six rows high. Leaning on the rail, calmly smoking a pipe, is a suntanned man of about his own age, looking out at the field with the careful kind of appraisal you only see in true lovers of the game. "Great day for soccer," Dolger says, coming to a stop near his shoulder. He is filled with it, all but bursting, and it feels so good he says it again, "Good soccer weather, conditions perfect."

He hopes this will lead into a talk about the upcoming game, some inside information as to who is who. Hopes, even, that he will have a chance to nonchalantly slip into the conversation the words that are part of what bubbles inside of him, *second-team All-American senior year.*

The man, though, hardly looks at him. When he does turn, it's with a scowl that makes the pipe sag below his chin and almost drop. "Snow tomorrow," he mumbles sourly, pointing nowhere.

"Well, up yours, buddy," Dolger wants to say—but even this moment isn't enough to dent his high spirits. He moves over to where he can get a better view of what is happening. The referee, a bowling pin of a man dressed all in black, brings the captains out for the coin toss. The tall girl on the blue-and-yellow team stares at her smaller counterpart as if she's trying some sort of mind game, intimidating her before play even begins. She wins the toss, jerks her thumb toward the south goal—the muddy goal, the one where scoring will come easiest.

There is some delay in actually starting—shoelaces to tie, the wrong number of players on the field, a problem with the clock. Dolger thinks about finding a phone to make his calls, then decides against it; he's only going to watch the first five minutes, so it hardly matters. If anything, the delay gives him a chance to appraise both teams, get a better fix on the matchups, the relative strengths.

The home team, while small, has distinct possibilities. On the front line, backing up to get ready for the kickoff, are three girls who aren't much more than skinny sticks, but speedy-looking sticks. The one on right wing, the one with short black curls, looks particularly so, a tomboy who can really scoot. Midfield seems shakier. One girl is tall and willowy, someone you could picture being named Ashley or Heather, but she stares dreamily off toward the clouds, hardly seems aware there's a game starting. Her partner, over on the left, wears shorts that flop down toward her ankles and flimsy sneakers rather than cleats. Deeper back are the fullbacks, who don't seem comfortable at all. Both are heavy and clumsy looking, buried in the back to hide them, and they don't promise much for the defense. The goalie, the one in camouflage, has the right look at any rate—lean, hungry, and anxious, especially the last.

The visitors, the blue-and-yellows, are an entirely different proposition. Their goalie has on a psychedelic sweatshirt and big orange mitts, which she cups around her mouth, yelling out a mix of encouragement and scorn. In front of her are two fullbacks who seem actual pillars, so tall are they, so strong, both wearing their sleeves rolled up over their biceps. The midfielders, by contrast, are small but clever looking, and one of them, while she waits for the kickoff, juggles a stone from one foot to the other without letting it drop.

It's the front line that really worries him, particularly the girl starting at center forward: the tall girl, the boomer, the one whose shots had all but torn the net off during warm-ups. Her hair falls down her back in an aggressive kind of ponytail which the pink bow does hardly anything to soften. Her lips are thin and pressed to whiteness; her cheeks are suntanned, but suntanned hard, as if they had recently gone from porcelain to brick and are now on their way to something even harder. She wears her shorts high, and why not, since her legs are like weapons—long-muscled, shapely, her thighs tensing and relaxing as she stands over the ball waiting for the referee's whistle to start. Unlike the other girls she has breasts, matronly breasts, bound and girdled for battle by a jersey that's far too small. Sherry is her name. The parents on her side call out her name, smug at possessing her.

At that moment he has his last fully coherent thought of the afternoon—how quick is the human propensity to take sides. Who were these girls to him? Nothing, and yet instantly they're everything, the red-and-black ones, the home team that is so obviously outclassed. His heart goes out to them, to the point where he can hardly focus on the other team at all. He remembers this from being a player—how anonymous a mob the other teams always seemed. A mist, a cloud, a maze Dolger had to butt through or glide past or somehow evade, scarcely human, until he saw one drop in pain from an injury or cry in despair when Dolger sneaked around him to score.

The delays are finally sorted out, the referee has the whistle in his mouth and his hand on his stopwatch, when there's a movement on his left where no one had been before, a scent, a woman's soft voice.

"It's George, isn't it? George Simms?"

This startles him, coming when it does, so it's all he can do not to jump. Turning, he sees a blonde, outdoorsy-looking woman in her thirties, wearing a suede coat the same brown color as the fallen leaves.

She smiles at his surprise, in a way that's obviously meant to be disarming. "Oh, that's an old line, isn't it?" she says. "Pretending I know you from way back when. But I could tell you weren't from around here." She points toward the field. "We're the hicks. We always lose."

He smiles absentmindedly—he's still waiting for the whistle. "Great day for soccer," he says.

"My daughter is halfback. Number seven?"

The Ashley girl—no surprise there.

"Do you have someone playing?" she asks, moving even closer.

He's about to bring out his usual line . . . *No kids, not yet* . . . then realizes how stupid it sounds, at his age. And besides, the whistle has finally gone off, the girls are running around in madcap patterns that make no sense, and he's anxious to be free of this intruder and concentrate on the game.

"Can I just stand here next to you for a little while?" the woman asks. "This thermos? There's schnapps inside if you want some. Everyone brings schnapps to the game. That's how we locals cope with defeat."

Is she teasing him, flirting? It's hard to know what she wants, but then she grimaces, brushes back her hair, comes out with an explanation on her own.

"My former husband is that fat one over there with the other team. The cowboy hat? He does that, stands with the enemy just to bug me. Well, I'm bugging him, standing next to a handsome stranger. Bugging him good." She takes a long swallow from her thermos, not even bothering to use the cup. "Eat shit, Henry," she says, staring across the field. "Eat shit, you cheap ugly meanhearted sonofabitch."

Dolger mumbles an excuse, then all but sprints down the line following the play. As tense as he had been for the kickoff, losing the first seconds makes him feel horribly disoriented, and his eyes race across the field trying to catch up. He'd had nightmares like this, ones where he was still playing striker and the game started without him and he was dropped into the middle of chaos without a chance of warming up, getting on top of it, spinning it to his purpose. But this stage doesn't last long. The ball emerges from a scrum of pink flailing legs over on the far side, and his eyes bore in on it, then pull back to determine everyone's relationship to that vital black-and-white core. Located, he feels much better. He squats down on his haunches, plucks a handful of grass, takes everything in.

The play is ragged at first, but this is to be expected. It's as if each girl must touch the ball with her foot before being persuaded of its reality; then, convinced, she could begin her job of urging it into motion. There are some wild looping crosses, some exuberant headers, the ball skittering away in a band of maple leaves with the galloping posse in hot pursuit. It doesn't take long for the magic of the game to assert itself, the old familiar geometry. Triangles, squares, diagonals, and the only trick is to anticipate all these, be there first at the point where the diagonal is driving, the apex of the triangle, the heart of the square. These girls haven't mastered geometry yet—that's understandable—and yet for those first few minutes the ball seems content to draw lines on its own, filling him with a gladness that all but makes him shout.

How he loves the game. How he loves it! He would have been content to watch forever under a sky so fine, feels he could do so if only he could draw back far enough, sit up on the highest of the risers or run to the edge of the meadow to climb the tallest tree. He stands up at any rate, the better to see past the parents, and he loses the pattern for a moment, the math gets away from him, and suddenly it's all wrong somehow. The home team is huddled over like they've been kicked in their stomachs, while the big girls in blue and yellow are turning cartwheels across the grass.

Sherry has scored the first goal. It happened so fast it seems already in the distant past—he's surprised he remembers seeing it at all. The ball had been moving in harmless little skips and bounces, but then a hard shape bulled past the softer ones, there was a stooping motion, a head bent intently toward a foot, the ball rocketing on a perfect line from the far right edge of the penalty area toward the top left corner of the goal. *Missed,* he decided, relieved, but his angle was wrong, because the ball bulged out the net, went on flying, then dropped vertically past the goalie's desperate and empty lunge.

One-nothing, visitors. He would have credited them with a good play if they had been better sports. It's not only the cartwheels, the arrogant high fives, but the way they so obviously sneer at the smaller team, as if this punishment is just the start. He can see their coach on the opposite sideline standing on the bench calling out numbers, wiggling his fingers, giving them a play. The home team, the red-and-black girls, slump back into formation, acting like they're used to this and somehow comfortable with it, as if being zapped is the only geometry they know.

Dolger glances down at his watch. Five minutes gone—time to make his calls. But he's caught up in things now, and instead of heading back toward the car he moves on toward midfield. Play has started up again, and for a moment it swirls past where he is standing, close enough that he can hear the girls pant and sputter, smell the perfumed sweat of them, hear them in quick little whispers call out each other's names. The ball is squeezed out past the sideline.

Instinctively, smoothly, he sticks his shoe out and flicks it up into the ballboy's arms.

"Blue!" the referee shouts, pointing downfield.

More parents have arrived. The little pockets on the sidelines thicken into a wall that is nearly continuous, so the sense of expanse disappears and the field now seems more like a boxing ring than it does a prairie. They seem evenly divided between those who care too much about the game and those who care nothing. The man with the pipe, the one who had looked so phlegmatic, cups his hands around his mouth, shouts the same thing over and over, "Who wants the ball! Who *wants* the ball, dammit!" Just beyond him is the blonde woman, who has apparently found herself a far more willing man to flirt with. They stand close enough that the buttons of her coat touch the zipper of his jacket, the two of them smiling and posing toward each other as if they're staring into mirrors. Beyond them— Well, he's tired of this already, actually disgusted, ashamed to be one of their number. Spectators were the enemy—any former player could tell you that—what with the heat of their passion on one hand, the ice of their indifference on the other.

He brushes past them until he stands on the corner of the field where he can see better. They're shutting Sherry down, he decides, glancing at his watch. But the moment he does this she winds up and one-times a shot in from well outside the box. And just a few minutes later she scores her third, this time on a header, the smaller girls falling away from her, intimidated. They actually looked scared, and why shouldn't they? She is so much bigger—had she been held back a year or what?

He has to admit she has talent, if only a fairly basic one. Her trick is to fake left by dipping her shoulder, then go right and shoot—and if the home coach were smarter he would put one of his midfielders on her with instruction to watch her right foot and ignore the rest of her body. He wondered if he should tell the coach this himself—as pleasant as the man seems, he doesn't know much about soccer. If he did, he would be yelling at the ref, protesting the bigger team's tactics. Sherry has skill, but the others depend on roughness—particularly the fullbacks, the ones with their sleeves rolled up, who like to wait until one of the smaller girls is making a run at goal before pinching in with their shoulders and bringing her down.

It's brutal, seeing this. Even the visitors' midfielders, speedy as they are, have been taught to kick the ball out of bounds whenever they are challenged, breaking up the red-and-black team's rhythm. It's negative tactics all the way, the kind that were ruining soccer, not only on this level but worldwide. It infuriates him, thinking about this. Didn't anyone care for the beauty of the game anymore, the grace?

Against all this the red-and-blacks do the best they can, especially the little girl with short black curls, whose good runs end time and time again when she is double-teamed or deliberately tripped. But she's a determined one, a plugger. After every fall she picks herself up, rearranges her shinguards, and goes off in pursuit of the ball, her skinny legs spinning. Dolger's heart goes out to her. He can picture having the care of a girl like that, giving her just the right amount of coaching so as to harness her speed; he can sense the way they would talk about a game afterward, how he would gently but firmly remind her of what she should do.

And his heart goes out to the Ashley girl, though in a completely different way. She plays with real abandon, her long blonde hair streaming behind like a decoration left in the air. She has a fluid, gliding sort of quality that takes routine chances and makes them into art—a coltish flourish to her headers, a dancer's follow-through to her kicks. She's the kind he would have been nuts about at that age. Even now, watching her, wishing her on, he can't help feeling that old forgotten need to show off, and it stirs him in a way that seems caught up somehow with the wide beauty of the clouds, the blowing leaves, the unfurled brilliance of the October sun.

It's four to zero before he decides there is no use punishing himself further. As things stand, the sales meeting is history, and he is already practicing his excuses as he detours back to the car. He'd gotten good at that lately, making excuses, dreaming things up. He is trying to think up an excuse for making excuses, taking a last idle glance around, when something so unexpected happens it changes everything and stops him literally in his tracks.

The home team scores a goal. The little black-haired girl, the speedy winger. She had been crunched by the fullbacks on a break-away, only this time instead of crumpling to the ground she keeps on running, the ball at her feet, and when the startled blue-and-yellow goalie rushes out, she makes a hopscotch kind of motion and tucks it by her into the net.

Four to one! He pumps his fist in the air, all but shouts. That's soccer, too, the sudden turn in fate. All the hometown girls leap in the air and cheer, but the girl who has scored isn't having any part of this; she rushes all serious back to her position, eager to get another one. On the other side, everything is confusion, a stunned disbelief, and Dolger realizes this is very likely the first goal they have allowed all year. Their coach stands well out on the field with his hands on his hips, screaming. The goalie, catching his tone, screams at her defenders, who yell at the midfielders, who turn to scold Sherry, think better of it, then hang their heads in a perfect pantomime of guilt.

This changes things for him, changes them considerably. For all his interest in the game he had kept a wall between what was happening there and his own involvement, but the goal by the little winger pierces it, lays it in ruins. He finds an open spot midway between the two benches, feeling a surge of adrenaline that makes his earlier excitement seem the merest drip. If anything, it's too much too soon—a sweaty kind of vertigo that drenches downward from his head. One of his coaches when he first started playing had warned him about becoming too passionately involved, even at eleven, and had suggested a trick to sober up. *Become the ball,* he had said, and while the other players had laughed at this, thought it silly, to the young Dolger it made immediate and perfect sense. In extremity, in moments of disorientation, he could identify with the solid leather roundness, its subtle indentation and give, even the pungent smell it would take on toward the end of a game, a com-pound mix of perspiration, boot polish, dirt, and grass. *Become the ball,* the coach had told him, *because no matter what happens out there the ball always comes back to earth.*

Sherry gets off a shot from the penalty area, but she's pressing now and it sails over the net. On the return upfield the little winger manages to get the ball again, and after a long run down the right side she crosses it beautifully to Ashley, who is open—for a second. The fullbacks pinch in on her but seem fooled by her flowing hair, because in the next moment she's clear of them streaking in on goal. Shoot, Dolger says to himself, his ankle cocking back. *Shoot!* But before she can, one of the midfielders appears on her right, running for all she is worth, and—seeing she's beaten—launches herself through the air in a feet-first tackle that rakes her cleats against Ashley's knees, bringing her down.

"That's a yellow card!" Dolger screams, thrusting his shoulders over the line. "Hey, ref! What is this, football? For God's sake, give her a yellow card!"

Had he really yelled? The hot ripple in his throat convinces him he had, but that is nothing compared to the angry sensation that runs down his knee in sympathy with the fallen girl. She picks herself up, limps gamely back toward play, while the referee, all oblivious, runs lead-footed and blind in the same direction.

This spoils things somehow, his yelling. The burning sensation gives way to a wet circle of dampness on the small of his back. Even the clouds seem to darken, so a matching chill presses down on him from above. He backs up from the line, telling himself this is ridiculous, that he'd become too involved—but at the same moment there is something tugging the other way, a vacuum left in the air by the soccer ball, the rush of the girls, sucking him in. He moves back to the line, cups his hands around his mouth, yells "Go red!" as loud as he can.

But neither team plays well in the next few minutes. A wimpy header, some sloppy throw-ins, a weak shot, and then, mercifully, the whistle blows for the half.

The home team rushes off the field in good spirits thanks to their goal. They sprawl on the ground around their grandfatherly coach, burying their legs under leaves until each becomes her own mound of scarlet and yellow. One of the mothers has tangerines for them— one of the girls sticks a wedge crossways in her mouth like an orange smile, and soon they're all doing this, giggling and laughing at how ludicrous they look.

Over by the other bench all is business. Their coach has them kneel around him in a circle while he draws diagrams on a chalkboard. Only Sherry stands apart from this. A stocky, red-faced woman, certainly her mother, gets right in her face, exhorting her, whipping her on—and then, in the very next second, kneels down and gives her legs a vigorous massage.

As a player Dolger had always tried for a moment of complete oblivion during halftime when he could let his mind and muscles go slack. He seeks this now, turns to look away from the girls out toward the field. Their smaller brothers, seeing their chance, boot the ball toward goal and scream their heads off, scaring away the dogs that are using the penalty area to crap. Dolger watches them, then goes off searching for a refreshment stand, somewhere he can slake his suddenly tremendous thirst. In the grass right in front of him, set there like a stubby little fountain, is a thermos someone has forgotten, and for lack of anything better he squats down, unscrews the cap, and takes a long sip. Whatever it is tastes of chocolate—he almost giggles in the innocent sweetness—and he's surprised and even shocked when the heavier taste of the schnapps kicks in. Still, he takes another swallow, then a third, then screws the cap back on with unusual concentration and places the thermos in the exact depression where he found it. Feeling stronger, but with no definite intention, he walks over toward the blue-and-yellow bench, stands there waiting to get the coach alone.

He's a young man, not yet out of his twenties; between the blazer he wears and the smooth blandness of his features, he resembles the kind who came to Dolger's house with religious tracts, though not nearly so polite. Judging by his compact build he had been a soccer player himself, maybe still plays in a men's league somewhere. Seeing this, Dolger feels a little softer toward him, as if he's a fellow member of a fraternity; the words *second-team All-American senior year* arrange themselves on the back of his tongue, ready to come out the moment they get their chance.

The coach gives his players their last instructions, then points them back to their positions on the field. With only a few seconds left before the half starts, Dolger approaches him, so wrapped up in this reasonable, avuncular mood his words come out much too softly.

"Say something?" the coach grunts, noticing him for the first time.

"It's just—" Dolger does his best to smile. "Hey, I'd rest that number nine of yours. The other side keeps rotating their players. I see you keep her in all the time. The thing to do is rest her, give the other kids a chance."

The coach stares at him with a bovine kind of shock. It takes seconds to dawn on him, what Dolger is saying, and a few seconds more before he finds the words to fling back, "Fuck you, old man," and then he turns and spits toward the grass.

And what's odd, the words don't affect Dolger, mean as they are. What affects him are the coach's eyes—how they're like a mirror held in front of Dolger so he can see himself as the coach must have, a funny, flat-headed guy in a jacket and tie carrying too much weight in his shoulders, too much redness in his face, and having no connection to what is going on. He withers under this. He tries again to smile, to find the words that might bring them back to that fellowship, but the best he can find is "Have it your way, coach." Very aware now of his posture, his stride, he walks down the sidelines trying to convince himself the whole episode hadn't taken place.

He keeps telling himself one thing: what is any of this compared to the game itself? That's what he loves above all, how each moment scrubs out those that have come just before, the ball rolling downfield into a perpetual, well-scoured present. The home team kicks off, the ball hits a hard spot and bounces, a defender tiptoes around some dog crap and gets left behind, someone else slips, someone stumbles, there's a mad scramble in the penalty area that makes him think of chorus girls engaged in a bitter shin fight—and then the ball is in the net, the score is four to two, and he can see the field all but tilt in the home team's favor.

"Yes!" he shouts, throwing up his arms.

He can't stand still now—he paces up and down the sideline, unable to stop the motion inside, hunting for a place where he can see past the parents to what is happening. It's obvious the Sherry girl is sulking—what angry thing had her mother said to her?—and without her leadership the big girls play uncertainly, getting mad at each other, colliding, giving up too soon on fifty-fifty balls, generally falling apart. At the same time the wind has come up, the sky blackened and turned colder under some fast-moving scud, and this seems to intimidate the blue-and-yellow players most, as if they're city kids, unused to having the elements breathe so directly on their necks.

The black-haired girl scores next, a neat little dribbler, and then—even before the shock of that fades—Ashley turns a pirouette, reverses herself, then curls the ball in from an impossible angle to tie the score. This seems to waken Sherry. Rather than slouching disconsolately after the play, she catches up with the ball near midfield, blows past three smaller girls, and lofts in a lob, putting her team back on top.

Ten minutes go by, twelve minutes, fourteen, and the game should be over, but the girls show no sign of slowing down, the coaches yell and gesticulate as before, and he realizes it's his own inner clock that has gone haywire, lost in the blowing black clouds, the darkness, these first, hard, punishing jabs of what will soon be November. The wind pushes the parents back into tight little knots, so they stand like herd animals near midfield, the steam from their thermoses horizontal over their shoulders. The setting sun finds a keyhole in the clouds, and a last shaft of amber shoots the entire length of the field, so it's as if the girls play at one goal, their shadows at the other.

Dolger goes back to find the abandoned thermos of schnapps, takes a hard swallow, hesitates, shrugs, drinks the rest down, then walks in choppy steps along the sideline two-thirds of the way toward the red-and-black goal. The only other spectator there is a short man with a trace of black mustache, pointing a furled umbrella toward the goalie as though it's a gun. For a second Dolger thinks it *is* a gun—there's that look in the man's eye, the squint of a sniper, the loner, the boyish man who suddenly runs amok. He's talking, his tissuey mouth shaping each word with careful deliberation, making sure it flies in the direction he aims.

"You hear me, goalie princess? You suck, you know that? You suck, and the ones in front of you suck even worse. Hey you, goalie sunshine. You suck, and the ones in front of you suck double."

Is he a parent, someone sent from the blue-and-yellows to make her cry? With his cheap black raincoat he looks like a visiting hooligan, the kind that stand in the terraces in decaying British stadiums urinating down each other's legs. He croons the same words over and over in a soft monotone, just loud enough so the goalie in camouflage can hear. And she *can* hear. She keeps glancing over at him, then tries hard to look away, moving by instinct further and further away from him so that she stands at the far corner of the goal now, well out of position, which had probably been his intention all along.

Dolger knows what he should do. Approach the man, yell at him, grab his raincoat and pull it over his shoulders, pummel him until he stops. But his encounter with the coach has made him wary, and after a minute or two of indecision he backs away, ashamed. Who knew who you were dealing with in this day and age? He had read of incidents at Little League games where spectators were sued just for voicing their opinions, and there were times back home when people flared into violence for no reason. He had heard about one occasion when an Italian defender, getting rough with another player, had contracted HIV, and there were soccer riots that had started over such arguments, with people crushed in stampedes against barbed-wire fences, poor people playing in barrios who shot each other over mistakes—and all these swarmed over him in a nausea that took on exactly the shape and substance of this raincoated man crooning abuse there in the dark.

Dolger had blown it now, with the missed phone calls, the temporary postponement of his life. But who would care? His doctor could find another prostate to check, Andrea would sparkle even more brilliantly at her party without him, there would be one less aging salesman for his company to lay off. The parents watching the game would have to forget their own concerns once it was over, find their daughters and put their arms around them, but who was there that he could comfort?

Even as a player he had felt something like this. Yes, he remembers it now, the feeling of disgust that came in the waning seconds of a game, the prospect of having to leave the clearness within the lines for the murkiness without. To fight it, he would have to double up on his concentration, slap himself, draw his muscles into alignment so as to focus on the job at hand. And wasn't something like this his responsibility right now? To pay attention right to the end? Out on the field the players have become nearly invisible, kicking at balls of darkness more than they are kicking at the ball itself.

"Upfield!" he shouts, coming to life.

Perhaps one minute left now—in the twilight he can just make out the referee squinting down at his watch. Ashley collects the ball near the blue-and-yellow penalty area, makes one of her ballet moves, then flicks the ball to the girl with curls, who has slanted toward goal, eluding the first tackle and heading straight toward the last defender, who has her squarely in her sights. Here it comes, Dolger decides—he can feel the sharp bony thunk of her on his ribs—but the defender miscalculates in the near darkness, and rather than hitting the black-haired girl with her cleats, she hits the ball, driving it between her own goalie's legs so that the score is tied.

The red-and-black team goes crazy, hugging one another, yelling, turning cartwheels of their own. A tie is a moral victory, a victory of major proportions, but at the very height of their elation Dolger recognizes a danger they are blind to. All the while the girls are celebrating the referee keeps looking down at his watch. Sherry, sensing there is still time, rushes the ball back to midfield and kicks off before the red-and-black girls even line up.

"Get back!" he screams, waving his arm.

But too late. Sherry feeds the ball to her winger, who flicks it right back, and then a second later she is around the last defender, a fat girl who makes a helpless stab at the ball and falls down. Alone now, thirty yards from goal, Sherry dribbles down the sideline just inside the chalk, needing only five or six steps more before she's in shooting range.

Dolger, realizing he alone can stop her, advances toward the murky edge of white, then stops as abruptly as a dog hitting an invisible fence, teetering there, caught between impulses. He has the angle on her, the geometry is on his side, all it will take is to jab his foot six inches across the barrier. In the darkness no one will see. But it's as if Sherry can read his intention, half formed as it is; she dips her shoulder to the left—and just as he sticks out his loafer expecting her to come back toward him, she dips her shoulder left again, cuts that way instead, draws her leg back and launches a vicious kick toward goal.

So hard and fast is her shot that, in his stupor, he is suddenly soaring downfield. *Become the ball,* his coach had told him, and he *is* the ball now, the seams of his face spinning sideways, the blocky asymmetry of his features causing him to wobble and crazily swerve. Below him he can see twenty-one girls leaning toward him like flowers toward a weak amber sun, frozen in yearning, the only motion coming from the goalie scrambling backwards to cover the open corner he's flying toward so fast—her face a mix of terror and hope. He longs with all his being to soften for her, to slow himself down, to fold himself into her youth, even as he senses the harsh logic of his inertia. Below him the crowd makes a snapping, sucking sound, then goes silent. He sees the goalie dip her knees slightly, then leap backwards and toward the side, but he senses it's too late, too desperate. He closes his eyes, braces himself for impact, expecting nothing better than the cold, sardonic clasp of twine, when he feels girlish hands on his face pressing in on his ears—tentative, grasping, then suddenly sure, yanking him down short of the goal line, pulling him into her, tumbling, grunting, sobbing, but not letting go.

Sheila M. Schwartz

Afterbirth

From *Ploughshares*

AT FIRST when the captain's voice came on over the intercom and made the announcement, she felt almost glad. Not gleeful exactly, but a sudden ching! of recognition coursed through her; events fell into place. She was glad she'd had her weekend at the hotel, glad for her swim in the hotel pool, for sleeping late, for the free hot coffee available in all the lobbies, tables laid out formally with linen napkins and china trimmed with gold leaf. She was glad, most of all, that she was flying alone; her husband and children hadn't come with her as they'd threatened to at the last minute. She was glad to be so selfless knowing that they were safe on the ground.

The captain's voice echoed her mood. It had a cheery lilt to it, like someone in a cartoon with a bubble over his head. It was his sight-seeing voice he used as they passed over the runway then abruptly surged upward again into the clouds above the lake. His tone seemed to imply that this just might be a Christmas miracle, the kind in a made-for-TV movie about the yin and yang of self-sacri-fice, as the engines churned forward, then picked up speed, the wings hovering and dipping like an uncertain insect. "Ah, well, folks," the captain said, "it looks like we've got a little problem here. Our landing gear light is shining red, and we don't know what it means. That's why we did that little dress rehearsal back there." He paused to chuckle at his own wit for a minute, dryly, then turned sober and reassuring. He banked the plane again for emphasis. "Now don't worry yet—it may not mean a thing. We'll just fly around for a little bit and check out some systems. Try to be patient with us, if you please."

Donna looked around to see what her reaction should be. No one else seemed to be panicked yet. An elderly couple across the aisle exchanged a look with her, a grim little smile that said, "We go through this every day." Other passengers, seasoned business travelers, were pretending to read their newspapers, thumbs paging casually, tenderly, through *The Wall Street Journal*. They were pretending to read computer printouts, legal briefs. Two seats up was a teenager who hadn't even heard the announcement. He had his Walkman on, turned up high enough for Donna to hear the bristle of drums, the angry thud of voices protesting some teenage issue— bad drugs, bad sex at the multiplex, exams without curves. She wondered if she ought to tell him, tap him on the shoulder gently and mouth it, "Honey—could you turn that down a bit? We're going to crash." (Donna had called everyone under thirty "honey" since her children were born, as if she'd suddenly and irrevocably catapulted into maturity, responsible for the frail moods of all souls. She practiced smiling when people were rude and ill-tempered, understanding for the first time how these were linked to a yearning for innocence, for the brick wall of mother love that would accept them.)

The boy swung his head back and forth, "No . . . no no no . . ." His smile was squeezed tight in a sullen orgasm of rebellion. "No . . . no no no . . ."

No no no no . . . , Donna mouthed to herself, but the captain interrupted, this time twinkling. "Yep! Still here, folks. Now just sit tight. We haven't found anything specific yet, and things are stacked up over the airport, anyway, as per usual. So we'll keep cruising. If you'd like another beverage, our personnel will be coming through the cabin to serve you."

At this cue the flight attendants broke their huddle at the cockpit. They clattered trays and carts, hoisted coffeepots, sprang soda tabs with a merry "Pffft!," jingled change for beer and whiskey, all the while smiling as if they were just here to perk up a weary office party. They moved quickly to fend off questions. They handed out extra bags of peanuts, as if this were one of the perks of crash landings. Their eyes were a geometry of evasion.

"And what would *you* like?" The flight attendant smiled, acting her part flawlessly—grace under pressure. "Coffee or tea? A beer, maybe? We're not charging for alcoholic beverages." And though Donna wanted to ask her, What do you *really* know? What did the captain tell you up there?, she did not want to be the one to ask nor to undo the carefully composed mood of the cabin. "Diet Pepsi," Donna said, "if you don't mind."

"No bother." The flight attendant nodded gravely as if it were not only appropriate but wise to choose, as one's last beverage on earth, something low-cal. Her gestures were a ballet of calm. "We're here to make you as comfortable as possible."

Donna had heard of masquerades like this one before. She'd heard of captains like this. Their bravery put ordinary humans to shame. In times of catastrophe, they could sound like a training manual. They could go through all the niceties of protocol as if death didn't mean a thing. They followed their procedures. They enunciated their last words clearly into the black box. There was a captain like that a couple of years ago she'd read about—somewhere over Iowa—who saved the lives of more than half the people on his plane by his expertise, his presence of mind. He was able to speak about the crash moments after the plane landed in a cornfield, able to explain how he'd decided on that particular site based on wind velocity, angle of engine failure, forward thrust and momentum, air to ground time. The empty field was a miracle, though, the God-given aspect of the situation. It opened up like a mirage just in the nick of time.

Of course, Donna thought, everyone knew there was nothing *but* cornfields in Iowa—what else would open up there? What interested Donna was how quickly the captain refocused the disaster into something positive. He didn't exactly gloss over the ninety-seven people who'd been killed, but he made it seem as if they'd beaten the odds, anyway. Two hundred and twelve people had been saved in a crash that might have killed everyone. He didn't bother to describe the burning bodies, entire families wiped out in one fell swoop. He didn't describe the particular horrors she'd read about later, the passenger accounts. One woman in particular had written an article for a parents' magazine, pleading with readers to pay for an extra seat on a plane trip to transport an infant in a carrier that could be secured with a seatbelt. Donna wondered if Captain Marvel had read *that* article, if he'd read the mother's description of her child's trusting look as she tried to soothe him before they crashed. "I love you," she murmured to him, her hand poised across his brow, as if to check for one last fever. "I love you, little Bobby, little dear one. You've had a beautiful life." Then she kissed him over and over until the end. She wasn't able to hold on to him when they struck the ground. He'd hurtled forward through time and space, a frail illustration of the laws of physics, the rest of his life condensed to a few brief seconds of fear. Donna wondered how a mother could survive such a thing.

She was glad that she might not have to. That was one of her greatest fears, the possibility of outliving her children, imagining the hundred different ways she could lose them: fire, car crash, inhaled balloons, the impervious marble of bathtubs, the magnetism of empty electrical sockets. The thought of a knife too close to the edge of the kitchen counter sometimes made her gasp right out loud.

Now she might be spared all these—though there still weren't any clear signs of doom from the flight attendants. They were hurrying through the aisles like precursors of the Christmas rush, balancing cups and trays, swinging sprays of tiny liquor bottles that chimed succinctly into the trash.

The plane itself seemed quiet as it plowed through the muffled darkness of clouds. The engines had smoothed to a hum, not loud and grinding like the plane she'd taken on the trip out to St. Louis. That one had needed a tune-up, she'd joked with a fellow passenger after landing, a man about ten years older than she. He had a tiny crease in his ear from a long-gone rhinestone, like a fossil imprint of his wild youth. She watched the discreet cascade of emotions that rippled across his face before he answered her: surprise, boredom, curiosity, lust, and, finally, lethargy. "Yeah. Well, that's what you get for flying a bankrupt airline," he said. He faced forward into the crowd of departing passengers and made his eyes glaze over.

She hadn't meant to pick him up or anything. It was just a remark to make while deplaning, her face pressed into the wool of someone's back as everyone crowded to get off. A thought like that hadn't occurred to her in years—she was a woman so thoroughly married, she'd lost all gender. Though she didn't mean that with any special bitterness. It was just the inescapable result of being married, of being a mother, of parading nakedly through the streets with a double-stroller.

And since she thought of herself that way, as a bad mystery ("The Case of the Revolting Mother"), it seemed ironic how this trip itself had come up. An old college friend had offered her a chance to be on a panel: "How Images of Women in the Helping Professions Have Changed Since the Feminist Movement of the '70's." She didn't really qualify for the panel—she had no image. She'd been a literacy volunteer before the children, had quit five years ago when Jackie was born, but she hadn't ever been a professional anything, had never done anything with vehemence or discipline except maybe waiting. She'd made a profession of that—waiting to grow up, waiting to leave home, waiting for her first love affair, her first husband, house, child. Her own mother had taught her to do this, had made her understand that happiness always seemed like a distant hill, just far enough away to look pleasant at twilight.

Like this trip. Something she'd anticipated for months, since her third child, Michael, had been born. It was an anniversary present from Tom, but she'd waited almost a whole year to do it, to be sure that as she walked out the door to the taxi, Michael's cries wouldn't draw her back. They circled her, but she shrugged them off, shrugged off the rationale behind Tom's gift—time to "rediscover" herself. *His* words. What could she find in a weekend? What could possibly be left?

She shivered now to think how eager she'd been to leave home, how it all might turn out to be a bad omen in a few short minutes— Tom's offer, the conference, her reunion with her friend, the man on the plane who'd snubbed her, the man at the conference who didn't. It had seemed like an opportunity at the time. Now it seemed like a mirage, a trap; it was her fault because she'd been so happy to leave her family. The plane was going to crash because of her, because she couldn't stand how much her children needed her, how they screamed every time she left the room, even if it was just to get their pajamas from the linen closet.

When she'd slammed the front door, departure day, it made an airtight seal. On her side, there was cool, clean air, trees as light-hearted as ghosts. On their side, sealed in amber, three despairing faces. Abandoned forever? Time was like that for children. A few minutes seemed like a lifetime.

She wondered if they'd gotten to the airport yet, Tom and the children, whether they were already waiting, her babies with their noses pressed to the glass, caroling: Mommy! Mommy! Mommy! They'd be wearing their new snowsuits, their tender faces haloed in bunny fur. She wondered how long they'd stand there watching for her plane before Tom dragged them away to check the board, what the word DELAYED would signify to them except that Mommy hadn't kept her promise; she was supposed to burst through the door right away like an angel and save them. Life for them was one rescue after another—from bore-dom, broken toys, premature bedtimes.

Someday they'd be too old to want her, and that would be worse. They'd be like that boy in the next row, oblivious, uncaring. His headphones were still on, and he was sound asleep, the static at the end of the tape whirred on and on, the mantra of all electrical equipment. Why didn't anyone wake him? Even the flight attend-ant speeding by, the jolt of her hip, an inadvertent nudge to his lolling head, didn't rouse him.

The flight attendants were gathered again at the door to the cockpit, waiting for further instructions, whispering the way nurses do outside the door of a terminal patient. Predictably the captain's voice reappeared again, not quite so cheery this time. It sounded strained, muffled, as if he'd placed a handkerchief over his mouth to hide his true identity.

"Sorry to keep you waiting," he sighed. "We're still checking our systems and coming up blank here, so we're going to try something a bit different. We're going to come around again over the airport and buzz the tower. They'll check us through their binoculars to see if our landing gear is intact. If it looks okay, we'll make one more pass again then proceed with our landing." The captain's voice dwindled. Even now he was unwilling to say what they'd do if their landing gear wasn't intact. "Sorry to keep you," he added.

Of course that was what the red light meant—no landing gear. Donna felt a chill yawn open inside her, a mouth to a secret cave. She tried to remember any similar cases she'd read of—a plane landing in that condition, what were their chances of surviving?—but all she could picture was an explosion, their plane, pregnant with passengers, bursting open, trailing fire as they skidded down the runway, plowing red searing scars into the tarmac.

Now everyone else seemed nervous, too. They tucked their heads down and checked their seatbelts. They stared out the darkening windows to grapple with fate, with clouds shifting form, disappearing into the night. Donna heard a rush of air that might have been the engines accelerating or the sudden whispering of everyone around her, lips forming wishful prayers. "I've been in worse situations," she heard someone say, but who? Not the teenager. He was as still as the moon. Not the old couple across the aisle. They were holding hands, peering at one of their tickets, maybe rereading the provisions for sudden death. What sorts of allowances would be made in such a case? Who would benefit?

Only the businessmen three rows back seemed to still be taking this in stride, though at a slightly higher pitch. They shook their heads as if this were just another part of their job description. They were swigging beers, rattling bags of potato chips, their faces flushed with scorn for the other passengers. It was as if this were an office party they didn't want to break up, a Xerox of other near-tragedies that could be averted by a loud voice, a jovial attitude. They were laughing to keep the mood from changing, telling stories of near-misses they'd had, crashes they'd avoided by accidental rebookings, malfunctions that didn't pan out, emergency landings.

"I've been on a lot of dud runs," one of them said.

"And I've been drilled in shit," said another, "and lived to do the deed!"

"What deed?" his friend across the aisle asked. "What the hell does that mean?"

Who knew? What did it matter?

They rambled on rapturously as if these were war stories or tales of sexual conquest. There were mountainous fogs they'd braved, shorn engines, battered wings, smokers in lavatories who set off alarms, were caught shamefaced with their pants down around their ankles stubbing out the evidence of their pleasure into their palms. There were baggage holds that split apart and cabins that lost pressure. There were drunken captains, incompetent ground crews who de-iced windows instead of wings. There was wind shear in their voices, tailspin in their eyes.

Of course all three of them had ordered several rounds of whiskey from the flight attendant on her last trip through. And then chasers. A few more chasers. All three wore London Fog raincoats buttoned and belted, ready to bolt when the plane came down. Their briefcases were poised across their laps, though the flight attendant chided them now to stow these safely in the overhead until they landed. *(When* they landed. *If* they landed.)

"Let's not get too grammatical," one of them said.

Which reminded his friend of another story which he told as soon as the flight attendant flickered back up the aisle. "I knew this guy once who boarded his live snake in the compartment in a lunchbox of all things. What an incredible jerk! I told him not to do it, but he claimed he didn't want to freeze it in baggage—it was a tropical snake! When we hit some turbulence, the compartment sprang open and out fell the snake—it had been crawling around in there loose the whole flight. A constrictor or something—long as my ass, long as a witch's tit." *(What* is that expression?) "At any rate, all hell broke loose. Somebody yelled, 'Help! Snakes! Terrorists!' One lady peed her pants—I swear! She wet the seat. You could see this big dark stain. That was one landing we made over water!"

The other two laughed uproariously, but Donna suddenly wanted to cry. What if they were really going to be killed? What if the last thing she heard was some horrible stupid story? What if she never saw her children again? Or Tom? She should concentrate on remembering them, press her feelings and memories into thumbprints, leaf stains. They probably had at least a half an hour left. Fifteen minutes, anyway, before they circled all the way over the airport and found their landing gear definitely gone.

Donna tried to picture them—Tom, with his arms around the children like a family portrait, grinning his gigantic smile, so sure that life was just right, that things would work out eventually if she wouldn't worry so much. Then she tried to review each of her children separately, their perfect limbs, their subterranean smiles, but they seemed to streak right past her without stopping, too small to be held. All she could clearly remember was the moment of their births, feeling them gush from her legs in a waterfall of pain, their tiny heads pushing, pushing, pushing her aside. Those were the only real moments of her life, it seemed, for the last five years. If not forever. The three births. Jackie. Allen. Michael. One right after another. Her life with Tom was over as soon as her life with them began. It was horrible but true—why bother to disguise it now? They both knew it, though they were too polite to say so. She would never think of Tom first ever again, would always feel that the best nights of her life were those first nights spent with each child, alone in the hospital room, their tiny lips pressed to her skin, soft as flowers; all night their infant moans of pleasure as she nursed them. They were perfect children untouched by memory. Perfectly safe. Perfectly hers.

Donna wondered if the other passengers were having thoughts like this. Weird thoughts. Desperate thoughts. What exactly were you supposed to be thinking at a time like this? Something profound, no doubt. Something that would change the course of your life forever, brief as that course might be. Dwelling on old sins, maybe. Or new ones. Maybe that's why they were so quiet.

She certainly had enough to keep *her* busy for the rest of the trip. That man at the conference, for instance. As different from Tom as she could make him. A lot like the businessmen behind her. A complete stranger. Horrible to her in most ways, frightening, even, with his briefcase filled with monetary funds and annuities, his eyes set thirty years ahead on retirement, as if what happened in between was neither principle nor interest.

They'd met at the pool, where she could see his skin stippled with scars, pockmarks, maybe. His white legs underwater thrashed as if there were a strong current. They grappled desperately with unseen forces. Donna had been a swimmer all her life and scorned people like this—hellbent on the rituals of exercise. They bought expensive swimsuits, put plugs in their ears, showered with gusto, strode to the edge of the pool, and peered down as if it were Niagara Falls. Then—plunge!—dove in with such a splash, the waves knocked everyone else out of the water. It was people like this who broke their necks diving into the wrong end. That was their idea of real get up and go.

Predictably he surfaced heartily, thrusting up an array of water, gulping air. His backwash dislodged her goggles. "Nice dive," she told him, and he was pleased.

"Thanks much," he said. His great round head nodded with slippery satisfaction. He was the least desirable man at the pool, so she chose him, to punish herself for what she was about to do.

"How about a drink?" he asked her, waiting around and waiting around until she'd showered and dried her hair. She didn't believe in saunas but lingered to try out the free soaps and lotions in their tiny bottles, neat as family heirlooms. It fascinated her, a bathroom like that, with carpeting and silvery wallpaper, silk flowers nodding in crystal vases—a locker room decorated for an assignation.

Like the restaurant where they went to grab a bite beforehand. No time to waste. Part of the hotel's package deal. Though it was only nine-thirty in the morning, the bar was already open and fluid with customers leaning over candles in red glass jars flickering knowledgeably, without warmth. Maybe it was the management's idea of romantic, implying checkered Parisian tablecloths and tree-lined boulevards from some bygone era. That was the meaning of the red carpet, the crystal chandeliers and brass sconces, a timeless bar for timelessly tacky love.

She didn't mind that they went there. She wanted it to be tacky. And fruitless. She planned in advance that he'd disgust her, to prove to herself, maybe, that touching someone other than Tom would make her sick. It was good that his arms were too thin, his chest was too hairy. She hoped that when it happened, after these last hollowed-out years of her marriage, his lips would feel sticky, like pieces of a burst balloon. He would kiss her too long here. Not long enough there. He'd hold her afterwards in a noncommittal way as if this were a demographic—the average length of post-coital grip. Wow! Wow!

That's what he said at the end but in a voice that rang of sex manuals. Do this. Do that. Express urgency.

There was no real way to explain what she'd done (what excuse could she possibly give? "At least I didn't have to pay for a babysitter"?), and now, maybe no need. When she looked out the window again, they were lowering through the clouds, coming closer to the airport once more, waiting for their moment of truth. Donna recognized features of the landscape they'd just passed a while ago, an hour ago maybe? Who knew how long it was when your mind was wandering free of responsibility, of logic. They passed over the usual grids of suburban neighborhoods just like hers: tree, lawn, house, tree lawn house, treelawnhouse—a series of what must be golf courses with tiny perfect ponds, miniscule flags waving, roads that looped around like elegant, handwritten O's. They crossed the marshy discarded fields that surrounded the airport, the glowering highway filled with rush-hour cars staring up as the plane roared over with the unreal magnitude of a blimp. So close. Donna could feel the magnetic pull of the landing strip (a battery of twirling lights from fire trucks already waiting for the crash), as they approached, the desire to kiss earth drew the plane downward, but they resisted; the plane rumbled over the tower slower than gravity, then shot upward again, expelling a loud groan.

The engines demurred, showed fear for the first time. "Goddammit," the captain muttered, "goddammit to hell," then realized the intercom was on and revised himself, "Oops!" as if this were a program for children and he might have to be recast. His voice wavered up and down a notch, searching for the right key. He cleared his throat. "Well, folks. Ahem," he said. (A-hem. Two syllables.) "I have some good news and some bad news. The bad news is—we're missing something. Part of our landing gear must have fallen off somewhere along the way. Folks over Des Moines probably thought they saw Kahoutec." He paused as if to let his audience recollect this forgotten comet of the seventies. A murmuring filled the plane, but not of recognition. "Also, the tower has figured out the runway here is too short for a gear-up landing, and we've now burned up too much fuel to go to another airport. The good news is—there have been many successful landings over water."

Water? A water landing? A shiver ran through them, a collective ripple of terror and reluctance.

The teenager two rows up screamed finally, but in his sleep, of all things, as if their bad karma had jumped ship and ignited him, made him dream his tapes were all snarled, unwinding for no reason into thin shining slivers that rustled onto the floor. Words tumbled from his mouth: *Help! Help! I hate you!* like an echo to all their thoughts.

Even the businessmen seemed unnerved for the first time. Puzzled. Their deadlines were tangled. Their calendars were really bolloxed up. A checklist of disappointment welled up on their faces: Death. Water. Death. Water. Death. Jesus Christ—not Death!

Death.

Clearly they weren't made for crash landings, though the flight attendant seemed to think so. She slid up the aisle smooth as glass to tap two of them on the shoulder, the two in the aisle seats, as soft and lightly as an angel, and pointed to the third in the window seat, her finger outstretched, serene, granting them pardon, or grace.

These men, her gesture seemed to say, were in the exit row—that was a privilege and an honor. These men were potential heroes— from where she stood, they were still neatly ironed. They could be guardians of the water slide, masters of the emergency chute *and* life rafts. The flight attendant warned them she'd be back in just a minute to give them further instructions, but they could reread their passenger safety cards in the meantime. They could hold themselves steady. Keep their heads up and look chipper. Smile those brushed white smiles.

Her words were light and frothy, much lighter than the air holding the plane up, still heavy enough to lift all three of them partway out of their seats. They leaned forward in unified protest, their smiles frozen in overdrive. "God Almighty," one of them muttered—the snake charmer. He screwed up his lips as if to spit, but nothing came out, just words made plain and grammatical by fear, "God Almighty—did she really mean that?"

"We're going to be pretty busy up here for a while," the captain announced, jumping in to divert their panic into smaller, more manageable streams. "It's going to take us some time to position ourselves, and the emergency ground crews are consulting with the Coast Guard about the best possible landing sites." He made it sound so simple, like a car pool, but he wasn't really fooling anyone.

All up and down the aisles there was motion, an animated universe of gestures like branches suddenly tossed by a hurricane, thrashing to get away, though the flight attendants warned them to stay in their seats with their belts fastened. The captain signed off again and left them alone without giving them any specific notion of time. Would he be back again? Did "some time" mean five minutes or two hours?

How much fuel did they have left? Maybe they would just cruise around until everyone had made his separate peace with God. Well—why not? She'd once been in a plane with engine trouble over Peru. That was long before she'd met Tom. She'd been a different person then high above the clouds, someone with a sense of mystery, who believed in magic beads and the advice of tea leaves. She'd gone to Peru on a whim to learn to "see," a phrase she'd borrowed from a popular mystic she barely understood. She'd had a couple of ambiguous moments (maybe spiritual, maybe not)—chewing coca leaves with an Indian on the train to Machu Picchu, again at the peak of a volcanic mountain she'd assumed was extinct until it rumbled. (She hadn't bothered to read her guidebook.)

Then there was that *real* moment, the one she'd thought was real, flying over the Andes, above a lake of clouds, when she was sure it was all over, felt the shining pinnacle of her body dissolving into the sun, had thought how light and casual it felt, like snow melting on a bright winter's day, pleasant almost—the way she'd repeated her own name out loud, several times, as if it might survive her. It had thrilled her then that no one knew she was on that plane, no one at all had the slightest idea where she was. Her entire history could be erased in a single minute, and there'd be nothing left to remember her. She was twenty-five years old and hadn't accomplished a single thing.

This time it was a completely different story. What *wouldn't* she leave behind? Everything she'd ever touched would become an artifact. Every word she'd ever said to her children would be a mystery.

If they could even remember what she'd said—words beyond "No, no, naughty!," words beyond "Don't touch!" Had she ever said anything meaningful, something they might remember as the years went by that would still glow for them like the birthday ring Tom had given her, a sapphire with rays of shifting light?

She tried to think, but space seemed to be roaring around her, as if it weren't infinite and desperately wide but small and crushing, shutting her in. She could only think of one conversation she'd had verbatim, with Jackie, her oldest boy—at Christmas, a year ago. They'd been walking around the neighborhood together looking at displays of lights when suddenly a meteor had fallen, had moved across the sky slowly and deliberately as if pushed by an unseen hand. Donna had gasped and exclaimed, "I can't believe it! I can't believe it! We saw the Christmas star!" Though Jackie had no idea what that was, he smiled for her, then exclaimed back, "That's nice, Mommy!" He still was young enough he'd say anything to please her. She tried hard to explain to him the star meant they were lucky; they were special. Maybe it meant they were blessed.

Now she saw it was just another crazy moment in a long line of them. It lifted her out of her skin for just a glimmer, and that was it.

All up and down the plane, they were remembering their own crazy moments as they stowed away their last belongings—books, magazines, extra jackets, needle-pointed pillows that whiled away the time. They wouldn't while away the time now. Barely time to remember who they were, where they'd been for the last twenty, thirty, sixty years. No way to define it except in glimmers, as she had done.

What were they thinking? What last memories? The old couple—were they remembering their grandchildren? What medications they'd forgotten to take that morning? Were the businessmen thinking about statistics? Or that special lunch at the Four Seasons, how lucky some of their clients were to eat caviar as casually as Spam?

It was bad to be bitter in one's last moments—that's what Tom would say. But how would he ever know? Nothing in the clouds to tell her what her attitude should be. They were a gray shroud, a thick, indecipherable tissue. They were still as an x-ray, silent as ice. As were her fellow passengers, riveted in their seats by expectation, facing straight forward, not speaking, not even swallowing. No one looked to see if there were life jackets underneath their seats; no one felt to see if their seatbelts were properly fastened. No one looked to find the nearest emergency exit, as if, even at this late hour, that would be the grossest possible lapse in taste, to seem as if you were wondering how you could be the first person to leave the plane.

Not that Donna had ever been much for good taste. She didn't care much if her children were muddy, if they used their forks and spoons to eat. Tom blamed her for things like that, for socks that never matched, for the tone of voice she sometimes used to yell at the children, and him ("I feel like a dog that just peed on the carpet—"); sometimes she thought he blamed her for everything, right from the moment they met, years before, at a barbecue to celebrate the summer solstice. It was two months late because the hosts had been too stoned to organize on time. As if that were *her* fault. The party was held at their farm, a never-say-die commune that had long since collapsed into private ownership. The members believed in total honesty, and that was how her friend had introduced her to Tom. "Now *this* is a woman worth sleeping with." That was marriage brokering in those days. It didn't seem to deter him. They went off to pick buckets of blueberries that stained their hands and lips dark as ink, a tribal rite—"We're marked for life," Tom had said.

This was clearly romantic, but later there was a pig roast, despite some vegetarians who objected, who took their tofu burgers and set up camp in another part of the field far away from where the pig smouldered in a deep pit plowed over with leaves and mud. Like a murder victim unearthed by accident. They dug the body up to eat it, subdivided the parts with a huge carving knife, waved forelegs, hindquarters. Donna and Tom sat next to each other and giggled at how weird it all was.

Though not as weird as the little 8mm film of a home birth brought along by a newlywed couple to celebrate the first harvest and offered proudly as a follow-up to the dessert of blueberry pie and ice cream. What was it supposed to be? Entertainment? Erotica?

That's how Tom had labeled it afterwards—"porno lite," though this really missed the essence. But so did the barbecue crowd, chanting: "New life! New life! Go! Go! Go!" as the screening progressed.

Still, the couple was proud. Their timing couldn't have been better. As luck would have it, the birth coincided with their wedding day—the film was still rolling from the ceremony when the bride felt the first contraction. She took off her wedding gown to labor right there in the field, got down on all fours to push the baby out into the billowing mess of her veil. Donna couldn't believe how the woman's haunches had clenched, unclenched, clenched, unclenched, in a demonstration of sheer animal fury. There was no sound, thank God, to explain her wide open mouth, but Donna could feel the screams as if they were her own as the woman swayed from side to side, grinding her belly into the earth.

Donna and Tom left before the placenta came out, after the top of the baby's head had popped in and out several times like a shy woodchuck peeping from its hole. That was one of the few times Tom was ever at a loss for words. Even at the birth of their own first child, he'd been composed, had whispered something into her ear about launching a new ship. Back then, though, he'd said, "Is it *me,* or is this the most disgusting thing you've ever seen?"

Back then Donna had agreed, but she didn't think so now. What could be more disgusting than dying before you were ready to?

That's what everyone else was thinking, she was certain, except for that crazy, comatose teenager still sleeping up there. Donna leaned forward in her seat, ready to wake him, just as the flight attendant passed by, already in the act. She ran one bright red fingernail across his forehead, then shook him by the shoulder for good measure. "Wake up, sir," she said firmly. "You can't sleep now. We need your attention."

The boy opened his eyes and cursed. "What the hell?" but she was already gliding away to another destination, another crisply performed task. "Damn," the boy muttered again, as if she'd interrupted something truly special—a memory of rollerblades or a bright green Mohawk, maybe the first time he told his parents to go screw themselves.

Nothing sentimental in *his* face. It was a map of pain and boredom—bored to be alive, bored in the U.S. of A., bored by the sound of rain pattering along the drainage ditch in his suburban cul-de-sac. A boy with just one parent. Or maybe four, six, eight. The wrong number, at any rate—all his exponents were mixed up. He was the kind of boy she was afraid her sons might grow up to be, the kind she always saw at shopping malls, too tall and skinny to be handsome, bent like a praying mantis over the record rack, worshipping the latest dance mixes, the type of boy who'd sit on the floor of a coffeehouse in the dirt and cigarette butts, enthralled by the sound of the espresso machine (hissing, hissing . . .); he probably liked to have his tongue vacuumed at the dentist, any sensation as long as it was unpleasant. A plane crash wouldn't bother him at all. He shrugged when the flight attendant warned him of what was to come. "Who cares?" he asked with such bitterness it was almost touching. "We're all gonna crash sooner or later." Then, bolstered by his own wit, he readjusted his headset, tucked the spongy earpieces tenderly back into the hollows of his ears, and closed his eyes, breathing deeply, face tilted to his airjet as if it were glue.

They were handing out final instructions, holding up the laminated cards that looked so simple. There was the plane cruising midair. There was the plane nestled in the ocean, waves lapping gently. There were the merry passengers taking their turns obediently, zipping down the chute like a great water slide adventure.

"This is your flotation device," the flight attendant said. She held up a seat cushion and waved it. "You'll want to take this with you on your way out. After we're safely in the water, you'll need to dislodge it and take it with you down the emergency slide. Don't take any belongings. You'll want to get out as quickly as possible.

This is the only thing you'll need—it will help you to remain on the surface of the water while we wait for rescue."

The flight attendant moved backwards several rows to give her spiel again. As she passed by, heat rose from her uniform like steam. (She was really nervous after all, despite the look on her face of frozen glee.) Her body trailed perfume—rose or lilac? She moved forward in a cloud of goodwill and determination. "Now *these* gentlemen," she said heartily when she reached the businessmen, "these fine gentlemen—" She waved her hand across them like a magic wand. "They're going to help you," she explained as she rotated a half-circle to face them. Her voice had a bright glare to it as she said, "You. You. *You.*"

She pointed to the one in the window seat. "You will open the emergency door when we land. And you," she tapped the middle one with her long fingernail, "will help him place the door in the row behind you. Don't throw it outside, or you might puncture the evacuation slide, which will deploy automatically." She nodded to the snake charmer across the aisle. "*You* will move to the window seat, and you will remove the door yourself and deposit it in the next row. After you do that, jump down the slide. The three of you, don't stay and try to assist people. You'll only block the passage for the other passengers."

She paused there, as if this were a moment in her script that deserved some thought. Donna marveled at her composure, the way her voice balanced on the ledge of a tall building. Her lipstick still gleamed thick as a layer of frosting. She could be dropped underwater, and she'd keep right on ticking. Though none of *them* could. They'd be at the bottom of the lake in just a few minutes, enshrined beneath the fierce upswellings of cold, of industrial waste, an occasional algal bloom. Their mouths would be clogged with ice, or fish, or stones. In summer the beer cans would rain down on their skulls, boats would roar across them, suntan lotion would seep towards them through the water slow as tears.

There was silence in the plane now, as if they'd all just shared the same bizarre fantasy, but the flight attendant didn't miss a beat. She treated this silence as if it were a loud and drunken outburst, as if she were waiting for the man to say, "Hell, no, lady—I won't do that. You're some crazy bitch if you think I'll do that—crazier than a witch's tit!" but he just shook his head—once, twice. His mouth was screwed up as if to spit, but nothing came out.

Donna felt sorry for the man. She nodded in sympathy like everyone else on the plane. Who was the flight attendant kidding? Even assuming that a safe water landing was possible, gentle as Icarus tumbling into the sea. She thought of a father watching from shore, his son burning up like a meteor, then of Tom shielding the children's eyes as the plane exploded. Luckily they'd be too far away to see her. If they saw anything, it would be like fireworks, like a far-off sparkler.

"This is a very important job," the flight attendant tried again, as devoted to her job as a mother. "It entails a great deal of responsibility," she added, as if this were something to add to a résumé later: 1) Dispatched rescue equipment. 2) Saved face in plane crash. She bent towards the man to pat his shoulder, but he turned away and pressed his face to the window. This made the flight attendant nod once more, agreeably. "Okay," she said. "That is perfectly all right. If you feel you are unable to perform your duties properly, then will you please change seats with someone who feels more confident? Can I have a volunteer?" She peered down the aisle expectantly, a glimmer of a smile on her face. Be brave, the smile said, be noble, be the kind of person you've always wanted to be! "We haven't much time," she chided.

As if to reaffirm this, Donna saw the lake appear below them, waves as sharp as fingerprints, the tiny festive dots of boats crawling over the hard surface of the water. She knew just how hard it would be when they hit, like iron, like Tom's face if she lived to tell him what she'd done that weekend, how she'd betrayed him as an experiment to see what it would feel like to do something absolutely wrong, to take on the shape of another life, a shadow that would glide between them, silent and dark, filling in the space her children had made that couldn't be explained, not the moments of crisis, not the moments of ecstasy, but those absolutely plain moments that were sheer as ice—tucking them in at night, washing their hair, pulling up their pants, their little socks that fell around their tiny ankles, pouring corn flakes into their bowls each morning, tenderly, measuring their sleep in hours, weeks, sometimes in seconds, reading them the same books over and over again ("Spot likes to chase his bouncy red ball . . ."), careful to vary the rhythms of her sentences, the pitch of her voice, patting a piece of bread with a smidgen of butter, a smidgen of jelly, smoothing her palm across each forehead as if she could instill something divine in them, make them healthy, better than she and Tom had ever been, better than they ever would be. "My children!" she thought. "My little babies." As if this were the most complete idea she'd ever had, the most enlightened.

"Okay," Donna said. "I'll do it. *I'll* do it. I'm willing," though the flight attendant didn't hear her. Everything was suddenly out of order, shaking to pieces as they went down, tipping over towards one wing, and then the other, unsure of gravity, where it might take them, the captain calling one last time over the intercom, "Hold on now, folks—this is a little sooner than we expected!" the teenager in front wagging his head back and forth as if this were some far-out beautiful rhythm, plane crash as performance art. He was shaking his shoulders. He was beating the armrests with both hands. He was yelling, "Yes! Yes! Do it, Mama! Do it to me, do it to me *now!*"

"You be quiet," the old lady across the aisle leaned over to glare at him. "Have some respect, young man," as if they were in a church, a reverent movie theater, and suddenly Donna knew it was okay. His craziness would save them. This was *his* crash, not theirs; he was the only one who believed in it. Everyone else still believed it couldn't happen to them, not today, not with so much unfinished business, so much misunderstood, not with a husband and three babies waiting down below, their lives not yet unfolded, crushed up in cocoons of adoration, still wet with joy and love.

Michael Chabon

Son of the Wolfman

From *Harper's Magazine*

WHEN THE MAN charged with being the so-called Reservoir Rapist was brought to justice, several of the women who had been his victims came forward and identified themselves in the newspapers. The suspect, eventually convicted and sentenced to fifteen years at Pelican Bay, was a popular coach and math instructor at a high school in the Valley. He had won a state award for excellence in teaching. Two dozen present and former students and players, as well as the principal of his school offered to testify on behalf of his good character at the trial. It was the man's solid position in the community, and the mishandling of a key piece of evidence, that led some of his victims to feel obliged to surrender the traditional veil of anonymity, which the LAPD and the newspapers had granted them, and tell their painful stories not merely to a jury but to the world at large. The second of the Reservoir Rapist's eight victims, however, was not among these women. She had been attacked on August 7, 1995, as she jogged at dusk around Lake Hollywood. This was the perpetrator's preferred time of day and one of three locations he favored in committing his attacks, the other two being the Stone Canyon and Franklin reservoirs; such regular habits led in the end to his eventual capture, on August 29. A day before the arrest, the faint pink proof of a cross, fixed in the developing fluid of her urine, informed the Reservoir Rapist's second victim, Cara Glanzman, that she was pregnant.

Cara, a casting agent, was married to Richard Case, a cameraman. They were both thirty-four years old. They had met and become lovers at Bucknell University and were married in 1985. In their twelve years together, neither had been unfaithful to the other, and in all that time Cara had never gotten pregnant, neither by accident nor when she was trying with all of her might. For the past five years this unbroken chain of menses had been a source of sorrow, dissension, tempest, and recrimination in Cara and Richard's marriage. On the day she was raped, in fact, Cara had called an attorney friend to discuss, in a vague, strangely hopeful way, the means and procedures of getting a divorce in California. After the attack her sense of punishment for having been so disloyal to Richard was powerful, and it is likely that even had she not found herself pregnant with Derrick James Cooper's child, she would never have counted herself among the women who finally spoke out.

The first thing Cara did after she had confirmed the pregnancy with her gynecologist was to make an appointment for an abortion. This was a decision made on the spur of the moment, as she sat on the crinkling slick paper of the examining table and felt her belly twist with revulsion for the blob of gray cells that was growing in her womb. Her doctor, whose efforts over the past five years had all been directed toward the opposite outcome, told her that he understood. He scheduled the operation for the following afternoon.

Over dinner that night, take-out Indian food, which they ate in bed because she was still unwilling to go out after dark, Cara told Richard that she was pregnant. He took the news with the same sad calm he had displayed since about three days after the attack, when he stopped calling the detective assigned to the case every few hours and dried his fitful tears for good. He gave Cara's hand a squeeze, then looked down at the plate balanced on the duvet in the declivity of his folded legs. He had quit his most recent job in mid-shoot and for the three weeks that followed the attack had done nothing but wait on Cara hand and foot, answering her every need. But beyond sympathetic noises and gentle reminders to eat, dress, and keep her appointments, he seemed to have almost nothing to say about what had happened to Cara. Often his silence hurt and disturbed her, but she persuaded herself that he had been struck dumb by grief, an emotion that he had never been able adequately to express.

In fact, Richard had been silenced by his own fear of what might happen if he ever dared to talk about what he was feeling. In his imagination, at odd moments of the day—changing stations on the radio, peeling back pages of the newspaper to get to the box scores—he tortured and killed the rapist, in glistening reds and purples. He snapped awake at three o'clock in the morning, in their ample and downy bed, with Cara pressed slumbering against him, horrified by the sham of her safety in his arms. The police, the lawyers, the newspaper reporters, the psychotherapists and social workers, all were buffoons, contemptible charlatans, and slackers. Worst of all, Richard discovered that his heart had been secretly fitted by a cruel hand with thin burning wires of disgust for his wife. How could he have begun to express any of this? And to whom?

That evening, as they ate their fugitive supper, Cara pressed him to say something. The looping phrase of proteins that they had tried so hard and for so long to produce themselves, spending years and running up medical bills in the tens of thousands of dollars, had finally been scrawled inside her, albeit by a vandal's hand, and now tomorrow, with ten minutes' work, it was going to be rubbed away. He must feel something.

Richard shrugged and toyed with his fork, turning it over and over as if looking for the silver mark. There had been so many times in the last few years when he had found himself, as now, on the verge of confessing to Cara that he did not, in his heart of hearts, really want to have children, that he was haunted by an unshakable sense that the barrenness of their marriage might, in fact, be more than literal.

Before he could get up the courage to tell her, however, that he would watch her doctor hose the bastard out of Cara's womb tomorrow not only with satisfaction but with relief, she leapt up from the bed, ran into the bathroom, and vomited up all the dal saag and chicken tikka masala she had just eaten. When Richard dutifully got up to go and keep her hair from falling down around her face, Cara yelled at him to close the door and leave her alone. Ten minutes later she emerged from the bathroom looking pale and desolate, but her manner was composed.

"I'm canceling the thing tomorrow," she told him.

At that point, having said nothing else for so long, he had no choice but to nod and say, automatically, "I understand."

Pregnancy suited Cara. Her bouts of nausea were intense and theatrical but passed within the first few weeks, leaving her feeling purged of much of the lingering stink and foul luster of the rape. She adopted a strict, protein-rich diet that excluded fats and sugars. She bought a juice machine and concocted amalgams of uncongenial fruits and vegetables that gave off a smell like the underside of a lawn mower at the end of a wet summer. She controlled what entered her body, oiled and flexed and soaked it in emollients, monitored its emissions. It responded precisely as her books told her it would. She put on weight at the recommended rate. Secondary symptoms, from the mapping of her swollen breasts in blue tracery to mild bouts of headaches and heartburn, appeared reassuringly on schedule.

For a time she marveled at her sense of well-being, the lightness of her moods, the nearly unwrinkled prospect that every day presented. In the wake of that afternoon at Lake Hollywood, which might have reduced her to nothing, she grew; every day there was more of her. And the baby, in spite of the evil instant of its origin— the smell of hot dust and Mexican sage in her nostrils, the winking star of pain behind her eyes as her head smacked the ground—she now felt to be composed entirely of her own materials and shaped by her hand. It was being built of her platelets and antibodies, strengthened by the calcium she took, irrigated by the eight squeeze bottles of water she daily consumed. She had quit her job; she was making her way through Trollope. By the end of her second trimester she could go for days on end without noticing that she was happy.

Over the same period of six months, Richard Case became lost. It was a measure, in his view, of the breadth of the gulf that separated

Cara and him that she could be so cheerfully oblivious of his lostness. His conversation, never expansive, dwindled to the curtness of a spaghetti-Western hero. His friends, whose company Richard had always viewed as the ballast carried in the hold of his marriage, began to leave him out of their plans. Something, as they put it to one another, was eating Richard. To them it was obvious: the rapist, tall, handsome, muscled, a former All-American who in his youth had set a state record for the 400 hurdles, had performed in one violent minute a feat that Richard in ten loving years had not once managed to pull off. It was worse than cuckoldry, because his rival was no rival at all. Derrick Cooper was beneath contempt, an animal, unworthy of any of the usual emotions of an injured husband. And so Richard was forced, as every day his wife's belly expanded, and her nipples darkened, and a mysterious purplish trail was blazed through the featureless country between her navel and pubis, into the awful position of envying evil, coveting its vigor. For a month or two he continued to go with his friends to the racetrack, to smoke cigars, and to play golf, but he took his losses too seriously, picked senseless fights, sulked, turned nasty. One Saturday his best friend found him weeping in a men's room at Santa Anita. After that Richard just worked. He accepted jobs that in the past he would have declined, merely to keep himself from having to come home. He gave up Dominican cigars in favor of cut-rate cigarettes.

He never went with Cara to the obstetrician or read any of the many books on pregnancy, birth, and infancy she brought home. When in her sixth month Cara announced her intention of attempting a natural childbirth with the assistance of a midwife, Richard said, as he always did at such moments, "It's your baby." A woman in the grip of a less powerful personal need for her baby might have objected, but Cara merely nodded and made an appointment for the following Tuesday with a midwife named Dorothy Pendleton, who had privileges at Cedars-Sinai.

That Monday Cara was in a car accident. She called Richard on the set, and he drove from the sound stage in Hollywood where he was shooting an Israeli kung-fu movie to her doctor's office in West Hollywood. She was uninjured except for a split cheek, and the doctor felt confident, based on an examination and a sonogram, that the fetus would be fine. Cara's car, however, was a total loss—she had been broadsided by a decommissioned hearse, of all things, a 1963 Cadillac. Richard, therefore, would have to drive her to the midwife's office the next day.

She did not present the matter as a request; she merely said, "You'll have to drive me to see Dorothy." They were on the way home from the doctor's office. Cara had her cellular telephone and her Filofax out and was busy rearranging the things the accident had forced her to rearrange. "The appointment's at nine."

Richard looked over at his wife. There was a large bandage taped to her face, and her left eye had swollen almost shut. He had a tube of antibiotic ointment in the pocket of his denim jacket, a sheaf of fresh bandages, and a printed sheet of care instructions he was to follow for the next three days. Ordinarily, he supposed, a man cared for his pregnant wife both out of love and a sense of duty and also because it was a way to share between them the weight of a burden mutually imposed. The last of these did not apply in their situation. The first had gotten lost somewhere between a shady bend in the trail under the gum trees at the north end of Lake Hollywood and the cold tile of the men's room at Santa Anita. All that remained now was duty. He had been transformed from Cara's husband into her houseboy.

"What do you even need a midwife for?" he said. "You have a doctor."

"I told you all this," Cara said mildly. "Midwives stay with you. They stroke you and massage you and talk to you. They put every-thing they have into trying to make sure you have the baby natu-rally. No C-section. No episiotomy. No drugs. I want to feel the baby come, Richie. I want to be able to push him out."

"What do you mean 'him'? I thought they couldn't tell the sex."

"They couldn't. I . . . I don't know why I said 'him.' Maybe I just . . . Everyone says, I mean, you know, old ladies and what-ever, they say I'm carrying high . . ."

Her voice trembled, and she drew in a sharp breath. They had come to the intersection, at the corner of Sunset and Poinsettia, where four hours earlier the bat-winged black hearse had plowed into Cara's car. Involuntarily she closed her eyes, tensing her shoulders. The muscles there were tender from her having braced herself against the impact of the crash. She cried out. Then she laughed. She was alive, and the crescent mass of her body, the cage of sturdy bones cushioned with fat, filled with the bag of bloody seawater, had done its job. The baby was alive, too.

"This is the corner, huh?"

"I had lunch at Authentic. I was coming up Poinsettia."

It had been Richard who discovered this classic West Hollywood shortcut, skirting the northbound traffic and stoplights of La Brea Boulevard, within a few weeks of their marriage and arrival in Los Angeles. They had lived then in a tiny one-bedroom bungalow around the corner from Pink's. The garage was rented out to a palmist who claimed to have once warned Bob Crane to mend his wild ways. The front porch had been overwhelmed years before by a salmon-pink bougainvillea, and a disheveled palm tree murmured in the back yard, battering the roof at night with inedible nuts. It had been fall, the only season in southern California that made any lasting claim on the emotions. The sunlight was as intermittent and wistful as retrospection, bringing the city into sharper focus while at the same time softening its contours. In the afternoons there was a smoky tinge of eastern, autumnal regret in the air that they only later learned was yearly blown down from raging wildfires in the hills. Cara had a bottom-tier job at a second-rate Hollywood talent agency; Richard was unemployed. Every morning he dropped her off at the office on Sunset and then spent the day driving around the city with the bulging Thomas Guide that had been her wedding gift to him. Although by then they had been lovers for nearly two years, at times Richard did not feel that he knew Cara at all well enough to have actually gone and married her, and the happy panic of those early days found an echo whenever he set out to find his way across that bland, encyclopedic grid of boulevards. When he picked Cara up at the end of the day they would go to Lucy's or Tommy Tang's, and he would trace out for her the route he had taken that day, losing himself among oil wells, palazzos, Hmong strip malls, and a million little bungalows like theirs, submerged in bougainvillea. They would drink Tecate from the can and arrive home just as the palmist's string of electric jalapeños were coming on in her window, over the neon hand, its fingers outspread in welcome or admonition. They had lived in that house for five years, innocent of Cara's basal temperature or the qualities of her vaginal mucus. Then they had moved to the Valley, buying a house with room for three children that overlooked the steel-bright reservoir.

"I can't believe you didn't see it," he said. "It was a fucking hearse."

For the first time, she caught or allowed herself to notice the jagged, broken note in his voice, the undercurrent of anger that had always been there but from which her layers of self-absorption, of sheer happy bulk, had so far insulated her.

"It wasn't my fault," she said.

"Still," he said, shaking his head. He was crying.

"Richard," she said. "Are you . . . ? What's the matter?"

The light turned to green. The car in front of them sat for an eighth of a second without moving. Richard slammed the horn with the heel of his hand.

"Nothing," he said, fighting back the bile rising in his throat. "Of course I'll drive you anywhere you need to go."

Midwives' experience of fathers is incidental but proficient, like a farmer's knowledge of bird migration or the behavior of clouds. Dorothy Pendleton had caught over two thousand babies in her career, and of these perhaps a thousand of the fathers had joined the mothers for at least one visit to her office, with a few hundred more showing up to do their mysterious duty at the birth. In the latter setting, in particular, men often revealed their characters, swiftly and without art. Dorothy had seen angry husbands before, trapped, taciturn, sarcastic, hot-tempered, frozen over, jittery, impassive, unemployed, workaholic, carrying the weight of all the generations of angry fathers before them, spoiled by the unfathomable action of bad luck on their ignorance of their own hearts. When she called Cara Glanzman and Richard Case in from the waiting room, Dorothy was alert at once to the dark crackling effluvium around Richard's head. He was sitting by himself on a love seat, slouched, curled into himself, slapping at the pages of a copy of *Yoga Journal*. Without stirring, he watched Cara get up and shake Dorothy's hand. When Dorothy turned to him, the lower half of his face produced a brief, thoughtless smile. His eyes, shadowed and hostile, sidled quickly away from her own.

"You aren't joining us?" Dorothy said in her gravelly voice. She was a small, broad woman, dressed in jeans and a man's pinstriped Oxford shirt whose tails were festooned with old laundry tags and spattered with blue paint. She looked dense, immovable, constructed of heavy materials and with a low center of gravity. Her big plastic eyeglasses, indeterminately pink and of a curvy elaborate style that had not been fashionable since the early 1980s, dangled from her neck on a length of knotty brown twine. Years of straddling the threshold of blessing and catastrophe had rendered her sensitive to all the fine shadings of family emotion but unfit to handle them with anything other than tactless accuracy. She turned to Cara. "Is there a problem?"

"I don't know," said Cara. "Richie?"

"You don't know?" said Richard. He looked genuinely shocked. Still he didn't stir from his seat. "Jesus. Yes, Dorothy, there is a little problem."

Dorothy nodded, glancing from one to the other of them, awaiting some further explanation that was not forthcoming.

"Cara," she said finally, "were you expecting Richard to join you for your appointment?"

"Not—well, no. I was supposed to drive myself."

"Richard," said Dorothy, as gently as she could manage, "I'm sure you want to help Cara have this baby."

Richard nodded and kept on nodding. He took a deep breath, threw down the magazine, and stood up.

"I'm sure I must," he said.

They went into the examination room, and Dorothy closed the door. She and another midwife shared three small rooms on the third floor of an old brick building on Melrose Avenue, to the west of the Paramount lot. The other midwife had New Age leanings, which Dorothy, without sharing, found congenial enough. She knew a good deal about herbs and the emotions of mothers, but she did not believe especially in crystals, meditation, creative visualization, or the inherent wisdom of preindustrial societies. Dorothy's mother and grandmother had both been midwives in a small town outside Texarkana, and twenty years of life on the West Coast had not rid her attitude toward pregnancy and labor of a callous East Texas air of husbandry and hard work. She pointed Richard to a battered armchair covered in gold Herculon, under a poster of the goddess Cybele with the milky whorl of the cosmos in her belly. She helped Cara up onto the examination table.

"I probably should have said something before," Cara said. "This baby. It isn't Richie's."

Richard's hands had settled on his knees. He stared at the stretched and distorted yellow daisies printed on the fabric of Cara's leggings.

"I see," said Dorothy. She regretted her earlier brusqueness with him, though there was nothing to be done about it now. Her sympathy for husbands was necessarily circumscribed by the simple need to conserve her energies for the principals in the business at hand. "That's hard."

"It's extra hard," Cara said. "Because, see . . . I was raped. By the, uh, by the Reservoir Rapist. You remember him." She lowered her voice. "Derrick James Cooper."

"Oh, dear God," Dorothy said. It was not the first time these circumstances had presented themselves in her office, but they were rare enough. It took a particular kind of woman, one at either of the absolute extremes of the spectrum of hope and despair, to carry a baby through from that kind of beginning. She had no idea what kind of a husband it took. "I'm sorry for both of you. Cara." She opened her arms and stepped toward the mother, and Cara's head fell against her shoulder. "Richard." Dorothy turned, not expecting Richard to accept a hug from her but obliged by her heart and sense of the proprieties to offer him one.

He looked up at her, chewing on his lower lip, and the fury that she saw in his eyes made her take a step closer to Cara, to the baby in her belly, which he so obviously hated with a passion he could not, as a decent man, permit himself to acknowledge.

"I'm all right," he said.

"I don't see how you could be," Dorothy said. "That baby in

there is the child of a monster who raped your wife. How can you possibly be all right with that? I wouldn't be."

She felt Cara stiffen. The hum of the air-conditioning filled the room.

"I still think I'm going to skip the hug," Richard said.

The examination proceeded. Cara displayed the pale hemisphere of her belly to Dorothy. She lay back and spread her legs, and Dorothy, a glove snapped over her hand, reached up into her and investigated the condition of her cervix. Dorothy took Cara's blood pressure and checked her pulse and then helped her onto the scale.

"You are perfect," Dorothy announced as Cara dressed herself. "You just keep on doing all the things you tell me you've been doing. Your baby is going to be perfect, too."

"What do you think it is?" Richard said, speaking for the first time since the examination had begun.

"Is? You mean the sex?"

"They couldn't tell on the ultrasound. But I figured, you're a midwife, maybe you have some kind of mystical secret way of knowing."

"As a matter of fact I am never wrong about that," Dorothy said. "Or so very rarely that it's the same as always being right."

"And?"

Dorothy put her right hand on Cara's belly. She was carrying high, which tradition said meant the baby was a boy, but this had nothing to do with Dorothy's certainty of the child's sex. She just had a feeling. There was nothing mystical about it.

"That's a little boy. A son."

Richard shook his head, face pinched, and let out a soft, hopeless gust of air through his teeth. He pulled Cara to her feet and handed her her purse.

"Son of the monster," he said. "Wolfman Junior."

Cara was due on the fourteenth of April. When the baby had not come by the twenty-first, she went down to Melrose to see Dorothy, who palpated her abdomen, massaged her perineum with jojoba oil, and told her to double the dose of a vile tincture of black and blue cohosh that Cara had been taking for the past week.

"How long will you let me go?" Cara said.

"It's not going to be an issue," Dorothy said.

"But if it is. How long?"

"I can't let you go much past two weeks. But don't worry about it. You're seventy-five percent effaced. Everything is nice and soft in there. You aren't going to go any two weeks."

On the twenty-fourth of April and again on the twenty-sixth, Cara and a friend drove into Laurel Canyon to dine at a restaurant whose house salad was locally reputed to contain a mystery leaf that sent women into labor. On the twenty-seventh, Dorothy met Cara at the office of her OB in West Hollywood. A non-stress test was performed. The condition of her amniotic sac and its contents was evaluated. The doctor was tight-lipped throughout, and his manner toward Dorothy Cara found sardonic and cold. She guessed that they had had words before Cara's arrival or were awaiting her departure before doing so. As he left to see his next patient, the doctor advised Cara to schedule an induction for the next day. "We don't want that baby to get much bigger."

He went out.

"I can get you two more days," said Dorothy, sounding dry and unconcerned but looking grave. "But I'm going out on a limb."

Cara nodded. She pulled on the loose-waisted black trousers and the matching black blouse that she had been wearing for the past two weeks. She stuffed her feet into her ragged black espadrilles. She tugged the headband from her head, shook out her hair, then fitted the headband back into place. She sighed and nodded again. She looked at her watch. Then she burst into tears.

"I don't want to be induced," she said. "If they induce me I'm going to need drugs."

"Not necessarily."

"And then I'll probably end up with a C-section."

"There's no reason to think so."

"This started out as something I had no control over, Dorothy. I don't want it to end like that."

"Everything starts out that way, dear," said Dorothy. "Ends that way, too."

"Not this."

Dorothy put her arm around Cara, and they sat there, side by side on the examining table. Dorothy relied on her corporeal solidity and steady nerves to comfort patients and was not inclined to soothing words. She said nothing for several minutes.

"Go home," she said at last. "Call your husband. Tell him you need his prostaglandins."

"Richie?" Cara said. "But he . . . he can't. He won't."

"Tell him this is his big chance," Dorothy said. "I imagine it's been a long time."

"Ten months," said Cara. "At least. I mean unless he's been with somebody else."

"Call him," Dorothy said. "He'll come."

Richard had moved out of the house when Cara was in her thirty-fifth week. Just as from the beginning of their troubles, there had been no decisive moment of rupture, no rhetorical firefight. He had merely spent longer and longer periods away from home, rising well before dawn to take his morning run around the reservoir, where the epitaph of their marriage had been written, and arriving home at night long after Cara had gone to sleep. In week thirty-four he had received an offer to film a commercial in Seattle. The shoot was scheduled for eight days. When it was over, Richard simply didn't come home. On Cara's due date he had telephoned to say that he was back in L.A., staying at his older brother Matthew's up in Camarillo. He was sleeping in a semi-converted garage behind Matthew's house, which he shared with Matthew's disaffected teenage son, Jeremy. Richard and Matthew had not gotten along as children and in adulthood had once gone seven and a half years without speaking. That Richie had turned to him now for help filled Cara with belated pity for her husband.

"He doesn't get home till pretty late, Aunt Cara," Jeremy told her when she called that afternoon from the doctor's office. "Like one or two."

"Can I call that late?"

"Fuck yeah. Hey, did you have your baby?"

"I'm trying," Cara said. "Please ask him to call me."

"Sure thing."

"No matter how late it is."

She went to Las Carnitas for dinner. Strolling mariachis entered and serenaded her in her magic shroud of solitude and girth. She stared down at her plate and ate a tenth of the food upon it. She went home and spent a few hours cutting out articles from *American Baby* and ordering baby merchandise from telephone catalogues in the amount of $512. At ten o'clock she set her alarm clock for one-thirty and went to bed. At one o'clock she was wakened from an uneasy sleep by a dream in which a shadowy, hirsute creature, bipedal and stooped, whom even within the dream itself she knew to be intended as a figure of or stand-in for Derrick James Cooper, mounted a plump guitarrón, smashing it against the ground. Cara shot up, garlic on her breath, heart racing, listening to the fading echoes in her body of the twanging of some great inner string.

The telephone rang.

"What's the matter, Cara?" Richard said. His voice was creased with fatigue. "Are you all right?"

"Richie," she said, though this was not what she had intended to say to him. "I miss you."

"Are you having the baby, Cara? Are you in labor now?"

"I don't know. I might be. I just felt something. Richie, can't you come over?"

"I'll be there in an hour," he said. "Hold on."

Over the next hour Cara waited for a reverberation or renewal of the twinge that had wakened her. She felt strange; her back ached, and her stomach was agitated and sour. She chewed a Gaviscon and lay propped up on the bed, listening for the sound of Richard's car. He arrived exactly an hour after he had hung up the telephone, dressed in ripped blue jeans and a bulging, ill-shaped, liver-colored sweater she had knit for him in the early days of their marriage.

"Anything?" he said.

She shook her head and started to cry again. He went over to her and, as he had so many times in the last year, held her, a little stiffly, as though afraid of contact with her belly, patting her back, murmuring that everything would be fine.

"No, it won't, Richie. They're going to have to cut me open. I know they will. It started off violent. I guess it has to end that way."

"Have you talked to Dorothy? Isn't there some kind of crazy

midwife thing they can do? Some root you can chew or something?"

Cara took hold of his shoulders and pushed him away from her
so that she could look him in the eye.

"Prostaglandins," she said. "And you've got them."

"I do?"

She looked down at his crotch, trying to give the gesture a slow
and humorous Mae West import.

"That can't be safe," Richard said.

"Dorothy prescribed it."

"I don't know, Cara. You and I—"

"Come on, Richie. Don't even think of it as sex. Just think of that
as an applicator, all right? A prostaglandin delivery system."

He sighed. He closed his eyes and wiped his open palms across
his face as though to work some life and circulation into it. The skin
around his eyes was as pale as a worn dollar bill.

"That's a turn-on," he said.

He took off his clothes. He had lost twenty-five pounds over the
past several months, and he saw the shock of this register on Cara's
face. He stood a moment at the side of the bed, uncertain how to
proceed. For so long she had been so protective of her body, conceal-
ing it in loose clothing, locking him out of the bathroom during her
showers and trips to the toilet, wincing and shying from any but the
gentlest demonstrations of his hands. When she was still relatively
slender and familiar he had not known how to touch her; now that
she loomed before him, lambent and enormous, he felt unequal to
the job.

She was wearing a pair of his sweatpants and a T-shirt, size extra
large, that featured the face of Gali Karpas, the Israeli kung-fu star,
and the words "Termination Zone." She slid the pants down to her
ankles and lifted the shirt over her head. Under the not quite familiar gaze of her husband, everything about her body embarrassed
her. Her breasts, mottled and veined, tumbled out and lay shining
atop the great lunar arc of her belly, dimpled by a tiny elbow or
knee. Her pubic bush had sent forth rhizoids, and coarse black curls
darkened her thighs and her abdomen nearly to the navel.

Richard sat back, looking at her belly. There was a complete miniature set of bones in there, a heart, a pleated brain charged with unimaginable thoughts. In a few hours or a day the passage he was about to enter would be stretched and used and inhabited by the blind, mute, and unknown witness to this act. The thought aroused him.

"Wow," Cara said, looking at his groin again. "Check that out."

"This is weird."

"Bad weird?" She looked up at Richard, reading in his face the unavoidable conclusion that the presence of the other man's child in her body had altered it so completely as to make her unrecognizable to him. A stranger, carrying a stranger in her womb, had asked him into her bed.

"Lie back," he said. "I'm going to do this to you."

She lowered herself down onto her elbows and lay, legs parted, looking at him. He reached out, cautiously, watching his hands as they assayed the taut, luminous skin of her belly.

"Quickly," she said, after a minute. "Don't take too long."

"Does it hurt?"

"Just—please—"

Thinking that she required lubrication, Richard reached into the drawer of the nightstand. For a moment he felt around blindly for the bottle of oil they had always kept there. In the instant before he turned to watch what his hand was doing, his middle finger jammed against the tip of the X-Acto knife that Cara had been using to cut out articles on nipple confusion and thrush. He cried out.

"Did you come?"

"Uh, yeah, I did," he said. "But mostly I cut my hand."

It was a deep, long cut that pulsed with blood. After an hour with ice and pressure they couldn't get it to stop, and Cara said that they had better go to the emergency room. She wrapped the wound in half a box of gauze and helped him dress. She threw on her clothes and followed him out to the driveway.

"We'll take the Honda," she said. "I'm driving."

They went out to the street. The sky was obscured by a low-lying fog, glowing pale orange as if lit from within, carrying an odor of salt and slick pavement. There was no one in the street and no sound except for the murmur of the Hollywood Freeway. Cara came around and opened the door for Richard, and drove him to the nearest hospital, one not especially renowned for its quality care.

"So was that the best sex of your life or what?" she asked him, laughing, as they waited at a red light. "I'll tell you something," he said. "It wasn't the worst."

The security guard at the doors to the emergency room had been working this shift for nearly three years and in that time had seen enough of the injuries and pain of the city of Los Angeles to render him immobile, smiling, very nearly inert. At 2:47 on the morning of April 28 a white Honda Accord pulled up, driven by a vastly pregnant woman. Then a man, clearly her husband, got out of the passenger side and walked, head down, past the guard. The sliding glass doors sighed open to admit him. The pregnant woman drove off toward the parking lot.

The guard frowned.

"Everything all right?" he asked Cara when she reappeared, her gait a slow contemplative roll, right arm held akimbo, right hand pressing her hip as though it pained her.

"I just had a really big contraction," she said. She made a show of wiping the sweat from her brow. "Whew." Her voice sounded happy, but to the guard she looked afraid.

"Well, you're in the right place, then."

"Not really," she said. "I'm supposed to be at Cedars. Pay phone?"

He directed her to the left of the triage desk. She lumbered inside and called Dorothy.

"I think I'm having the baby," she said. "No, I'm not. I don't know."

"Keep talking," said Dorothy.

"I'm calling from the emergency room." She named the hospital. "Richard cut his hand up. He . . . he came over . . . we . . ." A rippling sheet of hot foil unfurled in her abdomen. Cara lurched to one side. She caught herself and half-squatted on the floor beside the telephone, with the receiver in her hand, staring at the floor. She allowed the pain to permeate and inhabit her, praying with childish fervor for it to pass. The linoleum under her feet was ocher with pink and gray flecks. It gave off a smell of ashes and pine. Cara was aware of Dorothy's voice coming through the telephone, suggesting that she try to relax the hinge of her jaw, her shoulder blades, her hips. Then the contraction abandoned her, as swiftly as it had arrived. Cara pulled herself to her feet. Her fingers ached around the receiver. There was a spreading fan of pain in her lower back. Otherwise she felt absolutely fine.

"You're having your baby," Dorothy said.

"Are you sure? How can you tell?"

"I could hear it in your voice, dear."

"But I wasn't talking." Although now as she said this she could hear an echo of her voice a moment earlier, saying, *Okay . . . okay . . . okay.*

"I'll be there in twenty minutes," Dorothy said.

When Cara found Richard, he was being seen by a physician's assistant, a large, portly black man whose tag read Coley but who introduced himself as Nordell. Nordell's hair was elaborately braided and beaded. His hands were manicured and painted with French tips. He was pretending to find Richard attractive, or pretending to pretend. His hand was steady and his sutures marched across Richard's swollen fingertip as orderly as a line of ants. Richard looked pale and worried. He was pretending to be amused by Nordell.

"Don't worry, girlfriend, I already gave him plenty of shit for you," Nordell told Cara when she walked into the examination room. "Cutting his hand when you're about to have a baby. I said, boyfriend, this is not your opera."

"He has a lot of nerve," said Cara.

"My goodness, look at you. You are big. How do you even fit behind the wheel of your car?"

Richard laughed.

"You be quiet." Nordell pricked another hole in Richard's finger, then tugged the thread through on its hook. "When are you due?"

"Two weeks ago."

"Uh huh." He scowled at Richard. "Like she don't already have enough to worry about without you sticking your finger on a damn X-Acto knife."

Richard laughed again. He looked like he was about to be sick. "You all got a name picked out?"

"Not yet."

"Know what you're having?"

"We don't," said Cara. "The baby's legs were always in the way. But Richard would like a girl."

Richard looked at her. He had noticed when she came into the room that her face had altered, that the freckled pallor and fatigue had given way to a flush and a giddy luster in her eye that might have been happiness or apprehension.

"Come on," said Nordell. "Don't you want to have a son to grow up just like you?"

"That would be nice," Richard said.

Cara closed her eyes. Her hands crawled across her belly. She sank down to the floor, rocking on her heels. Nordell set down his suturing clamp and peeled off his gloves. He lowered himself to the floor beside Cara and put a hand on her shoulder.

"Come on, honey, I know you've been taking those breathing lessons. So breathe. Come on."

"Oh, Richie."

Richard sat on the table, watching Cara go into labor. He had not attended any but the first of the labor and delivery classes and had not the faintest idea of what was expected of him or what it now behooved him to do. This was true not just of the process of parturition but of all the duties and grand minutiae of fatherhood itself. The rape, the conception, the growing of the placenta, the nurturing and sheltering of the child in darkness, in its hammock of woven blood vessels, fed on secret broth—all of these had gone on with no involvement on his part. Until now he had taken the simple, unalterable fact of this rather brutally to heart. In this way he had managed to prevent the usual doubts and questions of the prospective father from arising in his mind. For a time, it was true, he had maintained a weak hope that the baby would be a girl. Vaguely he had envisioned a pair of skinny legs in pink high-topped sneakers, crooked upside down over a horizontal bar, a tumbling hem conveniently obscuring the face. When Dorothy had so confidently pronounced the baby a boy, however, Richard had actually felt a kind of black relief. At that moment, the child had effectively ceased to exist for him: it was merely the son of Cara's rapist, its blood snarled by the same bramble of chromosomes. In all the last ten months he had never once imagined balancing an entire human being on his forearm, never pondered the depths and puzzles of his relationship to his own father, never suffered the nightly clutch of fear for the future that haunts a man while his pregnant wife lies beside him with her heavy breath rattling in her throat. Now that the hour of birth was at hand he had no idea what to do with himself.

"Get down here," said Nordell. "Hold this poor child's hand."

Richard slid off the table and knelt beside Cara. He took her warm fingers in his own.

"Stay with me, Richie," Cara said.

"All right," said Richard. "Okay."

While Nordell hastily wrapped Richard's finger in gauze and tape, a wheelchair was brought for Cara. She was rolled off to admissions, her purse balanced on her knees. When Richard caught up to her a volunteer was just wheeling her onto the elevator.

"Where are we going?" Richard said.

"To labor and deliver," said the volunteer. "Fourth floor. Didn't you take the tour?"

Richard shook his head.

"This isn't our hospital," Cara said. "We took the tour at Cedars."

"I wish I had," Richard said, surprising himself.

When the labor triage nurse examined Cara, she found her to be one hundred percent effaced and nearly eight centimeters dilated.

"Whoa," she said. "Let's go have you this baby."

"Here?" Cara said, knowing she sounded childish. "But I . . ."

"But nothing," said the nurse. "You can have the next one at Cedars."

Cara was hurried into an algae-green gown and rolled down to what she and the nurse both referred to as an LDR. This was a good-sized room that had been decorated to resemble a junior suite in an airport hotel, pale gray and lavender, oak-laminate furniture, posters on the walls tranquilly advertising past seasons of the Santa Fe Chamber Music Festival. There was a hospital smell of air-conditioning, however, and so much diagnostic equipment crowded around the bed, so many wires and booms and monitors, that the room felt cramped, and the effect of pseudoluxury was spoiled. With all the gear and cables looming over Cara, the room looked to Richard like nothing so much as a soundstage.

"We forgot to bring a camera," he said. "I should shoot this, shouldn't I?"

"There's a vending machine on two," said the labor nurse, raising Cara's legs up toward her chest, spreading them apart. The outer labia were swollen and darkened to a tobacco-stain brown, gashed pink in the middle, as bright as bubble gum. "It has things like combs and toothpaste. I think it might have the kind of camera you throw away."

"Do I have time?"

"Probably. But you never know."

"Cara, do you want pictures of this? Should I go? I'll be right back. Cara?"

Cara didn't answer. She had slipped off into the world of her contractions, eyes shut, head rolled back, brow luminous with pain and concentration like the brow of Christ in a Crucifixion scene.

The nurse had lost interest in Richard and the camera question. She held one of Cara's hands in one of hers and stroked Cara's hair with the other. Their faces were close together, and the nurse was whispering something. Cara nodded, and bit her lip, and barked out an angry laugh. Richard stood there. He felt he ought to be helping Cara, but the nurse seemed to have everything under control. There was nothing for him to do and no room beside the bed.

"I'll be right back," he said.

He got lost on his way down to the second floor, and then when he reached two he got lost again trying to find the vending machine. It stood humming in a corridor outside the cafeteria, beside the men's room. Within its tall panel of glass doors, a carousel rotated when you pressed a button. It was well stocked with toiletry and sanitary items, along with a few games and novelties for bored children. There was one camera left. Richard fed a twenty-dollar bill into the machine and received no change.

When he got back to the room he stood with his fingers on the door handle. It was cold and dry and gave him a static shock when he grasped it. Through the door he heard Cara say, "Fuck," with a calmness that frightened him. He let go of the handle.

There was a squeaking of rubber soles, rapid and intent. Dorothy Pendleton was hurrying along the corridor toward him. She had pulled a set of rose surgical scrubs over her street clothes. They fit her badly across the chest, and one laundry-marked shirttail dangled free of the waistband. She was pinning her hair up behind her head, scattering bobby pins as she came.

"You did it," she said. "Good for you."

Richard was surprised to find that he was glad to see Dorothy. She looked intent but not flustered, rosy-cheeked, wide-awake. She gave off a pleasant smell of sugary coffee. Over one shoulder she carried a big leather sack covered in a worn patchwork of scraps of old kilims. He noticed, wedged in among the tubes of jojoba oil and the medical instruments, a rolled copy of *The Daily Racing Form.*

"Yeah, well, I'm just glad, you know, that my sperm finally came in handy for something," he said.

She nodded, then leaned into the door. "Good sperm," she said. She could see that he needed something from her, a word of wisdom from the midwife, a pair of hands to yank him breech-first and hypoxic back into the dazzle and clamor of the world. But she had already wasted enough of her attention on him, and she reached for the handle of the door.

Then she noticed the cardboard camera dangling from his hand. For some reason it touched her that he had found himself a camera to hide behind.

She stopped. She looked at him. She put a finger to his chest. "My father was a sheriff in Bowie County, Texas," she said.

He took a step backward, gazing down at the finger. Then he looked up again.

"Meaning?"

"Meaning get your ass into that room, deputy." She pushed open the door.

The first thing they heard was the rapid beating of the baby's heart through the fetal monitor. It filled the room with its simple news, echoing like a hammer on tin.

"You're just in time," said the labor nurse. "It's crowning."

"Dorothy. Richie." Cara's head lolled toward them, her cheeks streaked with tears and damp locks of hair, her eyes red, her face swollen and bruised looking. It was the face she had worn after the attack at Lake Hollywood, dazed with pain, seeking out his eyes. "Where did you go?" she asked him. She sounded angry. "Where did you go?"

Sheepishly he held up the camera.

"Jesus! Don't go away again!"

"I'm sorry," he said. A dark circle of hair had appeared between her legs, surrounded by the fiery pink ring of her straining labia. "I'm sorry!"

"Get him scrubbed," Dorothy said to the nurse. "He's catching the baby."

"What?" said Richard. He felt he ought to reassure Cara. "Not really."

"Really," said Dorothy. "Get scrubbed."

The nurse traded places with Dorothy at the foot of the bed and took Richard by the elbow. She tugged the shrink-wrapped camera from his grasp.

"Why don't you give that to me?" she said. "You go get scrubbed."

"I washed my hands before," Richard said, panicking a little.

"That's good," said Dorothy. "Now you can do it again."

Richard washed his hands in brown soap that stung the nostrils, then turned back to the room. Dorothy had her hand on the bed's controls, raising its back, helping Cara into a more upright position. Cara whispered something.

"What's that, honey?" said Dorothy.

"I said, Richard, I'm sorry too."

"What are you sorry about?" Dorothy said. "Good God."

"Everything," Cara said. And then, "Oh."

She growled and hummed, snapping her head from side to side. She hissed short whistling jets of air through her teeth. Dorothy glanced at the monitor. "Big one," she said. "Here we go."

She waved Richard over to her side. Richard hesitated.

Cara gripped the side rails of the bed. Her neck arched backward. A humming arose deep inside her chest and grew higher in pitch as it made its way upward until it burst as a short cry, ragged and harsh, from her lips.

"Whoop!" said Dorothy, drawing back her arms. "A stargazer! Hi, there!" She turned again to Richard, her hands cupped around something smeary and purple that was protruding from Cara's body. "Come on, move it. See this."

Richard approached the bed and saw that Dorothy balanced the baby's head between her broad palms. It had a thick black shock of hair. Its eyes were wide open, large and dark, pupils invisible, star-ing directly, Richard felt, at him. There was no bleariness, or swelling of the lower eyelids. No one, Richard felt, had ever quite looked at him this way, without emotion, without judgment. The consciousness of a great and irrevocable event came over him; ten months' worth of dread and longing filled him in a single unbear-able rush. Disastrous things had happened to him in his life; at other times, stretching far back into the interminable afternoons of his boyhood, he had experienced a sense of buoyant calm that did not seem entirely without foundation in the nature of things. Nothing awaited him in the days to come but the same uneven progression of disaster and contentment. And all those moments, past and future, seemed to him to be concentrated in that small, dark, pupilless gaze.

Dorothy worked her fingers in alongside the baby's shoulders. Her movements were brusque, sure, and indelicate. They reminded Richard of a cook's or a potter's. She took a deep breath, glanced at Cara, and then gave the baby a twist, turning it ninety degrees.

"Now," she said. "Give me your hands."

"But you don't really catch them, do you?" he said. "That's just a figure of speech."

"Don't you wish," said Dorothy. "Now get in there."

She dragged him into her place and stepped back. She took hold of his wrists and laid his hands on the baby's head. It was sticky and warm against his fingers.

"Just wait for the next contraction, Dad. Here it comes."

He waited, looking down at the baby's head, and then Cara grunted, and some final chain or stem binding the baby to her womb seemed to snap. With a soft slurping sound the entire child came squirting out into Richard's hands. Almost without thinking, he caught it. The nurse and Dorothy cheered. Cara started to cry. The baby's skin was the color of skimmed milk, smeared, glistening, flecked with bits of dark red. Its shoulders and back were covered in a faint down, matted and slick. It worked its tiny jaw, snorting and snuffling hungrily at the sharp first mouthfuls of air.

"What is it?" Cara said. "Is it a boy?"

"Wow," said Richard, holding the baby up to show Cara. "Check this out."

Dorothy nodded. "You have a son, Cara," she said. She took the baby from Richard and laid him on the collapsed tent of Cara's belly. Cara opened her eyes. "A big old hairy son."

Richard went around to stand beside his wife. He leaned in until his cheek was pressed against hers. They studied the wolfman's boy, and he regarded them.

"Do you think he's funny looking?" Richard said doubtfully. Then the nurse snapped a picture of the three of them, and they looked at her, blinking, blinded by the flash.

"Beautiful," said the nurse.

Pinckney Benedict

Miracle Boy

From *Esquire*

LIZARD and Geronimo and Eskimo Pie wanted to see the scars. Show us the scars, Miracle Boy, they said.

They cornered Miracle Boy after school one day, waited for him behind the shop-class shed, out beyond the baseball diamond, where the junior high's property bordered McClung's place. Miracle Boy always went home that way, over the fence stile and across the fields with his weird shuffling gait and the black-locust walking stick that his old man had made for him. His old man's place bordered McClung's on the other side.

Show us the scars. Lizard and Geronimo and Eskimo Pie knew all about the accident and Miracle Boy's reattached feet. The newspaper headline had named him Miracle Boy. MIRACLE BOY'S FEET REATTACHED IN EIGHT-HOUR SURGERY. Everybody in school knew, everybody in town. Theirs was not a big town. It had happened a number of years before, but an accident of that sort has a long memory.

Lizard and Geronimo and Eskimo Pie wanted to see where the feet had been sewn back on. They were interested to see what a miracle looked like. They knew about miracles from the Bible—the burning bush, Lazarus who walked again after death—and it got their curiosity up.

Miracle Boy didn't want to show them. He shook his head when they said to him, Show us the scars. He was a portly boy, soft and jiggly at his hips and belly from not being able to run around and play sports like other boys, like Lizard and Geronimo and Eskimo Pie. He was pigeon-toed and wearing heavy dark brogans that looked like they might have some therapeutic value. His black corduroy pants were too long for him and pooled around his ankles. He carried his locust walking stick in one hand.

Lizard and Geronimo and Eskimo Pie asked him one last time— they were being patient with him because he was a cripple—and then they knocked him down. Eskimo Pie sat on his head while the other two took off his pants and shoes and socks. They flung his socks and pants over the sagging woven-wire fence. One of the heavy white socks caught on the rusted single strand of bob-wire along the top of the fence. They tied the legs of his pants in a big knot before tossing them. They tied the laces of the heavy brogans together and pitched them high in the air, so that they caught and dangled from the electric line overhead. Miracle Boy said nothing while they were doing it. Eskimo Pie took his walking stick from him and threw it into the bushes.

They pinned Miracle Boy to the ground and examined his knotted ankles, the smooth lines of the scars, their pearly whiteness, the pink and red and purple of the swollen, painful-looking skin around them.

Don't look like any miracle to me, said Eskimo Pie. Miracle Boy wasn't fighting them. He was just lying there, looking in the other direction. McClung's Hereford steers had drifted over to the fence, excited by the goings-on, thinking maybe somebody was going to feed them. They were a good-looking bunch of whiteface cattle, smooth-hided and stocky, and they'd be going to market soon.

It just looks like a mess of old scars to me, Eskimo Pie said.

Eskimo Pie and Geronimo were brothers. Their old man had lost three quarters of his left hand to the downstroke of a hydraulic fence-post driver a while before, but that hadn't left anything much to reattach.

It's miracles around us every day, said Miracle Boy.

Lizard and Geronimo and Eskimo Pie stopped turning his feet this way and that like the intriguing feet of a dead man. Miracle Boy's voice was soft and piping, and they stopped to listen.

What's that? Geronimo wanted to know. He nudged Miracle Boy with his toe.

Jesus, he made the lame man to walk, Miracle Boy said. And Jesus, he made me to walk, too.

But you wasn't lame before, Geronimo said. Did Jesus take your feet off just so he could put them back on you?

Miracle Boy didn't say anything more. Lizard and Geronimo and Eskimo Pie noticed then that he was crying. His face was wet, shining with tears and mucus. They saw him bawling, without his shoes and socks and trousers, sprawled in his underpants on the ground, his walking stick caught in a pricker bush. They decided that this did not look good.

They were tempted to leave him, but instead they helped him up and retrieved his socks and unknotted his pants and assisted him into them. He was still crying as they did it. Eskimo Pie presented the walking stick to him with a flourish. They debated briefly whether to go after his shoes, dangling from the power line over-head. In the end, though, they decided that, having set him on his feet again, they had done enough.

Miracle Boy's old man was the one who cut Miracle Boy's feet off. He was chopping corn into silage. One of the front wheels of the Case 1370 Agri-King that he was driving broke through the crust of the cornfield into a snake's nest. Copperheads boiled up out of the ground. The tractor nose-dived, heeled hard over to one side, and Miracle Boy slid off the fender where he'd been riding.

Miracle Boy's old man couldn't believe what he had done. He shut off the tractor's power-takeoff and scrambled down from the high seat. He was sobbing. He pulled his boy out of the jaws of the silage chopper and saw that the chopper had taken his feet.

It's hard not to admire what he did next.

Thinking fast, he put his boy down, gently put his maimed boy down on the ground. He had to sweep panicked copperheads out of the way to do it. He made a tourniquet for one leg with his belt, made another with his blue bandanna that he kept in his back pocket. Then he went up the side of the silage wagon like a monkey. He began digging in the silage. He dug down into the wet heavy stuff with his bare hands.

From where he was lying on the ground, the boy could see the silage flying. He could tell that his feet were gone. He knew what his old man was looking for up there. He knew exactly.

Miracle Boy's old man called Lizard's mother on the telephone. He told Lizard's mother what Lizard and Geronimo and Eskimo Pie had done to Miracle Boy. He told her that they had taken Miracle Boy's shoes from him. That was the worst part of what they had done, he said, to steal a defenseless boy's shoes.

The next day, Miracle Boy's old man came by Lizard's house. He brought Miracle Boy with him. Lizard thought that probably Miracle Boy's old man was going to whip the tar out of him for his part in what had been done to Miracle Boy. He figured Miracle Boy was there to watch the beating. Lizard's own old man was gone, and his mother never laid a hand on him, so he figured that, on this occasion, Miracle Boy's old man would likely fill in.

Instead, Lizard's mother made them sit in the front room together, Lizard and Miracle Boy. She brought them cold Coca-Colas and grilled cheese sandwiches. She let them watch TV. An old movie was on; it was called *Dinosaurus!* Monsters tore at one another on the TV screen and chased tiny humans. Even though it was the kind of thing he would normally have liked, Lizard couldn't keep his mind on the movie. Miracle Boy sat in the crackling brown reclining chair that had belonged to Lizard's old man. The two of them ate from TV trays, and whenever Miracle Boy finished his glass of Coca-Cola, Lizard's mother brought him more. She brought Lizard more, too, and she looked at him with searching eyes, but Lizard could not read the message in her gaze.

By the third glassful of Coca-Cola, Lizard started to feel a little sick, but Miracle Boy went right on, drinking and watching *Dinosaurus!* with an enraptured expression on his face, occasionally belching quietly. Sometimes his lips moved, and Lizard thought he might be getting ready to say something, but he and Lizard never swapped a single word the whole time.

Miracle Boy's old man sat on the front porch of Lizard's house and looked out over the shrouded western slope of the Blue Ridge and swigged at the iced tea that Lizard's mother brought him, never moving from his seat until *Dinosaurus!* was over and it was time to take Miracle Boy away.

Geronimo and Eskimo Pie got a hiding from their old man. He used his two-inch-wide black bull-hide belt in his good hand, and he made them take their pants down for the beating, and he made them thank him for every stroke. They couldn't believe it when Lizard told them what his punishment had been. That, Geronimo told Lizard, is the difference between a house with a woman in charge and one with a man.

Lizard saw Miracle Boy's shoes every day, hanging on the electric wire over by McClung's property line, slung by their laces. He kept hoping the laces would weather and rot and break and the shoes would come down by themselves, and that way he wouldn't have to see them anymore, but they never did. When he was outside the school, his eyes were drawn to them. He figured that everybody in the school saw those shoes. Everybody knew whose shoes they were. Lizard figured that Miracle Boy must see them every day on his way home.

He wondered what Miracle Boy thought about that, his shoes hung up in the wires, on display like some kind of a trophy, in good weather and in bad. Nestled together nose to tail up in the air like dogs huddled for warmth. He wondered if Miracle Boy ever worried about those shoes.

He took up watching Miracle Boy in school for signs of worry. Miracle Boy kept on just like before. He wore a different pair of shoes these days, a brand-new pair of coal-black Keds that looked too big for him. He shuffled from place to place, his walking stick tapping against the vinyl tiles of the hallway floors as he went.

I'm going to go get the shoes, Lizard announced one day to

Geronimo and Eskimo Pie. It was spring by then, the weather alternating between warm and cold, dark days that were winter hanging on and spring days full of hard bright light. Baseball season, and the three of them were on the bench together. Geronimo and Eskimo Pie didn't seem to know what shoes Lizard was talking about. They were concentrating on the game.

Miracle Boy's shoes, Lizard said. Geronimo and Eskimo Pie looked up at them briefly. A breeze swung them first gently clockwise and just as gently counterclockwise.

You don't want to fool with those, Eskimo Pie said.

Lectrocute yourself, Geronimo said.

Or fall to your doom, one, Eskimo Pie said.

Lizard didn't say anything more about it to them. He kept his eyes on the shoes as they moved through their slow oscillation, and he watched the small figure of Miracle Boy, dressed in black like a preacher, bent like a question mark as he moved beneath the shoes, as he bobbed over the fence stile and hobbled across the brittle dead grass of the field beyond.

The trees are beginning to go gloriously to color in the windbreak up by the house. The weather is crisp, and the dry unchopped corn in the field around Miracle Boy and his old man chatters and rasps and seems to want to talk. Miracle Boy (though he is not Miracle Boy yet—that is minutes away) sits on the fender of the tractor, watching his old man.

Soon enough, Miracle Boy will be bird-dogging whitewings out of the stubble of this field. Soon enough, his old man will knock the fluttering doves out of the air with a blast of hot singing birdshot from his 12-gauge Remington side-by-side, and Miracle Boy will happily shag the busted birds for him. When the snow falls, Miracle Boy will go into the woods with his old man, after the corn-fat deer that are plentiful on the place. They will drop a salt lick in a clearing that he knows, by a quiet little stream, and they will wait together in the ice-rimed bracken, squatting patiently on their haunches, Miracle Boy and his old man, to kill the deer that come to the salt.

❏ ❏ ❏ ❏

Lizard made a study of the subject of the shoes. They were hung up maybe a yard out from one of the utility poles, so clearly the pole was the way to go. He had seen linemen scramble up the poles with ease, using their broad climbing slings and their spiked boots, but he had no idea where he could come by such gear.

In the end, he put on the tool belt that his old man had left behind, cinched it tight, holstered his old man's Tiplady hammer, and filled the pouch of the belt with sixtypenny nails. He left the house in the middle of the night, slipping out the window of his bedroom and clambering down the twisted silver maple that grew there. He walked and trotted the four miles down the state highway to the junior high school. It was a cold night there in the highlands of the Seneca Valley, and he nearly froze. He hid in the ditches by the side of the road whenever a vehicle went by. He didn't care for anyone to stop and offer him a ride or ask him what it was he thought he was doing.

He passed a number of houses on the way to the school. The lights were on in some of the houses and off in others. One of the houses was Miracle Boy's, he knew, a few hundred yards off the road in a grove of walnut trees, its back set against a worn-down knob of a hill. In the dark, the houses were hard to tell one from another. Lizard thought he knew which house was Miracle Boy's, but he couldn't be sure.

His plan was this: to drive one of the sixtypenny nails into the utility pole about three feet off the ground. Then to stand one-footed on that nail and drive in another some distance above it. Then he would stand on the second nail and drive a third, and so on, ascending nail by nail until he reached the humming trans-former at the top of the pole. Then, clinging to the transformer, he imagined, he would lean out from the pole and, one-handed, pluck the shoes from the wire, just like taking fruit off a tree.

The first nail went in well and held solid under his weight, and he hugged the pole tight, the wood rough and cool where it rubbed against the skin of his cheek. He fished in the pouch of nails, se-lected one, and drove it as well. He climbed onto it. His hands were beginning to tremble as he set and drove the third nail. He had to stand with his back bent at an awkward angle, his shoulder dug in hard against the pole, and already he could feel the strain grinding to life in his back and in the muscles of his forearm.

The next several nails were not hard to sink, and he soon found himself a dozen feet up, clinging to the pole. The moon had risen as he'd worked, and the landscape below was bright. He looked around him, at the baseball diamond, with its deep-worn base path and crumbling pitcher's mound and the soiled bags that served as bases. From his new vantage point, he noted with surprise the state of the roof of the shop shed, the tin scabby and blooming with rust, bowed and beginning to buckle. He had never noticed before what hard shape the place was in.

He straightened his back and fought off a yawn. He was getting tired and wished he could quit the job he had started. He looked up. There was no breeze, and the shoes hung as still as though they were shoes in a painting. He fumbled another nail out of the pouch, ran it through his hair to grease the point, mashed his shoulder against the unyielding pole, set the nail with his left hand, and banged it home.

And another, and another. His clothes grew grimy with creosote, and his eyes stung and watered. Whenever he looked down, he was surprised at how far above the ground he had climbed.

McClung's Herefords found him, and they stood in a shallow semicircle beneath the utility pole, cropping at the worthless grass that grew along the fence line. This was a different batch from the fall before. These were younger but similarly handsome animals, and Lizard welcomed their company. He felt lonesome up there on the pole. He thought momentarily of Miracle Boy, seated before the television, his gaze fixed on the set, his jaws moving, a half-eaten grilled cheese sandwich in his fingers.

The steers stood companionably close together, their solid barrel bodies touching lightly. Their smell came to him, concentrated and musty, like damp hot sawdust, and he considered how it would be to descend the pole and stand quietly among them. How warm. He imagined himself looping an arm over the neck of one of the steers, leaning his head against the hot skin of its densely muscled shoulder. A nail slithered from his numbing fingers, fell, and dinked musically off the forehead of the lead steer. The steer woofed, blinked, twitched its ears in annoyance. The Herefords wheeled and started off across the field, the moonlight silvering the curly hair along the ridgelines of their backs.

The nail on which Lizard was standing began to give dangerously beneath his weight, and he hurried to make his next foothold. He gripped the utility pole between his knees, clinging hard, trying to take the burden off the surrendering nail as it worked its way free of the wood. A rough splinter stung his thigh. He whacked at the wobbling nail that he held and caught the back of his hand instead, peeling skin from his knuckles. He sucked briefly at the bleeding scrapes and then went back to work, striking the nail with the side of the hammer's head. The heavy nail bent under the force of his blows, and he whimpered at the thought of falling. He struck it again, and the nail bit deep into the pine. Again, and it tested firm when he tugged on it.

He pulled himself up. Resting on the bent nail, he found himself at eye level with the transformer at the pole's top. Miracle Boy's shoes dangled a yard behind him. Lizard felt winded, and he took hold of the transformer. The cold metal cut into the flesh of his fingers. There was deadly current within the transformer, he knew, but still it felt like safety to him. He held fast, shifted his weight to his arms, tilted his head back to catch sight of the shoes. Overhead, the wires crossed the disk of the moon, and the moonlight shone on the wires, on the tarnished hardware that fixed them to the post, on the ceramic insulators. These wires run to every house in the valley, Lizard thought.

He craned his neck farther and found the shoes. Still there. The shoes were badly weathered. To Lizard, they looked a million years old, like something that ought to be on display in a museum somewhere, with a little white card identifying them. SHOES OF THE MIRACLE BOY. The uppers were cracked and swollen, pulling loose from the lowers, and the tongues protruded obscenely. Lizard put a tentative hand out toward them. Close, but no cigar.

He loosened his grip, leaned away from the pole. The arm with which he clung to the transformer trembled with the effort. Lizard trusted to his own strength to keep him from falling. He struggled to make himself taller. The tips of his outstretched fingers grazed the sole of one of the shoes and set them both to swinging. The shoes swung away from him and then back. He missed his grip, and they swung again. This time, he got a purchase on the nearest shoe.

He jerked, and the shoes held fast. Jerked again and felt the raveling laces begin to give. A third time, a pull nearly strong enough to dislodge him from his perch, and the laces parted. He drew one shoe to him as the other fell to the ground below with a dry thump. He wondered if the sound the shoe made when it hit was similar to the sound he might make. The shoe he held in his hand was the left.

In the moonlight, Lizard could see almost as well as in the day. He could make out McClung's cattle on the far side of the field, their hind ends toward him, and the trees of the windbreak beyond that, and beyond that the lighted windows of a house. It was, he knew, Miracle Boy's house. Set here and there in the shallow bowl of the Seneca Valley were the scattered lights of other houses. A car or a pickup truck crawled along the state road toward him. The red warning beacons of a microwave relay tower blinked at regular intervals on a hogback to the north.

Lizard was mildly surprised to realize that the valley in which he lived was such a narrow one. He could easily traverse it on foot in a day. The ridges crowded in on the levels. Everything that he knew was within the sight of his eyes. It was as though he lived in the cupped palm of a hand, he thought.

He tucked Miracle Boy's left shoe beneath his arm and began his descent.

When Lizard was little, his old man made toys for him. He made them out of wood: spinning tops and tiny saddle horses, trucks and guns, a cannon and caisson just like the one that sat on the lawn of the county courthouse. He fashioned a bull-roarer that made a tremendous howling when he whirled it overhead but that Lizard was too small to use; and what he called a Limber Jack, a little wooden doll of a man that would dance flat-footed while his father sang: "Was an old man near Hell did dwell, / If he ain't dead yet he's living there still."

Lizard's favorite toy was a Jacob's Ladder, a cunning arrangement of wooden blocks and leather strips about three feet long. When you tilted the top block just so, the block beneath it flipped over with a slight clacking sound, and the next block after that, and so on, cascading down the line. When all the blocks had finished their tumbling, the Jacob's Ladder was just as it had been before, though to Lizard it seemed that it ought to have been longer, or shorter, or anyhow changed.

He could play with it for hours, keeping his eye sharp on the line of end-swapping blocks purling out from his own hand like an infinite stream of water. He wanted to see the secret of it.

I believe he's a simpleton, his old man told his mother.

You think my boy wants anything to do with you little bastards?

Lizard wanted to explain that he was alone in this. That Geronimo and Eskimo Pie were at home asleep in their beds, that they knew nothing of what he was doing. Miracle Boy's old man stood behind the closed screen door of his house, his arms crossed over his chest, a cigarette snugged in the corner of his mouth. The hallway behind him was dark.

I don't necessarily want anything to do with him, Lizard said. I just brought him his shoes.

He held out the shoes, but Miracle Boy's old man didn't even look at them.

Your mommy may not know what you are, Miracle Boy's old man said, and his voice was tired and calm. But I do.

Lizard offered the shoes again.

You think he wants those things back? Miracle Boy's old man asked. He's got new shoes now. Different shoes.

Lizard said nothing. He stayed where he was.

Put them down there, Miracle Boy's old man said, nodding at a corner of the porch.

I'm sorry, Lizard said. He held on to the shoes. He felt like he was choking.

It's not me you need to be sorry to.

Miracle Boy appeared at the end of the dark hallway. Lizard could see him past the bulk of his old man's body. He was wearing canary-yellow pajamas. Lizard had never before seen him wear any color other than black.

Daddy? he said. The sleeves of the pj's were too long for his arms, they swallowed his hands, and the pajama legs lapped over his feet. He began to scuff his way down the hall toward the screen door. He moved deliberately. He did not have his walking stick with him, and he pressed one hand against the wall.

His old man kept his eyes fixed on Lizard. Go back to bed, Junior, he said in the same tired tone that he had used with Lizard before.

Daddy?

Miracle Boy brushed past his old man, who took a deferential step back. He came to the door and pressed his pudgy hands against the screen. He looked at Lizard with wide curious eyes. He was a bright yellow figure behind the mesh. He was like a bird or a butterfly. Lizard was surprised to see how small he was.

Miracle Boy pressed hard against the door. If it had not been latched, it would have opened and spilled him out onto the porch. He nodded eagerly at Lizard, shyly ducking his head. Lizard could not believe that Miracle Boy was happy to see him. Miracle Boy beckoned, crooking a finger at Lizard, and he was smiling, a strange small inward smile. Lizard did not move. In his head, he could hear his old man's voice, his long-gone old man, singing, accompanied by clattering percussion: the jigging wooden feet of the Limber Jack. Miracle Boy beckoned again, and this time Lizard took a single stumbling step forward. He held Miracle Boy's ruined shoes in front of him. He held them out before him like a gift.

T. Coraghessan Boyle

The Underground Gardens

From *The New Yorker*

But you do not know me if you think I am afraid.
—*Franz Kafka, "The Burrow."*

ALL HE KNEW, really, was digging. He dug to eat, to breathe, to live and sleep. He dug because the earth was there beneath his feet, and men paid him to move it. He dug because it was a sacrament, because it was honorable and holy. As a boy in Sicily, he had stood beside his brothers under the sun that was like a hammer and day after day stabbed his shovel into the skin of the ancient venerable earth of their father's orchards. As a young man in Boston and New York, he had burrowed like a rodent beneath streets and rivers, scouring the walls of subway tubes and aqueducts, dropping his pick, lifting his shovel, mining dirt. And now, twenty-six years old and with the deed to seventy bleak and hard-baked acres in his back pocket, he was in California. Digging.

FRIENDS! COME TO THE LAND OF FERTILITY WHERE THE SUN SHINES YEAR ROUND AND THE EARTH NEVER SUBMITS TO FROST! COME TO THE LAND THE ANGELS BLESSED! COME TO CALIFORNIA! WRITE NOW, c/o Euphrates Mead, Box 9, Fresno, California.

Yes, the land never froze, that was true and incontrovertible. But the sun scorched it till it was like stone, till it was as hard and impenetrable as the adobe brick the Indians and Mexicans piled up to make their shabby, dusty houses. This much Baldasare Forestiere discovered in the torporific summer of 1905, within days of disembarking from the train with his pick and shovel, his cardboard suitcase, and his meagre supply of dried pasta, flour, and beans. He'd come all the way across the country to redeem the land that would bloom with the serrate leaves and sweetly curling tendrils of his own grapes, the grapes of the Baldasare Forestiere Vineyards.

When he got down off the train, the air hot and sweet with the scent of things growing and multiplying, he was so filled with hope it was a kind of ecstasy. There were olive trees in California, orange and lemon and lime trees, spreading palms, fields of grapes and of cotton that had filled the rushing windows of the train with every kind of promise. No more sleet and snow for him, no more wet feet and overshoes or the grippe that took all the muscle out of your back and arms, but heat, good Sicilian heat, heat that baked you right down to the grateful marrow of your happy Sicilian bones.

The first thing he did was ask directions at the station, his English a labyrinth of looming verbs and truncated squawks that sounded strange in his ears but was serviceable for all that, and he soon found himself walking back in the direction he'd come, following the crucified grid of the tracks. Three miles south, then up a dry wash where two fire-scarred oaks came together like a pair of clasped arms—he couldn't miss it. At least, that was what the man on the platform had told him. He was a farmer, this man, unmistakably a farmer, in faded coveralls and a straw hat, long of nose and with two blue flecks for eyes in a blasted face. "That's where all the guineas are," he said. "That's where Mead sold 'em. Seventy acres, isn't it? That's what I figured. Same as the rest."

When he got there and set his cardboard suitcase in the dust, he couldn't help but pace off the whole seventy acres, the surveyor's map that Euphrates Mead had sent in the mail held out before him like a dowsing stick. The land was pale in a hundred shades of brown and a sere gray-green, and there was Russian thistle everywhere, the decayed thorny bones of it already crushed to chaff in his tracks. It crept down the open neck of his shirt and into his socks and shoes and the waist of his trousers, an itch of the land, abrasive and unforgiving. Overhead, vultures rose on the air currents like bits of winged ash. Lizards scuttered underfoot.

That night he ate sardines from a tin, licking the oil from his fingers and dipping soda crackers in the residue that collected in the corners, and then he spread a blanket under one of his new oak trees and slept as if he'd been knocked unconscious. In the morning he walked into town and bought a wheelbarrow. He filled the wheelbarrow with provisions and two five-gallon cans that had once held olive oil and now contained water—albeit an oleaginous and tinny-tasting variant of what he knew water to be. Then he hefted the twin handles of the new wheelbarrow till he felt the familiar flex of the muscles of his lower back, and he guided it all the long way back out to the future site of the Baldasare Forestiere Vineyards.

He'd always thought big, even when he was a boy wandering his father's orchards, the orchards that would never be his because of a simple confluence of biology and fate: his brothers had been born before him. If, God forbid, either Pietro or Domenico should die or emigrate to Argentina or Australia, there was always the other one to stand in his way. But Baldasare wasn't discouraged—he knew he was destined for greatness. Unlike his brothers, he had the gift of seeing things as they would one day be, of seeing himself in America, right here in Fresno, his seventy acres buried in grapes, the huge oak fermenting barrels rising above the cool cellar floors, his house of four rooms and a porch set on a hill and his wife on the porch, his four sons and three daughters sprinting like colts across the yard.

He didn't even stop to eat, that first day. Sweating until his eyes burned with the sting of salt, his hands molded to the shape of the wheelbarrow's polished handles, he made three more trips into town and back—twenty-four miles in all, and half of them pushing the overladen wheelbarrow. People saw him as they went about their business in carriages and farm wagons, a sun-seared little man in slept-in clothes following the tread of a single sagging tire along the shoulder of the broad dirt road. Even if he'd looked up, they probably wouldn't have nodded a greeting, but he never took his eyes off the unwavering line the tire cut in the dirt.

By the end of the week a one-room shanty stood beneath the oak, a place not much bigger than the bed he constructed of planks. It was a shelter, that was all, a space that separated him from the animals, that reminded him he was a man and not a beast. *Men are upright,* his father had told him when he was a boy, *and they have dominion over the beasts. Men live in houses, don't they? And where do the beasts live, mio figlio? In the ground, no? In a hole.*

It was some day of the following week when Baldasare began digging. (He didn't have a calendar and he didn't know Sunday from Monday, and, even if he had, where were the church and the priest to guide him?) He wanted the well to be right in front of the shack, beneath the tree where his house would one day stand, but he knew enough about water to know that it wouldn't be as easy as that. He spent a whole morning searching the immediate area, tracing dry watercourses, observing the way the hill under his shack and the one beside it abutted each other like the buttocks of a robust and fecund woman, until finally, right there, right in the cleft of the fundament, he pitched his shovel into the soil.

Two feet down he hit the hardpan. It didn't disconcert him, not at all—he never dreamed it would extend over all the seventy acres—and he attacked the rocky substrate with his pick until he was through it. As he dug deeper, he squared up the sides of his excavation with mortared rock and devised a pulley system to haul the buckets of superfluous earth clear of the hole. By the close of the second day, he needed a ladder. A week later, at fifty-two feet, he hit water, a pure sweet seep of it that got his shoes wet and climbed up the bottom rungs of his homemade ladder to a depth of four feet. And even as he set up the hand pump and exulted over the flow of shimmering water, he was contriving his irrigation system, his pipes, conduits, and channels, a water tank, a reservoir. Yes. And then, with trembling hands, he dug into the earth in the place where the first long row of canes would take root, and his new life, his life of disillusionment, began.

Three months later, when his savings had dwindled down to nothing, Baldasare became a laboring man all over again. He plowed another man's fields, planted another man's trees, dug irrigation channels and set grape canes for one stranger after another.

And on his own property, after those first few weeks of feverish activity, all he'd managed, after working the soil continuously and amending it with every scrap of leaf mold and bolus of chicken manure he could scrounge, was a vegetable garden so puny and circumscribed a housewife would have been ashamed of it. He'd dreamed of independence and what had he got but wage slavery all over again?

He was depressed. Gloomy. Brooding and morose. It wasn't so much Mr. Euphrates Mead who'd betrayed him as the earth, the earth itself. Plying his shovel, sweating in a long row of sweating men, he thought of suicide in all its gaudy and elaborate guises, his eyes closed forever on his worthless land and his worthless life. And then one rainy afternoon, sitting at the counter in Siagris's Drugstore with a cup of coffee and a hamburger sandwich, he had a vision that changed all that. The Vision was concrete, as palpable as flesh, and it moved with the grace and fluidity of a living woman, a woman he could almost reach out and . . . "Can I get you anything else?" she asked.

He was so surprised he answered her in Italian. Olive eyes, hair piled up on her head like a confection, skin you could eat with a spoon—but hadn't it been old Siagris, the hairy Greek, who'd fried his hamburger and set it down on the counter before him? Or was he dreaming?

She was giving him a look, a crease between her eyebrows, hands on hips. "What did you say?"

"I mean"—fumbling after his English—"no, no, thank you. But who, I mean?"

She was serene—a very model of serenity—though the other customers, men in suits, two boys and their mother lingering over ice cream, were watching her and quietly listening for her answer. "I'm Ariadne," she said. "Ariadne Siagris." She looked over her shoulder to the black-eyed man standing at the grill. "That's my uncle."

Baldasare was charmed—and a bit dazed, too. She was beautiful—or at least to his starved eyes she was—and he wanted to say something witty to her, something flirtatious, something that would let her know that he wasn't just another sorrowful Italian laborer with no more means or expectations than the price of the next hamburger sandwich but a man of substance, a landowner, the future proprietor of the Baldasare Forestiere Vineyards. But he couldn't think of anything, his mind had impacted, his tongue gone dead in the sleeve of his mouth. Then he felt his jaws opening of their own accord and heard himself saying, "Baldasare Forestiere, at your service."

He would always remember that moment, through all the digging and lifting and wheelbarrowing to come, because she looked hard at him, as if she could see right through to his bones, and then she turned up the corners of her mouth, pressed two fingers to her lips, and giggled.

That night, as he lay in his miserable bed in his miserable shack that was little more than a glorified chicken coop, he could think of nothing but her. Ariadne Siagris. She was the one. She was what he'd come to America for, and he spoke her name aloud as the rain beat at his crude roof and insinuated itself through a hundred slivers and cracks to drizzle down onto his already damp blankets, spoke her name aloud and made the solemnest pledge that she would one day be his bride. But it was cold, and the night beyond the walls was limitless and black, and his teeth were chattering so forcefully he could barely get the words out. He was mad, of course, and he knew it. How could he think he had a chance with her? What could he offer her, a girl like that who'd come all the way from Chicago, Illinois, to live with her uncle, the prosperous Greek—a school-educated girl used to fine things and books? Yes, he'd made inquiries—he'd done nothing but inquire since he'd left the drugstore that afternoon. Her parents were dead, killed at a railway crossing, and she was nineteen years old, with two younger sisters and three brothers, all of them farmed out to relatives. Ariadne. Ariadne Siagris.

The rain was relentless. It spoke and sighed and roared. He was wearing every stitch of clothing he possessed, wrapped in his blankets and huddled next to the coal-oil lamp, and still he froze, even here in California. It was an endless night, an insufferable night, but a night in which his mind was set free to roam the universe of his life, one thought piled atop another like bricks in a wall, until at some point, unaccountably, he was thinking of the tunnels he'd excavated in New York and Boston, how clean they were, how warm in winter and cool in summer, how they smelled, always, of the richness of the earth. Snow could be falling on the streets above, the gutters frozen, wind cutting into people's eyes, but below ground there was no weather, none at all. He thought about that, pictured it—the great arching tubes carved out of the earth and the locomotive with a train of cars standing there beneath the ground and all the passengers staring placidly out the windows—and then he was asleep.

The next morning, he began to dig again. The rain had gone, and the sun glistened like spilled oil over his seventy acres of mire and hardpan. He told himself he was digging a cellar—a proper cellar for the house he would one day build, because he hadn't given up, not yet, not Baldasare Forestiere—but even then, even as he spat on his hands and raised the pick above his head, he knew that there was more to it than that. The pick rose and fell, the shovel licked at the earth with all the probing intimacy of a tongue, and the wheelbarrow groaned under one load after another. Baldasare was digging. And he was happy, happier than he'd been since the day he stepped down from the train, because he was digging for her, for Ariadne.

But then the cellar was finished—a fine deep vaulted space in which he could not only stand erect, at his full height of five feet four inches, but thrust his right arm straight up over his head and still only just manage to touch the ceiling—and he found himself at a loss for what to do next. He could have squared up the corners and planed the walls with his spade till all the lines were rectilinear, but he didn't want that. That was the fashion of all the rooms he'd ever lived in, and as he scraped and smoothed and tamped he realized it didn't suit him. No, his cellar was dome-shaped, like the apse of the cathedral in which he'd worshipped as a boy, and its entrance was protected from the elements by a long broad ramp replete with gutters that drained into a small reflecting pool just outside the wooden door. And its roof, of course, was of hardpan, impervious to the rain and sun, and more durable than any shingle or tile.

He spent two days smoothing out the slope of the walls and

tidying and levelling the floor, working by the light of the coal-oil lamp while in the realm above the sky threw up a tatter of cloud and burned with a sun in the center of it till the next storm rolled in to snuff it out like a candle. When the rain came, it seemed like the most natural thing in the world to move his clothes and his bed and his homemade furniture down into the new cellar, which was snug and watertight. Besides, he reasoned, even as he fashioned himself a set of shelves and broke through the hardpan to run a stovepipe out into the circumambient air, what did he need a cellar for—a strict cellar, that is—if he couldn't grow the onions, apples, potatoes, and carrots to store in it?

Once the stove was installed and had baked all the moisture out of the place, he lay on the hard planks of his bed through a long rainy afternoon, smoking one cigarette after another and thinking about what his father had said—about the animals and how they lived in the ground, in holes. His father was a wise man. A man of character and substance. But he wasn't in California and he wasn't in love with Ariadne Siagris and he didn't have to live in a shack the pigeons would have rejected. It took him a while, but the conclusion Baldasare finally reached was that he was no animal—he was practical, that was all—and he barely surprised himself when he got up from the bed, fetched his shovel, and began to chip away at the east wall of his cellar. He could already see a hallway there, a broad grand hallway, straight as a plumb line and as graceful and sensible as the arches the Romans of antiquity put to such good use in their time. And beyond that, as the dirt began to fall and the wheelbarrow shuddered to receive it, he saw a kitchen and bedroom opening onto an atrium, he saw grape and wisteria vines snaking toward the light, camellias, ferns, and impatiens overflowing clay pots and baskets—and set firmly in the soil, twenty feet below the surface, an avocado tree, as heavy with fruit as any peddler's cart.

The winter wore on. There wasn't much hired work this time of year—the grapes had been picked and pressed, the vines cut back, the fig trees pruned, and the winter crops were in the ground. Baldasare had plenty of time on his hands. He wasn't idle—he just kept right on digging—nor was he destitute. Modest in his needs and frugal by habit, he'd saved practically everything he'd earned through the summer and fall, mending his own clothes, eating little more than boiled eggs and pasta, using his seventy acres as a place to trap rabbits and songbirds and to gather wood for his stove. His one indulgence was tobacco—that, and a weekly hamburger sandwich at Siagris's Drugstore.

Chewing, sipping coffee, smoking, he studied his future bride there, as keen as any scholar intent on his one true subject. He made little speeches to her in his head, casual remarks he practiced over and over till he got them right—or thought he did, anyway. Lingering over his coffee after cleaning the plate of crumbs with a dampened forefinger, he would wait till she came near with a glass or washcloth in hand, and he would blurt, "One thinks the weather will change, is that not true?" Or, "This is the most best sandwich of hamburger my mouth will ever receive." And she? She would show her teeth in a little equine smile, or she would giggle, then sometimes sneeze, covering her nose and mouth with one hand, as her late mother had no doubt taught her to do. All the while, Baldasare feasted on the sight of her. Sometimes he would sit there at the counter for two or three hours, until Siagris the Greek made an impatient remark, and he would rise in confusion, his face suffused with blood, bowing and apologizing, until he found his way to the door.

It was during this time of close scrutiny that he began to detect certain small imperfections in his bride-to-be. Despite her education, for instance, she seemed to have inordinate difficulty making change or reading the menu off the chalkboard on the wall behind her. She'd begun to put on weight, too, picking at bits of doughnut or fried potatoes the customers left on their plates. If she'd been substantial when Baldasare first laid eyes on her, she was much more than that now—stout, actually. As stout as Signora Cardino back home in Messina, who was said to drink olive oil instead of wine and to breakfast on sugared cream and cake. And then there were her eyes—or, rather, her right eye. It had a cast in it, and how he'd missed that on the day he was first smitten he couldn't say. But he had to look twice to notice the hairs on her chin—as stiff as a cat's whiskers and just as translucent—and, as far as he was concerned, the red blotches that had begun to appear on the perfect skin of her hands and throat might have been nothing more than odd splashes of marinara sauce, as if she'd got too close to the pot.

Another lover, less blinded by the light of certitude than Baldasare, might have found these blemishes a liability, but Baldasare treasured them. They were part of her, part of that quiddity that made her unique among women. He watched with satisfaction as her hips and buttocks swelled, so that even at nineteen she walked with a waddle, looked on with a soaring heart as the blotches spread from her throat to her cheeks and brow, and her right eye stared out of her head, across the room and out the window, surer each day that she was his. After all, who else would see in her what he saw and love her the way he did? Who but Baldasare Forestiere would come forward to declare himself? And he would declare himself soon—as soon as he finished digging.

Two years passed. He worked for other men and saved every cent of his wages, worse than any miser, and in his free time he dug. When he completed a passage or a room or carved his way to the sky for light, he could already see the next passage and the next room beyond that. He had a vision, yes, and he had Ariadne to think of, but even so he wasn't the sort to sit around idle. He didn't have the gift of letters, he didn't play violin or mouth organ, and he rarely visited his neighbors. The vaudeville theatre was a long way off, too far to walk, and he only went there once, with Lucca Albanese, a vineyard worker with whom he'd struck up a friendship. There were comedians and jugglers and pretty women dancing like birds in flight, but all the while he was regretting the fifteen-cent admission, and he never went back. No, he stayed home with his shovel and his vision, and many days he didn't know morning from night.

Saturdays, though, he kept sacred. Saturday was the day he walked the three miles to Siagris's Drugstore, through winter rains and summer heat that reached a hundred and sixteen degrees Fahrenheit. He prided himself on his constancy, and he was pleased to think that Ariadne looked forward to his weekly visits as much as he did. His place at the end of the counter was always vacant, as if reserved for him, and he relished the little smiles with which she greeted him and the sweet flow of familiar phrases that dropped so easily from her supple American lips: "So how've you been?" "Nice day." "Think it's coming on to rain?"

As time went on they became increasingly intimate. She told him of her uncle's back pain, the illness of her cat, her older brother's ascension to assistant floor supervisor at the Chicago Iron Works, and he told her of his ranch and of the spaciousness of his living quarters. "Twelve room," he said. "Twelve room, and all to myself." And then came the day when he asked her, in his runaway English, if she would come with him to the ranch for a picnic. "But not just the picnic," he said, "but also the scene, how do you say, the scene of the place, and my, my house, because I want—I need—you see, I . . ."

She was leaning over the counter, splotchy and huge. Her weight had stabilized in the past year—she'd reached her full growth, finally, at the age of twenty-one—and she floated above her feet like one of the airships the Germans so prized. "Yes," she said, and she giggled and sneezed. "I'd love to."

The following Sunday he came for her, lightly ascending the sun-bleached steps to the walkup above the drugstore where she lived with her uncle and aunt and their five children. It was a hot September morning, all of Fresno and the broad dusty valley beyond held in the grip of something stupendous, a blast of air so sere and scorching you would have thought the whole world was a pizza oven with the door open wide. Siagris the Greek answered his knock. He was in his shirtsleeves, and the sweat had made a washcloth of his garments, the white field of his shirt stuck like a postage stamp to the bulge of his belly. He didn't smile, but he didn't look displeased, either, and Baldasare understood the look: Siagris didn't like him, not one bit, and in other circumstances might have gone out of his way to squash him like a bug, but then he had a niece who took up space and ate like six nieces, and Baldasare could just maybe deliver him from that. "Come in," he said, and there was Baldasare, the cave dweller, in a room in a house two stories above the ground.

Up here, inside, it was even hotter. The Siagris children lay about like swatted flies, and Mrs. Siagris, her hair like some wild beast clawing at her scalp, poked her head around the corner from the kitchen. It was too hot to smile, so she grimaced instead and pulled her head back out of sight. And then, in the midst of this suffocating scene, the voice of a ventriloquist cried out, "He's here," and Ariadne appeared in the hallway.

She was all in white, with a hat the size of a tabletop perched on the mighty pile of her hair. He was melting already, in the heat, but when she focussed her wild eye on him and turned up her lips in the shyest of smiles, he melted a little more.

Outside, in the street, she gave him her arm, which was something of a problem, because she was so much taller, and he had to reach up awkwardly to take it. He was wearing his best suit of clothes, washed just the evening before, and the unfamiliar jacket clung to him like dead skin while the new celluloid collar gouged at his neck and the tie threatened to throttle him. They managed to walk the better part of a block before she put her feet together and came to a halt. "Where's your carriage?" she asked.

Carriage? Baldasare was puzzled. He didn't have a carriage—he didn't even have a horse. "I no got," he said, and he strained to give her his best smile. "We walk."

"Walk?" she echoed. "In this heat? You must be crazy."

"No," he said, "we walk," and he leaned forward and exerted the most delicate but insistent pressure on the monument of her arrested arm.

Her cheeks were splotched under the crisp arc of shadow the hatbrim threw over her face and her olive eyes seemed to snatch at his. "You mean," and her voice was scolding and intemperate, "you ain't even got a wagon? You with your big house you're always telling me about?"

The following Sunday, though it wounded him to throw his money away like some Park Avenue millionaire, he pulled up to Siagris's Drugstore in a hired cabriolet. It was a clear day, the sun high and merciless, and the same scenario played itself out in the walkup at the top of the stairs, except that this time Baldasare seemed to have things in hand. He was as short with Siagris as Siagris was with him, and he led Ariadne (who had refused the previous week to go farther than a bench in the park at the end of

the street) out the door, down the steps, and into the carriage like a
cavaliere of old.

Baldasare didn't like horses. They were big and crude and expensive and they always seemed to need grooming, shoeing, doctoring,
and oats, and the horse attached to the cabriolet was no exception. It
was a stupid, flatulent, broad-flanked, mouse-colored thing, and it
did its utmost to resist every touch of the reins and thwart every
desire of the man wielding them. Baldasare was in a sweat by the
time they reached his property, every square inch of his clothing
soaked through like a blotter, and his nerves were frayed raw. Nor
had he made any attempt at conversation during the drive, so riveted was he on the task at hand, and when they finally pulled up in
the shade of his favorite oak he turned to Ariadne and saw that she
hadn't exactly enjoyed the ride, either.

Her hat was askew, her mouth set in a thin unyielding line. She
was glistening with sweat, her hands like doughballs fried in lard,
and a thin integument of moistened dust clung to her features. She
gave him a concentrated frown. "Well, where is it?" she demanded.
"Why are we stopping here?"

His tongue ran ahead of him, even as he sprang down from the
carriage and scurried to her side to help her to alight. "This is what
I have want for to show you, and so long, because—well, because I
am making it for you."

He studied the expression of her face as she looked from the
disreputable shack to the hummock of the well and out over the
heat-blasted scrub to where the crown of his avocado tree rose
from the ground like an illusion. And then she saw the ramp
leading down to the cellar. She was stunned, he could see it in
her face and there was no denying it, but he watched her struggle to try on a smile and focus her eyes on his. "This is a prank,
ain't it? You're just fooling with me and your house is really over
there behind that hill"—pointing now from her perch atop the
carriage—"ain't it?"

"No, no," he said, "no. It's this, you see?" And he indicated the
ramp, the crown of the avocado, the bump where the inverted cone
of a new atrium broke the surface. "Twelve room, I tell you, twelve
room." He'd become insistent, and he had his hand on her arm,

trying to lead her down from the carriage—if only she would come, if only she would see—and he wanted to tell her how cool and fresh-smelling it was down there beneath the earth, and how cheap it was to build and expand, to construct a nursery, a sewing room, anything she wanted. All it took was a strong back and a shovel, and not one cent wasted on nails and lumber and shingles that fell apart after five years in the sun. He wanted to tell her, but the words wouldn't come, and he tried to articulate it all through the pressure of his hand on her arm, tugging, as if the whole world depended on her getting down from that carriage—and it did, it did!

"Let go!" she cried, snatching her arm away, and then she was sobbing, gasping for breath as if the superheated air were some other medium altogether and she were choking on it. "You said . . . *twelve rooms!*"

He tried to reach for her again—"Please," he begged, "please"— but she jerked back from him so violently the carriage nearly buckled on its springs. Her face was furious, streaked with tears and dirt. "You bully!" she cried. "You guinea, dago, wop! You're no better than a murderer!"

Three days later, in a single paragraph set off by a black border, the local paper announced her engagement to Hiram Broadbent, of Broadbent's Poultry & Eggs.

As engagement wasn't a marriage, that's what Baldasare was thinking when Lucca Albanese gave him the news. An engagement could be broken, like a promise or even a contract. There was hope yet, there had to be. "Who is this Hiram Broadbent?" he demanded.

They were sharing a meal of beans and vermicelli in Baldasare's subterranean kitchen, speaking in a low tragic Italian. Lucca had just read the announcement to him, the sharp-edged English words shearing at him like scissors and the pasta turning to cotton wadding in his throat. He was going to choke. He was going to vomit.

"Big, fat man," Lucca said. "Wears a straw hat winter and summer. He's a drunk, mean as the devil, but his father owns a chicken farm that supplies all the eggs for the local markets in Fresno, so he's always got money in his pocket. Hell, if you ever came out of your hole, you'd know who I'm talking about."

"You don't think—I mean, Ariadne wouldn't really . . . would she?"

Lucca ducked his head and worked his spoon in the plate. "You know what my father used to say when I was a boy in Catania?"

"What?"

"There're plenty of fish in the sea."

But that didn't matter to Baldasare—he wanted only one fish. Ariadne. Why had he been digging, if not for her? He'd created an underground palace, with the smoothest of corners and the most elegant turnings and capacious courtyards, just to give her space, to give her all the room she could want after having to live at her uncle's mercy in that cramped walkup over the drugstore. Didn't she complain about it all the time? If only she knew, if only she'd give him a chance and descend just once into the cool of the earth, he was sure she'd change her mind—she had to.

There was a problem, though. An insurmountable problem. She wouldn't see him. He came into the drugstore, hoping to make it all up to her, to convince her that he was the one, the only one, and she backed away from the counter, muttered a word to her uncle, and melted away through the sunstruck mouth of the back door. Siagris whirled around like an animal startled in a cave, his shoulders hunched and his head held low. "We don't want you in here anymore, understand?" he said. There was the sizzle of frying, the smell of onions, tuna fish, a row of surprised white faces staring up from pie and coffee. Siagris leaned into the counter and made his face as ugly as he could. *"Capisce?"*

Baldasare Forestiere was not a man to be easily discouraged. He thought of sending her a letter, but he'd never learned to write, and the idea of having someone write it for him filled him with shame. For the next few days he brooded over the problem, working all the while as a hired laborer, shovelling, lifting, pulling, bending, and as his body went through the familiar motions his mind was set free to achieve a sweated lucidity. By the end of the third day, he'd decided what to do.

That night, under cover of darkness, he pushed his wheelbarrow into town along the highway and found his way to the vacant lot behind the drugstore. Then he started digging. All night, as the constellations drifted in the immensity overhead until one by one they fled the sky, Baldasare plied his shovel, his pick, and his rake. By morning, at first light, the outline of his message was clearly visible from the second-story window of the walkup above the store. It was a heart, a valentine, a perfectly proportioned symbol of his love dug three feet deep in the ground and curving gracefully over the full area of what must have been a quarter-acre lot.

When the outline was finished, Baldasare started on the interior. In his mind's eye, he saw a heart-shaped crater there in the lot, six feet deep at least, with walls as smooth as cement, a hole that would show Ariadne the depth of the vacancy she'd left in him. He was coming up the ramp he'd shaped of earth with a full wheelbarrow to spread over the corners of the lot, when he glanced up to see Siagris and two of his children standing there peering down at him. Siagris's hands were on his hips. He looked more incredulous than anything else. "What in Christ's name do you think you're doing?" he sputtered.

Baldasare, swinging wide with his load of dirt so that Siagris and the children had to take a quick step back, didn't even hesitate. He just kept going to a point in the upper corner of the frame where he was dumping and raking out the dirt. "Digging," he said over his shoulder.

"But you can't. This is private property. You can't just dig up people's yards, don't you know that? Eh? Don't you know anything?"

Baldasare didn't want a confrontation. He was a decent man, mild and pacifistic, but he was determined, too. As he came by again with the empty wheelbarrow and eased it down the ramp, he said, "Tell her to look. She is the one. For her I do this."

After that, he was deaf to all pleas, threats, and remonstrations, patiently digging, shoring up his walls, spreading his dirt. The sun climbed in the sky. He stopped only to take an occasional drink from a jug of water or to sit on his overturned wheelbarrow and silently eat a sandwich from a store of them wrapped in butcher's paper. He worked through the day, tireless, and though the sheriff came and threatened him, even the sheriff couldn't say with any certainty who owned the lot Baldasare was defacing—couldn't say, that is, without checking the records down at the courthouse, which he was going to do first thing in the morning, Baldasare could be sure of that.

It began to get dark. Baldasare had cleared the entire cutout of his heart to a depth of three feet, and he wasn't even close to quitting. Six feet, he was thinking, that's what it would take, and who could blame him if he kept glancing up at the unrevealing window of the apartment atop the drugstore in the hope of catching a glimpse of his inamorata there? If she was watching, if she knew what he was doing for love of her, if she saw the lean muscles of his arms strain and his back flex, she gave no sign of it. Undeterred, Baldasare dug on.

And then there came a moment, and it must have been past midnight, the neighborhood as silent as the grave and Baldasare working by the light of a waxing moon, when two men appeared at the northern edge of the excavation, right where the lobes of the heart came together in an elegant loop. "Hey, wop," one of them yelled down to where Baldasare stood. "I don't know who you think you are, but you're embarrassing my fiancée, and I mean to put an end to it."

The man's shadow under that cold moon was immense—it could have been the shadow of a bear or a buffalo. The other shadow was thinner, but broad across the shoulders—where it counted—and it danced on shadowy feet. There was no sound but the slice of Baldasare's shovel and the slap of the dirt as it dropped into the wheelbarrow.

He was a small man, Baldasare, but the hundreds of tons of dirt he'd moved in his lifetime had made iron of his limbs, and when they fell on him he fought like a man twice his size. Still, the odds were against him, and Hiram Broadbent, fuelled by good Kentucky bourbon and with the timely assistance of Calvin Thompson, a farrier and amateur boxer, was able to beat him to the ground. And, once he was down, Broadbent and Thompson kicked him with their heavy boots until he stirred no more.

When Baldasare was released from the hospital, he was a changed man—or at least to the degree that the image of Ariadne Siagris no longer infested his brain. He went back home and sat in a bentwood rocker and stared at the sculpted dirt walls of the kitchen, which gave onto the atrium and the striated trunk of its lone avocado tree. His right arm was in a sling, with a cast on it from the elbow down, and he was bound up beneath his shirt like an Egyptian mummy with all the tape it took to keep his cracked ribs in place. After a week or so—his mourning period, as he later referred to it—he found himself one evening in the last and deepest of his rooms, the one at the end of the passage that led to the new atrium, where he was thinking of planting a lemon tree or maybe a quince. It was preternaturally quiet. The earth seemed to breathe with and for him.

And then suddenly he began to see things, all sorts of things—a rush of raw design and finished image that flickered across the wall before him like one of Edison's moving pictures. What he saw was a seventy-acre underground warren that beckoned him on, a maze like no other, with fishponds and gardens open to the sky above, and more, much more—a gift shop and an Italian restaurant with views of subterranean grottoes and a lot for parking the carriages and automobiles of the patrons who would flock there to see what he'd accomplished in his time on earth. It was a complete vision, more eloquent than any set of blueprints or elevations, and it staggered him. He was a young man still, healing by the day, and while he had a long way to go, at least now he knew where he was going. *Baldasare Forestiere*'s *Underground Gardens,* he said to himself, trying out the name, and then he said it aloud: "Baldasare Forestiere's Underground Gardens."

Standing there in the everlasting silence beneath the earth, he reached out a hand to the wall in front of him, his left hand, pronating the palm as if to bless some holy place. And then, awkwardly at first, but with increasing grace and agility, he began to dig.

Kiana Davenport

Fork Used in Eating Reverend Baker

From *Story*

MONTHS LATER, when armed soldiers patrolled the streets, she would remember the omens. A fire walker with steel rods through his cheeks had predicted the year would end in disaster, the islands would be laid waste by a curse. Educated Fijians had laughed at his prediction, shrugging off the odd cyclone and shark attack.

Their country was the showpiece of the South Pacific, leader of independent island nations, with the highest standard of living. Still, uncommon things began to occur. French tourists were killed by a pack of wild dogs, a teenage girl grew horns. On the north shore of Viti Levu, Fiji's principal island, three infants disappeared from their cribs.

In that early spring of 1987, in Suva, capital city of Fiji, Annabel Koro and her cousin, Jemese, often dined together at Draughts, a club for local professionals that increasingly drew foreigners. One night, candlelight glancing in spurts off her dark, glowing shoulders, Annabel leaned in toward her friends.

"There's a Hindi who owns curry stands near Queen's Road. Yet I see him and his family at the symphony, the museum, the tennis club."

It unsettled her, the notion that this person whom she regarded as the "curry man" was visible in her life on more important planes.

"Hindi dogs who can't remember their place." Jemese was refer-
ring to that era when Indians, first imported by the Brits as inden-
tured labor to Fiji, were called *coolies, Koli* meaning "dog" in Fijian.

"They've already taken over banking and business," Annabel
said. "If the Labour Party wins the elections, we'll be second citizens
in our own country. Granted, the party is the champion of the poor,
and it would be good for the economy. But it will be bad for native
Fijians if Indians get power."

"No matter, we will still own the land," Jemese promised. "And
we *Taukei* will show how *land* is more important than capital."

The ultra-nationalist *Taukei* movement—with a goal of "racially
pure" Fiji purged of Indian influence—was steadily growing.

"If you remember clearly," Annabel said, *"land* is what cut off my
education. And my life."

Years back, in the bamboo forests of Nubutautau, she and Jemese
had been the chosen. Privileged grandchildren of an important
chief, they were sent to boarding school in New Zealand, then on to
university, the boy to Australia where lizards walked upright like
men, the girl to California.

After earning his degree, Jemese came home to practice law and,
engaged in a corporate-fraud case, splintered the nose of the white
defense counsel who called him "nigger." He kept swinging at
whites for several years until he was disbarred. Now he had set up a
paralegal business, counseling locals on land rights and taxes. Other
than that, occasional visits home to his children and wife in
Nubutautau. Occasional prostitutes. Mostly, he stayed alone.

Annabel earned a degree from Stanford and completed a year of
medical school. In her second year, her mother had suddenly died
and, summoned home by her grandfather, the girl was told their
land-owning clan needed more heirs. A marriage was arranged. On
her wedding day, Annabel looked at her husband, thinking *This is
where my life ends.* Now she was divorced, a biology professor at the
local university, while her daughter studied medicine abroad.

Conversation at the table slowly changed hands. A woman
laughed, nipples pressed against her shirt. Annabel saw through the
eyes of the men they thought the woman beautiful. Annabel's skin
was lighter, but she was ten years older. At forty-four, her face was

still lovely, lips voluptuous, the top lip upturned like a girl. She moved with wild grace, drawing men's glances. But her breasts were beginning to sag, and at night her ankles swelled. It had been three years since her last lover.

From the clutch of foreigners in the bar, a powerfully built man with blue-black skin stared at her. He was wearing a safari suit, a black man's version of a white man in the tropics, the suit so immaculate and crisp, it could have stood there by itself. He smiled, confusing her. He must have been forty, he could have been thirty, but something about him lacked youth. He sent over a round of drinks, moving forward cautiously.

"You're the only lively group in this place!" His voice a basso profundo. "May I join you?"

Jemese stiffened like an animal sensing danger. The man was so massive, yet his manner so relaxed, Jemese found himself intrigued. His name was Numan Shaki, just arrived from British Columbia, part of a design and engineering group completing a $50 million wood-processing plant up toward Lautoka. The trees would come from foothills of the highlands, near Annabel and Jemese's village.

"I've heard of Nubutautau." Numan grinned. "Your people ate missionaries."

"With good reason," Jemese said. "They tried to clothe our women! Actually, it was necessary to eat wild spinach with those chaps. Something about white flesh that constipates."

People laughed, but Annabel spoke earnestly. "We're quite proud of that history. We only resent it when people say our ancestors ate missionaries' *shoes* as well. In the Fiji Museum, you'll see the fork my people used to eat Reverend Baker."

"Perhaps you can take me there," he said.

Next day Numan rang Annabel's flat, inviting her to dinner. At New Peking Restaurant, she explained how Fijians called wonton "short soup" and noodles "long soup."

"And missionaries, 'long pig,' " he joked.

Numan was South African, from Umtata, in the Transkei. After university in England, he had stowed away on a ship to Tangiers.

"My father expected me to become the president of South Africa. But I decided to see the world."

His engineering firm, he said, now sent him to places like South Yemen, Central America. During dinner he taught her the word for meat in seven languages, and nine Dutch words for cleanliness. Watching his huge, graceful hands against white linen, Annabel wondered why he had chosen her. There were younger and prettier women in Suva. There were the prostitutes at the Dragon, and Man Friday's, desperate things who made love in alleys bent over garbage cans.

After dinner, she gave him tea and sent him away. The second night he stayed. Watching her brown skin grow pale against his blue-blackness, Annabel wondered again why he was with her. Later, she watched him sleep with his eyes open, as if they were painted on his head.

Despite a faint lime cologne, his sweat had a scent that would stiffen hair on a hunting dog's back, different from the sweet, salty smell of Fijians. A potent, tigerish smell that made her want him again and again. He woke turning to her, her groans exciting him, like the groans of banana trees as sap is forced into the fruit. When he was gone, she remembered him as a trick figure hidden in a dream.

Convulsed as it was with traffic, the city made Numan tense. On weekends they drove off to humid little villages with ancient hotels, mildewed furnishings, natives hanging agog in the windows. Yet Numan showed an inordinate interest in each place—the view, the facilities, and number of rooms. This puzzled Annabel, then she dismissed it as they tossed and snuffled on musty, Victorian beds.

One night, north of Nadi, they found a seedy bordello of an inn called Maugham's. Half-bald parrots in oxidizing cages, a barman sneezing blood, hookers draped over what had been a conscious man. They seemed to be biting hunks of his flesh as they slid off his neck chains and rings with their teeth. Over the bar a sign warned: IN CASE FIRE GO LEFT GO RIGHT. IF BURN, NO INSURE. In a corner, spiderwebs hugged an old Steinway that still had miraculous tone. Numan sat down and ceremoniously flexed his fingers, dredging up old sentimentals: "Star Dust," "Deep Purple," "Ruby." He played so well, even the hookers were silent.

Months later, Annabel would remember that night, a decrepit

hotel, Numan lulling young whores to sleep with his playing. She would remember it so specifically because, watching his fingers brush scorched, ivory keys, it occurred to her that she had never seen him truly relaxed, that they seldom had real conversations. She had a sense of a man holding back information.

Numan seemed curious about her cousin, Jemese, a handsome man in an injured way: mahogany skin, crinkly hair, eyes with a sadness that stood its ground. Annabel described him as smart, possibly brilliant, but his temper had stood in the way of success. Trying to rebuild his credibility and someday enter Parliament, Jemese had won the position of clerk to the Senate, assistant to the House of Representatives. He was also made trustee of the keys to the Parliament building, overseeing crowds in the spectators' gallery when Parliament was in session.

Hearing this, Numan asked Jemese to give them a tour of the Parliament chamber, panelled with woods from all over the Pacific. One day when Parliament was not in session, Jemese led them into the chamber, vast as a church.

"The woods here are symbolic," he said. "One kind of wood from almost every country in the Commonwealth."

The Speaker's chair was Indian teak, the desk, English oak. The members' benches, Fijian *yaka.* They studied a huge horseshoe table, the surface a golden wood shot with dark streaks. The dispatch boxes were New Zealand *kauri,* the division-glass stand, Australian mahogany.

"I find wood soothing," Numan whispered. "So tranquil."

The soft glow emanating from benches and walls made Annabel yawn. She watched Numan move almost dreamily through the chamber, stroking tables, hands sliding up and down doors and walls.

Later, sipping Fiji Bitters at Draughts, he kept pulling the conversation back to the chamber: how many spectators it held, how many doors, exits, and entrances.

"Your cousin's overqualified for that job. Why, precisely, is he there?"

She told of Jemese being disbarred. "In Australia, he was exposed to brutal racism. It's here too, of course. We look down on the

Indians, they look down on us. It's a kind of symbiosis between the cultures, we've been living together for so long. Of course, whites look down on *all* of us. That was Jemese's problem. He couldn't follow the drill."

In early April, she and Jemese went home to Nubutautau to counsel elders on Fiji's coming national elections. Some natives felt the present government had grown corrupt, that the opposing Labor Party would vastly improve the economy. Driving halfway round the island, they maneuvered paved roads that turned to gravel, spiraling up into cool, jungled mountains, where gravel turned to dirt. Near sundown, they left Jemese's car in a clearing and, in amber light, began the long hike to their village.

Deep in the jungle interior, they struggled through mud and vine toward the Sigatoka River, then up a steep ridge of spear grass and slippery ravines. Green became a denser green. This jungle was older, thicker, bounding them in leathery umbrellas of the prehistoric *balabala* and bamboo trees forty feet high. Large, green, crested iguanas blinked slowly, recording their passing. Overhead, gaudy parrots flew in pairs.

In a sudden plain of windswept grasses stood a grouping of traditional thatched pyramids. Nubutautau. Her village looked so small, Annabel felt she could hold it in her hand. Yet her umbilical cord was buried in this soil. Here was genesis, geological calm. The subtle irritation of torches through trees, her clan running to meet them, shouting *Bula! Bula!* the greeting of good health, good life. They crowded round, kissing the cousins Fiji-style by sniffing their faces. Ancient women danced to and fro, distended earlobes dangling like dark taffy down the sides of their heads, weighted with bamboo cylinders holding tobacco and talismans.

Elders shouted tongue-storms of welcome, leading them to the house of their grandfather, chief of their clan. Bending at the waist, calling *Tama, Tama,* the greeting of respect, Annabel and Jemese presented him with *yaqona,* pepper roots, from which the narcotic, ceremonial drink *kava* was made. The family sat cross-legged on mats, the chief made a welcoming speech. The preparation and drinking of *kava* began.

During the welcoming feast of a full-grown pig, Annabel looked affectionately at her clan women, wooden forks absent-mindedly stuck in their bushy hair while they ate with their fingers, bare feet calloused so thick they struck matches against them. Most women were missing front teeth, where husbands had punched them. Drunk on *kava,* Jemese began teasing Annabel about dating a foreigner. People abruptly stopped eating; they seemed to stop breathing.

Her grandfather stared at her. "Our kind not good enough? You choose pale skin?"

Annabel laughed. "Grandfather, he's South African, black as coal! An engineer at Lautoka Mill."

Grandfather shook his head, snowy from the drizzle of years. "Still, a stranger. This is not our way."

It was *her* way, a way she had chosen long ago, divorcing her husband, sending her daughter off to England to study. Her grandfather felt the girl should have stayed home, married, borne children. He had made a grave mistake in educating Annabel. He wondered how the gods would make him pay.

That night in her father's house, she sank into a cocoon of woven blankets. Cool jungle drafts and smoke of cooking fires sifted through her dreams. Years ago when she left this place, she was a girl who knew how to kill and skin small game without scoring the pelts. At boarding school in New Zealand, Annabel wore her first pair of shoes. She learned to use a telephone. And, to survive far from blood she could trust, she became many-selved. One of those selves was a girl who could no longer recite her descent line, forgot her jungle hiding-and-hunting skills, learned how to lighten her skin with rice talcum. Another self lied, denying her cannibal history, denying her grandmother sewed with needles of human bone.

Years later, when she returned from Stanford, she came home to her people a miracle. But somewhere in the breaking out and sailing forth, her many selves had begot other selves. Her mother was dead, she was a different person, and so she came home and mourned for two.

Annabel lay dreaming of Numan Shaki and woke with her cheek burning, the sensation of having been slapped. Through the window, she saw the green ghost of her mother running barefoot up a tree. Born on a night of red lightning, the woman had possessed double *mana,* able to forecast droughts and tidal waves by reading melted-down animal fats. She once drove a thief to suicide by urinating in his footprint. Stalked by the dead man's tribe, she had been poisoned to death.

But some nights Annabel's father was seen dancing with his wife in moonlight. Afterward he recalled nothing, but he carried a green and guilty smell. Now Annabel fell into another dream. Her mother rubbing the head of Numan Shaki with saliva of wild boar, an old cure for malignance and evil. Outside, the moan of the forest was a dirge.

She and Jemese spent a week addressing elders on the coming elections. They spoke in support of Prime Minister Mara, a native Fijian, the prime minister since 1970, when Fiji won its independence. Oxford-educated, a Western sympathizer, Mara was known as a pawn of the superpowers, as having grown rich and corrupt while Fiji's economy sagged. Still, Jemese warned, if the opposition Labor Party won, the country would fall into the hands of Indian "opportunists and radicals." They would welcome trade with the Russians, they would steal Fijian lands! Elders listened like children, for Jemese was thought to possess almost as much wisdom as their chief, whose title he would inherit. They followed behind him, touching objects he had touched.

On the drive back to Suva, Annabel brooded on Numan Shaki, wondering what her mother had tried to tell her in the dream. She had slept with him for weeks, and one night she had asked him what he thought of love.

His voice had been gentle, but his words jumped out and bit her. "I'm not the man for you. After some of the things I've seen, normal life seems bloody *silly.* Anyway, one day soon I shall leave."

Still, she didn't stop with him. He seemed to represent a part of her she could not come to terms with.

Now Jemese glanced at her, reading her mind. "You'll be sensible, won't you? You won't get carried away."

"I am carried away. I *want* to be carried away."

"Annabel, stick to your own kind. Men you can trust."

"Like my ex-husband? I was nothing to him, a maid he could sleep with and punch about."

"Rubbish!" He shifted gears impatiently. "You insulted your husband, he bored you. All local men bore you. You should have stayed in America, all that challenge and aggression."

She thought of the oppressiveness of American cities. "I didn't want to stay. I just wanted a medical degree, a *future*. There are so few things I have ever really wanted. And what about *you,* and your prostitutes? You hardly visit your wife and children. Do they mean so little to you?"

He slowed down, keeping his eyes straight ahead. "Some sins we commit . . . so we won't commit others."

She thought of the years he had guided her through crowded rooms and stood at her side, gently touching the small of her back. The hopeless valor with which he had tried to shield her from the world. Quite possibly, Jemese was the only man who had ever truly loved her.

He reached across for her hand. "Look. Numan seems a decent sort, but he's a transient. They pass through the islands like frigate birds. Anyway . . . there's something about him that makes me uneasy."

On Election Day, Timoci Bavadra, Indian leader of the leftist Labour Party, defeated Mara, becoming Fiji's new prime minister. The nation erupted in violence. Government buildings were firebombed. Leftist students holding victory parades were attacked and viciously beaten. Fumes of melting tires from incinerated cars left people blinded, groping on their knees. Indian women were dragged from their homes, handcuffed to trees, and gang-raped, their vocal cords slashed.

In the chaos, packs of wild dogs, like rivers of fur, swarmed into graveyards, exhuming fresh corpses. Their coats grew shiny from the diet of human bones until soldiers ambushed them with grenades. The city became a minefield of concrete and metal fragments, dog parts, mounds of congealed blood the soil refused.

Disheveled and drunk, Jemese took the floor at Draughts. "It's over for us, Bavadra will hand us to the Soviets on a plate! He's already offered them fishing rights in our waters. Next, they'll level our forests for wood chips."

A Bavadra supporter challenged him. "It's either the Russians or the Yanks. When the U.S. is kicked out of the Philippines, they'll need new military bases. We'll end up like Manila, whorehouse of the Pacific!"

Numan Shaki stood and spoke out with disdain. "You people amaze me with your precious ideals. I've seen people dying in the thousands, crawling over their young for water, a piece of bread. *Hundreds* of thousands. You sit here in perfect health." He shook his head, disgusted. "What's the difference, Soviets or Yanks, as long as your children don't starve to death."

Next day Annabel maneuvered through streets patrolled by armed soldiers and sat on a beach, watching Jemese teach his pet mongoose to play dead. Smoke curling up the sky, they listened to sirens in the distance.

"I think it's finished with Numan."

"Good. You had nothing in common but lust."

"Don't be so clever and cynical. I'm over forty. I'm alone!"

"Annabel. We're *all* alone." Jemese took her gently by the shoulders. "I'm going back to Nubutautau. There I have pride. I am useful."

She sobbed like a child. *"Isi,* Jemese, *isi.* What will become of me without you?"

"Come home," he said. "Teach our women to stand up, to have opinions. Give them a voice of their own."

His wife and children were in Nubutautau. She traced his jawline with her finger, shaking her head no.

Jemese hugged her, and openly wept. *"Isalei,* Annabel."

Two days later, Bavadra's new government was crushed in a bloodless coup. Round the world, newspaper headlines announced: First Military Takeover in the History of the South Pacific.

Walking out of class that day, Annabel heard sirens and screams. She tore at a young man's sleeve.

"What is it?"

"They've kidnapped Bavadra from Parliament!"

Now military trucks blocked all roads. Cars flew by on sidewalks, knocking people down. Remembering Jemese had gone that morning to clear out his office at the Parliament building, Annabel started running. In front of Parliament, Fiji military forces had formed a cordon with fixed bayonets. People knelt, covering their faces.

"Jemese Koro!" She shouted his name over and over.

A man leaned close and whispered. "I was there . . . in the spectators' gallery when soldiers broke in with machine guns. They took Bavadra and his cabinet. Jemese Koro, too."

"They?" She cried. *"Who?"*

He shook his head, that was all he knew.

Hours later in her flat, she knelt before the radio, slowly turning the dial. Nothing but static, all stations shut down. And then the phone rang, a reporter who had been in the press gallery during the abduction.

". . . It was led by Lieutenant Colonel Sitiveni Rabuka, a *Taukei* nationalist. They've taken over the government."

"What have they done with my cousin?" Annabel cried.

The man hesitated. ". . . At first I didn't understand it. Your cousin and Rabuka are both *Taukei,* both *against* Bavadra. Now, I think Jemese suspected something bigger than our own military was behind the coup. Some outside force. I saw him yell at one of the terrorists, as if recognizing him. He tried to pull off his mask. That's why they took him."

She had never been so still.

"Miss Koro, except for Colonel Rabuka, those soldiers were *not* Fiji forces. Too big. Different body language. From what I could see, they were black. Can you think of any foreigners, people your cousin might have known?"

Her tongue felt like rubber. "He knew everyone . . . he had many interests."

Next morning, an underground paper described the coup. Soldiers in battle dress and gas masks, armed with M16 machine guns, had followed Rabuka into Parliament. Believed to be international mercenaries, they spoke only with hand signals, hustling Prime Minister Bavadra, twenty-eight members of his cabinet and party coalition, and Jemese Koro, a bystander, outside to waiting vans. Their destination was not known. At noon, Rabuka shut down newspapers and took control of broadcast stations. Suspending the Constitution, he cut all links with the outside world.

Annabel tried reaching Numan Shaki at Lautoka Mill. Each time, she was disconnected. Her students brought news from the underground that the hostages had been driven north of Nadi. They were now prisoners in an old hotel called Maugham's. Military helicopters were landing and taking off from there. She pushed through crowds to Jemese's flat and held his clothes against her face. His mongoose whined, deranged by his absence, its nose wet and vulnerable like a human heart.

That night, a personal aide of Rabuka stood at her door. He entered cautiously, inspecting every room, then spoke quietly. Trying to escape, Jemese Koro had leapt from the hotel balcony into the sea, near a cove known for shark attacks. Annabel laughed like a madwoman. Jemese wasn't a swimmer, he was terrified of the sea.

She crossed the room. She punched his chest. "Who pushed him! Rabuka? The mercenaries? You?"

The aide threw her to the floor. "Where is your proof? Your so-called *mercenaries.*"

A week later, Bavadra and his party were released unharmed. Knowing Nubutautau had heard the news, Annabel sent word for the village to pray. There was no proof, no body, surely Jemese was alive. One night, while her clan tongue-stormed and grieved in the highlands, scarring their limbs with splintered bones, she set his mongoose free at the edge of town. Then she sat at Jemese's writing desk with a razor, making small hesitation cuts in her wrists. She sat for two days, unable to plunge past herself and do it.

Four weeks after the coup, deposed Prime Minister Bavadra testified in Washington, D.C., submitting documents proving the masked soldiers who pulled off the coup were South African mercenaries, hired by the CIA. The United States was concerned that the Soviets were becoming too friendly with Fiji, that Bavadra's Labour Party would allow the Russians to take over trade. South African blacks had been used because they "blended" with locals. The leader had been planted in Fiji months before the takeover, posing as an engineer at a mill near Lautoka. His soldiers were flown into Fiji two nights before the coup.

Annabel studied her face in a mirror. She had lost her jungle instinct, her hiding-and-hunting skills. She had forgotten how to distinguish between what was fascinating and what was deadly.

Inside the Fiji Museum, she stared at Jemese's favorite display, the ornate fork used in eating Reverend Baker, symbol of fierce *Taukei* pride, reminder that they were the eaters of man. She looked at beautifully carved dishes used to serve the reverend, at the extraordinary diversity of instruments of death. A throwing club of smooth black wood inlaid with ivory stars and crescent moons. Masterworks in ebony-like *vesi* wood, carved, polished, baroque. Bludgeons. Cudgels. Battle-axes. A seven-foot, razor-sharp spear used by the fiercest warriors in Fiji's history, called "The white man does not run fast enough."

Knowing it was time, she left for Nubutautau. Skirting roadblocks, hiding in ditches when military trucks passed, she walked all night to foothills where the jungle began. For a while she lay down, drawing strength from the sap and drizzle of plants. Then she pushed on, beneath lush jungle canopy, stroking the bark of trees like a long-distance swimmer making contact with shore.

For twenty years, she had fought this place, not letting it claim her. She had even instilled in her daughter the need to run from here. Now, at dawn, she watched naked children ride umbrella leaves down the river, hoping someday her daughter would return, hoping she could teach her daughter's daughter ancient hiding-and-hunting skills. She would recite to her their descent line, their cannibal history. She would enrich her with *vaka Viti,* the Fijian way.

Exhausted, she leaned against a tree, wondering how she could relearn these things. How did one proceed? Something tapped her rib cage. A glowing form knifed the jungle in flight.

"Mama!"

She came like a storm, raining green on everything.

"Jemese is dead," Annabel cried. "And I am dust. Mama, tell me what to do . . ."

The woman shook her head and wept. She touched a finger to

her daughter's cheek, then slowly dissolved. Annabel saw men approaching from her village.

"Bula!" she shouted. *"Bula!"*

They stood holding spears, blocking her progress. Seeing her grandfather in the distance, she called out again.

"Grandfather! Forgive me. Let me mourn with you."

He stared at her, then turned his back and walked away. Slowly, a human wall staked with spears grew across the jungle. Something swift bit into her. A blade the blue of deep ravines hung between her ribs. The handle quivered, ebony fraught with inlaid stars.

She went down on one knee. Something large and infinitely old blinked up at her. She felt the incredible immobility of things. Nothing moved, but the eyes of the iguana.

Charlotte Forbes

Sign

From *New Orleans Review*

THE SIGN could come in the form of a tap on the shoulder or a great lavender light or a speeding car or just an everyday object that will rise up and say very clearly what it is about me or about Tom or about me and Tom that keeps killing the babies. That sign is all I am looking for now and I am looking everywhere because that is where it may come from too.

Tom is a good man. Good, but bullheaded. Forever smoking his cigars, taking his nightly walks along the streets of our town which is 94 minutes from the city by commuter train and full of white Victorian houses with wide gleaming windows, protected from the world by a river and a crescent of woods. Everything a baby needs to be happy.

A cigar in the mouth makes a man look like an English lord in a smoking jacket or a card shark. It makes Tom look like a card shark, especially when he wears a dark shirt and slicks his hair back and always because of his eyes which narrow and dart about looking for luck.

Luck doesn't grow on trees, you've got to make your own sometimes. Tom says this a lot now, which is why we moved to this town five months ago and why he bought the dark blue Cadillac of a stroller from Reggie for twenty bucks on Thanksgiving night. *You can't ignore serendipity,* Tom said when he set down his prize stroller, which was like new, in the front hall and stared at it as though it was a lone star in the night sky. *Reggie's going to bring by a highchair too.*

Doesn't Tom know these things have nothing to do with why the babies don't live?

Right now the baby inside me is the size of a walnut the expecting book says, it may have eyes but they can't see. Tom can see her though. At night when I collapse on my back in the dark of the bed and the hard moonlight streams in on us, he kneels above me and lifts away the blue tulips growing up my flannel nightgown and stares right into my belly which is flat like always and sees a saucer-eyed girl with cheeks galore who will climb up on his lap and eat moo shu pork and fish-shaped almond cookies with him and say, daddy, you're the greatest.

I hope it works out for you that way, I tell him, though I don't think he should count on it.

When I look at my belly I don't see anything.

I did see Reggie walking up the street with the highchair. He was no older than me and tall, with a large face that was covered with a dark beard, there was nothing harsh about him though and he set the highchair down on the porch like it was a basket of eggs and rang the bell. I waited a moment and then opened the front door.

Mornin Ma'am, he nodded. He was gentle in the way only big creatures, whales or elephants, can be.

What's your name? was all I could think to say, though I already knew.

It took him a minute but he looked me in the eye and told me his name and a few other things, that he used to live in the city, that he's likely just passing through this town although he's been here four months now and that he collects cans and picks the trash and does odd jobs. There was a drawl to his speech and he spoke slowly as though nothing deep down was driving him to do one thing over another.

I bought the highchair and hired him to paint the baby's room.

Just like that? Tom said when I told him. Tom came home from work and took off his $200 shoes and his Armani jacket which is what you have to wear when you're vice president of the Searle

Corporation and you don't have a heart for it. His eyes shot around his Victorian kingdom, its mahogany wainscoting and stained glass windows that brooded and glimmered in the light, they sensed something out of place and fixed on me. So I told him about Reggie. *He'll be great,* I added.

Tom frowned. *I don't want this guy working here when you're all alone.*

We've had plenty of workmen here when you're at the office.

He's a drifter.

That's no crime, I wanted to say, no more than a log commits a crime when it lets the river take it. Though I simply said, *He can paint.*

I don't like it. We don't know this guy from Adam.

You don't have the time to do the painting. It has to get done. For the baby, I said.

I don't like it. Tom started to say something else, instead he just shook his head and went downstairs to his workshop.

When I want Reggie he could be one of three places, working at the used book shop or picking the trash or anywhere else. Reggie told me to ask the twins. They wash cars at the gas station on the next block and when I ask them they stand too close and stare into my face, bewildered as if I'm a wounded swallow that's just fallen from the sky. Then it's always the same thing. *Oh yeah, Donald Trump. We'll go get him.*

It just proves how industrious Reggie is, I tell Tom. *And he'll come in the evenings when you're here too.* What I don't tell Tom is when Reggie is late or when he stands us up.

It was Whopper Night at Burger King, Reggie will say.

Reggie. You know you'll get dinner here. Don't you like my cooking? Sorry, Miss Emily.

No one has ever called me that, I'm not a spinster and I'm not from the South and I know I should ask him to stop, but I don't. When Reggie comes in the door his eyes are puffy red as if he's been crying, or maybe it's because of the cold, it's even too cold to snow.

It's the kind of cold you want to smack back. I can only stay out a half hour, in the mornings I walk out from town over the high dirt road to the hills. Tom says don't go, it's too far for you to go now. You're right, dear, I say. Then I go.

There are no cars on the road and I stand for as long as I can before the fields and the wall of woods at the edge of town, the hills rise and fall like breath with a sugary glaze over them. When I do this I take the three babies that died inside me and the baby growing there now and flatten them up like sheets of cardboard and squish them up against the back of my mind so I can wait for the sign. And eventually I will see it, big and dark as a spot on the hills, the sign that will tell me why my babies don't live.

Only Reggie's first night gave me trouble. Reggie was early, Tom wasn't back from the city yet but his voice was, *I don't want him here with you alone* played in my head and made my stomach queasy though maybe the queasiness was the baby growing.

Reggie was in the baby's room above the kitchen where I was washing lettuce for dinner, supposedly he was working but if he were moving I could tell. It was quiet, just the trickle of water over the greens, no other sound in the house. My hands started to shake, I felt hot in the forehead, I hid the cleaver under the red-and-white checked dishtowels in the drawer and started upstairs, if the stairs were alive I would've killed them for creaking. The upstairs hall was dark and cold and it froze me to a spot so I couldn't flee if I had to, my ears strained to make something of the quiet and out of it came Reggie muttering to himself, then a transistor radio sputtering *O Come All Ye Faithful,* then Reggie again, singing over the radio's tinny words in a voice that was low and rich and heavy with prayer.

I am as bad as Tom.

It took Reggie a week but he smoothed and scraped and spackled the walls until you could slide a hand over them and mistake them for silk, he painted them the pink of peony petals and fixed the radiator, put on a new door, hung pictures of Cinderella and Snow White.

Even Tom had to admit a baby would be thrilled to sleep there. *You were right. The guy can paint,* Tom admitted when he came home from work early one night and handed me a bunch of daisies. After Tom gives me a hard time, he buys me daisies. That just makes it worse. I don't trust flowers that sprang from the mind of a greeting card designer, flowers are license to do more of the same anyway, so just don't bother I want to say. If you really knew me, you'd buy me cut amaryllis the color of raspberries and twist some ivy through them and stick them in a big-bellied clear vase and leave it in the sunlight on the kitchen table and never refer to it directly.

Sometimes I think the sign is about me and Tom, that there's only enough love between us to grow a baby to the size of a grapefruit.

When Reggie finished the nursery, I asked him to stay and replaster and paint the guest bedroom. He pawed the ground like a nervous horse. *I don't know, Miss Emily. I got to be moving on.* I told him I'd throw in dinner too, he pulled at his beard and looked around the room. *OK. But then I gotta be moving on.*

What I liked about Reggie was the noise. After the first night, I said he could come in the afternoon, and whenever Reggie was working in the nursery, I stayed in the kitchen right below him. I put the oak rocking chair from the parlor right in the middle of the kitchen. I could hear every movement, the footsteps, sometimes padding along, sometimes creaking the floorboards, the cans dragging across the floor, drawers opening, bangs and bumps. If I folded my hands over my belly and rocked hard and closed my eyes tight enough, I could trick myself into feeling the movements were inside me, that it wasn't Reggie stomping across the floor, but tiny feet picking their way though the gray fluid, it wasn't some workman hammering the wall, it was my baby's fist punching its way to life. I thought I could feel those things, but maybe I was just glad there was someone else in the house.

When Reggie moved across the hall to work on the guest room, I followed underneath. More sounds. Dragging, dropping, thumps. The scraping away of the old plaster was the best, little bursts of sound that said, *I'm here, I'm here, I'm here . . .*

How'd the sonogram go today? Tom came rushing in the back door on one of those scraping afternoons and threw his briefcase on the kitchen counter. *I tried to call you but there was no answer.*

I had forgotten all about the appointment, I kept sitting in the rocking chair and didn't open my eyes. *Oh, fine. Everything's fine.* I believed it, so the lie was all right.

When I did open my eyes I saw Tom frowning, I thought he had read my mind but it was only because he noticed there were three places set at the table. *Now he's going to eat with us too?*

Smoothing out walls is hard work, when Reggie came to dinner there was plaster dust all over him like he'd fallen in a vat of flour, he tracked filmy white footsteps over the parlor floor and into the kitchen.

Christ, Tom muttered and made a face.

The three of us ate dinner at the round oak table in the kitchen, I turned the overhead light off and lit the candles, it's easier to talk without all that light. Reggie always sat tall in his chair, his body twitching slightly like a dog wagging his tail cause he knows his bowl of food is coming soon, when I put Reggie's plate before him he didn't lunge at it, only when I started eating would he dig in, his momma has taught him this I can tell, and he would never say there's too much ginger in the stirfry or the onions are overdone. I knew how he would kiss me too, he'd put his hand on my cheek or stroke my hair or look into my eyes, he'd do something gentle like that first I'm almost sure.

Thoughts like that are a sign I am an unfit mother.

I'm still playing Pick, too. When Tom and I are at a restaurant I am listening to him but in my head I am playing Pick with the men eating quietly with their own wives, which means pick the one you would go to bed with and say why, to yourself of course. And last year Tom's brother followed me into the kitchen at the lake house, everyone else was out on the lawn drinking beer and eating barbe-cued chicken, he took the platter of coleslaw from my hands and set it down on the counter and looked at me for a full minute and said, *I hear you're a great kisser,* and I showed him.

A baby shouldn't have a tart for a mother.

That's what I was thinking when Tom yelled up to me from his workshop. *Emily, where's my screwdriver? The big Phillips screwdriver with the red handle?*

Oh, I gave it to Reggie. He needed it to fix a table he found in the trash.

Damn it, Emily. Don't loan out my things. How many times do I have to tell you?

He'll bring it back tomorrow. I'm sure. I made my voice sound cheery, but I didn't tell Tom that I gave that screwdriver to Reggie a week ago and hadn't thought about it since.

Another thing I didn't tell Tom, I was walking the river path one afternoon thinking about signs but there were none, just gray water and leftover snow and bare black trees and a black road carved into the mountain across the way. Coming toward me was a man pushing a grocery cart, the cart was piled with bottles and plastic shopping bags full of something, sneakers dangled from the cart bottom, the wheels went in all directions over the frozen rutty ground and the man was talking to himself, cursing. I had to pass him but as I came closer, the sight of him made me shrink back and run the other way: he didn't see me but I know it was Reggie.

Tom never got used to Reggie. During the 10 days he plastered and painted the guest room Reggie stayed for dinner each night, kale or buckwheat noodles or tofu stir fries was what I served. *Those Big Macs are junk, you shouldn't be eating junk, it makes you weak,* I did tell him that, I gave him second helpings of vegetables too. He always took them, though only after a long sigh. *I used to work in the city too,* Reggie said to Tom one night and named a big brokerage house. *Too much pressure, man,* Reggie took a big gulp of water. *Too much pressure.*

Right, he was probably the janitor, Tom said to me later, but I know that's why Tom kept sneaking looks at Reggie during dinner. He wanted to know if something had snapped in Reggie's mind and whether it could happen to him, too. There was no stopping Tom, his eyes kept darting around the room and lighting on Reggie so finally I cleared my throat and spoke up. *I know a dozen people around here who would hire you in a second,* I said to Reggie. *The woman in the stone house at the end of the street . . .*

Tom didn't even let me finish the sentence. *Watch out, Reggie,* he said. *She'll have your whole life planned out for you.* He was laughing of course, and when Reggie squirmed in his chair and rested his fork on top of the tofu casserole and stared at his plate, Tom had to say, *It's a joke.*

I always packed up the leftovers for Reggie. One morning at the bottom of the driveway I found a little explosion of bulghur wheat and corn kernels and tofu chunks, it was no accident, I could see it came from a pure premeditated splat against the ground, it was brilliant in its way and complete, like a painting. So I walked around it and went on. I didn't tell Tom.

When the guest room was done I asked Reggie to stay and redo the floors in the extra bedroom that would be a den. He didn't say yes or no, but just went into the den and began moving the furniture out into the hall.

When is this going to stop? Tom said. *That room is fine as it is.*

It almost did stop because for four days I didn't see Reggie. When he came back he didn't look at me, he just grunted and went upstairs and closed the den door, and I didn't hear a sound but the vacuum sucking at the floor.

Reggie didn't stay for dinner that night, he had something to do he said, that made five nights in a row I thought he was coming for dinner and he didn't. Tom and I sat at the table in the kitchen by ourselves, there was too much food for just us, I left the overhead light on and I served everything on one plate, it's easier to clean up, everything ran together but I didn't care.

Tom reached over and took my hand. *I'm sorry you're disappointed about Reggie. But it's better this way, believe me,* Tom's voice was soft and low and he stroked my cheek, he kept stroking it and his fingers felt warm and familiar, I could feel the whorls on his fingertips and they calmed me. His hand slid over my shoulder and down my arm into my hand and he pulled me up and led me downstairs to his workshop. It was beautiful what he made, fit for a princess, a set of drawers in a butterscotch wood with dark swirls racing through it, it wasn't a wood I knew, it couldn't have come from a tree but from a dream of a tree and there were fluted columns at the sides and the whole thing gleamed like a light was shining on it from far away.

What makes you think it's going to be a girl? I couldn't help myself, I spat the words at him.

Tom bowed his head. *I hope it's a girl. If it's a girl I'll get to see what you were like from day one.*

I started to turn away but Tom pulled me back, my face landed below his neck, my nose jammed into his collarbone. *Come on Emily, we'll do it this time. Please try.* His breathing was fast and jerky like he was crying, even though I knew it wouldn't do any good I whispered *OK*.

The next morning, which is today, Tom was at work in the city, I was upstairs folding the laundry, the doorbell rang as if it would explode unless I answered it. It was Reggie, his eyes were glazed like when Tom gives him beers, he had on an army coat and he was shivering and hopping from one foot to the other to keep warm. *Miss Emily. Goin' on your walk this morning?*

Yeah. Though I didn't know Reggie knew about my walks.

Come on. I'll go too.

Tom's Yankees jacket was on the coat rack by the door and I grabbed it and his yellow knit cap that said *Pizza* in red and we raced up Quill Street and over the high school track to get to the dirt road that led to the woods. We weren't talking, I had to trot to keep up with his stride, his eyes were straight ahead and our breaths were clouds of frost, one big, one little.

Slow down Reggie. What's the rush?

Reggie didn't say anything.

A snow had fallen, the sun was strong and it hit the snow and bounced back and around so everything was bright white, so bright the only place your eyes could look was the sky.

There, over there, Reggie pointed to the clearing at the edge of the woods. *That's where you go isn't it? Coming out here everyday to look at nothing.* He laughed a crazy laugh, the laugh of a loon on a Maine lake and it ripped a hole in the white silence and ran all over the field and in and out of the woods. Reggie's laugh was the only sound too, no car swooshing by on the road to relieve the silence, not a bird calling, not the thud of an icicle slipping from a branch onto the snow. There was nothing, nothing alive but me and Reggie standing knee deep in the snow and the laugh had made him someone else.

Reggie, stop it. You're scaring me.

Shut up. Bitch!

The shape of his face changed, I watched his mouth twist up and his eyes go somewhere else, I watched him reach inside his Army jacket. What he took out was the screwdriver, Tom's Phillips head screwdriver.

The sun is so bright it's even shining up the dull lead of the screwdriver. In my mind I can feel the pain already but when it comes it won't register immediately, then it will be in my stomach and my chest and maybe in my back, a sharpness so new I won't even recognize it as pain. The blood will come, beautiful against the white snow, vivid, blood warm enough to melt the snow and seep down into it and bleed into a wide pink lake.

I feel my belly for the last time now, my jacket is open and my belly is flatter than before, not even a hint of a curve, the walnut inside me has already begun to shrivel and die like they all did. The babies were smart not to come, with their little wisps of eyes they saw the sign even before it had been given a shape.

Soon the sirens will scream and the red lights on top of the blue and white cars will flash. Detectives will swarm the hillside. One thing I'm happy for, when they find my body and roll it over, the whites of my eyes will be spotless as snow. Tom and the police and the townspeople will shake their heads and cover their faces. But if they look at me, they can take comfort in my eyes. If they can bring themselves to look at me they will see my eyes are amazingly clear and bright and if they look for more than a second they may even see it's the clarity and brightness that only come to the eyes when death makes sense.

Julia Whitty

A Tortoise for the Queen of Tonga

From *Harper's Magazine*

S HE DIED in the Palace Gardens in 1966 of extreme old age and a heart that had swelled insupportably large from nearly two centuries of loneliness. For a day no one noticed, not because she was neglected but because her metabolism was inert enough that immobility did not arouse suspicions. The crabs discovered her first, hordes of frenetic, land-dwelling red crabs with pincers for cutlery. The dogs found her next, but because they neither bayed nor howled they kept the secret to themselves. Only when the pigs got wind of it and began to squeal with excitement did the Queen's gardener rouse himself from the shade under a casuarina tree and stroll on the slow heels of detached curiosity toward the community of living things that had gathered to feast on the remains of the dead tortoise.

"Tu'i Malila is dead," the gardener announced to the Queen's secretary.

"Your Royal Highness," said the Queen's secretary to the King, "Tu'i Malila is dead."

"Royal Wife and Queen," said the King to the Queen, "Tu'i Malila is dead."

The Queen did not rise from her wrought-iron chaise under the banyan tree, but she did signal to her ladies-in-waiting to stop swirling the palm-frond fans around her head as her huge moon-face quivered and her dark eyes puddled up with tears.

For more than two decades the tortoise lay where she died, long after the pigs had been spit-roasted and the *'umu* ovens had been dug to charbroil the funeral feast, which drew the nobility in from all over Tongatapu in her honor. In the course of time, her empty carapace became as much a feature of the Palace Gardens as the huge Norfolk Island pines and the red gingerbread gables of the wooden palace. Royal princes and princesses used her empty shell as a jungle gym, a hilltop fortress, a private retreat. In 1988 she was moved to the new Tonga National Center outside Nuku'alofa, where her remains were displayed alongside portraits of the monarchs. Visitors wondered at the vast parchment of her shell, its surface scarred, chipped, burned, and in places worn as thin as a fingernail from her encounters with pirates, explorers, missionaries, kings, and queens.

Captain James Cook bought the giant tortoise in 1776 from a Dutch merchant in Cape Town, South Africa, as he embarked on his third and final Pacific voyage. She was not yet an adult, though she was probably thirty years old, her skin young and supple with the soft patina of sea glass. The Dutch merchant had bought her from English pirates, who had wrenched her from her home on the atoll of Aldabra off the coast of Africa. She had spent weeks in the dark bellies of various ships, trussed, unwatered and unfed, panicking at the strange motion of the sea, the perpetual blackness, the stench of men, the attacks of sea lice and rats. The sailors had no concept of her as a living thing. They kicked her and laughed. They dripped hot lamp oil on her. She retreated into an hallucinogenic state; in her mind's eye she could see the yellow light of Aldabra, the turquoise sea, the glassy sky decorated with the black kites of soaring frigate birds.

Captain Cook took her aboard along with a menagerie of sheep, goats, cattle, horses, and chickens that turned his ship, *Resolution,* into a floating ark. She was part of his oceangoing savings account, able to survive up to a year in the hold without food or water. When called upon, she would become turtle soup. His men lowered her into the dank hold. The hatches dropped down onto darkness. *Resolution* plunged into the mountainous waves of the southerly sailing route fearfully called the Roaring Forties. The ship began to leak. Squalls tore the mizzen topmast off. The horses tap-danced day and night. The sheep shivered and died. When a fog as dense as smoke settled over the sea, *Resolution* and her companion ship, *Discovery,* maintained contact with each other by the steady firing of their guns.

In Tonga, William Bligh, the young master of Cook's ship, oversaw the tricky business of getting the tortoise off the ship and onto a launch. Two sailors ran the deck winch. Three sailors waited below in the open boat. The tortoise emerged from the darkness with her head drawn deep into her shell and her eyes squeezed shut. "A dozen lashes to any fool who drops it," shouted Bligh as the ropes shifted and the tortoise took a list to starboard. The sailors heaved. The knots slipped. The tortoise crashed onto the boat's thwart, chipping a bony plate on the left side of her carapace.

Captain Cook accepted a gift a day from the Tu'i Tonga, the King of the Islands of Tonga, which Cook called "The Friendly Isles." He accepted a sacred red feather bonnet, bowls of intoxicating *kava* drink, and exquisitely made *tapa* paintings on bark. The King in return took few gifts, showing no interest in the novelties that his people borrowed with infuriating regularity from *Resolution*: cats, muskets, buttons, nails, anchors. The King did not care for such things. He accepted only one small glass bowl, some livestock, and the tortoise: "For my wife," he said.

The Queen adored the tortoise from the start. She loved the tortoise's eyes, dark as mirrors. She loved the way the tortoise stretched her long neck and tilted her head and hissed. The sound was soft and undemanding, but it never failed to catch the Queen of Tonga's ear, even above the perpetual sibilance of the court. Nearly a year had passed since the tortoise had been taken from Aldabra, and when she arrived on Tonga she was emaciated and dehydrated. The Queen understood this at once and undertook to feed her by hand, offering tempting gardenia blossoms, bananas, coconut milk, and—wonder of wonders—the tart fruit from the Polynesian screw pine. This screw pine was so much like the screw pine from Aldabra that when the tortoise ate it the yellow flesh frothed up on her lipless mouth and damp rings formed around her eyes. *"Lelei taha,"* said the Queen, recognizing the tortoise's favorite: this one is the best. Then the Queen sent a summons to bring in screw-pine fruit from all over Tongatapu, and toward the end of the fruiting season, from as far away as Vava'u. The tortoise responded to these feasts by swelling back into her skin so that the wrinkles and sags disappeared.

The tortoise grew fat. The Queen admired her fatness. The Queen was also fat, the fattest person in the islands other than her husband, the King. The Queen felt a communality with the tortoise's girth. She realized that the tortoise met every criterion for Tongan royalty: hugeness, ponderousness, dignity, silence. The tortoise began to join the King and Queen for their stroll down the beach each morning. The Queen loved the cut of their three stately bodies moving in corpulent elegance from the clutter of shade beneath one palm tree to another. To an outsider they looked like a trio creeping underwater against a hard current. "The tortoise lives *fakatonga,"* said the Queen: the Tongan way. "We will call him Tu'i Malila"—King Malila. The royal title guaranteed the tortoise's future. Of all the animals that Cook bestowed or lent to the Tongans, only the tortoise survived the cooking fires.

In early summer the seabirds known as sooty terns returned by the thousands to Tongatapu, swirling in on the long red streamers of sunset, singing their *wide-awake, wide-awake* calls. Tongans by the twos and threes sat on the resting mounds called *esi*, staring out to sea, admiring the lines of the birds' wings as they hovered then plunged through the surface of the water, rising with shiny anchovies in their bills.

The tortoise took to joining the Queen on the beach each afternoon as Tongan slaves cast webs across the shallows, gathering in jeweled reef fish for the royal tables. Warriors drove canoes with synchronous cuts of their paddles. Girls slithered naked through the water. The King bobbed on the waves, nude, brown, enormous, buoyant, terns butterflying around him.

The ladies-in-waiting removed the Queen's *ta'ovala,* the pandanus mat, then guided her by the elbows to the water's edge. With each demi-step her flesh liquefied and rippled. Rolls of fat surged into motion, cascading up and down her body. The King raised his head from his pillow on the waves and watched admiringly.

The tortoise learned to join them in the water, her shell sinking down until only its crown remained dry. Her long neck snaked up through the surface for each breath. She let the warm water flood the secret folds of her skin, in her armpits, under her tail, inside her shell. Underwater, she studied the Queen's buttocks, huge, dimpled, swaying in the surge. The King's hair dangled like the tentacles of a jellyfish. Clouds of neon-blue chromis fish rose up to greet her. Sometimes a sea turtle flew past, thrusting long flippers backward. Then the tortoise would piston with her legs, trying to sink away into the blue world. But she was a creature of the land, with feet, not flippers. She could never dive, could only thrash the surface until the white bubbles boiled up around her, blinding her.

The tortoise felt her loneliness most in the season when the sea turtles came ashore. Although their realm was the ocean, they returned to their ancient birth islands once a year to lay their eggs. The sight of their smooth shells evoked ancient needs in the tortoise. She found herself drawn to the island's sandy plateaus, where she dug holes and laid clutches of infertile eggs. On summer nights she felt a magnetic attraction to fields of volcanic boulders. In the darkness, the boulders resembled giant tortoises. The tortoise's shell recorded the first of many deep abrasions from squeezing in between them.

The Queen was admiring the smoky luster reflecting off the tortoise's shell when the news arrived. "The Captain Cook is dead," said the King to the Queen. "He has died in the islands far to the north." The Queen had never been to Hawaii, but she knew about it.

"He died in battle with a king," said the King. "He was cooked on a slow fire and eaten, and some of his bones are now kept in a stone *langi* burial tomb, where they are worshiped."

The Queen nodded. It was a fitting end for a grand enemy. The King himself could expect no better in battle. The Queen remembered Cook's white wigs and frogged jackets. She remembered his kindness in leaving her Tu'i Malila. She wondered what he had tasted like.

Late every summer when the sea turtles dragged themselves ashore to lay their eggs, the Tongans gathered on the beaches at night, waiting as a slice of the moon tumbled slowly through the sky. The turtles squeezed out clutches of jelly-like eggs and covered them with sand. The Tongans cut into a few select nests and gathered the eggs for the royal table. The King liked to pop an egg into each cheek and squeeze it against his teeth until it burst and the salty proto-turtle fluid gushed out. The Queen liked to roll one around on her tongue until the outer membrane of the egg grew as thin as tissue paper and the inner jelly dissolved. The King ate four times as many eggs as the Queen, and since the purpose of the eggs was aphrodisiacal he was soon aroused to a tower of passion. The ladies-in-waiting were called in to remove the Queen's clothing. The King's valets were called in to help him out of his clothes and onto the sleeping mats on the floor. Their mountains of flesh quivered around them.

The sea-turtle tracks disappeared in the tides of the winter solstice. The spring equinox brought the flowering of the poison-fish tree. The Queen's sixth child was born—her sixth son. The Queen was disappointed. Sons were wonderful. Sons were worthy and strong and often handsome. But they were not daughters. The Queen did what many a daughterless Tongan family did: she declared her youngest child *fakaleiti*—like a lady. He was named Lini, a girl's name. He was dressed like a girl. He was put out to play with the girls. He was called "she." The Queen crooned to him about skin potions and hair ornaments. She taught him to weave flowers into garlands. She arranged for him to learn to dance the *tau'olunga,* the slow, sinuous solo dance of the women. As he grew, Lini learned to seduce men with the cant of his slim hips and the smolder in his pretty eyes. His brothers teased him, but they also admired him. He was not a warrior, but he was bolder and rougher than a girl, and there was the feeling that he would do wonderfully painful things to them if asked to. The King did not mind. The Queen had already given him five manly sons. He had other wives and through them other sons. His seed was broadcast plentifully.

In the heat of midday Lini and the tortoise napped together in the dark air under a banyan tree. The tortoise slept with her head and legs pulled into her shell. Lini lay on his side with his *tupenu* skirt pulled up over his head. He dreamed of warrior-men, their skin oiled, the muscles on their backs flexing as they rowed through the surf. The tortoise dreamed of tortoises bedded together in sand bunkers on Aldabra.

"Lini," said the Queen, shaking her son's shoulder. She sank onto her huge haunches, fat draping like curtains of brown velvet from her legs. Her ladies-in-waiting shooed the flies away with fans of white tropic-bird feathers. "An Englishman named William Bligh has returned. He has come back to the South Seas as captain of his own ship. He has been at Tahiti. His men drank *kava,* danced the *tamure,* got tattooed, got married. But his men threw him off his ship near Tonga." The Queen dug bright yellow beloperone flowers from a fold in her skirt and fed them to the tortoise. The tortoise hissed, remembering the ships, the cruelty.

In the winter the humpback whales returned to Tonga. They came up from Antarctic waters. They breached and tail-lobbed among the coral reefs. They sang epic songs that set the surface of the lagoons vibrating. The Tongans sat on the beaches or floated in the waves, listening to the whistles, rumbles, whoops, gurgles, trills, and flutters. The tortoise rested in the shade beneath a palm tree and remembered Aldabra, where the whales sang so loudly that flying fish erupted from the water and soared onto the beaches, where the tortoises stepped gingerly around them.

❏ ❏ ❏ ❏

Lini grew into a beautiful young woman. His shoulders were wide and strong. His hips were slim, and the muscles on his legs were taut as carved ironwood. He flirted mercilessly with the unmarried warriors. He seduced them with stories of courageous men and beautiful women who resembled men. Sometimes, on moonless nights, Lini and the tortoise sat on the beach together watching the stars circle overhead. Lini told their stories, pointing out the constellations to the tortoise. "That one is the sun god Tangaloa, and that is his human love, Va'epopua. He has caught her while she is collecting shellfish. He makes love to her, and their son becomes the first Tu'i Tonga, the first King of Tonga." On spring nights the huge bats called flying foxes mated on the wing above them, their courtship flights casting black shadows across the moonlit sand. Then Lini would take off his clothes and run down to the sea and strike out with strong arms to the line of silver surf breaking on the reef. The tortoise would stare out to the starry horizon. Sometimes, when Lini got back to shore, a young warrior would be waiting, and Lini would take him by the hand and lead him into the mangroves on the edge of the lagoon. Then the tortoise dug her bed in the sand and slept.

The seasons of the whales and turtles came and went. The King grew into an old, old man, and then at the end of one rainy season he died. It took six warriors to lift his immense corpse onto the funeral bier. His sons grieved, then to alleviate their grief they went to war against the Fijians. One after another each was killed in battle until only Lini, safe at home, was left. "Tu'i Malila," Lini whispered to the tortoise, "now I will never be Queen." He let the warm tears roll over the edges of his eyes and down his cheeks. He let them bead up in his eyelashes so that when he looked out on the turquoise lagoon the light shimmered and sparkled. He laid his head down beside the tortoise and peered into the dark interior where her head was hiding. His grief echoed inside her shell.

Lini renounced his *fakaleiti* status. He was elected King. He asked his mother to remain Queen. He gave the tortoise a permanent seat next to him at the royal *kava* circle, where she munched coconut meat and watched *kailao* war dances by torchlight, remembering the forest fires on Aldabra, which the Spanish had set to flush out islanders for the slave trade. Lini, as King, grew fat. He wore red-and-green capes made from the plucked feathers of thousands of blue-crowned lorikeets. He was carried everywhere in a hand-barrow.

The Queen died in the season when the baby sea turtles emerged from the sand and crabbed their way down to the sea. The frigate birds jostled for position in the air, sweeping across the sand on paper-thin wings, flipping the hatchlings off the beach and into their gullets.

The Queen stared out to the turquoise waters of the lagoon. "Is it the sea turtles?" she asked, wondering about the clouds of frigate birds. Her ladies-in-waiting wept and nodded. "Lini," she said to the son whom she had always regarded as a daughter, "now you must find a Queen." She reached out for the tortoise's head. "And don't forget to bring screw-pine fruit from Vava'u."

The funeral feast lasted for a week. Everything that could be caught was roasted in *'umu* ovens and eaten: pigs, bats, chickens, terns, dogs, tuna, crabs. *Ma'ulu'ulu* dances were choreographed, using seated female dancers who moved only their graceful hands to eulogize the Queen's life. Musicians beat sharkskin drums through the night. The priests performed round-the-clock obsequies beside her cadaver on a raised platform. Lini visited often, his huge girth humbly clothed in an ancient *ta'ovala* mat that had been handed down from mother to son to wife to son for five generations. The tortoise rested her head in his lap.

An Englishman named George Vason came to visit Lini, the King, on a winter day when water leaked from heavy skies and the spirals of waterspouts menaced the horizon. Lini, befitting a King, said nothing.

"I would like to marry a Tongan," said the Englishman in his slow, accented Tongan, "if it pleases Your Highness, Your Royal Highness."

The King worked his way down a banana, eating some, biting some off for the tortoise.

"I believe I am worthy, Sire."

The tortoise hissed, remembering the smell of white men.

The Englishman drew back. "You know you can eat that thing," he said, pointing to the tortoise, but the King only reached for another banana. The Englishman tried again: "I know that I came as a missionary, and I believed in the Bible." The rain moved on-shore in a black wave. Attendants held huge pandanus leaves above the King. The Englishman flinched under the hard slaps of the raindrops. "But I no longer believe that. Now I believe in Tangaloa, the sun god. I have renounced Christianity."

The King looked up from his third banana and studied the Englishman, with his strange blue eyes. The man had arrived uninvited along with nine others from the London Missionary Society. None had converted a single Tongan. Three had failed to survive the Tongans. Six had escaped to Australia. The last, George Vason, was here before him, yellow hair dripping down his face.

The King broke eye contact, reached for another banana, gave the tortoise the first bite.

"I *love* this woman," said the Englishman, looking away. The tortoise left the King's side, ambled to the man, reached out her long neck. Without thinking, the Englishman patted her. "Go on then," said the King. "Marry. Settle here. Live *fakatonga* with your woman."

Eight beautiful, near-naked warriors carried the King to his own wedding. All were brown as teak, skins glistening with coconut oil, muscles rippling. They wore yellow hibiscus blossoms in their hair. The King rode in titanic splendor on a stretcher made of pigskin and pandanus. His vast girth was smothered under mountains of flowers and fruits. He snacked on roasted yams during the ride.

His thirteen-year-old Queen was tiny by comparison, brown and lithe, with delicate arms and small breasts. She could barely look at the King, at his gigantic dimensions. The tortoise ambled toward her, tilting her head. The new Queen giggled. Her teeth were white and smooth. Her eyes sparkled with reflected torchlight. She stole a glance at the King, but he was admiring his warriors, who in turn were admiring her.

The new Queen loved the tortoise. She loved her wise, patient eyes, her stately gait, her affection. The new Queen joined the tortoise on the tortoise's morning walks down the beach. At first the young Queen sprinted ahead, laughing and skipping. But the tortoise soon paced her by her own slow example.

The new Queen took her duties seriously. She began to consume frequent, large meals. She learned to never go anywhere without a bunch of bananas or a fistful of crabs' legs to munch on. She drank gallons of coconut milk to make her skin shine. She slurped dozens of oysters, fat as little tongues, off their half shells. She ate *feke* and *'ufi* and bowl after bowl of *faikakai*. The people of Tonga noted it, even those from neighboring islands, and nodded their heads in approval. "The Queen is fattening," they said, "for the King." The new Queen outgrew all her old *ta'ovala* mats, and the King solemnly awarded her one that had belonged to the old Queen, his mother. "This will be handed down to our children," he said shyly, looking down, then adding quickly: "Your feet are doing well. Even your toes are getting fat." The Queen blushed and smiled and tried to grab his hand as he was turning to leave, but her reflexes were slowed by her weight and she missed.

"I am not fat enough," worried the Queen as the King walked away. "I am not yet fat enough for the King to love."

The Queen grew fatter, fatter than the old Queen. She was the fattest person in the islands other than the King. The King admired her, but only from a distance. The Queen began to pine. She gnawed on her fingernails. She drummed her fingers on her knees. Her appetite waned. She waved away plates of jellied stingray. She chewed, but did not swallow, the platters of steamed bats' wings. She took long walks down the beaches—slowly, yes—but without any food to fortify her. Her hard-earned pounds began to evaporate.

The tortoise went with the Queen out to the beach for a nighttime swim. The King bobbed in the waves. The Queen, ever more listless, did not notice. The tortoise kicked at the sand, excavating a clutch of turtle eggs. The Queen, without thinking, wiped one clean, popped it in her mouth. She carried the remainder down to the water's edge, unwrapped her clothes. In the moonlight, her skin was silver, the shadows in her cleavages were velvety black. The King watched as the waves climbed the Queen's legs and crumpled back into the sea. He wheezed.

Startled, the Queen jumped, then waved, then glanced at the turtle eggs in her hand. She hesitated, but only for a moment, before wading toward the King and gently placing an egg on his tongue, then another and another.

All throughout that night, as the tortoise studied the stars and dozed, the royal love of Tonga, like the love of whales, played out on the buoyant bed of the sea.

The King and Queen met often in the phosphorescent water at night. Consequently the Queen had daughters, one after another, cherubic babies with hair like black gorgonian corals and laughing eyes. The Queen raised them in a feast of love. She nibbled on their toes, tickled their arms, blew blubbery kisses into their fat stomachs. The princesses slathered affection on the tortoise. They built entire fantasy worlds around her: Tu'i Malila was a whale-god washed up and dying and in need of a princess to kiss him back to life; Tu'i Malila was a handsome prince bewitched by a lizard-spirit who would release him from his spell if only a beautiful girl sang out her heart to him. The girls wore a faint saddle into the tortoise's back from taking so many rides. They polished her shell to a translucent sheen from the constant caress of their hands.

Sometimes when the cares of state allowed, Lini joined them. Alone with his girls and the tortoise, he danced the *tau'olunga* again, showing them the slow, sinuous moves. When the princesses lay on their backs under banana trees, sun streaming into their eyes, he joined in: idling and laughing and dreaming of being queens.

The seasons of the sea turtles came and went. The seasons of the flying foxes cartwheeled past. The constellations rolled through the sky, told their stories, dipped from sight, told them again. Then one year, in the season of the humpback whales, Lini died. The Queen followed not long after, in the time before the rains, when the land crabs migrated by the millions from the forests to the sea.

Afterward there was drought, and sometimes wildfires.

Once a fire singed the edges of the tortoise's shell.

Occasionally typhoons roared in from the west, shattering the perfect tempo of living.

The years came and went with the fluid rhythm of the barracuda in the lagoon: finning into the outgoing tide, backpedaling into the incoming tide. One after another the kings and queens of Tonga rose up, then disappeared from the face of time.

The tracks of the sooty terns blew away on the southeast trade winds. The tracks of the pack rats braided across the beaches in their stead. The Tongans had never seen rats before. They marveled at the way these wingless bats came into their houses, took away shiny things the islanders wanted, and left old clam shells behind in trade. *Palangi kovi,* they called them: lousy foreigners.

The Wesleyan missionaries (in whose boats the rats had come) also arrived with the seeming purpose of taking away things the Tongans loved and replacing them with things they didn't, like clothing. The missionaries were not taken seriously by the people of Tonga, who teased them and threatened to eat them. But then the King of Tonga, George Tupou I, developed a weakness for sermons and converted, abandoning his *ta'ovala* mat for a black wool suit and top hat.

The King outlawed the worship of the old gods. He mandated the Christianization of all the islanders. He made the people wear clothes. The Tongans vented their frustration by killing rats. The tortoise, stepping slowly around the piles of dead rodents on the beach, remembered the creatures aboard *Resolution* who had nipped the flesh on her tail and under her legs all those years ago. The Wesleyan missionaries saw the power of the rats and threatened the Tongans with grisly stories of rats in a place called Hell. Rebelliously, the Tongans tried eating the rats but discovered they made better fishing lures and set them alive in the water, where their thrashings attracted the fatal curiosity of octopuses.

❏ ❏ ❏ ❏

The Queen, King George Tupou I's wife, gave up daytime swimming, since it required too much unveiling of skin and the eyes of the Wesleyans were everywhere. But at night, she and the tortoise went down to the beach and lumbered in secret from mangrove to mangrove until they could launch onto the waves, buoyant as ships, water splashing over the Queen's brown skin and the tortoise's hull. Sometimes they could hear the sermons from onshore. The Queen always sighed in the water. The tortoise always stretched out her neck and let the water trickle into the secret folds of her skin, now withered with age and sun.

An island erupted from the sea to the north of Tongatapu, breathing smoke, cinder, and pumice. Fonuafo'ou, or New Land, the Tongans called it. Picnic canoes full of families set off from the islands to see it. King George Tupou I and the Queen chugged out aboard a steam-driven pearl boat, the two of them solemnly dressed in black, black smoke dusting the skies behind them. Shirley Baker, an Englishman, stood beside the King. He had come to Tonga as a Wesleyan missionary, had climbed the ranks to become the King's confidant, and now was Prime Minister. As the island hove into sight, sulfuric and dismal, Shirley Baker declared it "God's magnificent work." The Queen, hiking the black wool dress over her wide hips so that her feet could breathe, whispered to the King that she thought it looked more like the work of the devil, whoever he was.

The seasons of the humpback whales came and went, the whales lolling at the passes into the lagoon, wing flippers rearing into the air, shivering there, then flopping back to the surface with slaps that rang like cannon fire. The whaling ships came, responded with cannons of their own, firing deep into the recesses of blubber and bone. Blood washed ashore on the waves.

When the whales were gone for good, the whalers disappeared from the cobalt blue sea outside the lagoon. The rendering plant on the beach collapsed into a pile of rust. The Tongans who were born too late to ever hear the songs of the whales made the old people mimic them, made them screw up their faces and flick their tongues in and out of their mouths and whoop and gurgle. But without the amplification of the sea, the sound was unconvincing. The tortoise stared out to where the silver feet of the sun danced on the water, and remembered the power of the leviathans who had lifted the ocean onto their backs and fountained it up into the air.

Princess Salote, the eldest great-granddaughter of King George Tupou I, liked to ride belly-down on top of the tortoise, skinny arms and legs hooked under the edge of the tortoise's shell, laughing and giggling while they made infinitesimal progress toward the beach. Salote and the tortoise went everywhere together. Each Sunday, during choir practice, the tortoise climbed the wooden steps of the royal chapel, then lodged herself inside the too-small doorway while Salote sang a-cappella hymns imported from England. It took all twelve choir members to dislodge the tortoise from the door at the end of each practice, the tortoise's shell sawing an ever deeper track into the frame until one day she sawed her way through and ambulated right up to the steps of the choir where Salote sat, eyes flickering steadily between heaven and the tortoise as she sang.

Salote tended the tortoise like a child. She rubbed coconut oil into the tortoise's leathered skin, scrubbed her shell with fish scales, cleaned the space between the tortoise's huge toes with musk parrot feathers brought from 'Eua. The tortoise lay her head in the Princess's lap and listened to the Princess's stories of beautiful nuns and handsome priests. Sometimes, when the Princess and the tortoise napped together under the huge arms of the *mape* tree, the Princess confided to the tortoise how she would like to become a nun when she grew up, and renounce the royalty of Tonga in exchange for the royalty of heaven.

News came that the island called Fonuafo'ou, or New Land, had disappeared. Picnic canoes full of families set off to see where it no longer stood. Salote went out aboard a packet boat with the King, the Queen, a clot of cousins, and a photographer from Scotland who had come to the South Seas to make his reputation, à la Gauguin, only to find everyone clothed in whalebone and cotton and not a breast in sight. The sea made them all sick. When they got to the place where Fonuafo'ou used to be, the royal party lined up, clutching the rail. The photographer exposed a single shot of them, queasy and green against a snarl of whitecaps.

Salote's father, the King, died. From the edge of his deathbed in the royal palace, Salote looked out the windows and saw the sooty terns fanning the blue sky with black wings. Within hours the news was radioed to the outer islands, and canoes full of nobles began arriving at Tongatapu. For three days they huddled together in the gazebo in the Palace Gardens before emerging with a decision: since there was no Prince to become King, Princess Salote, eighteen years old, would become Queen.

She appeared at her coronation wearing an ancient *ta'ovala* mat, a red-and-green lorikeet-feather cape, and a small golden crucifix on her brown throat. The people of Tonga were impressed. Despite being female and as skinny as a sea snake, the new Queen appeared, somehow, spiritually weighty. The tortoise stood at her side, bedecked with garlands of hibiscus, her long neck weaving back and forth.

The coronation feast lasted two weeks. Spring lamb was shipped in from New Zealand and sides of beef from Australia. The King of England sent a silver chafing dish. Queen Salote sat in a wicker throne at the head of the royal table while the shadows of palm fronds sawed back and forth across the lawn. She fed the tortoise cubes of mango from her own plate, eating little herself. The members of the coronation party could not fail to notice the new Queen's meager appetite. They urged the royal cooks to try harder. New dishes were invented on the spot. But the Queen smiled and shook her head, demurely rejecting her own earthly appetites.

The Queen would not fatten. She established schools and medical clinics across the islands. She personally taught children to read. In the evenings, when her work was done, she swayed in a hammock in the Palace Gardens, an arm draped over the side, caressing the tortoise's neck as she swung by.

One year during the season of the sea turtles when the tortoise made her private pilgrimage to the fields of volcanic boulders, the

Queen followed. She wandered the maze of stone, watching the tortoise lumber through the tight angles and dead-end alleys. She listened to the low screech of sound as the rocks carved their way into the tortoise's hull. She let her fingers wander over the new etchings in the tortoise's carapace, feeling their sharp edges. She pondered the slow decades of the tortoise's sorrow.

The Queen made a decision. She would let her own unhappiness sink to the bottom of her life like a tadpole in the watery cup of a bromeliad plant: alive but awaiting transformation. She began to eat. She made the weekly rounds of all her maternity clinics accompanied by an attendant with a basket of pickled *'ota ika*. She taught reading classes with an array of *fingota* fresh from the lagoon spread out on a blanket at her feet. She swung in her hammock at night with a packet of taro leaves stuffed with warm *manioke* balanced on her chest, munching. She grew fat, so fat that when she sang in the choir her chins bobbled like wattles and her voice took on the timber of a low wind in the taro fields.

On summer afternoons the tortoise swam with her in the lagoon, the Queen resplendent in a huge Indian-cotton bathing dress that swirled like loose ink in the water.

The Queen fell in love. She married. She had children, one after another. The tortoise reveled in the affections of a new generation of princes and princesses.

The years came and went like the fingerling waves inside the lagoon, tickling the stilt roots of the mangroves, stepping away.

The seasons of the moon tumbled acrobatically through the sky.

The new island called Fonuafo'ou began to rise again. The Tongans watched its fiery progress from the ferry that ran between Tongatapu and Niuafo'ou.

The turtle boats waited for moonless nights, when the sea turtles swam up the sandy beaches and kicked open the hollows of their nests. The fishermen followed, scooping the turtles from the beach, trussing them, tossing them on their backs into the bottom of their dinghies, rowing them to ships offshore.

The visits of the sea turtles became rare, and rarer, until they stopped altogether. Then the old people of Tonga entertained the young people with stories of turtle eggs, how different love had been with them around. The tortoise sat on an *'esi* resting mound, staring out to sea. The Queen, afloat on the waves, could no longer entice her into the water, not even with handfuls of late-season screw-pine fruit.

The Queen flew to England for the coronation of that Queen. It rained incessantly. The Queen of England lived in opulence, but she had no tortoise. The Queen of Tonga shared her snapshots with the Queen of England, showing her Tu'i Malila, King Malila, older and wiser than the wind itself.

The tortoise, sleepy with age, napped under the shade of the palm trees in the Palace Gardens. The royal grand princesses and grand princes played on top of her, painting her shell with Magic Markers, sliding down into the soft cushions of sand castles built at her feet. In her dreams, the tortoise smelled the dune grasses of the Indian Ocean. She heard the snoring of other tortoises, who, in her aging memory, now resembled volcanic rocks.

The Queen, ancient as a wave-worn coconut, died in the rainy season when the irregular thud of dropping mangoes kept time between the peals of thunder. Not only the people of Tonga mourned. Heads of state from around the world sent condolences. Planes carrying flowers from abroad bumped to the ground on Tongan runways made of white coral rubble.

The tortoise accompanied the funeral procession to the royal cemetery, her shell bedecked with pure white gardenias. When the people filed away, the tortoise stayed behind, listening to the water drum against her shell. She stayed there through the night, and the next one, and the next. She stayed until the end of the rains started the geckos chirping and mating on the underside of every palm frond in the islands. She drifted through the dry season, while her memories played out inside the interior of her shell: the sounds of guns firing in the fog, the sight of a young man dancing the *tau'olunga,* the smell of human sweat, the burning torches of *kailao* war dances, a young girl's white teeth. Deep in the core of all her dreams was a memory of something long ago lost, now finally forgotten.

The screw-pine trees fruited, then faded. The land crabs came and went, cleaning out the tortoise's massive hull until the pack rats could carry off her bones. The new Queen visited the empty carapace in the garden and polished it with coconut oil, fingers probing all the old scars and cracks, reading the hieroglyphs of history.

Annie Proulx

The Mud Below

From *The New Yorker*

OKLAHOMA

RODEO NIGHT in a hot little Okie town, and Diamond Felts was inside a metal chute a long way from the scratch on Wyoming dirt he named as home, sitting on the back of Bull 82N, a loose-skinned brindle-Brahma cross identified in the program as Little Kisses. There was a sultry feeling of weather. He kept his butt cocked to one side, his feet up on the chute rails so the bull couldn't grind his leg, brad him up, so if it thrashed he could get over the top in a hurry. The time came closer, and he slapped his face forcefully, bringing the adrenaline roses up on his cheeks, glanced down at his pullers, and said, "I guess." Rito, neck gleaming with sweat, caught the free end of the bull rope with a metal hook, brought it delicately to his hand from under the bull's belly, climbed up the rails, ready to pull it taut.

"Aw, this's a sumbuck," he said. "Give you the sample card."

Diamond took the end, made his wrap, brought the rope around the back of his hand and over the palm a second time, wove it between his third and fourth fingers, pounded the rosined glove fingers down over it and into his palm. He laid the tail of the rope across the bull's back and looped the excess, but it wasn't right— everything had gone a little slack. He undid the wrap and started over, making the loop smaller, waiting while they pulled again. In the arena, a clown fired a pink cannon, the fizzing discharge diminished by a deep stir of thunder from the south, Texas T-storm on the roll.

Night performances had their own hot charge—the glare, the stiff-legged parade of cowboy dolls in sparkle-fringed chaps, the spotlight that bucked over the squinting contestants and the half-roostered crowd. They were at the end of the night now. The bull beneath him breathed, shifted roughly.

In the first go-round he'd drawn a bull he knew and got a good scald on him. He'd been in a slump for weeks, wire stretched tight, but things were turning back his way. He'd come off that animal in a flying dismount, sparked a little clapping that quickly died; the watchers knew as well as he that if he burst into flames and sang an operatic aria after the whistle it would make no damn difference.

He drew O.K. bulls and rode them in the next rounds, scores in the high seventies, fixed his eyes on the outside shoulder of the welly bull that tried to drop him, then at the short-go draw he pulled Kisses, rank and salty, big as a boxcar of coal. On that one, all you could do was your best and hope for a little sweet luck; if you got the luck, he was money.

The announcer's voice rattled in the speakers above the enclosed arena. "Now folks, it ain't the Constitution or the Bill a Rights that made this a great country. It was God who created the mountains and plains and the evenin sunset and put us here and let us look at them. Amen and God bless the Markin flag. And right now we got a bull rider from Redsled, Wyomin, twenty-three-year-old Diamond Felts, who might be wonderin if he'll ever see that beautiful scenery again. Folks, Diamond Felts weighs one hundred and thirty pounds. Little Kisses weighs two thousand ten pounds. He is a big, big bull, and he is thirty-eight and one, last year's Dodge City Bull Riders' choice. Only one man has stayed on this big bad bull's back for eight seconds, and that was Marty Casebolt, at Reno, and you better believe that man got all the money. Will he be rode tonight? Folks, we're goin a find out in just a minute, soon as our cowboy's ready. And listen at that rain, folks, let's give thanks we're in a enclosed arena or it would be deep mud below."

Diamond glanced back at the flank man, moved up on his rope, nodded, jerking his head up and down rapidly. "Let's go, let's go."

The chute gate swung open and the bull squatted, leaped into the waiting silence, and, a paroxysm of twists, belly rolls and spins, skipping, bucking, and whirling, powerful drop, gave him the whole menu.

REDSLED, WYOMING

Diamond Felts, a constellation of moles on his left cheek, dark hair cropped to the skull, was more than good-looking when cleaned up and combed, in fresh shirt and his neckerchief printed with blue stars, but for most of his life he had not known it. Five feet three, rapping, tapping, nail-biting, he radiated unease. Diamond was a virgin at eighteen—not many of either sex in his senior class in that condition—and his tries at changing the situation went wrong and, as far as his despairing thought carried him, would always go wrong in the forest of tall girls. There were small women out there, but in the privacy of his head it was the six-footers he mounted.

All his life, he had heard himself called Half-Pint, Baby Boy, Shorty, Kid, Tiny, Little Guy, Sawed-Off. His mother never let up, always had the needle ready, even the time when she had come into the upstairs hall and caught him stepping naked from the bathroom she said, "Well, at least you didn't get shortchanged that way, did you?"

In the spring of his final year of school he drummed his fingers on Wallace Winter's pickup, listening to its swan-necked owner pump up a story, trying for the laugh, when a knothead they knew only as Leecil—God save the one who said Lucille—walked up and said, "Either one a you want a work this weekend? The old man's fixin a brand, and he's short-handed." He winked his dime-size eyes. His blunt face was corrugated with plum-colored acne and among the angry wellings grew a few blond whiskers. Diamond couldn't see how he shaved without bleeding to death. The smell of livestock was strong.

"He sure picked the wrong weekend," said Wallace. "Basketball game, parties, fucking, drinking, drugs, car wrecks, cops, food poisoning, fights. Didn't you tell him?"

"He didn't ask me. Tolt me get some guys. Anyway, it's good weather now. Stormt the weekend for a month." Leecil spit.

Wallace pretended serious consideration. "Scratch the weekend, I guess we get paid." He winked at Diamond, who grimaced to tell him that Leecil was not one to be teased.

"Yeah, six per, you guys. Me and my brothers got a work for nothin for the ranch. Anyway, we give or take quit at suppertime, so you can still do your stuff. Party, whatever." He wasn't going to any town blowout.

"I never did ranch work," Diamond said. "My mama grew up on a ranch and hated it. Only took us up there once, and I bet we didn't stay an hour," remembering an expanse of hoof-churned mud, his grandfather turning away, a muscular, sweaty Uncle John in chaps and filthy hat swatting him on the butt and saying something to his mother that made her mad.

"Don't matter. It's just work. Git the calves into the chute, brand em, fix em, vaccinate em, git em out."

"Fix em," said Diamond.

Leecil made an eloquent gesture at his crotch.

"It could be weirdly interesting," said Wallace. "I got something that will make it weirdly interesting."

"You don't want a git ironed out too much, have to lay down in the mud," said Leecil severely.

"No," said Wallace. "I fucking don't want to do that. O.K., I'm in. What the hell."

Diamond nodded.

Leecil cracked his mouthful of perfect teeth. "Know where our place is at? There's a bunch of different turn-offs. Here's how you go," and he drew a complicated map on the back of a returned quiz, red-marked F. That solved one puzzle; Leecil's last name was Bewd. Wallace looked at Diamond. The Bewd tribe, scattered from Fan Creek to Pine Bluffs, filled a double-X space in the local pantheon of troublemakers.

"7 A.M.," said Leecil.

❑ ❑ ❑ ❑

The good weather washed out. The weekend was a windy, overcast cacophony of bawling, manure-caked animals, mud, dirt, lifting, punching the needle, the stink of burning hair that he thought would never get out of his nose. Two crotch scratchers from school showed up; Diamond had seen them around, but he did not know them and thought of them as losers for no reason but that they were inarticulate and lived out on dirt-road ranches—friends of Leecil. Como Bewd, a grizzled man wearing a kidney belt, pointed this way and that as Leecil and his brothers worked the calves from pasture to corral to holding pen to chute and the yellow-hot electric branding iron to cutting table, where the ranch hand Lovis bent forward with his knife and with the other hand pulled the skin of the scrotum tight over one testicle and made a long outside cut through skin and membrane, yanked out the hot balls, dropped them into a bucket, and waited for the next calf. The dogs sniffed around, the omnipresent flies razzed and turmoiled, three saddled horses shifted from leg to leg under a tree and occasionally nickered.

Diamond glanced again and again at Como Bewd. The man's forehead showed a fence of zigzag scars like white barbed wire. He caught the stare and winked.

"Looking at my decorations? My brother run over me with his truck when I was your age. Took the skin off from ear to here. I was all clawed up. I was scalloped."

They finished late Sunday afternoon, and Como Bewd counted out their pay carefully and slowly, added an extra five to each pile, said they'd done a pretty fair job, then, to Leecil, said, "How about it?"

"You want a have some fun?" said Leecil to Diamond and Wallace. The others were already walking to a small corral some distance away.

"Like what?" said Wallace.

Diamond had a flash that there was a woman in the corral.

"Bull ridin. Dad's got some good buckin bulls. Our rodeo class come out last month and rode em. Couldn't hardly stay on one of em."

"I'll watch," said Wallace, in his ironic side-of-mouth voice.

Diamond considered rodeo classes the last resort of concrete heads who couldn't figure out how to hold a basketball. "Oh man," he said. "Bulls. I don't guess so."

Leecil Bewd ran ahead to the corral. There was a side pen and in it were three bulls, two of them pawing dirt. A chute opened into the corral. One of the crotch scratchers was in there already, jumping around, ready to play bullfighter and toll a bull away from a tossed rider.

To Diamond, the bulls looked murderous and wild, but even the ranch hands had a futile go at riding them. Leecil's father, bounced down in three seconds, hit the ground on his behind, the kidney belt riding up his chest.

"Try it," said Leecil, mouth bloody from a face slam, spitting.

"Aw, not me," said Wallace. "I got a life in front of me."

"Yeah," said Diamond. "Yeah, I guess I'll give it a go."

"Atta boy, atta boy," said Como Bewd, and handed him a rosined left glove. "Ever been on a bull?"

"No, sir," said Diamond, no boots, no spurs, no chaps, T-shirted and hatless. Leecil's old man told him to hold his free hand up, not to touch the bull or himself with it, keep his shoulders forward and his chin down, hold on with his feet and legs and left hand, above all not to think, and, when he got bucked off, no matter what was broke, get up quick and run like hell for the fence. He helped him make the wrap, ease down on the animal, said, "Shake your face and get out there," and, grinning, blood-speckled Lovis opened the chute gate, waiting to see the town kid dumped and dive-bombed.

But Diamond stayed on until someone counting eight hit the rail with the length of pipe to signal time. He flew off, landed on his feet, stumbling headlong but not falling in a run for the rails. He hauled himself up, panting from the exertion and the intense nervy rush. He'd been shot out of the cannon. The shock of the violent motion, the lightning shifts of balance, the feeling of power as though he were the bull and not the rider, even the fright, fulfilled some greedy physical hunger in him he hadn't known was there. The experience had been exhilarating and unbearably personal.

"You know what," said Como Bewd. "You might make a bull rider."

❑ ❑ ❑ ❑

Monday morning on the school bus, Diamond went for Leecil sitting in the back with one of the crotch scratchers. Leecil touched thumb and forefinger in a circle, winked.

"I need to talk to you. I want to know how to get into it. The bull riding. Rodeo."

"Don't think so," said the crotch scratcher. "First time you git stacked up, you'll yip for mama."

"He won't," said Leecil, and to Diamond, "You bet it ain't no picnic. Don't look for no picnic—you are goin a git tore up."

That night, he told his mother he was going to bull-riding school in California. Kaylee Felts managed a tourist store, High West—Vintage Cowboy Gear, Western Antiques, Spurs, Collectibles. A chain headquartered in Denver. She had told him there was probably a place in the business for him after college, one of the other stores if he wanted to see the world.

"What is this, some kid thing you kept to yourself all this time? No. You're going to college. I worked to bring you boys up in town, get you out of the mud, give you a chance to make something out of yourselves. You're just going to throw everything away to be a rodeo bum?"

"Well, I'm going to rodeo," he answered. "I'm going to ride bulls."

"Don't you get it?" she said. "Rodeo's for ranch boys who don't have the opportunities you do. The stupidest ones are the bull riders. We get them in the shop every week trying to sell us those pot-metal buckles or their dirty chaps."

"Doing it," he said. It could not be explained.

TEXAS

At the California bull-riding school, he rode thirty animals in a week, invested in a case of sports tape, watched videos until he fell asleep sitting up. The instructor's tireless nasal voice called, "Push on it, you can't never think you're goin a lose, don't look into the well, find your balance point, once you're tapped, get right back into the pocket, don't never quit."

Back in Wyoming, he found a room in Cheyenne, a junk job,

bought his permit, and started running the Mountain Circuit. He made his P.R.C.A. ticket in a month, thought he was in sweet clover. Somebody told him it was beginner's luck. He ran into Leecil Bewd at almost every rodeo, got drunk with him twice, and, after a time of red-eye solo driving, always broke, too much month and not enough money, hooked up with him and they travelled together, riding the jumps, covering bulls from one little rodeo to another, eating road dust. He had chosen a rough, bruising life and with it confused philosophies of striving to win and apologizing for it when he did. But there was a dark lightning in his gut now, a feeling of blazing real existence.

It worked pretty well for a year and then Leecil quit. It had been a scorching, dirty afternoon at the Greeley fairgrounds. Leecil squirted water from a gas-station hose over his head and neck, drove with the window cranked down, the dry wind sucking up the moisture immediately. The venomous blue sky threw heat.

"I wasn't packin enough in my shorts today to ride that trash," said Leecil. "Say what, the juice ain't worth the squeeze. Made up my mind while I was rollin in the dirt. I used a think I wanted a rodeo more than anything. But shoot, I gotta say I hate it. I don't got that thing you got, the style, the fuck-it-all-I-love-it thing. I miss the ranch bad. The old man's on my mind. He got some medical problem, can't hardly make his water good, told my brother there's blood in his bull stuff. They're doin tests. And there's Renata. What I'm tryin a say is, I'm cuttin out on you. Anyway, guess what, goin a get married."

"What do you mean? You knock Renata up?" It was all going at speed.

"Aw, yeah. It's O.K."

"Well, shit, Leecil. Won't be much fun now." He was surprised that it was true. He knew he had little talent for friends or affection, stood armored against love, though when it did come down on him later it came like an axe and he was slaughtered by it. "I never had a girl stick with me more than two hours. I don't know how you get past that two hours," he said.

Leecil looked at him.

After Leecil quit, he moved to Texas, where there was a rodeo every night for a fast driver, red-eyed from staring at pin headlights miles distant, alternately dark and burning as the road rose and fell away.

The second year, he was getting some notice and making money until a day or so before the big Fourth of July weekend. He came off a great ride and landed hard on his feet with his right knee sharply flexed, tore the ligaments and damaged cartilage. He was a fast healer, but it put him out for the summer. When he was off the crutches, bored and limping around on a cane, he thought about Redsled. The doctor said the hot springs there might be a good idea. He picked up a night ride with Tee Dove, a Texas bull rider, the big car slingshot toward a black hump of range, dazzle of morning an hour behind the rim, not a dozen words exchanged.

"It's a bone game," Tee Dove said, and Diamond, thinking he meant injuries, nodded.

REDSLED

For the first time in two years, he sat at his mother's table. She said, "Bless this food, amen, oh boy, I knew you'd be back one of these days. And look at you. Just take a look at you. Like you climbed out of a ditch." She was dolled up. Her hair was long and streaked blond, crimped like Chinese noodles, and her eyelids were iridescent blue.

They ate in silence, forks clicking among the pieces of cucumber and tomato. He disliked cucumber. She got up, clattered small plates with gold rims onto the table, brought out a supermarket lemon-meringue pie, began to cut it with the silver pie server.

"All right," said Diamond, "calf-slobber pie."

Pearl, his ten-year-old brother, let out a bark.

She stopped cutting and fixed him with a stare. "You can talk ugly when you're with your rodeo bums, but when you are home keep your tongue decent."

He looked at her, seeing the cold blame. "I'll pass on that pie."

"I think all of us will after that unforgettable image."

She went out then, some kind of Western-junk meeting at the Redsled Inn, sticking him with the dishes. It was as if he'd never left.

He came down late the next morning. Pearl was sitting at the kitchen table reading a comic book. He was wearing the T-shirt Diamond had sent. It read "Give Blood, Ride Bulls." It was too small.

"Mama's gone to the shop. She said you should eat cereal, not eggs. Eggs have cholesterol. I saw you on TV once. I saw you get bucked off."

Diamond fried two eggs in butter and ate them out of the pan, fried two more. He looked for coffee, but there was only a jar of instant dust.

"I'm going to get a buckle like yours when I'm eighteen," Pearl said. "And I'm not going to get bucked off because I'll hold on with the grip of death. Like this." And he made a white-knuckled fist.

"This ain't a terrific buckle."

"I'm going to tell Mama you said 'ain't.' "

"For Christ's sake, that's how everybody talks. Except for one old booger steer roper. You want an egg?"

"I hate eggs. They aren't good for you. Ain't good for you. How does the old booger talk? Does he say 'calf-slobber pie'?"

"Why do you think she buys eggs if nobody's supposed to eat them? The old booger's religious. Always reading pamphlets about Jesus. Actually he's not old. He's no older than me. He's younger than me. He don't never say 'ain't.' He don't say 'shit' or 'fuck' or 'cunt' or 'prick' or 'goddam.' He says 'Good Lord' when he's pissed off or gets slammed up the side of his head."

Pearl laughed immoderately, excited by the forbidden words and low-down grammar spoken in their mother's kitchen.

"Rodeo's full of Jesus freaks. And double and triple sets of brothers. All kinds of Texas cousins. There's some fucking strange guys in it. It's like a magic show sometimes, with prayers and jujus and crosses and amulets and superstitions. Anybody does anything good, makes a good ride, it's not them, it's their mystical-power connection helping them out." He yawned, began to rub the bad knee. "So, you're going to hold on tight and not get bucked off?"

"Yeah. Really tight."

"I'll have to remember to try that," said Diamond.

On Thursday night after supper, she said to Diamond, "I've got something I want you to see. We'll just take us a little ride."

"Can I come?" said Pearl.

"No. This is something I want your brother to see. Watch TV. We'll be back in an hour."

"What is it," said Diamond, remembering the dark smear on the street she had brought him to years before. She had pointed, said, he didn't look both ways. He knew it would be something like that. He should not have come back.

She drove past the scrap-metal pile and the bentonite plant and, at the edge of town, crossed the railroad tracks where the road turned into rough dirt cutting through prairie. Under a yellow sunset stood several low metal buildings. The windows reflected the bright honey-colored west.

She said. "Hondo Gunsch? You know that name?"

"No." But he had heard it somewhere.

"Here," she said, pulling up in front of the largest building. Thousands of insects barely larger than dust motes floated in the luteous air. She walked quickly, he followed, dotting along.

"Hello," she called into the dark hallway. A light snapped on. A man in a white shirt came through a door, his pocket stiffened with a piece of plastic to hold his ballpoint pens. He had a black hat, brim bent like the wings of a crow, and a face crowded with freckles, spectacles, beard, and mustache.

"Hey there, Kaylee." The man looked at her as though she were hot buttered toast.

"This is Shorty, wants to be a rodeo star. Shorty, this is Kerry Moore."

Diamond shook the man's hand. It was an exchange of hostilities.

"Hondo's out in the tack room," said the man, looking at her. He laughed. "Always in the tack room. He'd sleep there if we let him. Come on out here."

He opened a door into a large, square room at the end of the stables. The last light fell through high windows, gilding bridles, and reins hanging on the wall. A small refrigerator hummed behind a desk, and on the wall above it Diamond saw a framed magazine cover, *Boots 'n Bronks,* August, 1960, showing a saddle-bronc rider, straight, square, and tucked on a high-twisted horse, spurs raked all the way up to the cantle, his outflung arm in front of him. His hat was gone and his mouth open in a crazy smile. A banner read "GUNSCH TAKES CHEYENNE SB CROWN." The horses back was humped, his nose pointed down, hind legs straight in a powerful jump and five feet of daylight between the descending front hooves and the ground.

In the middle of the room, an elderly man worked leather cream into a saddle; he wore a straw hat with the brim rolled high on the sides. There was something wrong in the set of the shoulders, the forward slope of his torso from the hips. The room smelled of apples, and Diamond saw a basket of them on the floor.

"Hondo, we got visitors." The man looked past them at nothing, revealing a flat bulb of a crushed nose, a dished cheekbone, the great dent above the left eye, which seemed sightless. His mouth was pursed with concentration. There was a pack of cigarettes in his shirt pocket. There was a kind of carved-wood quietude about him, common to those who have been a long time without sex, out of the traffic of the world.

"This here's Kaylee Felts and Shorty, stopped by to say howdy. Shorty's into rodeo. Guess you know something about rodeo, don't you, Hondo?" He spoke loudly, as though the man were deaf.

The bronc rider said nothing, his blue, sweet gaze returning to the saddle, the right hand holding a piece of lamb's wool, beginning again to move back and forth over the leather.

"He don't say much," said Moore. "He has a lot of difficulty but he keeps tryin. He's got plenty of try, haven't you, Hondo?"

The man was silent, working the leather. How many years since he had spurred a horse's shoulders, toes pointed east and west?

"Hondo, looks like you ought to change them sorry old floppy stirrup leathers one day," said Moore in a commanding tone. The bronc rider gave no sign he had heard.

"Well," said Diamond's mother after a long minute of watching the sinewy hands, "it was wonderful to meet you, Hondo. Good luck." She glanced at Moore, and Diamond could see a message fly but didn't know their language.

They walked outside, the man and woman together, Diamond following, so deeply angered he staggered.

"Yeah. He's kind a deaf, old Hondo. He was a hot saddle-bronc rider on his way to the top. Took the money two years runnin at Cheyenne. Then some dinky little rodeo up around Meeteetse, his horse threw a fit in the chute, went over backwards, Hondo went down, got his head stepped on. Oh, 1961, and he been cleanin saddles for the Bar J since then. Thirty-seven years. That's a long, long time. He was twenty-six when it happened. Smart as anybody. Well, if you rodeo, you're a rooster on Tuesday, feather duster on Wednesday. But, like I say, he's still got all the try in the world. We sure think a lot a Hondo."

They stood silently watching Diamond get into the car.

"I'll call you," said the man, and she nodded.

Diamond glared out the window at the plain, the railroad tracks, the pawnshop, the Safeway, the Broken Arrow bar, Custom Cowboy, the vacuum-cleaner shop. The sun was down, and a velvety dusk coated the street, the bar neons spelling good times.

As she turned onto the river road, she said, "I would take you to see a corpse to get you out of rodeo."

"You won't take me to see anything again."

The glassy black river slowed between dim willows. She drove very slowly.

"My God," she shouted suddenly, "what you've cost me!"

"What! What have I cost you?" The words shot out like flame from the mouth of a fire-eater.

The low beams of cars coming toward them in the dusk lit the wet run of her tears. There was no answer until she turned into the last street, then, in a guttural, adult woman's voice, raw and deep, as he had never heard it, she said, *"Everything."*

He was out of the car before it stopped, limping up the stairs, stuffing clothes in his duffelbag. He called a taxi to take him to the cracker-box airport, where he sat for five hours until a flight with connections to Calgary left.

CODY, WYOMING

He bought a thirdhand truck, an old Texas hoopy, travelled alone for a few months, needing the solitary distances, blowing past mesas and red buttes piled like meat, humped and horned, and on the highway chunks of mule deer, hair the buckskin color of winter grass, flesh like rough breaks in red country, playas of dried blood.

He almost always had a girl in the motel bed with him, making up for years of nothing, a half-hour painkiller but without the rush and thrill he got from a bull ride. There was no sweet time when it was over. He wanted to get gone. The in-and-out girls wasped it around that he was quick on the trigger, an arrogant little prick.

"Hit the delete button on you, buddy," flipping the whorish blond hair.

What they said didn't matter because there was an endless supply of them by now and because he knew he was getting down the page and into the fine print of this way of living. There was nobody in his life to slow him down with love. Sometimes riding the bull was the least part of it, but only the turbulent ride gave him the indescribable rush, shot him mainline with crazy-ass elation. In the arena, everything was real because none of it was real except the chance to get dead. The charged bolt came, he thought, because he wasn't dead.

One night in Cody, running out to the parking lot to beat the traffic, Pake Bitts, a big Jesus-loving steer roper, yelled out to him "You goin a Roswell?"

"Yeah." Pake Bitts was a big stout guy with white-blond hair and high color. A sticker, "Praise God," was peeling loose from his gear bag.

"Can I git a ride? My dee truck quit on me up in Livinston. Had to rent a puny car, thing couldn't hardly haul my trailer. Burned out the transmission."

"You bet. Let's go. If you're ready." They hitched up Bitts's horse trailer, left the rental car standing.

"Fog it, brother, we're short on time," said the roper, jumping in.

Diamond had the wheels spattering gravel before he closed the door.

He thought it would be bad, a lot of roadside prayers and upcast eyes, but Pake Bitts was steady, watched the gas gauge, took care of business, and didn't preach.

Big and little, they went on together to Mollala, Roswell, Guthrie, Kaycee, Baker, and Bend. After a few weeks, Pake said that if Diamond wanted a permanent travelling partner he was up for it. Diamond said yeah, although he knew that only a few states still allowed steer roping and that Pake would have to cover long, empty ground, his main territory in the livestock country of Oklahoma, Wyoming, Oregon, and New Mexico. Their schedules did not fit into the same box without patient adjustment. But Pake knew a hundred dirt-road shortcuts. He steered them through scabland and slope country, in and out of the tiger shits, over the tawny plain still grooved with pilgrim wagon ruts, into early darkness and the first storm laying down black ice, ragged webs of dry rain that never hit the ground, through small-town traffic, band of horses in morning fog, two redheaded cowboys moving a house that filled the roadway, and Pake busting around and into the ditch to get past, leaving junk yards and Mexican cafés behind, turning into midnight motel entrances with "Ring Office Bell" signs or pulling off onto the black prairie for a stunned hour of sleep.

Bitts came from Rawlins, Wyoming, and always wanted to get to the next rodeo and grab at the money, was interested in no woman but his big-legged, pregnant wife, Nancy, a heavy Christian girl, studying, said Bitts, for her degree in geology. "You wont a have a good talk," he said, "have one with Nancy. Good Lord, she can tell you all about rock formations."

"How can a geologist believe that the earth was created in seven days?"

"Shoot, she's a Christian geologist. Nothin is impossible for God, and he could do it all in seven days, fossils, the whole nine. Life is full a wonders." He laid a chew of long-cut into his cheek for even he had his vices.

"How did you get into it," asked Diamond. "Grow up on a ranch?"

"Never lived on a ranch. Grew up in Huntsville, Texas. You know what's there?"

"Big prison."

"Right. Huntsville had a real good prison rodeo program for years. My dad took me. He got me started in a Little Britches program. My granddad Bitts was in Huntsville, too. Did most of his ropin there. He had a tattoo of a rope around his neck and piggin strings around his wrists. But he seen the light after a few years and took Jesus into his heart, and that passed on down to my dad and to me. And I try to live a Christian life and help others."

They drove in silence for half an hour, light overcast dulling the basin grass to the shades of dirty pennies. Then Pake started in again.

"Bringin me to somethin I wont a say to you. About your bull ridin. About rodeo? See, the bull is not supposed a be your role model, he is your opponent and you have to get the best a him, same as the steer is my opponent and I have to pump up and git everything right to catch and thow em or I won't thow em."

"Hey, I know that." He'd known, too, that there would be a damn sermon sooner or later.

"No, you don't. Because if you did you wouldn't be playin the bull night after night. You would be a man lookin for someone to marry and raise up a family with. You'd take Jesus for a role model, not a dee ornery bull. Which you can't deny you done. You got a quit off playin the bull."

"I didn't think Jesus was a married man."

"Maybe not a married man, but he was a cowboy, the original rodeo cowboy. It says it right in the Bible. It's in Matthew, Mark, Luke, and John." He adopted a sanctimonious tone: "Go into the village in which, at your enterin, ye shall find a colt tied, on which yet never so man sat; loose him and bring him here. The Lord hath need a him. And they brought him to Jesus, and they cast their garments upon the colt, and they set Jesus on it. Now, if that ain't a description a bareback ridin I don't know what is."

"I ride a bull, the bull's my partner, and if bulls could drive you can bet there'd be one sitting behind the wheel right now. I don't know how you figure all this stuff about me."

"Easy. Myron Sasser's my half brother." He rolled down the window and spit. "Dad had a little bull in him, too. But he got over it."

Pake started in again a day or two later. Diamond was sick of hearing about Jesus and family values. Pake had said, "You got a kid brother, that right? How come he ain't never at none of these rodeos lookin at his big brother? And your daddy and mama?"

"Pull over a minute."

Bitts eased the truck over on the hard prairie verge, threw it into park, misguessing that Diamond wanted to piss, got out himself, unzipping.

"Wait," said Diamond, standing where the light fell hard on him. "I want you to take a good look at me. You see me?" He turned sideways and back, faced Bitts. "That's all there is. What you see. Now do your business and let's get down the road."

CHEYENNE, WYOMING

He had a wide-legged walk now as though there was swinging weight between his thighs. He dived headlong into the easy girls. He wanted the tall ones. In that bullish condition he had tangled legs with the wife of Myron Sasser, his second travelling partner. He couldn't regret it now. It had happened. He had been in Cheyenne in Myron's truck and Myron's wife was with them, sitting in the back seat of the club cab. All of them were hungry. Myron pulled into the Burger Bar. He left the truck running, the radio loud.

"How many you want, Diamond, two or three? Londa, you want onions with yours?"

They had picked her up at Myron's parents' house in Pueblo the day before. She was five-eleven, long brown curls like Buffalo Bill, had looked at Diamond and said to Myron, "You didn't say he was hardly fryin size. Hey there, Chip."

"That's me," he said, "smaller than the little end of nothing whittled to a point," smiled through murder.

She showed them a heart-shaped waffle iron she had bought at a yard sale. It was not electric; it was a gadget from the days of the wood-burning range. The handles were of twisted wire. She promised Myron a Valentine breakfast.

"I'll get this," said Myron and went into the Burger Bar.

Diamond waited with her in the truck, aroused by her orchidaceous female smell. Through the glass window they could see Myron standing near the end of a long line. He thought of what she'd said, moved out of the front seat and into the back with her and pinned her, wrestled her 36-inseam jeans down to her ankles and got it in, like fucking sandpaper, and his stomach growling with hunger the whole time. She was not willing. She bucked and shoved and struggled and cursed him, she was dry, but he wasn't going to stop then. Something fell off the seat with a hard sound.

"My waffle iron," she said and nearly derailed him. He finished in five or six crashing strokes and it was done. He was back in the front seat before Myron reached the head of the line.

"I heard it called a lot of things," he said, "but never a waffle iron," and laughed until he choked. He felt fine.

She cried angrily in the seat behind him, pulling at her clothes.

"Hey," he said. "Hush up. It didn't hurt you. I'm too damn small to hurt a big girl like you, right? I'm the one should be crying—could have burred it off." He couldn't believe it when she opened the door and jumped down, ran into the Burger Bar, threw herself at Myron. He saw Myron putting his head over to listen to her, glancing out at the parking lot where he could see nothing, wiping the tears from her face with a paper napkin he took from the counter, and then charging toward the door with squared, snarling mouth. Diamond got out of the truck. Might as well meet it head on.

"What a you done to Londa?"

"Same thing you did to that wormy Texas buckle bunny the other night." He didn't have anything against Myron Sasser except that he was a humorless fascist who picked his nose and left pliant knobs of snot on the steering wheel, but he wanted the big girl to get it clear and loud.

"You little pissant shit," said Myron and came windmilling at him. Diamond had him flat on the macadam, face in a spilled milkshake, but in seconds more lay beside him knocked colder than a wedge by the waffle iron.

OKLAHOMA

Little Kisses, Bull 82N, let the hammer down. In the sixth second, the bull stopped dead, then shifted one way and immediately back again, and Diamond was lost, flying to the left and over the animal's shoulder, his eye catching the bull's wet glare, but his hand had turned upside down and was jammed. He was hung up and good.

"Stay on your feet," he said aloud, "jump, amen."

The bull was crazy to get rid of him and the clanging bell. Diamond was jerked off the ground with every lunge, snapped like a towel. The rope was in a half-twist, binding his folded fingers against the bull's back, and he could not turn his hand over and open the fingers. Everything in him strained to touch the ground with his feet, but the bull was too big and he was too small. The bullfighters darted like terriers. The animal whipped him from the Arctic Circle to the Mexico border with every plunge. There was bull hair in his mouth. His arm was being pulled from its socket. It went on and on. This time he was going to die in front of shouting strangers. The bull's drop lifted him high, and the bullfighter, waiting for the chance, thrust his hand up under Diamond's arm, rammed the tail of the rope through, and jerked. The fingers of his glove opened and he fell cartwheeling away from hooves. Then the bull was on him, hooking. He curled, got his good arm over his head.

"Oh man, get up, this's a mean one," someone far away called and he was running on all fours, rump in the air, to the metal rails, a clown there, the bull already gone. The audience suddenly laughed and out of the corner of his eye he saw the other clown mocking his stagger. He pressed against the rails, back to the audience, dazed, unable to move. They were waiting for him to get out of the arena. Beyond the beating rain a siren sounded faint and sad.

A hand patted him twice on the right shoulder, someone said, "Can you walk?" Trembling, he tried to nod his head and could not. His left arm hung limp. He profoundly believed that death had marked him out, then had ridden him almost to the buzzer, but had somehow wrecked. The man got in under his right arm, someone else grasped him around the waist, half carried him to a room where a local saw-bones sat swinging one foot and smoking a cigarette. No sports-medicine team here. He thought dully that he did not want to be looked at by a doctor who smoked.

From the arena, the announcer's voice echoed as though in a culvert, "What a ride folks, far as it went, but all for nothing, a zero for Diamond Felts, but you got a be proud a what this young man stands for, don't let him go away without a big hand, he's goin a be all right, and now here's Dunny Scotus from Whipup, Texas—"

He could smell the doctor's clouded breath, his own rank stench. He was slippery with sweat and the roaring pain.

"Can you move your arm? Are your fingers numb? Can you feel this? O.K., let's get this shirt off." He set the jaws of his scissors at the cuff and began to cut up the sleeve.

"That's a fifty-dollar shirt," whispered Diamond. It was a new one, with a design of red feathers and black arrows across the sleeves and breast.

"Believe me, you wouldn't appreciate it if I tried to pull your arm out of the sleeve." The scissors worked across the front yoke and the ruined shirt fell away. The air felt cold on his wet skin. He shook and shook. It was a bad-luck shirt now anyway.

"There you go," said the doctor. "Dislocated shoulder. Humerus displaced forward from the shoulder socket. I want an X-ray first."

"Can't you—"

"X-ray."

In the mobile X-ray unit a fattish woman red-peppered with freckles guided him into position as though he held a vial of nitro-glycerine, then led him back to the doctor.

"All right, I'm going to try to reposition the humerus." The doctor's chin was against the back of his shoulder, his hands taking the useless arm, powerful smell of tobacco. "This will hurt for a minute. I'm going to manipulate this—"

"Jesus *CHRIST!*" The pain was excruciating and violent. The tears rolled down his hot face and he couldn't help it.

"Cowboy up," said the doctor sardonically.

Pake Bitts walked in, looked at him with interest.

"Got hung up, hah? I didn't see it but they said you got hung up pretty good. Twenty-eight seconds. They'll put you on the videos. Thunderstorm out there." He was damp from the shower. He spoke to the doctor. "Throw his shoulder out? Can he drive? It's his turn a drive. We gotta be in south Texas two o'clock tomorrow afternoon."

The doctor finished wrapping the cast, lit another cigarette. "I wouldn't want to do it—right hand's all he's got. Dislocated shoulder, it's not just a question of pop it back in and away you go. He could need surgery. There's injured ligaments, internal bleeding, swelling, pain, could be some nerve damage. He's hurting. He's going to be in the cast for a month. If he's going to drive, one-handed or with his teeth, I can't give him codeine and you'd better not let him take any, either. You may want to call your insurance company."

"What insurance?" said Pake. Then, "You ought a quit off smokin." And to Diamond, "Well, the good Lord spared you. When can we get out a here? Hey, you see how they spelled my name? Good Lord." He yawned hugely, had driven all the last night coming down from Idaho.

"Give me ten. Let me get in the shower, steady up. You get my rope and war bag. I'll be O.K. to drive. I just need ten."

The doctor said, "On your way, pal."

Someone else was coming in, a deep cut over his left eyebrow, finger pressed below the cut to keep the blood out of his rapidly swelling eyes, and he was saying, "Just tape it up, tape the fuckin eyes open, I'm gettin on one."

He undressed one-handed in the grimy concrete shower room, having trouble with the four-buckle chaps and his boot straps. The pain came in long ocean rollers. He couldn't get on the other side of it. There was someone in one of the shower stalls, leaning his forehead against the concrete, hands flat against the wall and taking hot water on the back of his neck.

Diamond saw himself in the spotted mirror, two black eyes, bloody nostrils, his abraded right cheek, his hair dark with sweat, bull hairs stuck to his dirty, tear-streaked face, a bruise from armpit to buttocks. He was dizzy with the pain, and a huge weariness overtook him. The euphoric charge had never kicked in this time. If he were dead this might be hell—smoking doctors and rank bulls, eight hundred miles of night road ahead, hurting all the way.

The cascade of water stopped and Tee Dove came out of the shower, hair plastered flat. He was ancient, Diamond knew, thirty-six, an old man for bull riding but still doing it. His sallow-cheeked face was a map of surgical repair, and he carried enough body scars to open a store. A few months earlier Diamond had seen him, broken nose draining dark blood, take two yellow pencils and push one into each nostril, maneuvering them until the smashed cartilage and nasal bones were forced back into position.

Dove rubbed his scarred torso with his ragged but lucky towel, showed his fox teeth to Diamond, said, "Ain't it a bone game, bro."

Outside the rain had stopped, the truck gleamed wet, gutters flooded with runoff. Pake Bitts was in the passenger seat, already asleep. He woke when Diamond, bare-chested, bare-footed, pulled the seat forward, threw in the cut shirt, fumbled one-handed in his duffelbag for an oversized sweatshirt he could get over the cast, jammed into his old athletic shoes, got in, and started the engine.

"You O.K. to drive? You hold out two, three hours while I get some sleep. I'll take it the rest a the way. You drive the whole road is not a necessity by no means."

"It's O.K. How did they spell your name?"

"C-a-k-e. Cake Bitts. Nance'll laugh her head off over that one. Burn a rag, brother, we're runnin' late."

And he was asleep again, calloused hand resting on his thigh palm up and a little open as though to receive something.

Just over the Texas border, he pulled into an all-night truck stop and filled the tank, bought two high-caffeine colas and drank them, washing down his keep-awakes and pain-stoppers. He walked past the cash registers and aisles of junk food to the telephones, fumbled the phone card from his wallet and dialled. It would be two-thirty in Redsled.

She answered on the first ring. Her voice was clear. She was awake.

"It's me," he said. "Diamond."

"Shorty?" she said. "What?"

"Listen, there's no way I can put this that's gentle or polite. Who was my father?"

"What do you mean? Shirley Custer Felts. You know that."

"No," he said. "I don't know that." Shirley Custer Felts had walked out ten years before. "Get the fuck out of the way were his last words to me. Get the fuck out of the way, you little bastard. You ain't no kid of mine."

"That dirty man," she said. "He set you up like a time bomb."

"I'm no time bomb. I'm just asking you, who was he?"

"I told you." As she spoke, he heard a deep smothered cough over the wire.

"I don't believe you. Third time, who was my father?"

He waited.

"Who you got there, Mama? The big slob with the black hat?"

"Nobody," she said and hung up. He didn't know which question she'd answered.

He was still standing there when Pake Bitts came in, shuffling and yawning.

"You wont me a drive now?" He pounded the heel of his hand on his forehead.

"No, get you some sleep."

"Aw, yeah. Piss on the fire, boy, and let's go."

He was O.K. to drive. He would drive all the way. He could do it now, this time, many more times to come. Yet it was as though some bearing had seized up inside him and burned out. It had been not the phone call but the flat minute pressed against the rail, when he could not walk out of the arena.

He pulled back onto the empty road. There were a few ranch lights miles away, the black sky against the black terrain drawing them into the hem of the starry curtain. As he drove toward the clangor and flash of the noon arena, he considered the old saddle-bronco rider rubbing leather for thirty-seven years, Leecil riding off into the mosquito-clouded sunset, the ranch hand bent over a calf, slitting the scrotal sac. The course of life's events seemed slower than the knife but not less thorough.

There was more to it than that, he supposed, and heard again her hoarse, charged voice saying, *"Everything."* It was all a hard, fast ride that ended in the mud. He passed a coal train in the dark, the dense rectangles that were the cars gliding against indigo night, another, and another. Very slowly, as slowly as light comes on a clouded morning, the euphoric heat flushed through him, or maybe just the memory of it.

Contributors' Notes

PETER BAIDA grew up in Baltimore, lives in New York City, and works as director, direct mail fund-raising, at Memorial Sloan-Kettering Cancer Center. He has published fiction in *The Gettysburg Review, American Literary Review, Western Humanities Review, Confrontation,* and elsewhere, and nonfiction in *The Atlantic, American Heritage, The American Scholar,* and elsewhere. He is the author of *Poor Richard's Legacy: American Business Values from Benjamin Franklin to Donald Trump.*

" 'A Nurse's Story' was inspired by 'Sisters, Can You Spare a Dime,' a nonfiction account of a nurses' strike that appeared in the July 10, 1995, issue of *The Nation.*

" 'A Nurse's Story' is a whole-life rather than a slice-of-life story. What pleases me most about it is that it captures, as well as I could, the life of a decent woman. I don't usually like happy endings, but I like the one in this story. I also like and admire my main character, Mary McDonald. If you feel good when you finish reading this story, you can thank Mary. Many of my stories are angry, but Mary would not let me write an angry story.

"Sometimes I find it helpful to have some scene by a better writer in mind while I work on scenes in my fiction. For instance, I was thinking about the gravediggers' scene in *Hamlet* when I wrote the embalming scene in 'A Nurse's Story.' I don't think that this is stealing, just intelligent borrowing. The last scene in 'A Nurse's Story' (Mary's family at her deathbed) was inspired by the scene in *The Wizard of Oz* when Dorothy awakens back in Kansas, surrounded by the farmhands whom we recognize as the Scarecrow, the Cowardly Lion, and the Tin Man.

"For a year or so I knew that I wanted to write a story about a nurses' strike, but I could not find a form that fit the story. Once I decided to begin near the end of Mary's life, and to move back and forth in Mary's mind, everything seemed to fall into place. The key, I think, is that the story moves forward both in the present (through Mary's conversations with Eunice) and in Mary's memories.

"A note of encouragement for middle-aged writers: I was forty-six when I wrote 'A Nurse's Story,' and had published exactly one story in the previous twenty years. A discouraging note: twenty-two editors rejected the story before Peter Stitt took it for *The Gettysburg Review*. Thinking about the twenty-two rejections, I wonder: What are editors looking for? How good does a story have to be to get published in the 1990s?

" 'A Nurse's Story' is dedicated to my wife, Diane Cole, and to my son Edward. In about ten years, when he is old enough to read it, Edward may wish to know that he appears in the story—not in the form of a little boy but in the form of the girl Coretta, making a fuss when her mother declares that the time has come to leave the playground. I'm sorry, Edward, if you dislike being transformed into a girl, but that's what happens in stories."

PINCKNEY BENEDICT grew up on his family's dairy farm in the mountains of southern West Virginia. He has published two collections of short fiction and a novel. His stories have appeared, among other places, in *Esquire, Pushcart XXI: Best of the Small Presses, Zoetrope All-Story, Ontario Review, Story,* and *The Oxford Book of American Short Stories.* He is an associate professor in the Creative Writing Program at Hollins University in Roanoke, Virginia.

"I remember being afraid (I was a clumsy kid) of catching my arms or my legs in the machinery around the farm and having them torn off. So probably 'Miracle Boy' is my way, as an adult, of reassuring myself: saying, 'Well, it didn't happen, and if it had happened, it would have been okay, because they'd have been reattached, and anyway I'd have been graceful about the whole thing.' "

T. CORAGHESSAN BOYLE: "My temptation here is to speak about myself in the third person, but I'm going to resist it. Quite simply, I am honored to be included in this august annual volume for the third time, especially as I am a longtime aficionado of the short story. I have published seven novels, the most recent of which is *Riven Rock,* and five volumes of short stories, including, this past year, a collected volume of sixty-eight pieces called *T. C. Boyle Stories*. I have been the recipient of a number of awards and honors, for which I am deeply grateful, including the 1988 PEN/Faulkner Award for *World's End* and the 1997 Prix Médicis Étranger for *The Tortilla Curtain*.

" 'The Underground Gardens' is one of a group stories I did not include in the collected volume, but have instead reserved for the next collection, *After the Plague,* which should appear in 2001. Baldasare Forestiere is a figure from history, and he did indeed carve out the underground gardens of Fresno, which remain as a tourist attraction. I knew only the bare bones of his biography, and interpolated from there. What would provoke a man to such extreme behavior, I wondered, and why go underground? The answer, for my fiction, at least, was love. What else? The actual Baldasare was apparently rejected by his inamorata in Sicily, who did not want to return with him to Fresno; my Baldasare had both a happier and a sadder fate."

MICHAEL CHABON: "I was born in 1963, in Washington, D.C., and, after several early dislocations brought about by my physician father's various medical residencies and his hitch in the U.S. Public Health Service, raised in the Maryland suburbs—specifically in Columbia, a mildly utopian 'New Town.' My childhood was itself rather utopian, to a point.

"After my parents' divorce, my father moved to Pittsburgh, a chance that has since determined not only my college career (a year at Carnegie-Mellon, then three at Pitt) but the settings of my first two novels (*The Mysteries of Pittsburgh* and *Wonder Boys*) and a number of my stories (collected in *A Model World and Other Stories*). I got an M.F.A. in Creative Writing at U.C. Irvine, and have spent most of the past fifteen years in Southern California, with brief sojourns in Washington State, Florida, and New York State. Since 1997 I have been living in Berkeley, where I am on the point of finishing my third novel, *Kavalier & Clay,* due next year from Random House. 'Son of the Wolfman' has also appeared in my second collection of stories, *Werewolves in Their Youth*.

" 'Son of the Wolfman' arose in part from a sudden easy familiarity with pregnancy, labor, delivery, midwifery, and the mysteries of *courage* that I derived from the gestations and births of my own two children. God only knows where the rest of it came from."

MICHAEL CUNNINGHAM is the author of the novels *A Home at the End of the World, Flesh and Blood,* and *The Hours,* which won both the 1999 PEN/Faulkner Award and the 1999 Pulitzer Prize. His stories have appeared in *The New Yorker, DoubleTake, The Atlantic Monthly*, and *The Paris Review,* as well as *The Penguin Book of Gay Short Stories* and *The KGB Bar Reader.* He has received fellowships from the Guggenheim and Whiting foundations. He teaches in the M.F.A. program at Columbia University.

"I almost always begin a novel or story convinced that I've got a good, simple idea in mind, that I know exactly what will happen, and that this time, finally, the work will go quickly, will be free of false starts and blind alleys, and will be finished, essentially, in one draft. That has never occurred, and yet I persist so obdurately in the illusion that I've come to accept it as necessary. If I have to trick myself into writing, so be it.

" 'Mister Brother' started with the title, which is rare for me. I generally write whatever I write, see what it turns out to be, and then give it a name, which again seems like a necessary part of my process but is, in practice, very much like waiting to name the baby until he or she turns thirty-five. The title 'Mister Brother' presented itself mysteriously one afternoon while I was doing errands, and once I'd decided that it would concern a boy who's in love with his older brother I believed I would simply set one sentence rapidly on top of another until it was done. Two months later, after countless discarded drafts, I had a seven-page story."

KIANA DAVENPORT is *hapa haole,* half Native Hawai'ian, half Anglo-American. She is the author of the novels *Shark Dialogues* and most recently *Song of the Exile.* Her short fiction has been published worldwide.

"In 1987, traveling from Honolulu to Auckland, I stopped to visit friends in Fiji. During my stay, the prime minister and his cabinet were kidnapped. It was the first military coup in the history of the South Pacific. Radio stations were shut down. Parts of Suva city were in flames. People were killed.

"The potential layers of deception in this event have haunted me: a prime minister deceiving his people, the military leader of the coup deceiving and murdering his friend, a mercenary deceiving his mistress, a woman deceiving her clan. 'Fork Used in Eating Reverend Baker' is also a cautionary tale: an educated woman turns her back on her culture and loses her jungle instincts, her hiding-and-hunting skills. She can no longer discern what is merely fascinating and what is deadly."

CHARLOTTE FORBES lives in New York with her husband and daughter. Her stories have appeared in *Other Voices, Sycamore Review, New Delta Review,* and other magazines.

"I once knew a Reggie, who like the Reggie in the story was a drifter. My husband hired him to do some odd jobs and to help restore some religious statues he had come upon. We both took to Reggie, he had a brilliance and vulnerability that were irresistible. Then two or three odd things happened that sent my imagination into overdrive."

CARY HOLLADAY, a native of Virginia, is the author of two short-story collections, *The Palace of Wasted Footsteps* (University of Missouri Press, 1998) and *The People Down South* (University of Illinois Press, 1989). She lives in Memphis.

"I found the term 'merry-go-sorry,' which serves as the title for this story, in an old copy of *The Book of Lists.* It's an ancient word that means a tale containing both good news and bad. As soon as I saw it, I recognized it as a principle underlying my own way of storytelling.

"In trying to come to terms with the horrific subject matter of this particular story, I gained a greater understanding of Memphis, Arkansas, and the Delta region: a proud, defiant, emotional culture where tragedies stay fiercely fresh in recollection, prayer, and debate."

PAM HOUSTON is the author of two books of short stories, *Cowboys Are My Weakness* and *Waltzing the Cat,* as well as a forthcoming book of essays, *A Little More About Me.* She lives at nine thousand feet above sea level in Colorado, near the headwaters of the Rio Grande.

"I wrote 'Cataract' not long after a near-fatal trip of my own down Cataract Canyon. I was very aware, the whole time I was writing it, that since it was my second river story, its reason to be needed to be something other than the life and death drama of surviving a river accident, though the story certainly contains its share of that. I got very interested in the boy's boat/girl's boat nature of the trip, in the very complicated, rarely spoken, and often divergent reasons men and women find themselves risking their lives in the outdoors. As always, I was driven into the story by the metaphoric potential of the place-names of the Colorado Plateau: The Doll's House, Spanish Bottom, Upheaval Dome, and most intriguing of all, The Land Behind the Rocks. I was worried, during the writing, about the length of the denouement, the way it winds around river bend after river bend, pages after the story has reached its climax. As it turns out, those are the pages in which the story really happens, when everything about it that surprised me takes place."

JHUMPA LAHIRI's fiction has appeared in *The New Yorker, Agni, Epoch, The Louisville Review, Story Quarterly,* and elsewhere. She is the author of *Interpreter of Maladies,* a collection of short stories, published by Houghton Mifflin.

" 'Interpreter of Maladies' began as a title without a story. The title came to me after bumping into an acquaintance who told me that his job was to interpret on behalf of Russian-speaking patients for a doctor in Brookline, Massachusetts. I wrote the phrase on a piece of paper at the back of my agenda, and for four years I tried to write a story to go with it. One day, on the same piece of paper, I wrote, 'monkeys stole the driver's clothes,' which was what had happened when I was touring in the north of India with my family, and our driver had set some laundry to dry on the roof of his car. Eventually, these two phrases set the story in motion."

ALICE MUNRO: "I have written several books of short stories, many stories originally appearing in *The New Yorker* and also in *Saturday Night* (Canada), *The Atlantic Monthly, Granta,* and several times in *Best American Short Stories.* I live in Ontario and British Columbia.

"The story started with an anecdote heard about a visit to a house like this, by a woman who had known it in her childhood, and the discovery of this sort of dreary, humdrum/sinister scene within. It just grew from there, the way my stories grow, so I can hardly recover the process later."

CHAIM POTOK was born and raised in New York City. He is the author of *The Chosen, My Name Is Asher Lev, Davita's Harp,* and *I Am the Clay,* among others. His most recent book is *Zebra and Other Stories.*

"Every story I write must have a core of truth, the base of a heretofore unexplored mountain. Language, imagination, and a nearly lunatic focused will are some of the equipment for the climb.

"The core in 'Moon': my son, who plays the drums; close friends, who are noted physicians; an Asian boy, who spoke in a nearby school; and the rage that seems to possess so many young people today. Those elements aroused me, seized me, drew me toward the mountain. You stumble and climb, driven by an incomprehensible urgency, by a passion for mapping new worlds with language and the alchemical fires of the imagination. And by the exhilarating prospect of reaching the crest: the story in its final form: one more fragment of the world explored and given some measure of gratifying or fearful meaning."

ANNIE PROULX lives and writes in Wyoming.

"The title 'The Mud Below' is taken from the title of a song by Tom Russell, 'The Sky Above, the Mud Below,' and used with his kind permission."

GERALD REILLY: "I was born and raised in New Jersey, where I currently live. Other recent stories have appeared in *Prairie Schooner, The Virginia Quarterly Review,* and *Image,* among other places. The stories are part of a collection entitled *The Zen Adulterer.*

"Among other things, 'Nixon Under the Bodhi Tree' is about managing inner landscapes. In this age of talk radio and twenty-four-hour cable news, we're full of opinions about people and things we know nothing about. I have passed the requisite hours seething about this or that affront to my sense of cosmic justice. Even after twenty-five years, the bombing of Cambodia still inhabits a special place in my imagination as a symbol for human callousness and national amnesia.

"Death and suffering tend to cut through all the static and chatter. They don't guarantee wisdom, but they certainly can add a bit of perspective. As I look back at the story, what appears its chief success is maintaining focus on the life-and-death question. Dallas Boyd's acting role is completely of a piece with the specifics of his meditations."

GEORGE SAUNDERS teaches in the Creative Writing Program at Syracuse University and is the author of *CivilWarLand in Bad Decline,* a collection of stories.

"I don't have much to say about 'Sea Oak,' except thanks from the heart to Bill Buford and Meghan O'Rourke at *The New Yorker* for helping me so much with it. Their brilliance and generosity and clearheadedness were greatly appreciated. Also thanks to Larry Dark for including the story in this collection."

ROBERT SCHIRMER is the author of the collection *Living with Strangers,* which won New York University's Bobst Award for Emerging Writers. He's been the recipient of a Pushcart Prize and a fellowship from The Chesterfield Film Company's Writers Film Project. He lives in Brooklyn, where he's working on a novel and a second collection of stories.

"I was in a serious house fire in 1986. At the time I was living with a woman in a relationship that was not working out for many reasons, but neither one of us had the will to break it off. Our fire came at night and burned the crate filled with my stories (not the crippling blow to world literature I had imagined it was then). When the fire finished with the stories, it moved on to the rest of the house. A couple of months later we broke up, and it seems to me now, looking back, that we saw the truth about our relationship that night, standing out in the cold October night in various stages of undress, exposed to the pitying stares of the Murray, Kentucky, Fire Department. An uneasy mixture of adrenaline, clarity, and dread take over a person caught at random in a cataclysmic event. You have the feeling you've been jarred awake from a life you've been dreaming, but now the sleepwalking is over and you're accountable for getting on with things. Or at least that's been my experience.

"The memory of the fire returned to me with special vividness several years later, when I was living and writing in Los Angeles during the city's disaster years (L.A. riots, Malibu fires, Northridge earthquake). I was almost broke and trying to write a romantic screenplay about star-crossed lovers for my agent at the time, who kept advising me to make the action "big." But every time I tried to write one of the screenplay's soft "big" romantic moments, I felt goofy and artificial, a poseur trying to write Jello. I found much more compelling an image that had lodged itself in my brain, of a man and woman running out of a burning house with smoke rising off their clothes and hair. I pictured the image not from the perspective of the couple, but from that of an onlooker with his own life who might be driving by on the road. My deadline came and went, my heart locked itself against the Jello screenplay, I had moved from almost broke to unequivocally so, and a friend of mine involved in a destructive relationship with a woman felt "too far in" to break it off, so he married her instead. *The bones of this man will soon be visible in pale light* . . . the words came to me in a kind of whisper, so I jotted them down quickly while I could still hear them and wrote the first draft of 'Burning.' Then, with money I received unexpectedly from the option on a different screenplay, I packed my life into boxes and moved to New York."

SHEILA M. SCHWARTZ is the author of *Imagine a Great White Light,* a winner of the Pushcart Editors Book Award. She teaches in the

Creative Writing Program at Cleveland State University. She recently completed a novel, *Lies Will Take You Somewhere* . . .

"I think of this story as a kind of 'Occurrence at Owl Creek Bridge' only higher up in the air. It was inspired by a plane trip which ended with our landing gear being in question. We actually buzzed the control tower so that little men with binoculars could point upward and say, *Yep. It's there!* or *Sorry. You guys are doomed.* I have to admit that I was terrified to the point of prayer and a whole lot of sweating. The only thing that calmed me down was the thought that at least my children weren't with me. I began the story with this idea—that a woman could feel lucky to be dying as long as her children weren't. I hadn't realized until then that it was possible to *begin* a story with a revelation as well as end with one."

DAVID FOSTER WALLACE is the author of four fiction books, the most recent of which is *Brief Interviews with Hideous Men.* He lives in Bloomington, Illinois.

"This was not a real fun piece to do. For one thing, I kept falling into periods of violent dislike for the protagonist and wanting to have scenes in the story where like huge spikes come out of nowhere and impale her through the right eyesocket. This is not a great head to be in w/r/t one's protagonist, obviously. A couple 'close friends' of mine have posited that maybe I disliked her so much because she reminded me of certain qualities/tendencies in myself that I reject or deplore, etc. This theory is still under review."

W. D. WETHERELL holds the Strauss Living Award from the American Academy of Arts and Letters, enabling him to devote five years to writing. His books include *Chekhov's Sister, Wherever That Great Heart May Be,* and *North of Now.*

"When you're writing about a game, it's hard not to take sides, fix the outcome—I sympathize with my hero all the way. And my hunch is that anyone looking to write the classic sports story in this day and age, be it about soccer or basketball or hockey, should look toward women's sports; when it comes to metaphor, symbolism, action, that's where the real excitement is, forget about the men."

JULIA WHITTY's stories have appeared in *Harper's Magazine, Story, Prairie Schooner, The Virginia Quarterly Review,* and elsewhere. She received the Bernice Slote Award for fiction in 1996, and is currently at work completing a collection of short stories as well as a novel.

"I originally thought that 'A Tortoise for the Queen of Tonga' would be a novella, spanning two hundred years of change in the

South Pacific. But the themes quickly repeated themselves and in the end I found that all could be said in a short story, while still maintaining the languid tempo of the centuries. Having met giant tortoises in the Seychelles and in the Galápagos, I already knew that they were fine protagonists: slow, dignified, affectionate, and wise."

JURORS

SHERMAN ALEXIE is a Spokane/Coeur d'Alene Indian from Wellpinit, Washington, on the Spokane Indian reservation. He earned a 1994 Lila Wallace–*Reader's Digest* Writers' Award, was a citation winner for the PEN/Hemingway Award for the Best First Book of Fiction, and was named one of *Granta*'s Best of the Young American Novelists. Alexie's novels include *Indian Killer* and *Reservation Blues,* which won him the Before Columbus Foundation's American Book Award. His collection of short stories, *The Lone Ranger and Tonto Fistfight in Heaven,* served as the basis for the film *Smoke Signals.* Alexie's books of poetry include *The Business of Fancydancing, Old Shirts & New Skins, First Indian on the Moon,* and *The Summer of Black Widows.* He is the winner of the Taos Poetry Circus 1998 World Heavyweight Championship Poetry Bout.

STEPHEN KING was born in Portland, Maine. He made his first short-story sale to a mass-market men's magazine shortly after graduating from the University of Maine. He continued to write while teaching high school English, until the successful publication of *Carrie* allowed him to leave teaching and write full time. *Hearts in Atlantis* is his most recent novel. He lives with his wife Tabitha in Bangor, Maine.

LORRIE MOORE is the author of two novels and three collections of stories, the most recent of which is *Birds of America.* She lives in Madison, Wisconsin.

Series Editor: This is the third volume of *Prize Stories: The O. Henry Awards* edited by **Larry Dark,** who has also compiled and edited four previous anthologies: *Literary Outtakes, The Literary Ghost, The Literary Lover,* and *The Literary Traveler.* He works at *Business Week* magazine, is married to writer Alice Elliott Dark, and lives in New Jersey.

Short-Listed Stories

ADRIAN, CHRIS, "Horse and Horseman," *Zoetrope: All-Story,* Vol. 2, No. 3

Two Haitian sisters sneak out of their parents' Miami house to attend voodoo rituals. The older sister pursues voodoo because she wants to put to rest the spirit of her beloved older brother and convinces her younger sister to participate in a ritual in which she will become the bride of a voodoo deity.

ALEXANDER, ANDREW, "Little Bitty Pretty One," *Mississippi Review,* Vol. 26, No. 3

A girl orders a pet monkey from the back of a catalog, but when it arrives it's sickly and depressed.

BALLANTINE, POE, "The Mayfly Glimmer Before Last Call," *The Sun,* Issue 275

An aimless young man is followed West from Niagara Falls by a beautiful woman, who before had been unattainable to him. They see each other often, but only toward the end of her visit is a short-lived romance kindled.

BOYLE, T. CORAGHESSAN, "Juliana Cloth," *The New Yorker,* January 19, 1998

A cloth salesman in an African village spreads AIDS through his method of bartering for a beautiful cloth. Though an unattractive woman is spared, she courts risks through her attraction to a handsome and promiscuous young man.

BRADFORD, ARTHUR, "Mollusks," *McSweeney's,* Autumn 1998

Two friends find a three-foot-long slug in the glove compartment of an abandoned car. One of them insists on taking it home, believing he can make his fortune with the creature. But while he's trying to cash in on the slug, the other fellow makes a play for his friend's wife.

BURGIN, RICHARD, "The Usher Twins," *Another Chicago Magazine,* No. 34

A woman unhappy in her marriage impulsively writes a letter to a man she hasn't seen for twenty years, whom she had a crush on and a flirtation with when she was a teenager. The letters and phone calls escalate until she is faced with the possibility of leaving her children and her domineering husband for a man who is essentially a stranger to her.

BYERS, MICHAEL, "Dirigibles," *Glimmer Train Stories,* Spring 1998, Issue 26

A retired couple living in the country are visited by an old friend from the days they ran a ferry boat out of Seattle. The husband brings out home movies to show the friend, but inadvertently shows an old and embarrassingly intimate family movie.

CLARK, JOSEPH, "Public Burning," *Zoetrope: All-Story,* Vol. 2, No. 1

A graduate student sets up a ranch house with microphones and surveillance cameras in order to study the typical white suburban family, becoming obsessively preoccupied with them and learning some disturbing things about them in the process.

COEN, ETHAN, "The Boys," *The New Yorker,* July 6, 1998

On a family trip, a father finds himself at the mercy of his odd young sons and their strange habits, which range from a diet of jelly omelets to irrational tantrums.

DIVAKARUNI, CHITRA B., "Mrs. Dutta Writes a Letter," *The Atlantic Monthly,* April 1998

A widow leaves her native India to be with her son and his family in California. For a while, they politely endure her old-country ways, but she soon catches on to the fact that they view her presence as being disruptive rather than helpful.

DOWNING, BRANDON, "The Heights of Alan Alexander," *Chelsea,* 63

The story of a marriage is conveyed through a series of elliptical, fragmentary scenes.

DUBUS, ANDRE, "Riding North," *Oxford Magazine,* Vol. XII

Not long after the Civil War, a stranger rides up to a farm in California and shoots and kills a man, then rapes the man's twenty-year-old daughter, before riding off on a stolen horse. A black man rides up and, after helping the woman to bury her father, goes off to hunt down the killer.

ENGLANDER, NATHAN, "The Twenty-seventh Man," *Story,* Summer 1998

Twenty-seven Russian writers are rounded up on Stalin's orders. Most of them are famous, but among them is an unknown, a young man who has spent his life alone in a room, compulsively writing— and who just might be the greatest talent of them all.

FREEMAN, CASTLE JR., "Another Part of the Present," *New England Review,* Vol. 19, No. 4

A college boy who spends his summers in rural Vermont with his cousin falls under the spell of the cousin's girlfriend, an aspiring actress. She's taken up with the cousin because he saved her from a fire that burned down her summer-stock playhouse and dorm.

GAITSKILL, MARY, "A Dream of Men," *The New Yorker,* November 23, 1998

A day in the life of a forty-year-old woman who works at a medical clinic in Houston. Her father has recently died and she recalls his last days. Among the highlights of the day: a lingering, disturbing dream; a forty-three-year-old patient who proudly admits she is a virgin; office chat about Monica Lewinsky; and a car full of loud, vibrant young Hispanic men.

GAUTREAUX, TIM, "The Piano Tuner," *Harper's Magazine,* September 1998

A Louisiana piano tuner strikes up a friendship with a frail woman living alone in her family's decaying farmhouse, a talented piano player skirting the edge of a breakdown.

GAY, WILLIAM, "I Hate to See That Evening Sun Go Down," *The Georgia Review,* Vol. LII, No. 3

An old man checks himself out of a nursing home and returns to his house, only to find that it has been rented out by his lawyer son. He takes up residence in the tenant house and tries to harass the present tenants into moving out.

HIGGINS, GEORGE V., "A Martini for Father McBride," *Michigan Quarterly Review,* Vol. XXXVII, No. 1

When asked to relate the worst news he ever heard, a priest tells of how he discovered the shocking secret behind his sister's estrangement from his mother.

HOFFMAN, ALICE, "The Man Who Could Eat Fire," *StoryQuarterly,* No. 33

During the Vietnam War era, a mentally unbalanced but brilliant young man renting a cottage on the grounds of an estate falls in love with a wealthy young woman who has ties to radical groups. She gets him to help her build bombs in the cellar of the cottage.

HOLLADAY, CARY, "Heaven," *The Kenyon Review,* Vol. XX, No. 1

In 1918, a prophesying horse plunks out the answers to questions on an enormous typewriter-like contraption kept in a barn.

HOLMES, CHARLOTTE, "Agnes Landowski: Her Art and Life," *New Letters,* Vol. 64, No. 4

A revealing self-portrait figures prominently in the story of an artist's life and the life of her ex-husband, who owns the picture.

HUDDLE, DAVID, "La Tour Dreams of the Wolf Girl," *American Short Fiction,* Vol. 8, No. 30

In two parallel plot lines, an ex-lover returns causing a married man to leave his wife of twelve years and the wife, an art historian, imagines the seventeenth-century painter Georges de La Tour, at the end of his life and career, painting a beautiful model with an affliction known as wolf shoulder.

IAGNEMMA, KARL, "A Little Advance," *Playboy,* September 1998

A slacker who works at a 7-Eleven and makes sculptures out of rusty car parts accompanies his rich girlfriend home for Christmas and meets her eccentric, born-again brother.

JARMAN, MARK ANTHONY, "Burn Man on a Texas Porch," *The Georgia Review,* Vol. LII, No. 3

A man is badly burned in a propane explosion while on vacation in Texas. He takes jobs that allow him to work with his face hidden and reflects on his bad fortune.

JULAVITS, HEIDI, "Marry the One Who Gets There First," *Esquire,* April 1998

Descriptions of and elaborations on thirty-six photographs taken during the weekend of a wedding reveal the behind-the-scenes story of the couple and members of the wedding party.

KOHLER, SHEILA, "Africans," *Story,* Autumn 1998

A young newly wed South African woman retains the loyal Zulu servant who helped raise her. But his loyalty is tested by turmoil in her marriage.

LENNON, J. ROBERT, "Twelve Terrors," *Fiction,* Vol. 15, No. 1

Episodes ranging from childhood nightmares and fears to adult anxieties.

LONG, DAVID, "Morphine," *The New Yorker,* July 20, 1998

A small town doctor in 1959 indulges himself in two ways: by making regular journal entries every night and by once a month shooting up with morphine. One night, while under the effects of the drug, the doctor gets an emergency call and helps a boy with a severe ear infection, repaying an old debt.

MacMillan, Ian, "The Fourth Rescue," *The Laurel Review*, Vol. 32, No. 1

An innocent young man from upstate New York, working as a lifeguard in Staten Island after serving time in a boys' home for a crime he didn't commit, performs a heroic rescue.

Martin, Charles Philip, "Lau the Tailor," *Mānoa*, Vol. 10, No. 1

The owner of a Hong Kong tailor shop hires a tailor who has the uncanny ability to take the measure of someone by sight alone and to make beautiful clothes that correspond to significant moments in the person's life.

McCaddon, Beauvis, "The Candy Spoon," *The Virginia Quarterly Review*, Vol. 74, No. 4

After thirty years of marriage, a wife still can't forgive her husband for accidentally setting fire to her honeymoon clothes. The husband has never amounted to much and the wife supports the family through her dress shop and candy making. He makes a fool of himself and gets shot in the leg pursuing a woman who isn't interested in him.

Millhauser, Steven, "Flying Carpets," *The Paris Review*, No. 145

A young boy is given a magic carpet. At first he uses it cautiously, then becomes more daring. Ultimately summer draws to a close and the boy tires of the carpet. It ends up packed away and gathering dust.

Munro, Alice, "Before the Change," *The New Yorker*, August 24 & 31, 1998

Set in 1960 and told in the form of unsent letters from a young woman to her former fiancé. The woman has temporarily moved back in with her aging, cantankerous father, a still-practicing physician and secret abortionist.

Munro, Alice, "Cortes Island," *The New Yorker*, October 12, 1998

A newly married couple rents a basement flat in Vancouver. The wife wants to be a writer and goes out looking for a job. The landlord's parents also live in the building and the woman is hired to look after the husband, partly disabled from a stroke. He gets her to read to him from old scrapbooks that point to a dark secret.

NELSON, KENT, "Galimatia," *Shenandoah,* Vol. 48, No. 3

A man recalls when he was sixteen and a young woman named Galimatia moved to the Naja reservation where his tribe lived. He became fascinated with her, but rumors circulated about the woman, causing him to keep his distance.

NOVAKOVICH, JOSIP, "Bruno," *The Kenyon Review,* Vol. XX, No. 1

Croatia, 1948. A ten-year-old boy comes down with tuberculosis contracted from drinking raw milk from an infected cow. Under the sway of the illness he draws great pictures and develops an erotic attachment to his stepmother. He is saved by a delivery of medicine from UNICEF at the insistence of his father, despite the dangers of asking for help from the West.

ORRINGER, JULIE, "What We Save," *The Yale Review,* Vol. 86, No. 1

A woman dying of cancer takes her daughters to DisneyWorld to meet up with her high school sweetheart, his wife, and two sons.

OZICK, CYNTHIA, "Actors," *The New Yorker,* October 5, 1998

An aging New York character actor gets a part playing a Jewish King Lear. He grows a beard and goes to meet the writer's inspiration for the role—a legendary Yiddish actor living in a nursing home.

PRITCHARD, MELISSA, "Port de Bras," *The Southern Review,* Vol. 34, No. 2

An awkward, overweight twelve-year-old girl befriends a beautiful, graceful girl in her ballet class and succumbs to the other girl's flights of fancy.

PROULX, ANNIE, "The Bunchgrass Edge of the World," *The New Yorker,* November 30, 1998

An overweight young woman living on an isolated cattle ranch with her parents takes on increased responsibilities when her brother runs off and her father takes ill. An old tractor in disrepair starts to talk to her. Eventually, she meets the son of the cattle buyer and they marry.

SCHAFFERT, TIMOTHY, "Wolves at Bay," *Prairie Schooner,* Vol. 72, No. 2

Two girls—their father dead, their mother in Mexico—live with their grandmother in her rarely visited "antiques" store on a highway in the plains. It's Easter and their car has hit a large bird on the way home from church. The store is visited by a strange trove of bird-watching women.

SHUKMAN, HENRY, "Mortimer of the Maghreb," *The Missouri Review,* Vol. XXI, No. 2

A once world-renowned journalist goes off to cover a civil war in Morocco. Nothing happens for days and he writes letters to his ex-wife about the war. Then he witnesses the brutal murder of two POWs and discovers that the rebels are trying to manipulate him into writing the story of the war their way.

STERN, STEVEN, "The Wedding Jester," *New England Review,* Vol. 19, No. 3

A famous Jewish writer, middle-aged and divorced, escorts his widowed mother to a wedding in a Catskills resort. An attractive divorcee and her widowed father, a retired furrier, attach themselves to the man and his mother. During the ceremony, the bride becomes possessed by a dybbuk—the ghost of a Jewish comic. And the writer leads an exorcism.

UPDIKE, JOHN, "Licks of Love in the Heart of the Cold War," *The Atlantic Monthly,* May 1998

In the fifties a renowned bluegrass banjo player is sent on a goodwill tour of the Soviet Union. Before parting he has a tryst with a voluptuous but mentally unstable secretary in the State Department who keeps sending him delusional love letters in the packets he receives while on tour.

VILLANUEVA, MARIANNE, "Silence," *The Threepenny Review,* No. 72

A young woman in an abusive marriage silently endures.

WALLACE, DAVID FOSTER, "Brief Interviews with Hideous Men," *Harper's Magazine,* October 1998

Numbered interviews with unnamed men, regarding either hideous behavior, hideous attitudes, or hideous things they have suffered.

WALLACE, DAVID FOSTER, "Yet Another Example of the Porousness of Certain Borders (VIII)," *McSweeney's,* Autumn 1998

A man on parole accompanies his surgically disfigured mother on the bus ride to her lawyer's office.

WALTER, VICTOR, "A Bell for Rome," *New England Review,* Vol. 19, No. 1

A Jewish bell maker in twelfth-century Rome is invited to play chess with a cardinal, who commissions him to make a bell for Santa Maria in Trastevere.

WARNER, SHARON OARD, "The Object Lesson," *Prairie Schooner,* Vol. 72, No. 2

A working single mother tries to teach her teenage boy a lesson by making him wash his own sheets after she discovers stains caused by the boy and his girlfriend.

WILLIAMS, JOY, "Substance," *The Paris Review,* **No. 148**
A friend who has committed suicide leaves an odd assortment of possessions to his friends. One woman gets his dog, Broom. Though she doesn't want the dog, she also refuses to give him up to her dead friend's brother.

1999 Magazine Award:
The New Yorker

FOR THE SECOND YEAR in a row, *The New Yorker* is the winner of the O. Henry Award for the magazine publishing the best fiction. Given the large number and high quality of short stories published by *The New Yorker* year in and year out, it will no doubt win many more of these awards. *Harper's Magazine,* with three O. Henry Award–winning stories, and *The Gettysburg Review,* with two (including the first-prize winner), were strong contenders for this honor and deserve recognition for the excellent quality of fiction they published during the course of the year.

The New Yorker has four O. Henry Award–winning stories in this collection, more than any other magazine: the third-prize winning "Save the Reaper" by Alice Munro, "The Underground Gardens" by T. Coraghessan Boyle, "The Mud Below" by Annie Proulx, and "Sea Oak" by George Saunders. Eight short-listed stories and the magazine's continued devotion to literary fiction, as evidenced by the number and variety of stories it published and the two annual double issues devoted to fiction it produced in 1998, add additional support to the selection of *The New Yorker* as this year's prizewinner for magazines. Congratulations to Editor-in-Chief David Remnick, Fiction Editor Bill Buford, the rest of the fiction staff, and the writers published in *The New Yorker* during the course of the year.

Magazines Consulted

Entries entirely in boldface and with their titles in all-capital letters denote publications with prizewinning stories. Asterisks following titles denote magazines with short-listed stories. The information presented is up-to-date as of the time *Prize Stories 1999: The O. Henry Awards* went to press. For further information, including links to magazine Web sites, visit the O. Henry Awards Web site at:

www.boldtype.com/ohenry

Magazines that wish to be added to the list and to have the stories they publish considered for O. Henry Awards may send subscriptions or all issues containing fiction to the series editor at:

P.O. Box 739
Montclair, NJ 07042

All other correspondence should be sent care of Anchor Books or, via e-mail, to Ohenrypriz@aol.com.

Please note: It is the responsibility of the editors of each magazine to make sure that issues are sent to the series editor. If none are received during the course of the year, a publication may no longer be listed as a Magazine Consulted for the series.

Acorn Whistle
907 Brewster Avenue
Beloit, WI 53511
Fred Burwell, Editor
Publishes one or two issues a
year.

African American Review
Stalker Hall 213
Indiana State University
Terre Haute, IN 47809
Joe Weixlmann, Editor
web.indstate.edu/artsci/AAR
Quarterly with a focus on African
American literature and culture.
Averages one short story per
issue.

AGNI
236 Bay Street Road
Boston University Writing
Program
Boston, MA 02115
Askold Melnyczuk, Editor
webdelsol.com/AGNI

AIM Magazine
P.O. Box 1174
Maywood, IL 60153
"America's Intercultural Magazine"
Quarterly.

Alabama Literary Review
Smith 253
Troy State University
Troy, AL 36082
Theron Montgomery, Chief Editor
Published annually.

ALASKA QUARTERLY REVIEW
University of Alaska Anchorage
3211 Providence Drive
Anchorage, AK 99508
Ronald Spatz, Editor
www.uaa.alaska.edu/aqr

Alligator Juniper
Prescott College
220 Grove Avenue
Prescott, AZ 86301
Melanie Bishop, Managing Editor
Annual.

Amelia
329 "E" Street
Bakersfield, CA 93304-2031
Frederick A. Raborg, Jr., Editor
Quarterly. Includes supplements:
Cicada *and* SPSM&H.

American Letters and Commentary
850 Park Avenue
Suite 5B
New York, NY 10021
Jeanne Marie Beaumont, Anna
Rabinowitz, Editors
www.amletters.org
Annual.

American Literary Review
University of North Texas
P.O. Box 13827
Denton, TX 76203
Lee Martin, Editor
www.engl.unt.edu/alr
Biannual.

American Short Fiction*
University of Texas Press
Journals Division
Box 7819
Austin, TX 78713-7819
Joseph E. Kruppa, Editor
journals@uts.cc.utexas.edu
www.utexas.edu/utpress/journals/
jasf.html
Quarterly. No longer publishing.

American Voice
332 West Broadway
Suite 1215
Louisville, KY 40202
Frederick Smock, Editor
www.kfw.org/KFW/AmVoice.html
Triannual publication.

American Way
P.O. Box 619640
DFW Airport
Texas 75261-9640
Chuck Thompson, Senior Editor
American Airlines' inflight
magazine. Published twice a
month. No longer publishing
fiction.

Another Chicago Magazine*
Left Field Press
3709 North Kenmore
Chicago, IL 60613
Barry Silesky, Editor and Publisher
Antietam Review
41 S. Potomac Street
Hagerstown, MD 21740
Susanne Kass, Executive Editor
The Antioch Review
P.O. Box 148
Yellow Springs, OH 45387
Robert S, Fogarty Editor
Quarterly.
Appalachian Heritage
Berea College
Berea, KY 40404
Sidney Saylor Farr, Editor
Sydney_Farr@Berea.edu
www.berea.edu/Library/AH/
Current_Issue.html
*Quarterly of Southern Appalachian
life and culture.*
Arkansas Review
Dept. of English & Philosophy
Box 1890
Arkansas State University
State University, AR 72467
William Clements, Editor
delta@toltec.astate.edu
www.clt.astate.edu/arkreview
Formerly the Kansas Quarterly. *"A
Journal of Delta Studies."
Triannual.*
Ascent
English Dept.
Concordia College
901 8th Street S
Moorhead, MN 56562
W. Scott Olsen, Editor
ascent@cord.edu
www.cord.edu/dept/english/ascent
Triannual.
Atlanta Review
P.O. Box 8248
Atlanta, GA 30306
Daniel Veach, Editor and Publisher
Biannual.

The Atlantic Monthly*
77 N. Washington Street
Boston, MA 02114
C. Michael Curtis, Senior Editor
www.TheAtlantic.com
The Baffler
P.O. Box 378293
Chicago, IL 60637
Thomas Frank, Editor-in-Chief
Barnabe Mountain Review
P.O. Box 529
Lagunitas, CA 94938
Gerald Fleming, Editor
*Annual, first published in 1995,
which plans to cease publication
after its fifth issue.*
Bellowing Ark
P.O. Box 55564
Shoreline, WA 98155
Robert R Ward, Editor
Bimonthly.
Beloit Fiction Journal
Box 11
Beloit College
700 College Street
Beloit, WI 53511
Fred Burwell, Editor-in-Chief
Biannual.
Big Sky Journal
P.O. Box 1069
Bozeman, MT 59771
Allen Jones, Editor
bsj@mcn.net
*Glossy Montana magazine
published five times a year.*
**Black Dirt: A Journal of
Contemporary Writing**
Elgin Community College
1700 Spartan Drive
Elgin, IL 60123-7193
Rachel Tecza, Fiction Editor
Biannual. Formerly known as
Farmer's Market.

Black Warrior Review
University of Alabama
P.O. Box 862936
Tuscaloosa, AL 35486-0027
Christopher Chambers, Editor
www.sa.ua.edu/osm/bwr
Biannual.

Blood & Aphorisms
P.O. Box 702, Station P
Toronto, Ontario
M5S 2Y4, Canada
Michelle Alfano, Dennis Block,
Fiction Editors
fiction@interlog.com
www.interlog.com/~fiction
Quarterly.

BOMB
594 Broadway, 9th Floor
New York, NY 10012
Betsy Sussler, Editor-in-Chief
editor@bombsite.com
www.bombsite.com
*Quarterly magazine profiling
artists, writers, actors, directors,
and musicians, with a downtown
New York City slant. Fiction
appears in* First Proof, *a literary
supplement.*

Border Crossings
500-70 Arthur Street
Winnipeg, Manitoba
R3B IG7 Canada
Meeka Walsh, Editor
border@escape.ca
Magazine of the arts. Quarterly.

The Boston Book Review
30 Brattle Street, 4th Floor
Cambridge, MA 02138
Theoharis Constantine Theoharis,
Editor
BBR-Info@BostonBookReview.com
www.BostonBookReview.com
*A book review that also publishes
fiction, poetry, and essays.
Published ten times a year—
monthly with double issues in
January and July.*

Boston Review
E53-407, MIT
Cambridge, MA 02139
Joshua Cohen, Editor-in-Chief
bostonreview@mit.edu
bostonrview.mit.edu
*"A political and literary forum."
Published six times a year.*

Boulevard
4579 Laclede Avenue
Suite 332
St. Louis, MO 63108-2103
Richard Burgin, Editor
Triannual.

The Briar Cliff Review
3303 Rebecca Street
P.O. Box 2100
Sioux City, IA 51104-2100
Tricia Currans-Sheehen, Editor

The Bridge
14050 Vernon Street
Oak Park, MI 48237
Jack Zucker, Editor
Biannual.

Buffalo Spree
3993 Harlem Road
P.O. Box 38
Buffalo, NY 14226
Johanna Hall Van de Mark, Editor
*Buffalo, NY–area quarterly arts
magazine.*

Button
Box 26
Lunenburg, MA 01462
Sally Cragin, Editor/Publisher
Buttonx26@aol.com
*"New England's tiniest magazine
of poetry, fiction, and gracious
living." Biannual.*

Callaloo
English Dept.
322 Bryan Hall
University of Virginia
Charlottesville, VA 22903
Charles H. Rowell, Editor
www.muse.jhu.edu/journals/cal
A quarterly journal of African American and African arts and letters.

Calyx
P.O. Box B
Corvalis, OR 97399-0539
Editorial collective
calyx@proaxis.com
www.proaxis.com/~calyx
Triannual journal of art and literature by women.

The Carolina Quarterly
Greenlaw Hall CB#3520
University of North Carolina
Chapel Hill, NC 27599-3520
rotating editorship
cquarter@email.unc.edu
www.unc.edu/student/orgs/cquarter
Triannual.

The Chariton Review
Truman State University
Kirskville, MO 63501
Jim Barnes, Editor
Biannual.

Chattahoochee Review
2101 Womack Road
Dunwoody, Georgia 30338-4497
Lawrence Hetrick, Editor
www.gpc.peachnet.edu/~twadley/cr/index.htm
Quarterly.

Chelsea*
P.O. Box 773
Cooper Station
New York, NY 10276-0773
Richard Foerster, Editor
Biannual.

Chicago Review
5801 South Kenwood Avenue
Chicago, Ill 60637-1794
Andrew Rathman, Editor
humanities.uchicago.edu/humanities/review
Quarterly.

Cimarron Review
205 Morrill Hall
Oklahoma State University
Stillwater, OK 74078-0135
E. P. Walkiewicz, Editor
Quarterly.

City Primeval
P.O. Box 30064
Seattle, WA 98103
David Ross, Editor
Quarterly featuring "Narratives of Urban Reality."

Clackamas Literary Review
Clackamas Community College
19600 South Molalla Avenue
Oregon City, OR
Jeff Knorr and Tim Schell, Editors
www.clackamas.cc.or.us/clr
Biannual.

Colorado Review
Colorado State University
Dept. of English
Fort Collins, CO 80523
David Milofsky, Editor
creview@vines.colostate.edu
www.colostate.edu/Depts/English/pubs/colrev/colrev.htm
Biannual.

Columbia: A Journal of Literature and Art
415 Dodge Hall
Columbia University
2960 Broadway
New York, NY 10027
Rotating editorship
arts-litjournal@columbia.edu
www.columbia.edu/cu/arts/writing/columbiajournal/columbiafr.html
Student-run biannual.

Commentary
165 East 56th Street
New York, NY 10022
Neal Kozodoy, Editor
Commentary@compuserve.com
*Monthly, politically conservative
Jewish magazine.*

Communities
P.O. Box 169
Masonville, CO 80541-0169
Diana Leafe Christian, Editor
communities@ic.org
www.ic.org
*Quarterly "Journal of Cooperative
Living."*

Concho River Review
English Dept.
Angelo State University
San Angelo, TX 76909
James A. Moore, General Editor
Biannual.

Confrontation
English Dept.
C. W. Post Campus of Long Island
Univ.
Brookville, NY 11548
Martin Tucker, Editor-in-Chief

Conjunctions
21 East 10th Street
New York, NY 10003
Bradford Morrow, Editor
www.conjunctions.com
Biannual.

Crab Orchard Review
Southern Illinois University at
Carbondale
Carbondale, IL 62901-4503
Richard Peterson, Editor
www.siu.edu/~crborchd
Biannual.

Crazyhorse
Dept. of English
University of Arkansas at Little
Rock
2801 S. University
Little Rock, AR 72204
Ralph Burns, Editor
www.ualr.edu/~english/
CHHOME.htm
Biannual.

The Cream City Review
University of Wisconsin-Milwaukee
P.O. Box 413
Milwaukee, WI 53201
rotating editorship
www.uwm.edu/Dept/English/CCR/
about.html
Biannual.

The Crescent Review
Box 15069
Chevy Chase, MD 20825-5069
J. Timothy Holland, Editor
www.thecrescentreview.com
Triannual.

CUTBANK
Dept. of English
University of Montana
Missoula, MT 59812
rotating editorship
cutbank@selway.umt.edu
www.umt.edu/cutbank/
default.htm
Biannual.

Dead Snake Apotheosis
87-3193 Road H
Captain Cook, HI 96704
Carol Greenhouse, Editor
DEAD Eds@aol.com
Biannual. Est. 1998.

Denver Quarterly
English Dept.
University of Denver
Denver, CO 80208
Bin Ramke, Editor
www.du.edu/english/
DQuarterly.htm

Dominion Review
Old Dominion University
English Dept., BAL 220
Norfolk, VA 23529-0078
rotating editorship
webdelsol.com/dreview
Annual.

DOUBLETAKE
55 Davis Square
Somerville, MA 02144
Robert Coles, Editor
dtmag@aol.com
www.doubletakemagazine.org
Beautifully produced quarterly
devoted to photography and
literature. New address.

Epoch
251 Goldwin Smith Hall
Cornell University
Ithaca, NY 14853-3201
Michael Koch, Editor
Triannual. 1997 O. Henry Award
Winner, Best Magazine.

ESQUIRE*
250 West 55th Street
New York, NY 10019
Adrienne Miller, Literary Editor
www.esquiremag.com
Monthly with annual summer
reading issue.

Event
Douglas College
Box 2503
New Westminster, British
Columbia
V3L 5B2, Canada
Calvin Wharton, Editor
Triannual.

FICTION*
English Dept.
The City College of New York
New York, NY 10031
Mark Jay Mirsky, Editor
www.ccny.cuny.edu/Fiction/
fiction.htm
All-fiction format.

Fiction International
English and Comparative
Literature Dept.
San Diego State University
San Diego, CA 92182
Harold Jaffe, Editor
Annual.

The Fiddlehead
University of New Brunswick
P.O. Box 4400
Fredericton, New Brunswick
Canada E3B 5A3
Don McKay, Editor
Quarterly.

Fish Stories
3540 N. Southport Avenue #493
Chicago, IL 60657
Amy G. Davis, Editor-in-Chief
Annual. Publication currently
suspended.

Five Fingers Review
P.O. Box 12955
Berkeley, CA 94712-3955
Jaime Robles, Editor
vladstutu@aol.com

Five Points
English Dept.
Georgia State University
University Plaza
Athens, GA 30303-3083
David Bottoms, Pam Durban,
Editors
www.gsu.edu/~wwweng/fivepoints
Triannual.

The Florida Review
Dept. of English
University of Central Florida
Orlando, FL 32816
Russ Kesler, Editor
pegasus.cc.ucf.edu/~english/
floridareview/home.htm
Biannual.

Flyway
206 Ross Hall
English Dept.
Iowa State University
Ames, IA 50011
Debra Marquart, Editor

Fourteen Hills
Creative Writing Dept.
San Francisco State University
1600 Holloway Avenue
San Francisco, CA 94132-1722
rotating editorship
hills@sfsu.edu
userwww.sfsu.edu/~hills
Biannual.

Fugue
Brink Hall, Room 200
English Dept.
University of Idaho
Moscow, ID 83844-1102
www.uidaho.edu/LS/Eng/Fugue.
*Irregularly published, rotating
editorship.*

Gargoyle
1508 U Street, NW
Washington, DC 20009
Richard Peabody, Lucinda
Ebersole, Editors
atticus@atticusbooks.com
www.atticusbooks.com/
gargoyle.html
Published irregularly.

Geist
1014 Homer Street #103
Vancouver, British Columbia
V6B 2W9 Canada
Stephen Osborne, Publisher
geist@geist.com
*"The Canadian Magazine of Ideas
and Culture." Quarterly.*

THE GEORGIA REVIEW*
The University of Georgia
Athens, GA 30602-9009
Stanley W. Lindberg, Editor
www.uga.edu/garev
Quarterly.

THE GETTYSBURG REVIEW
Gettysburg College
Gettysburg, PA 17325
Peter Stitt, Editor
(www.gettysburg.edu/academics/
gettysburg_review)
Quarterly.

Glimmer Train Stories*
812 SW Madison Street
Suite 504
Portland, OR 97205-2900
Linda Burmeister Davies, Susan
Burmeister-Brown, Editors
www.glimmertrain.com
Quarterly. Fiction and interviews.

Global City Review
Simon H. Rifkind Center for the
Humanities
The City College of New York
138th St. and Convent Ave.
New York, NY 10031
Linsey Abrams, Editor
webdelsol.com/GlobalCity
*Nifty, pocket-size format. Annual
as of 1997.*

GQ
350 Madison Avenue
New York, NY 10017
gqmag@aol.com
www.gq.com
Monthly.

Grain
Box 1154
Regina, Saskatchewan
Canada S4P 3B4
J. Jill Robinson, Editor
grain.mag@sk.sympatico.ca
www.skywriter.com/grain25
Quarterly.

Grand Street
131 Varick Street
Room 906
New York, NY 10013
Jean Stein, Editor
www.voyagerco.com/gs
Quarterly arts magazine.

Granta
1755 Broadway, 5th floor
New York, NY 10019-3780
Ian Jack, Editor
www.granta.com
*London-based international
quarterly.*

The Green Hills Literary Lantern
Box 375
Trenton, MO 64683
Jack Smith, Ken Reger, Senior
Editors
Annual.

Green Mountains Review
Johnson State College
Johnson, VT 05656
Tony Whedon, Fiction Editor
Biannual.

The Greensboro Review
English Dept.
University of North Carolina at
Greensboro
Greensboro, NC 27412
Jim Clark, Editor
www.uncg.edu/eng/mfa/
grhmpg.htm
Biannual.

Gulf Coast
English Dept.
University of Houston
4800 Calhoun Road
Houston, TX 77204-3012
Biannual.

Gulf Stream
English Dept.
FIU-North Miami Campus
3000 NE 151 Street
North Miami, FL 33181-3000
Lynn Barrett, Editor

Habersham Review
Piedmont College
Demorest, GA 30535-0010
Frank Gannon, Editor
Biannual.

Hampton Shorts
P.O. Box 1229
Water Mill, NY 11976
Barbara Stone, Editor
*"Fiction plus from the Hamptons
and The East End."*

HAPPY
240 East 35th Street
Suite 11A
New York, NY 10116
Bayard, Editor
Offbeat quarterly.

HARPER'S MAGAZINE*
666 Broadway
New York, NY 10012
Lewis Lapham, Editor
www.harpers.org
Monthly.

Hayden's Ferry Review
Box 871502
Arizona State University
Tempe, AZ 85287-1502
rotating editorship
HFR@asu.edu
news.vpsa.asu.edu/hfr/hfr.html
Biannual.

High Plains Literary Review
180 Adams Street
Suite 250
Denver, CO 80206
Robert O. Greer, Jr., Editor-in-
Chief
Triannual.

The Hudson Review
684 Park Avenue
New York, NY 10021
Paula Deitz, Editor
Quarterly.

The Idaho Review
Boise State University
English Dept.
1910 University Drive
Boise, ID 83725
Mitch Wieland, Editor-in-Chief
Annual, inaugurated in 1998.

IMAGE
P.O. Box 674
Kennett Square, PA 19348
**Gregory Wolfe, Publisher and
Editor**
gwolfe@compuserve.com
www.imagejournal.org
*"A Journal of the Arts and
Religion." Quarterly.*

Indiana Review
465 Ballantine
Bloomington, IN 47405
rotating editorship
www.indiana.edu/~ireview/
home.html
Biannual.

Ink Magazine
P.O. Box 52558
264 Bloor Street West
Toronto, ON
M5S 1V0 Canada
John Degan, Editor
Quarterly.

Interim
English Dept.
University of Nevada
Las Vegas, NV 89154
James Hazen, Editor
Biannual.

The Iowa Review
308 English/Philosophy Building
University of Iowa
Iowa City, IA 52242-1492
David Hamilton, Mary Hussmann,
Editors
www.uiowa.edu/~english/
iowareview
Triannual.

Iowa Woman
P.O. Box 680
Iowa City, IA 52244-0680
Rebecca Childers, Editor

The Journal
The Ohio State University
English Dept.
164 West 17th Avenue
Columbus, OH 43210
Kathy Fagan, Michelle Herman,
Editors
www.cohums.ohio-state.edu/
english/journals/the_journal/
homepage.htm
Biannual.

Kalliope
Florida Community College at
Jacksonville
3939 Roosevelt Boulevard
Jacksonville, FL 32205
Mary Sue Koeppel, Editor
www.fccj.org/learningresource/
kalliope.htm
Triannual journal of women's art.

Karamu
English Dept.
Eastern Illinois University
Charleston, IL 61920
Peggy Brayfield, Editor
Annual.

The Kenyon Review*
Kenyon College
Gambier, OH 43022
David H. Lynn, Editor
kenyonreview@kenyon.edu
www.kenyonreview.com
Triannual.

Kiosk
State University of New York at
Buffalo
English Dept.
306 Clemens Hall
Buffalo, NY 14260
rotating editorship
Annual.

The Laurel Review*
English Dept.
Northwest Missouri State
University
Maryville, MO 64468
William Trowbridge, David Slater,
Beth Richards, Co-Editors
Biannual.

Literal Latté
Suite 240
61 East 8th Street
New York, NY 10003
Jenine Gordon Bockman,
Publisher and Editor
Litlatte@aol.com
www.literal-latte.com
Bimonthly.

The Literary Review
285 Madison Avenue
Madison, NJ 07940
Walter Cummins, Editor-in-Chief
tlr@fdu.edu
www.webdelsol.com/tlr
Quarterly.

Louisiana Literature
Box 792
Southeastern Louisiana University
Hammond, LA 70402
David C. Hanson, Editor
Biannual.

The Madison Review
University of Wisconsin
English Dept., Helen C. White Hall
600 North Park Street
Madison, WI 53706
rotating editorship
Biannual.

The Malahat Review
University of Victorla
Box 1700
Victoria, British Columbia
V8W 2Y2 Canada
Derk Wynand, Editor
malahat@uvic.ca
web.uvic.ca/malahat
Quarterly.

Mānoa*
English Dept.
University of Hawai'i
Honolulu, HI 96822
Frank Stewart, Editor
www2.hawaii.edu/mjournal
Biannual.

The Massachusetts Review
Memorial Hall
University of Massachusetts
Amherst, MA 01003
Jules Chametzky, Mary Heath,
Paul Jenkins, Editors
www.litline.org/mr/massreview.html
Quarterly.

McSweeney's*
394A Ninth Street
Brooklyn, NY 11215
David Eggers, Editor
mcsweeneys@earthlink.net
www.mcsweeneys.net
*Est. 1998. Cutting-edge quarterly
humor magazine. Known by many
aliases and featuring amusing
marginalia.*

Meridian
University of Virginia
English Dept.
Charlottesville, VA 22903
rotating editorship
meridian@virginia.edu
www.engl.virginia.edu/meridian
Biannual, student-run.

Michigan Quarterly Review*
The University of Michigan
3032 Rackham Building
915 E. Washington Street
Ann Arbor, MI 48109-1070
Laurence Goldstein, Editor
www.umich.edu/~mqr

Mid-American Review
English Dept.
Bowling Green State University
Bowling Green, OH 43403
George Looney, Editor-in-Chief
Biannual.

Midstream
110 East 59th Street, 4th Floor
New York, NY 10022
Joel Carmichael, Editor
*Monthly with focus on Jewish
issues and Zionist concerns.*

The Minnesota Review
English Dept.
University of Missouri-Columbia
107 Tate Hall
Columbia, MO 65211
Jeffrey Williams, Editor
Non-Minnesota-based biannual.

Mississippi Review*
University of Southern Mississippi
Southern Station, P.O. Box 5144
Hattiesburg, MS 39406-5144
Frederick Barthelme, Editor
sushi.st.usm.edu/mrw/index.html
*Internet version publishes full text
stories and poems monthly, many
of which are not included in
regular issues of the magazine.
One of the first literary Web sites
and still among the best.*

The Missouri Review*
1507 Hillcrest Hall
University of Missouri
Columbia, Missouri 65211
Speer Morgan, Editor
moreview@showme.missouri.edu
www.missourireview.org
Triannual.

Ms.
135 West 50th Street
16th Floor
New York, NY 10020
Marcia Ann Gillespie,
Editor-in-Chief
ms@echonyc.com
Focus on feminist issues.

The Nebraska Review
Writers' Workshop
Fine Arts Building 212
University of Nebraska at Omaha
Omaha, NE 68182-0324
Art Homer, Richard Duggin,
Editors
unomaha.edu/~nereview
Biannual.

New Delta Review
English Dept.
Louisiana State University
Baton Rouge, LA 70803-5001
rotating editorship
wwwndr@unix1.sncc.lsu.edu
www.lsu.edu:80/guests/wwwndr
Biannual.

New England Review*
Middlebury College
Middlebury, VT 05753
Stephen Donadio, Editor
NEReview@middlebury.edu
www.middlebury.edu/~nereview
Quarterly.

New Letters*
University of Missouri–Kansas City
5101 Rockhill Road
Kansas City, MO 64110
James McKinley, Editor-in-Chief
cctr.umkc.edu/newletters
Quarterly.

New Millennium Writings
P.O. Box 2463
Knoxville, TN 37901
Don Williams, Editor
www.mach2.com/books/williams/
index.html
Biannual.

NEW ORLEANS REVIEW
Box 195
Loyola University
New Orleans, LA 70118
Ralph Adamo, Editor
noreview@beta.loyno.edu
Quarterly.

The New Renaissance
26 Heath Road #11
Arlington, MA 02174-3614
Louise T. Reynolds, Editor-in-Chief
Biannual.

New York Stories
English Dept.
La Guardia Community College/
CUNY
31-10 Thomson Ave.
Long Island City, NY 11101
Michael Blaine, Editor-in-Chief
Triannual. Inaugural issue in 1998.

THE NEW YORKER*
25 West 43rd Street
New York, NY 10036
Bill Buford, Fiction Editor
www.newyorker.com
Esteemed weekly with special fiction issues in June and December. Magazine Award winner for 1998 and 1999.

Nimrod
The University of Tulsa
600 S. College
Tulsa, OK 74104-3184
Francine Ringold, Editor-in-Chief
www.utulsa.edu/Nimrod
Biannual.

The North American Review
University of Northern Iowa
1222 West 27th Street
Cedar Falls, IA 50614
Robley Wilson, Editor
nar@uni.edu
www.webdelsol.com/
NorthAmReview/NAR
Bimonthly founded in 1815.

North Carolina Literary Review
English Dept.
East Carolina University
Greenville, NC 27858-4353
Thomas E. Douglas, Margaret Bauer, Editors
BauerM@mail.ECU.edu
Nicely produced and illustrated annual.

North Dakota Quarterly
The University of North Dakota
Grand Forks, ND 58202-7209
Robert W. Lewis, Editor
ndq@sage.und.nodak.edu

Northeast Corridor
English Dept.
Beaver College
450 S. Easton Road
Glenside, PA 19038-3295
Susan Balée, Editor
Biannual.

Northwest Review
369 PLC
University of Oregon
Eugene, OR 97403
John Witte, Editor
Triannual.

Notre Dame Review
Creative Writing Program
English Dept.
University of Notre Dame
Notre Dame, IN 46556
John Matthias, William O'Rourke, Editors
English.ndreview.1@nd.edu
www.nd.edu/~ndr/review.htm
Biannual.

Oasis
P.O. Box 626
Largo, FL 33779-0626
Neal Storrs, Editor
oasislit@aol.com
www.litline.org/html/oasis.html
Quirky quarterly.

The Ohio Review
Ellis Hall
Ohio University
Athens, Ohio 45701-2979
Wayne Dodd, Editor
Biannual.

Ontario Review
9 Honey Brook Drive
Princeton, NJ 08540
Raymond J. Smith, Editor
www.ontarioreviewpress.com
Biannual.

Open City
225 Lafayette Street
New York, NY 10012
Thomas Beller, Daniel Pinchbeck, Editors
ocmagazine@aol.com
www.opencity.org
Downtown annual.

Other Voices
English Dept. (MC 162)
University of Illinois at Chicago
601 South Morgan Street
Chicago, IL 60607-7120
Lois Hauselman, Executive Editor
Biannual with all-fiction format.

Owen Wistar Review
University of Wyoming
Student Publications
Box 3625
Laramie, WY 82071
rotating editorship
Annual.

The Oxford American
P.O. Box 1156
Oxford, MS 38655
Marc Smirnoff, Editor
oxam@watervalley.net
*John Grisham–backed magazine
with Southern focus. Bimonthly.*

Oxford Magazine*
English Dept.
356 Bachelor Hall
Miami University
Oxford, OH 45056
rotating editorship
Oxmag@geocities.com
www.muohio.edu/creativewriting/
oxmag.html

Oyster Boy Review
103B Hanna Street
Carrboro, NC 27510
Damon Sauve, Editor
oyster-boy@sunsite.unc.edu
sunsite.unc.edu/ob
*Triannual with full text available
online.*

The Paris Review*
541 East 72nd Street
New York, NY 10021
George Plimpton, Editor
www.parisreview.com
Quarterly.

Parting Gifts
3413 Wilshire Drive
Greensboro, NC 27408
Robert Bixby, Editor
rbixby@aol.com
users.aol.com/marchst

Partisan Review
236 Bay State Road
Boston, MA 02215
William Phillips, Editor-in-Chief
www.webdelsol.com/
Partisan_Review
Quarterly.

Passages North
English Dept.
Northern Michigan University
1401 Presque Isle Avenue
Marquette, MI 49007-5363
Anne Ohman Youngs, Editor-in-
Chief
Biannual.

Phoebe
George Mason University
4400 University Drive
Fairfax, VA 22030-4444
rotating editorship
phoebe@gmu.edu
www.gmu.edu/pubs/phoebe
Biannual, student-edited.

Playboy*
Playboy Building
919 North Michigan Avenue
Chicago, IL 60611
Alice Turner, Fiction Editor
editor@playboy.com
www.playboy.com
*Monthly. "I still only read it for the
stories."*

Pleiades
English and Philosophy Depts.
Central Missouri State University
Warrensburg, MO 64093
R. M. Kinder, Kevin Prufer, Editors
kdp8106@cmsuz.cmsu.edu
cmsuvmb.cmsu.edu/
englphil.pleiades.html
Biannual.

PLOUGHSHARES
100 Beacon Street
Boston, MA 02116
Don Lee, Editor
www.emerson.edu/ploughshares
Triannual. Guest-edited by
prominent writers.
Potomac Review
P.O. Box 354
Port Tobacco, MD 20677
Eli Flam, Editor and Publisher
www.meral.com/potomac
Quarterly.
Potpourri
P.O. Box 8278
Prairie Village, KS 66208-0278
Polly W. Swafford, Senior Editor
Potpourpub@aol.com
www.potpourri.org
Quarterly.
Pottersfield Portfolio
P.O. Box 40, Station A
Sydney, Nova Scotia
B1P 6G9 Canada
Douglas Arthur Brown, Managing
Editor
www.chebucto.ns.ca/Culture/
WFNS/Pottersfield/potters.html
Triannual.
Prairie Fire
423-100 Arthur Street
Winnipeg, Manitoba
R3B 1H3 Canada
Andris Taskins, Editor
Quarterly.
Prairie Schooner*
201 Andrews Hall
University of Nebraska
Lincoln, NE 68588-0334
Hilda Raz, Editor
www.unl.edu/schooner/psmain.htm
Quarterly.

Press
125 West 72nd Street
Suite 3-M
New York, NY 10023
Daniel J. Roberts, Editor
www.paradasia.com/press
Quarterly.
Prism International
Creative Writing Dept.
University of British Columbia
Vancouver, British Columbia
V6T 1Z1 Canada
rotating editorship
prism@unixg.ubc.ca
www.arts.ubc.ca/prism
Quarterly.
Puerto del Sol
P.O. Box 30001
Dept. 3E
New Mexico State University
Las Cruces, NM 88003-8001
Kevin McIlvoy, Editor-in-Chief
Biannual.
Quarry Magazine
P.O. Box 1061
Kingston, Ontario
K7L 4Y5 Canada
Rob Payne, Editor-in-Chief
Quarterly.
Quarterly West
200 S. Central Campus Drive
Room 317
University of Utah
Salt Lake City, UT 84112
Margot Schlipp, Editor
www.webdelsol.com/
Quarterly_West
Biannual.
Raritan
Rutgers University
31 Mine Street
New Brunswick, NJ 08903
Richard Poirier, Editor-in-Chief
Quarterly. Edited by former O.
Henry Awards series editor
(1961–66).

REAL
Stephen F. Austin State University
P.O. Box 13007, SFA Station
Nagodoches, TX 75962
W. Dale Hearell, Editor

Red Rock Review
English Dept., J2A
Community College Southern
Nevada
3200 East Cheyenne Avenue
North Las Vegas, NV 89030
Richard Logsdon, Editor-in-Chief
Biannual.

Redbook
224 West 57th Street
New York, NY 10019
Dawn Raffel, Books and Fiction
Editor
*Monthly women's magazine.
Stopped publishing fiction but may
resume.*

Rio Grande Review
Hudspeth Hall
University of Texas at El Paso
El Paso, Texas 79968
M. Elena Carillo, Editor
Biannual.

River Styx
634 N. Grand Boulevard, #12
St. Louis, MO 63103-1002
Richard Newman, Editor
www.riverstyx.org/contents.html
Triannual.

Rosebud
P.O. Box 459
Cambridge, WI 53523
Roderick Clark, Editor
www.hyperionstudio.com/rosebud
Quarterly.

St. Anthony Messenger
1615 Republic Street
Cincinnati, OH 45210-1298
Jack Wintz, O.F.M., Editor
www.AmericanCatholic.org
StAnthony@AmericanCatholic.org
*Monthly magazie published by
Franciscans, with about one story
per issue.*

Salamander
48 Ackers Avenue
Brookline, MA 02445-4160
Jennifer Barber, Editor
Biannual.

Salmagundi
Skidmore College
Saratoga Springs, NY 12866
Robert Boyers, Editor-in-Chief
Quarterly.

Salt Hill
Syracuse University
English Dept.
Syracuse, NY 13244
rotating editorship
jsparker@mailbox.syr.edu
www-hl.syr.edu/cwp
Biannual.

Santa Monica Review
Santa Monica College
1900 Pico Boulevard
Santa Monica, CA 90405
Lee Montgomery, Editor
Biannual.

The Seattle Review
Padelford Hall
Box 354330
University of Washington
Seattle, WA 98195
Colleen J. McElroy, Editor
Biannual.

Seven Days
29 Church Street
P.O. Box 1164
Burlington, VT 05042-1164
Paula Routly, Co-publisher
*Free weekly newspaper in the
Burlington, Vt., area. Occasional
fiction.*

The Sewanee Review
University of the South
Sewanee, TN 37375
George Core, Editor
www.sewanee.edu/sreview/
home.html
Quarterly.

Shenandoah*
Troubador Theater, 2nd floor
Washington and Lee University
Lexington, VA 24450
R. T. Smith, Editor
www.wlu.edu/~shenando
Quarterly.

Snake Nation Review
110 #2 West Force Street
Valdosta, GA 31601
Robert George, Editor
Triannual.

Sonora Review
English Dept.
University of Arizona
Tucson, AZ 85721
rotating editorship
www.coh.arizona.edu/sonora
sonora@u.arizona.edu
Biannual.

South Dakota Review
Box 111
University Exchange
Vermillion, SD 57069
Brian Bedard, Editor
www.litline.org/html/sdreview.html
Quarterly.

Southern Exposure
P.O. Box 531
Durham, NC 27702
Jordan Green, Fiction Editor
southern_exposure@14south.org
*A quarterly journal of Southern
politics and culture that publishes
some fiction.*

Southern Humanities Review
9088 Haley Center
Auburn University
Auburn, AL 36849
Dan R. Latimer, Virginia M.
Kouidis, Editors
www.auburn.edu/academic/
liberal_arts/english/shr/home.htm
Quarterly.

The Southern Review*
43 Allen Hall
Louisiana State University
Baton Rouge, LA 70803-5005
James Olney, Dave Smith, Editors
unix1.sncc.lsu.edu/guests/wwwtsr
Quarterly.

Southwest Review
Southern Methodist University
307 Fondren Library West
Dallas, TX 75275
Willard Spiegelman, Editor-in-Chief
Quarterly.

Spelunker Flophouse
P.O. Box 617742
Chicago, IL 60661
Chris Kubica, Wendy Morgan,
Editors
spelunkerf@aol.com,
sflophouse@aol.com
members.aol.com/spelunkerf/
index.html
Quarterly. Started in 1997.

STORY*
1507 Dana Avenue
Cincinnati, OH 45207
Lois Rosenthal, Editor
www.writersdigest.com/
catalogue/mag_frame.html
Quarterly. All fiction.

StoryQuarterly*
P.O. Box 1416
Northbrook, IL 60065
Anne Brashler, M.M.M. Hayes,
Directing Editors
Not quarterly, but annual.

The Sun*
107 North Robertson Street
Chapel Hill, NC 27516
Sy Safransky, Editor
www.thesunmagazine.org
Monthly.

Sycamore Review
English Dept.
1356 Heavilon Hall
Purdue University
West Lafayette, IN 47907
Sarah Griffiths, Editor-in-Chief
sycamore@expert.cc.purdue.edu
www.sla.purdue.edu/academic/
engl/sycamore
Biannual.

Talking River Review
Division of Literature and
Languages
Lewis-Clark State College
500 8th Avenue
Lewiston, ID 83501
www.lcsc.edu/TalkingRiverReview
Student-run biannual.

Tamaqua
Humanities Dept.
Parkland College
2400 West Bradley Avenue
Champaign, IL 61821-1899
Bruce Morgan, Editor-in-Chief
Biannual.

The Texas Review
English Dept.
Sam Houston State University
Huntsville, TX 77341
Paul Ruffin, Editor
www.whsu.edu/~eng_www/trp.html
Biannual.

Thema
Box 87479
Metairie, LA 70011-8747
Virginia Howard, Editor
www.litline.org/html/thema.html
For every issue, a theme.
Biannual.

Third Coast
English Dept.
Western Michigan University
Kalamazoo, MI 49008-5092
rotating editorship
www.wmich.edu/thirdcoast
Biannual.

13th Moon
English Dept.
SUNY
Albany, NY 12222
Judith Emlyn Johnson, Editor
A feminist literary magazine.

The Threepenny Review*
P.O. Box 9131
Berkeley, CA 94709
Wendy Lesser, Editor
www.litline.org/html/
threepenny.html
Quarterly.

Tikkun
60 West 87th Street
New York, NY 10024
Thane Rosenbaum, Fiction Editor
magazine@tikkun.org
www.tikkun.org
*"A Bimonthly Jewish Critique of
Politics, Culture & Society."*

Trafika
P.O. Box 250822
New York, NY 10025-1536
Scott Lewis, Krister Swartz, Jeffrey
Young, Editors
*Also has editorial office in Czech
Republic.*

TriQuarterly
Northwestern University
2020 Ridge Avenue
Evanston, IL 60208-4302
Susan Firestone Hahn, Editor
triquarterly.nwu.edu
Triannual.

The Urbanite
P.O. Box 4737
Davenport, IA 52808
Mark McLaughlin, Editor
"Surreal & Lively & Bizarre."
Published irregularly.

Urbanus
P.O. Box 192921
San Francisco, CA 94119-2921
Peter Driszhal, Editor
*Published "approximately 3 times
a year."*

The Virginia Quarterly Review*
One West Range
Charlottesville, VA 22903
Staige D. Blackford, Editor
www.virginia.edu/vqr

Wascana Review
English Dept.
University of Regina
Regina, Saskatchewan
S4S 0A2 Canada
Kathleen Wall, Editor
Biannual.

Washington Review
P.O. Box 50132
Washington, DC 20091-0132
Heather Fuller, Literary Editor
www.litline.org/html/
washingtonreview.html
*Bimonthly D.C. journal of arts and
literature.*

Washington Square
Creative Writing Program
New York University
19 University Place, 3rd Floor
New York, NY 10003-4556
rotating editorship
Student-run annual.

Weber Studies
Weber State College
Ogden, UT 84408-1214
Sherwin W. Howard, Editor
weberstudies.weber.edu
*Triquarterly. "Voices and
viewpoints of the contemporary
west."*

Wellspring
4080 83rd Avenue North
Suite A
Brooklyn Park, MN 55443
Meg Miller, Editor/Publisher

West Branch
Bucknell Hall
Bucknell University
Lewisburg, PA 17837
Karl Patten, Robert Love Taylor,
Editors
Biannual.

West Coast Line
2027 East Academic Annex
Simon Fraser University
Burnaby, British Columbia
V5A 1S6 Canada
Roy Miki, Editor
www.sfu.ca/west-coast-line
Triannual.

Western Humanities Review
University of Utah
Salt Lake City, UT 84112
Barry Weller, Editor
Quarterly.

Whetstone
P.O. Box 1266
Barrington, IL 60011-1266
Sandra Berris, Marsha Portnoy,
Jean Tolle, Editors
Annual.

Whiskey Island Magazine
University Center
Cleveland State University
1860 East 22nd Street
Cleveland, OH 44114
rotating editorship
whiskeyisland@popmail.
csuohio.edu
www.csuohio.edu/whiskey-island
Biannual.

Willow Springs
526 5th Street, MS-1
Eastern Washington University
Cheney, WA 99004
Christopher Howell, Editor
Biannual.

Wind
P.O. Box 24548
Lexington, KY 40524
Charlie Hughes, Leatha Kendrick,
Editors
lit-arts.com/wind/magazine.htm
Biannual.

Windsor Review
English Dept.
University of Windsor
Windsor, Ontario
N9B 3P4 Canada
Alistair MacLeod, Fiction Editor
uwreview@uwindsor.ca
Biannual.

Witness
Oakland Community College
Orchard Ridge Campus
27055 Orchard Lake Road
Farmington Hills, MI 48334
Peter Stine, Editor
Biannual.

The Worcester Review
6 Chatham Street
Worcester, MA 01609
Rodger Martin, Managing Editor
www.geocities.com/paris/leftbank/
6433
Annual.

Wordplay
P.O. Box 2248
South Portland, ME 04116-2248
Helen Peppe, Editor-in-Chief
Quarterly.

Writers' Forum
University of Colorado
P.O. Box 7150
Colorado Springs, CO 80933-7150
C. Kenneth Pellow, Editor-in-Chief
Annual.

WV: Magazine of the Emerging Writer
5 West 63rd Street
New York, NY 10023
Kathleen Warnock, Managing
Editor
WrtrsVoice@aol.com
hometown.aol.com/wrtrsvoice/
WVmag.html
Quarterly launched in 1998.

Xavier Review
Xavier University
Box 110C
New Orleans, LA 70125
Thomas Bonner, Jr., Editor
Biannual.

Xconnect: Writers of the Information Age
P.O. Box 2317
Philadelphia, PA 19103
David Deifer, Publisher/Editor
xconnect@ccat.sas.upenn.edu
ccat.sas.upenn.edu/~xconnect
Pronounced "Cross connect."
Annual print version of triannual
Web 'zine.

The Yale Review*
Yale University
P.O. Box 208243
New Haven, CT 06250-8243
J. D. McClatchy, Editor
Quarterly.

Yankee
Yankee Publishing, Inc.
Dublin, NH 03444
Judson D. Hale, Sr., Editor
Monthly magazine devoted to New
England. Occasional fiction.

Zoetrope: All-Story*
126 Fifth Avenue
Suite 300
New York, NY 10011
Adrienne Brodeur, Editor-in-Chief
Quarterly. Established by movie
director Francis Ford Coppola.
Short stories, essays on stories,
reprints of classic stories adapted
for the screen, and commissioned
stories. Web site provides full-text
stories and allows for online
submissions, provided users first
read and rate five stories. An
online community with message
boards and live chat.

ZYZZYVA
41 Sutter Street
Suite 1400
San Francisco, CA 94104-4903
Howard Junker, Editor
ZYZZYVAINC@aol.com
www.zyzzyva.org
Triannual. West Coast writers and artists.

Permissions